ZANE PRE

HARM
DONE

Dear Reader:

Get ready for a journey of blackmail, suspense and romance in this tale surrounding a college professor whose love life is an adventurous ride.

Shariece is surrounded by scandal as her younger love interest is a student in her class. But it's not only her cougar role that raises eyebrows; it's her affair with Emjay, her best friend Leandra's son. While they believe their relationship is a secret, they soon realize all is not as secure as it seems.

Shariece's ex-boyfriend, Myrick, is thrown in the mix and once released from prison, he becomes a serious threat. His obsession with her leads him on a destructive mission to snare her back into his dangerous web.

This entertaining story will keep readers on the edge of their seats with its twists and turns and continuous surprises. And steamy scenes abound in this tantalizing novel with an urban flair.

If you haven't read Shane Allison's debut novel, *You're the One I Want*, an excerpt is included at the end.

As always, thanks for supporting myself and the Strebor Books family. We strive to bring you the most cutting-edge, out-of-the-box material on the market. You can find me on Facebook @AuthorZane.

Blessings,

Zane

Publisher
Strebor Books
www.simonandschuster.com

ZANE PRESENTS

HARM DONE

SHANE ALLISON

STREBOR BOOKS

NEW YORK LONDON TORONTO SYDNEY

Strebor Books
P.O. Box 55471
Atlanta, GA 30308
www.simonandschuster.com

© 2017 by Shane Allison

ISBN 978-1-59309-654-0
ISBN 978-1-47679-827-1 (ebook)
LCCN 2017941826

First Strebor Books trade paperback edition August 2017

Cover design: www.mariondesigns.com
Cover photograph: © Keith Saunders/Keith Saunders Photos

10 9 8 7 6 5 4 3 2 1

Manufactured in the United States of America

For information regarding special discounts for bulk purchases, please contact Simon & Schuster Special Sales at 1-866-506-1949

The Simon & Schuster Speakers Bureau can bring authors to your live event. For more information or to book an event, contact the Simon & Schuster Speakers Bureau at 1-866-248-3049 or visit our website at www.simonspeakers.com.

This novel is dedicated to Vytautas Pliura who always believed that I could. Continue to rest in peace. I love you.

ACKNOWLEDGMENTS

I want to thank Zane and Charmaine Parker for believing in me and the characters in *Harm Done*. You are forever my sisters. Mad Love.

ONE
SHARIECE

"Don't stop. Goddamn, don't stop," I moaned. "Oh shit, yeah, right there." The pussy eating work Emjay was putting down on me was enough to make my pedicured, fire engine-red painted toes curl. Literally. For someone who was only twenty years old, Emjay was a pro at cunnilingus. He circled my nipples with the tips of his fingers as he sucked the delicate, sweet pink of my pussy, tonguing my core, applying the right amount of pressure. "Oh, fuck, you're gonna make me…" Emjay glanced up at me with a smug look, relishing that he knew all the spots to send me into orbit. When he started to suck on the lips of my pussy as if there was a sweet prize awaiting him once he reached the center, I purred. "Yeah, like that, that's good, right there, baby, damn." Emjay moaned as he sucked and licked on my clit. He had me good, my plump, sugar-brown thighs hiked on his shoulders. I ran my hands over his fingers that stimulated my nipples, his fingers along my luscious lips. I sucked them as if they were his dick, applying pressure. Emjay was bone-hard, dick thumping against the white cotton of his underwear. He smelled of Axe shower gel. I loved how the manly aroma infiltrated me like his fingers in my pussy, like his thick, candy bar-brown dick. I wanted to ravish him, lick the skin off if I could have. Emjay moaned as he worked his dick, feasting on my pussy.

I fisted the bed sheets. I couldn't hold out much longer. I buried his head deeper, screaming, "Eat my pussy!" I love talking dirty when I'm horny. He worked me over until I came, my nectar oozing like liquid candy. Emjay rose up off the balls of his knees and walked to where I was lying flat on my back. I took him into my mouth, licking, sucking, massaging his dick with my fingers. "I'm gonna come," he warned. It had been weeks since we'd fucked, being that we'd had to be careful about being seen together. I tightened my lips around his mushroom tip, around the vein-induced shaft. I didn't stop until he had given me what I want. Minutes within, Emjay spurted thick, creamy webs of semen across my face and lips. I don't mind cum on my face. He knew I wasn't one of these spoiled, pretty girls who think they're too good to suck dick. I licked his juices from the tap of his dick. "Damn, baby, that's good," he whispered under his breath as I milked out every drop, watching the last remnants of semen plummet from his teardrop-shaped pee slit. Emjay's dick already started to go limp when we heard a knock at his apartment door.

"Who the hell is that?" I whispered.

Emjay slipped on some shorts before he went to go see who was knocking at the door.

"Fuck, it's Mama."

You would have thought my ass was on fire the way I hauled up out of bed. I began to get dressed. Emjay was funny the way he ran his skinny behind around the apartment like a chicken with its head cut off.

"What the hell is she doing here?"

"I forgot that I told her that I would have breakfast with her today."

"Interesting how you failed to mention that," I said, as I pulled on my skirt. Leandra always had the worst timing.

"Emjay, I know you're in there. I can hear you walking around."

"Damn, where are my panties?"

"Don't look at me. I don't know." Emjay kicked his drawers under the bed.

"Emjay!" Leandra yelled.

"*Chill out, woman, damn,*" I said.

"I'm coming, Ma. I just got out of the shower."

"Open the door, boy. Got me out here yelling in this hall."

Leandra started jiggling the knob as if by some possibility, Emjay may have left the door unlocked. I was glad he didn't.

"You gotta hide." I grabbed my shoes and ducked into the closet. "Hold up, you forgot this." He tossed my purse at me like it was a damn football, causing some of my personals to tumble out. I hid in the closet like I was some kind of dirty secret. I watched through the slit of the closet door at Emjay take one last look around before he finally let Leandra, my best friend of eleven years, into his studio apartment.

Damn, what is that smell? My nose led me to a pair of old Adidas that smelled of ass, feet and blue cheese. I plugged my index finger under my nose in an effort to drown out the stench. Here I was, a grown-ass, forty-two-year-old woman, hiding in my best friend son's closet. I gently began retrieving the contents that had dropped out of my brown genuine leather Coach, no thanks to Emjay's ass. After all that whooping and hollering she was doing outside of his door, he'd let her in. As I scanned the room through the slit of the closet, I noticed my iPhone 6 sitting on one of the bedside tables next to an empty champagne glass.

"Emjay, you know how I hate standing outside in the hallway, yelling at you. Your neighbors are going to think I'm a straight-up fool."

"Good morning to you too, Mama," Emjay said, giving Leandra a kiss on the cheek. He stood there shirtless and barefooted, with his hands shoved in the front pockets of his skinny jeans. I stared at my phone hoping, praying that Emjay saw the phone before Leandra did. She was with me at Best Buy the day I'd purchased it. You would never know that Leandra was forty by looking at her. It's like I always say, "black don't crack."

Lee looked good in her tangerine-orange capris with top and orange sandals. The color looked good against her mocha skin. Her makeup was flawless and there wasn't a hair out of place from the curly extensions that hung over her shoulders and down her back. The capris were slightly tight, but Leandra liked her clothes tight to show off her curvy assets. Some had mistaken her for Emjay's sister, a compliment she relished.

"You're not wet."

"What?"

"You said you just got out of the shower, but you're not wet."

"Oh, I just dried off."

Leandra looked at him like she could see clean through his lie.

"Get the phone," I whispered under my breath. "Don't let her see the phone, Emjay, damn."

"Are you okay? You seem...different."

"Um, yeah, it's like nine in the morning on a Saturday."

"Oh, I forgot," Leandra said, pursing her lips, "you don't get your tail up before noon."

"Glad you remembered."

"You'll be fine once you get some breakfast in you."

Emjay glanced over at the closet where I hid; scanning the

room for anything Leandra was at risk to find. He did a double-take when he saw my phone.

"Jesus, this place is a mess. Emjay, how can you live like this?" As Leandra started picking up tossed clothes off the floor, Emjay eased over to the nightstand and pushed my phone behind a stack of books.

"I've been busy with school. I haven't had time to straighten up."

"Oh, I almost forgot to tell you. Guess who came into the shop last week?"

Oh Lord, here she goes.

"Brooke Canfield."

"Who?"

"Don't tell me you don't remember Brooke. Ya'll were play-mates as children. You had the biggest crush on her in middle school, remember?"

"Yeah, that was like eight years ago, Ma."

"She's studying nursing at Keiser College. Girl's going to be making money hand over fist when she's done. I can't believe she's still single—smart girl like her."

"Ma, I know what you're trying to do. Quit it."

"I'm just saying she—"

"Are you ready?" Emjay interrupted. "Those pecan pancakes you like at the Golden Corral are going to be gone if we don't bounce."

"We're not going with you all half naked. Put some clothes on." The sound of Leandra's voice was getting on my last nerve.

"You oughta get sick of walking around looking like you should be out on the street begging for change."

My heartbeat quickened when she started for the closet. Emjay stopped her, and ushered her back toward the center of the apartment.

"Ma, I got this. Here, why don't you, um…water the plants." While her attention was on the ferns that sat on his window sill, Emjay quickly pulled a white polo from the rack.

"You got one plant and that thing looking like it's on life support. And here you are talking about getting a dog, and you can't even take care of a plant." One thing about Leandra, she could easily get preoccupied.

She turned around and looked at Emjay with a peculiar expression. "Are you sure you're all right?"

"No, I'm hungry, and you keep going on about that plant."

"Well, okay. We can leave, but I'm going to come back here and gather up all your dirty clothes, and take them back to the house to wash."

"Fine, whatever, now can we go eat, please, before I keel over from hunger?"

After Leandra's constant nagging, they finally left. I pushed the door open, anxious to free myself from Emjay's funky-smelling closet. "That's it. That's the first and the last time I hide in a closet for him or anybody," I said out loud. "What the hell do I look like, some sorority slut? I'm a grown-ass woman. I don't hide and I don't sneak." I finished getting dressed, buttoning my top, and then slipping my size tens in black Anne Klein heels. "I need to have my college-educated head examined for getting involved with not only the son of my best friend, but a damn student at the junior college where I teach."

I grabbed my iPhone that nearly got me caught, off the bedside table and dropped it in my purse. I watched from one of Emjay's windows of his apartment at Leandra pull off in her cream Cadillac Escalade before I made the walk of shame down the steps that led outside to the front of Chapel Hill Apartments. I eased into my Buick, checking in the rearview mirror; my perm had been sweated out from the freak nasty fucking he had given me last night. I was still thinking of his head buried between my thick thighs only thirty minutes earlier.

TWO
SHARIECE

worked my ass off trying to get this teaching job as an English instructor at Tallahassee Community College after I had applied and was turned down by five universities in Florida. They went on about how great my resume was and wished they could hire me, but couldn't due to budget cuts in their departments. With the ink still wet on my Master of Fine Arts from Florida Atlantic University, along with three years of teaching experience, I asked myself, "Who do I have to blow to get a j-o-b in this town?"

After searching the employment website at Tallahassee Community College for weeks on end, I saw that the Communications and Humanities Department was in search of an instructor to teach two freshman composition courses and one creative writing class. The only criteria were that you needed experience, and hold a master's or Ph.D. in the field. Instead of going through Human Resources where I risked my application and resume ending up in some slush pile, I walked my credentials directly to the English Department where I met the director, Dr. Rochelle Payne. This sister was the embodiment of a plus-size diva, wearing a black, white and red tweed suit that I would have killed for. She had light-brown eyes, thick, red lips like mine, and flawless skin. Had she told me she used to model, I wouldn't have been surprised with those pretty, white teeth. I have a gap in the front of mine that I'm still self-conscious as hell about, but that would be taken care of once I had some money to get the gap fixed. I was ready for whatever Dr. Payne had for me. I answered all of her questions with the utmost of professionalism. She informed me that there was an error on the department site about the number of courses: there were a total of five, including three freshman composition classes and two introduction to English literature. I told her that I was fine with the course load and then thought, *Damn, there go my weekends.* But considering I had credit card bills, a house and car note, I wasn't going to raise a fuss.

The interview didn't last long, which kind of made me nervous. I thought to compliment her on her suit as a last-ditch effort to get the teaching job, but decided against it, not wanting to come off like a kiss-ass. I figured this woman had an entire staff to kiss her ass; she didn't need another brownnoser. We shook hands, smiled at each other, and that was it. Rochelle informed me that she was considering other applicants, but would let me know that following week if I got the teaching job. I felt confident about the interview, yet the last thing I wanted to do was get my hopes up or jinx it by telling myself I was going to get the job. I kept my fingers and toes crossed, and hoped for the best.

I should have gone to nursing school like my cousins Takara and Eboni. I could have been working for some hot, rich doctor in Atlanta somewhere pulling major cake, instead of living in some third-rate townhouse on the East Side. I could have been driving an Escalade instead of pushing a fourteen-year-old Buick down the street with no air conditioning. That car kept me sweating. It's more trouble than what I paid for it. If I got this teaching job, I was going to park that shit in a ditch and walk to the nearest car lot. I had my eyes on a silver Toyota F7. It was probably about thirty grand, yeah, but I'd make it work. A week had passed. I was putting in applications, passing out resumes like flyers. I had gotten the call from Rochelle on a Friday morning, standing over my printer as it spat out a hundred copies of my resume.

"Ms. Houston, hello, this is Dr. Payne." She sounded so pleasant on the phone.

"Dr. Payne, good morning," I said, closing my eyes, crossing my fingers with the hope she was calling to give me good news.

"I am calling to offer you the writing instructor position if you are still interested."

I literally jumped for joy, causing a couple of hair rollers to fall out of my hair.

"Absolutely, yes, of course. I'm still interested."

"Wonderful. Can you come to my office Monday morning, and we can discuss a contract and details of the position? How does nine a.m. sound?"

"Sounds great. I'll be there."

"Wonderful. I'll see you on Monday, nine a.m."

"Thank you, Dr. Payne."

"Call me Rochelle."

"Thank you. Have a good weekend, Rochelle."

Leandra was the first person I shared the news with. We went to the Silver Slipper and celebrated with shots.

Rochelle informed me that the classes were held Mondays, Wednesdays and Fridays at 8 a.m., with ten to twenty students per class. She reminded me that the position was part time, and that if a full-time position opened up, I would be placed on a list of other candidates. I didn't care if it was only for a few hours of the day. I had a job, an actual career.

The first day of the fall semester, I was a ball of nerves. With a few stories published in a few literary magazines and some placed in three anthologies by Zane, one of my favorite authors, my literary resume wasn't too shabby. I kept telling myself that I was a smart, educated, talented sister who could take on anything that was thrown at her. I was dressed to the nines in my white bell bottoms, and black blouse with a red broach to set the whole outfit off. I checked myself in the mirror probably ten times that morning, making sure that not a hair extension was out of place. I always say, just because you don't make a million dollars, don't mean you can't look like a million dollars.

When I arrived on campus, the lot was filled with cars. It was hard to believe that only a week before, the school looked near deserted. With my faculty pass, I pushed my SUV into the lot segregated from student parking—one of the perks I was enjoying. My days as a student driving around a campus for forty-five minutes to find a parking space were over. The campus was buzzing with students armed with backpacks and plastic bags of textbooks and stationery. My office was located on the first floor of the department building with a view of the adjoining buildings. It wasn't much with its bland, gray carpeting and white cinderblock walls. A desk faced me as I walked through the door of my new office with a flat-screen Dell computer. The office wasn't much, but I would soon give it the Shariece Houston touch that it so desperately needed.

I was making preparations for my first class of the day when Rochelle walked in. "Good morning."

"Hey, good morning."

"How are you settling in?"

"So far, so good. I'm just trying to get some things situated and organized."

Rochelle wore a smoke-gray pants suit with a white blouse. I had seen the same suit at Belk for $200, which told me this woman made some money. She looked at me and probably knew I was an off-the-rack, T.J. Maxx kind of chick.

"I just wanted to stop by and welcome you to FAMU and to the department. There will be a faculty meeting on Friday—a meet-and-greet, really. Some finger food and wine, nothing major."

"That sounds nice. Count me in."

"Great. Well, I will let you get back to work. If you need anything like supplies, you can call my secretary. If you have any questions or concerns, don't hesitate to call me."

"Thank you, Dr.—I mean…Rochelle."

It was a quarter 'til nine and I didn't have much time. Anything that needed to be done would have to wait. With a stack of syllabuses nestled in my arms, I went to my first class that was located conveniently on the first floor of the department. "Good morning," I said, as I walked toward the desk that faced the dry erase board.

"Good morning," a few of them grumbled.

They clearly were not fully awake yet, so I repeated again, "I said, good morning, class." I spoke slightly louder in a need to wake up the collegiate sleepyheads.

"GOOD MORNING!"

"That's better. I should have brought some coffee, to wake ya'll up."

They all laughed as they fished notebooks and pens out of their backpacks. I introduced myself and started passing out the syllabus explaining what I expected from them for the semester.

"If you come to class on time, work hard, do the assignments, go to your writing lab, I don't see any reason why you all shouldn't make an A in my class. I won't make it easy, so don't expect this is one of those classes you think you can half step and get an easy A in. I'm about making this semester as successful as possible for all of you."

After I had stressed how much I hated students coming to my class late, Emjay walked through my door with nothing in his hand but a black-and-white composition book. Needless to say, I was surprised to see him. He sat in the first row near the door sporting blue baggy jeans and a blue and gold T-shirt that said *Enyce* down the left side in big white letters. Emjay wasn't a kid anymore, but a fully grown young man. He had thick bubble-gum-pink lips and apple butter-brown skin. He was fine as hell, a thought I made sure I kept to myself. It was crazy how much he looked like his daddy. He wasn't on my roll, so I figured he must have added my class late. It was nice to see a familiar face, yes, but I knew he didn't think that just because he was Leandra's son, that I was going to give his young behind special treatment. If anything, my expectations of him would be in the ballpark of the nosebleed section. Leandra could have at least given me a heads-up. I figured she didn't know if he added the class at the last minute, or maybe she did know and just wanted to shock me with one of her surprises she enjoyed springing on me.

As weeks passed, Emjay proved to me that he didn't expect handouts or special treatment because he was Leandra's boy. He did the assignments and participated in class, which was twenty percent of everyone's final grade. Emjay still needed to work on getting to class on time. That was the only thing I gave him a break on. I was pleased to tell Leandra how well he was doing. It wasn't easy seeing him sitting there three days a week looking all scrumptious, his hand resting haphazardly on his crotch. I started thinking about Emjay more than a teacher should of her student, fantasizing about us having sex, him eating me out under my desk during my office hours. Because of Emjay, I consistently had my fingers in my pussy, wishing it was his mouth, or his banana-thick dick stretching my sugar walls.

I exercised self-control when he made visits to my office. I would sit across from him and get lost in his light-brown eyes. Emjay's cologne infiltrated my office, and lingered for hours after his departure. I felt guilty about having these thoughts about my best friend's son; Leandra would have been livid if she ever found out about us. I wish I could have said that when we first began our affair, it was by accident, and that Emjay tripped and fell between my legs, but that's not how it happened.

It was a Wednesday afternoon. Emjay had an appointment to speak with me about an essay he was at work on and wanted my opinion. He'd looked handsome in his purple Polo with gray cargo shorts and white low-top Chuck Taylors. The purple juxtaposed nicely against his skin. His hair was cut low and brushed into waves. He'd smelled of Tom Ford's Noir. Sitting at the desk in front of me, Emjay had handed me his essay to peruse. Even though my kitty-cat was purring for his dick, I'd had to keep things professional. I would have glanced between his legs if I hadn't thought he'd notice me checking out his bulge. I would have given anything to whip his dick out of those shorts and throw my lips around his appendage. Damn, of all the teachers Emjay could have chosen, he'd ended up in front of me.

"I didn't know you were teaching this course. It said 'To Be Announced' next to the class." Emjay could have easily gone to the department, and requested a specific instructor if he had wanted.

"This is pretty good."

"You really think so?"

"Yeah, I mean, it could use some fleshing out in some places, but it flows nicely; you get to the point. It's a great start."

"What do you think of this part right here?" he'd asked, sauntering around my desk to where I was sitting. I had started to notice little things about Emjay as he went on about his essay like the dip in his shoulder blades, the stubble from his freshly shaven face, the hair on his arms, the way his skinny fingers traipsed along the paper, fingers I had often dreamt of sucking on among other things. His dick was only centimeters away from my hand. I had wanted to say fuck it, drop to my knees, unzip his shorts, pull it out and show that I was an all-day dick-sucking kind of bitch, but I'd digressed. I'd leaned into him, causing my breasts to graze against his arm. I knew it was wrong, but a woman wants what she wants.

"Ma wanted me to ask if you have any plans for Thanksgiving. She wants me to invite you over for dinner." Was Leandra serious? Sure, it wouldn't have been weird at all to be sitting across the table of my best friend's son whom I so happened to be screwing.

I had planned to merely cuddle up at the house, and watch the Macy's Thanksgiving Parade, maybe get around to reading that new Cairo novel I had bought six weeks ago, but never found the time to start. I could have heard Leandra: "Girl, why are you always so antisocial?" The thought of showing up on her doorstep, all decked out for turkey and sweet potato pie, had made me giggle. "Tell her yeah, I can come."

"Cool," Emjay had said.

"So how have you been doing in your other classes?"

"I should get a B in Western Civilization, an A in Algebra and a B in Oceanography, and hopefully an A in your class if I'm lucky." He had looked at me with those baby-brown eyes knowing exactly what he was doing.

"I haven't finished grading yet, but seeing that you've worked so hard this semester, I don't see why you shouldn't get a passing grade in my class, Emjay."

"Just passing?"

"The rest is up to you."

"Because I'm willing to do anything to do well," he'd said, looking at me seductively. Emjay's touch sent jolts of sextricity up my body as he'd glided his hand up my inner thigh. "I mean, I'm down for whatever you need me to do, Ms. Houston." I'd pulled my legs ajar as he'd made his way up to my honey pot. He'd cut me a slick smile when he'd discovered I didn't have any panties on, that there was nothing but a set of black sheer pantyhose between his fingers and my pussy. I had slid my skirt up exposing myself.

"Go lock the door."

Emjay had done what I'd asked, jiggling the knob, making sure that we couldn't be disturbed. He had come back around to where I was sitting. I had cocked my right leg on top of the desk. He'd licked his lips as he tore a hole through the silk black material, exposing me. He'd sucked his middle finger, and then gently had inserted it inside me. I'd unbuttoned my blouse, yanked at satin until one of my breasts had popped free from my black bra. I had caressed my nipple for stimulation as Emjay had fingered me. I had given into temptation.

"I see how you look at me in class."

"How do you mean?" I had asked like I didn't have a clue.

"You know exactly what I mean." Emjay had slid his fingers out of my pussy and brought them to his mouth, sucking my juices off the tips. "Damn, tasty-sweet." I was so used to pleasuring myself with plastic dicks, I had forgotten how pleasing someone else's touch could be. A line had been crossed, and there was no turning back. I hadn't felt that good since my days with Myrick, my psycho ex who thankfully was rotting in a Florida State Prison. Emjay was about to unleash his dick from his shorts when the phone had rung.

Fuck.

"Don't answer it," he had pleaded.

I'd picked up the phone anyway figuring it might be an important call that I needed to take.

"Hello."

"Hey, girl, what's up?"

It was Leandra. The woman had the worst timing.

Emjay had plucked out his fingers wet with my juices, and had dropped to his knees, giving me a look like I was in for the best sex of my life.

"Hey, what are you doing?" I had struggled to keep my composure as Emjay began tongue-tickling my pussy lips.

"I was in the area, and wanted to see if you wanted to get some lunch. There's something I want to talk to you about."

"What is it?"

Oh my God, yes, right there. I had gripped the arm of my desk chair.

"No, trust, you're going to be knocked off your ass."

Where the hell did Emjay learn to eat pussy like this? "All right, where do you want to meet?"

"Actually, I'm about to turn into the parking lot on campus." I had jerked up, pushing Emjay's head from between my thighs. He had looked annoyed like a baby who had been snatched from his mama's nipple.

"It's your mother," I had mouthed.

Emjay had sat up off his knees and had wiped his mouth with the back of his hand.

"You're here right now?"

"Yeah, I'm pulling in now."

"Okay, I'll see you in a few minutes," I'd said, frantically tugging my skirt down over my ass. "Leandra's on her way here to my office."

"Shit."

"You gotta go." I had scrambled to my feet.

"When can I see you again?"

"That's not a good idea." I had tucked the shirt tail of my blouse back into my skirt.

"We can't. If anyone ever found out, I could lose my job, and Emjay, I need this job, Emjay."

"We'll be careful."

"There's no such thing. Look what happened to that lady in Nebraska for sleeping with her student."

"That's different, Shariece. I'm an adult."

"Leandra would kill me if she ever found out."

"I'm a grown-ass man. My mother can't tell me who I can and can't see."

I had looked Emjay dead in his eyes. "Listen to me. This can't happen again." He had glanced off like he was a child being scolded. "You gotta go. Leandra should be walking in the building right about now."

"Can I call you?"

"No. You need to go."

"I will if you say I can call you."

"Fine, but don't call my office phone."

"Can I get a kiss before I go?"

"Emjay, don't play with me."

He had grabbed his backpack, unlocked the door and left. I had taken a can of air freshener and had started to spray in an attempt to mask the scent of sex with a peach blossom aroma. Only minutes after Emjay's departure, Leandra had walked into my office.

"What's up, 'Riece?" she had announced.

"Just finishing up some grading."

"I ran into Emjay down the hall. How's my baby boy doing?" Leandra had taken a seat in front of my desk.

"Pretty good. He gets his assignments in on time, and he's attentive."

"Emjay tells me he wants to be a big-time writer like you. I'm always catching him scribbling in that notebook of his. He read a poem he had written about me. It was so sweet. You should see his apartment. Books everywhere: on shelves, on his desk, even on his bathroom floor. I told him he needs to write a novel."

"Keep nourishing his talent. It'll open up a whole lot of doors for him if he keeps writing." Leandra would have been beating my ass right then had she caught us.

"That would be something else, 'Riece, a writer in the family."

"So what is it you want to tell me?"

"Come on, let's go to lunch. Where do you want to eat?"

"Leandra, for real? Girl, what is it?" I had grinned.

"I met somebody."

"Oh Lord. Not another loser from Blackpeople.com."

"Some of the guys on there are pretty nice."

"Much like the last guy you met."

Leandra's luck with men was for shit—one loser after the other wanting her for sex, if not money, sometimes both.

"How was I supposed to know he had five baby mamas?"

"Hey, I'm just looking out for you."

"Whatever, Taj isn't like that."

"We don't think any of them are like that when we first meet them. Look what happened with me and Myrick."

"Okay, Oprah, before you judge the brother, you should at least let me fill you in."

"I'm listening."

"Keep your mind open until we get some food. I'm so hungry I could eat an ox. All I had to eat this morning was a sausage biscuit from Mickey D's."

"Well, let's go get you fed before your blood sugar bottoms out." I shoved the rest of the ungraded papers and my planner in my brown leather satchel, grabbed my purse and switched off the lights.

"Whose car are we taking, yours or mine?" I had asked.

"We can take my Escalade." Leandra was always quick to let me know that she was more well off than me. She thought that just because she owned a hair salon, drove an Escalade and had a three-bedroom home on the North Side of town, it made her somebody. She was the type who measured her success by how many toys she owned, but she knew that had never impressed me, and I couldn't care less that she had a Jacuzzi and a fifty-inch flat-screen TV.

Leandra and I had met at a Weight Watchers meeting. When my last boyfriend had left me for some low-budget stripper, I had drowned my sorrows in a gallon of Ben & Jerry's Chunky Monkey for a week and ballooned to 200 pounds. Once I was able to pull myself from the double cheeseburgers and super-size fries, it was time for a new and improved me. I didn't want to be toothpick-thin, but at a healthy weight and still keep my figure. Leandra had just come out of a bad situation herself. It turned out we had so much in common. We liked the same movies, the same TV shows; we had similar taste in fashion. From our initial meeting, we became fast friends, going to mixers, grown folks' night at The Moon, talking tirelessly on the phone for hours like two teenagers until sometimes two in the morning. We were like sisters, and there was nothing we wouldn't do for each other.

"So what are you in the mood for: chicken wraps, fish tacos, tofu burgers?"

"I was thinking of some smothered pork chops at Kacey's Chicken. They have that all-you-can-eat buffet during the week."

I'd looked at Leandra like she was crazy.

"Don't give me that look, 'Riece. I'm hungry."

"Whatever happened to your dream of wanting to get into a size twelve again?"

"Ain't no harm in one smothered pork chop. I'll just get on the treadmill and burn it off."

"I'm not going to let you mess up over a moment of weakness. How about we go to Crispers instead? They have good Caesar salads."

Leandra had locked her hand at the wide waistline she was trying to shrink. "Girl, I am not in the mood to graze. Last I looked, I'm not a rabbit. A bitch needs meat every now and then."

When we had arrived, we both had ordered the Asiago salad with chicken and raisins with an unsweetened tea. "Just *pretend* its smothered pork chops." I had laughed.

"I hate you," she'd said, stuffing her face with soda crackers.

"So you were telling me about this new guy you met."

"Okay, you know that new club downtown called Mint Lounge?"

"The one you've been trying to get me to go with you to for the past two weeks, yes."

"You know I don't play that staying-at-home shit with all these single men out here."

"So you met this guy. What's his name again?"

"Taj. Isn't that the sexiest name you've ever heard?"

"As in Taj Mahal?"

"See, you tried it," Leandra had said, laughing. "No, it's short for Tajnaranja."

"Hearing you say his name makes my tongue hurt. Where do you find these men?"

"Let's see what you say when you meet him. He's six-four, caramel skin, dark-brown eyes, and a body from heaven."

I had twirled my straw around in my glass of raspberry sweet tea. "Does he have a job?"

"He's a photographer at *Tallahassee Magazine*."

"Interesting. I'm listening."

"He models sometimes, too."

"Runway or catalog?"

"Catalog mostly, but he's done a few runway shows in New York."

"How old is he?" Leandra had paused and taken a sip from her tea. "Leandra?"

"He's twenty-two."

I nearly had choked on my breadstick when she'd told me Taj's age. "What?"

"I know he's a little young."

"A little?"

"He's sweet, Shariece, and such a gentleman. I thought men like him were extinct. Girl, he listens to me. He actually cares what I have to say."

As soon as she'd told me how young Taj was, the rest of what Leandra was saying fell on deaf ears. Who was I to judge her being that I was messing around with her son?

"He's coming to dinner on Friday."

I had sat there swirling my straw in my drink when the waiter had arrived with our salads. "Who has the Asiago salad?"

"Shariece? Earth to Shariece?" I'd heard Leandra say.

"Huh?" I had looked up at the waiter holding my food. "Oh, sorry, yes, that's me."

Leandra had cut Jason, the redheaded, blue-eyed waiter, a flirty smile as he'd set her plate in front of her.

"Is there anything else I can get for you ladies?"

"No, I think we're good, thank you," I'd said.

Leandra was checking out Jason as he'd sprinted back to the kitchen with an empty serving tray.

"He's fine for a white boy."

"You a trip." I had laughed.

"Don't act like you wouldn't mind going all reverse cowgirl on that young piece."

I had glanced at Jason in the kitchen as he scrambled to prepare someone's order.

"He's all right," I had said, forking salad, chunks of chicken and raisins in my mouth.

"Okay, so did you hear me?"

"What?"

"I'm inviting Taj over for dinner and I want you to join us. I want Emjay to meet him too."

"I don't know, Leandra. I have to finish grading these papers; my house is a mess..."

"C'mon, 'Riece. I want to know what you and Emjay think of him."

"Well, if it means that much to you."

Leandra had smiled big, clapping gleefully like that time I'd agreed to go with her to take this pottery making class at Michaels last year. "Yes. Thank you, girl."

"Leandra, are you sure about this guy? I mean, what do you really know about him?"

"Shariece, you need to relax."

"I'm just looking out for you."

"It's been what, two years since that Myrick craziness?" Leandra had asked.

"This isn't about me. I don't want you to get hurt, that's all."

"I've had to hear your cautionary tales about men ever since

Myrick got locked up. You got to get over what happened, move on with your life. Men are like buses. A new one comes along every fifteen minutes."

"I'm over that psycho. I have a job. I'm making my own money. If this isn't me getting over him, I don't know what is."

"He's rotting in a state prison now. Put his crazy-ass in your rearview."

I had felt like I was being scolded by my mother.

"Remember what we said on New Year's night?"

"Fresh new beginnings, I know."

"Fresh new everything. Leave that 2014 drama in 2014."

"Are you done lecturing me, Iyanla Vanzant?"

Leandra had thrown up her hands. "Class dismissed."

"But I hear, you, girl, and you're right. There are too many good men out here for me to be harping on one man."

"That's my girl."

"So does Tajna...Tajnee..."

"Tajnaranja," she had corrected. "Call him Taj for short."

"Does Taj have a brother he could set me up with?"

THREE
SHARIECE

had officially slammed the door in Love's face after that mess with Myrick. I'd admitted that I used to be hardheaded when it came to men. Most of them were "hit it and quit its," and after I got what I wanted out of them, they got kicked to the curve, their names never remembered. I didn't see anything wrong with getting my freak nasty on every now and then. Men do that shit and they're kings, but if a woman does it, she's a slut. Fuck that double standard. Men think if they treat you to lobster and cheese biscuits, then they're entitled to some pussy, but I was quick to set a brother straight. After a while, the one-night stands get old. Most of the men I met were from pickup bars and grown folk nights at a number of clubs around town.

I'd met Myrick at this club called Top Flight on the South Side of town. That night, I was being hit on by just about every loser in the club. After three Vodka Cranberries, and the fact that none of the men in the club lived up to my standards, I had decided to call it a night. It was pouring rain. It had been raining for three days straight. It'd reminded me how much I hated Florida and how Tallahassee only worked on two cylinders: hot and wet. Either it was raining all the time or it was hot as hell. I was wearing this new dress I'd bought from Macy's, one of my splurge purchases when I had a little disposable spending change, and black platform heels courtesy of Belladonna. After a night of watered-down drinks and tacky pickup lines, I had wanted to get out of the shoes that were putting a killing on my feet, and soak them in a warm bubble bath. I had gotten tired of waiting for the rain to slack up, so I'd decided to make a run to my car. As I'd pulled my weave behind my back, this beautiful, dark-skinned brother had held his umbrella over me. "Need a lift?" He'd had a nice smile with pretty white teeth and luscious lips.

"My car's right over here." He was exactly what I needed that night. Running in platforms is nothing cute, so I'd taken him up on his offer.

"You ready?" Myrick had asked.

"Let's do it."

We were shoulder to shoulder; creeping to my car like the rain was something we couldn't let touch our skin. I took in the faint aroma of Polo Red permeating off his body as we walked to my car. I hoped he wasn't some weirdo rapist with a taste for big girls. I thought of how long it would take me to grab the pepper spray from my purse. When we got to my car, I started digging frantically for my keys.

"Sorry. I know they're in here."

"Take your time."

I thought to myself, *Shariece, you are such a dizzy bitch*.

"I'm Myrick, by the way," he said, extending his hand out.

I stopped looking for my keys to take the time to introduce myself. "Shariece."

"Nice to meet you."

"Ah, here they are."

I shoved my key into the hole of the driver's side door.

"I know that you have probably been getting this question all night, but I've had my eyes on you all night, but was too shy to approach you. I guess this rain presented the perfect opportunity. I would love to take you out sometime."

Now this was the first that a man ever bothered to offer me *his* number. It was quite different, but I was feeling him.

"But I don't know you."

"True, but if I let a beautiful sister like you get away without giving you my number, I might regret it for the rest of my life."

His line wasn't the most original, but Myrick had heart.

"Do you have a pen?"

He padded his shirt and jean pockets, looking for something to write with.

"Hold on," I said, and took a pen out of the side pouch of my purse and handed it to him. Myrick jotted my number on his palm as I read it off.

"Now if you go home and accidently wash that off your hand, it's on you." I smiled.

"I won't. I've already memorized it. I'll call you. Maybe we can have dinner."

Myrick was not only cute, but a gentleman, so that earned him a few brownie points.

"We'll see."

"That's all I ask, pretty lady. Well, let me let you get out of this rain. Have a good night, drive safe."

"You too. Stay dry."

Two days later, Myrick and I'd had dinner at this Italian restaurant Bella Bella. Their raviolis were the best I'd ever had. I made a mental note to take Leandra there who thinks calzones from Sbarro is real Italian.

The first date had ended with a goodnight; the second date had concluded with a kiss. By the third date, we were comfortable enough with one another that a little touch here and tickle there ensued. I could tell Myrick was getting anxious. I had tortured the man long enough, so by the fourth date, it was time to let him taste my candy.

Myrick had taken me to dinner at Silver Slipper the night we had consummated our relationship. I was rocking these blue-black, low-waist jeans that accentuated my booty nicely. I wore this white blouse that hung seductively off one shoulder, something to keep his dick hard. We got back to my place, and didn't even make it past the sofa before things got hot and heavy. And my coochie was wet and down for whatever. We were kissing, Myrick feeling my breasts, sucking on my nipples. If having a rock-hard dick was a law, Myrick would have been tried and convicted. When we got to my bedroom, I smeared myself on the bed. My jeans and fuchsia panties were off faster than you could say "scantily clad."

"Turn over," he said. What was he going to do? I didn't ask, but just did what he wanted.

"Get up on your knees."

Oh shit.

I arched my back that made my ass arch. I was startled by the first touch of Myrick's tongue lapping at my booty hole. *Damn, he never said anything about being freaky.*

I had never had so much as a dick anywhere near my asshole, not to mention a man's tongue. Not that men haven't tried to ass-fuck me, talking all pretty, but I was quick to let them know that my starfish was exit only. Myrick's tongue was ticklish and slick as he teased the ring of my anus. He pried my cheeks apart, smothering his face in. He sucked and slurped, giving equal attention to my pussy.

"You ready for this dick?"

"Yes."

"What's that, baby?"

Myrick kept on licking my spot like it was a strawberry pudding pop. "Give it to me."

"You want it? You want this dick?"

His dirty talk had me horny as hell.

"Beg me."

"Yes."

"Beg me to fuck you."

"Please."

"Please, what?"

"Fuck me."

"You want it?"

"Yes."

"You want Myrick's dick?"

"Yes. I want your dick, Myrick. Fuck me."

"Are you on the pill, baby?"

I was taken aback by his question. "Yeah."

I felt the meaty tip of his dick graze against my pussy lips, and then enter me. Myrick didn't waste any time dicking me down.

"You like that?"

"You like how this dick feels in that pussy?"

"Damn, baby."

"You got some sweet pussy."

"Fuck me."

"Whose pussy is this?"

"Yours."

"What, I didn't hear you."

"Yours. This pussy is yours!"

"Turn over for me on your back. I want you to look at me while I fuck you, baby."

He tossed my legs up over my shoulders, and slipped his dick like a dirty secret back inside me. Myrick fucked me better than any man I had been with before. We fucked twice, sometimes three times a day. He would be sitting watching TV, and I would whip out his dick and start sucking it right there in the living room. "Damn, I like it when you get freak nasty like that."

I was so in love with him, I didn't think about how fast we were going. As months passed, and our relationship grew, Myrick started to get clingy, calling, if not texting me several times a day, wanting to know my every move and whereabouts. I had come home from work one night to find Myrick sitting on my stoop. I had worked a ten-hour shift at Target and was not in the mood for his mess.

"Myrick, what are you doing here? I told you I would call you."

He'd looked like he hadn't slept in days.

"I know, but I just wanted to see you. You've been working so much. I've missed you."

The smell of alcohol was hot on his breath. "Have you been drinking?"

Myrick took me into his arms. I pushed him off of me like something smelly and stinking. "You're drunk. You need to go home and sleep it off."

"What I need is my girlfriend to not be such a bitch," he said, tugging me by the arm like I was some rag doll.

I had a small thing of mace on my key chain, and was ready to pepper-spray his ass. "You need to get your fucking hands off me."

"Or what? What the fuck you go'n do?"

I held up the mace and sprayed Myrick in the face. I frantically unlocked the door and ran inside. I slammed the door behind me and locked it, leaving him rubbing pepper spray out of his eyes. "Fuckin' bitch!" He banged on my door.

"Go home, Myrick, before I call the cops!" I watched him from my living room window.

"Shariece, open this goddamn door!"

After about forty-five minutes, he got into his truck and screeched out of the lot. As far as I was concerned, we were over. Leandra went down with me to the police station where I filed a restraining order against his psychotic ass, but that only made things worse. On a couple of occasions, I found my tires slashed. Two-hundred and forty dollars—that shit set me back. He would crank call me and say, "How do you like, bitch?"

"Stay the hell away from me, you crazy fuck!"

"Next time it will be you I slash."

"Fuck you, Myrick!" I hung up and drove over to Leandra's.

"He's not going to stop. The only thing a man like that knows is a bullet to the head," Leandra said.

I had no idea how right Leandra was when Myrick and I came to a final head. I had just gotten home from work, tired as hell. Every muscle in my body ached. When I got home, I threw my purse on the sofa and dragged myself to my bedroom like a zombie out of a bad horror movie. I couldn't wait to wash the stink of the day off of me. I sensed a large figure behind me when I flicked on the bathroom light. Before I could turn around, I felt a hand muffle my mouth. I couldn't scream. From the smell of his cologne, I knew it was Myrick. He grabbed me tight around my midsection as we struggled.

"Hey, baby girl. Miss me?" I pawed at his hand over my mouth, scratching at his skin in hopes that the pain would be too much that he would let me go.

"Stop struggling, bitch." Afraid for my life, I did what Myrick wanted. My heart was pounding crazy in my chest thinking I was about to die.

"Baby, did you really think that a piece of paper would keep me away from you?" Myrick slid his hand up along my inner thigh, between my legs. I clamped my legs around his intruding hand in protest. "Nothing is going to keep me away from the woman I love." I never envisioned that I would die by the hands of a crazy-ass man, but that's exactly how I was going to meet my maker. "Why'd you go to the cops? We could have talked about this, worked things out like a normal couple, but you started overreacting, getting the damn cops and that bitch Leandra involved in our business." Myrick tugged at my pants until the button popped from the waistline. "We can work things out, right?" Myrick yanked my pants down past my ass and slid his hand down into my panties, parting my legs with brute force. I could hear him unzip his jeans. I knew what he had in mind. I stood to be raped if I didn't do something quick. "Come back to me, Shariece. You're mine and a restraining order isn't going to change that." I shook my head in agreement. "Good girl. Now if I let you go, you promise not to scream?"

I caressed his hand lovingly and nodded. Myrick dropped his hand from my mouth. I didn't scream knowing that he would kill me if I did. I turned around, looked at him, his face sweaty with a murderous expression. "You're right, Myrick. I'm sorry, baby. I did overreact." I fondled his dick to distract him. "Let's forget any of this ever happened, okay?"

"That's what's—" With a swift kick to his balls, I shut him up. A man's nuts are his Achilles heel. "Ah, fuckin' bitch!" The crystal vase that was given to me as a birthday gift from Leandra sat on the bedroom dresser. I took it and smashed it over Myrick's head, hard enough to knock him unconscious. I thought to continue hitting him with the vase until he was dead, but I decided that he wasn't worth ruining a pretty vase over, so I went for my cell phone to dial 9-1-1.

I called Leandra afterward, and she got to my house before the cops' slow asses did.

"Shariece!" I heard Leandra yell from outside my door. I was sitting on the end of the bed with the vase in my hand in case Myrick came to. "In here." Leandra gasped to Myrick lying on my bedroom floor, bleeding from his head. "Girl, is he…"

"He's alive."

"Are you okay?"

"He must have jimmied the lock." Leandra came over to hug me as I was on the brink of tears. Cop cars and ambulances filled the driveway. My nosey-ass neighbors gathered around the scene. I wondered where they were when I was screaming for my life. That's black folks for you: don't hear, see or say shit. Myrick was still out of it when the EMTs lifted him handcuffed into the ambulance. This white lady cop interrogated me like I had done something wrong. "I don't know how he got in. I told you he didn't have a key to my place." After I gave them a statement, they told me I could go. "There's no way I'm staying in that house tonight."

"Girl, you can stay with me as long as you want," Leandra said.

I went to the hearing to see Myrick sentenced. The judge gave him five years in prison for not only violating his restraining order, but the cops found out that he had three warrants for numerous offenses. As far as I was concerned, five years was not long enough for that sick bastard. He gave me a sinister stare as the bailiff took him away. I turned away. I couldn't stand to look at the man who damn-near killed me. After Myrick, I was done with the club and bar scene, and swore off men until this thing with Emjay happened. I made a promise to myself that I would never allow a man to have that much control over me again.

FOUR
LEANDRA

Emjay made a beeline to the new Air Jordans when we strolled into Foot Locker. Funny how I end up spending money when I bring him to the mall. "Ma, these are the ones I was talking about right here," Emjay said, picking up one of the shoes on display.

"I'm scared to look at the price of these ugly things." The shoes were black and white with red stripes and some kind of lightning-bolt design. I took the shoe and studied the price sticker on the sole. *One-hundred-twenty-eight dollars.* "For this price, you better be able to fly to the moon."

Emjay chuckled, looking at me with an excited expression, knowing that I would break down and buy them.

"I promise, Ma, if you get me these I will pay you back."

"Pay me back with what? You first have to get a job."

"I will pay you back every cent when I get a job."

"Which will be when?"

"I'm putting in applications. I went on an interview at Subway on Monday."

"And how did it go?"

"I thought it went well. They said they would give me a call next week, that they're still interviewing people."

"How are y'all doing today?" a salesgirl with pretty mahogany skin, a long, slick weave pulled back in a pony said as Emjay practically drooled over the pricey Nikes.

I looked at Emjay, and he back at me with a please-Ma look on his cute, looks-just-like-his-daddy expression. "How you doing? Can we see these in a size thirteen?"

"I'll go check in the back."

We took a seat and waited for her to bring the shoes out. "Zandra's cute."

"Who?"

"The salesgirl."

"How do you know her name?"

"That's what it says on her name tag: *Zandra*." Emjay shrugged his shoulders.

"You think she's cute?"

"Oh God, Ma, seriously?" Emjay smiled.

"I'm just asking."

"I don't know. I guess, yeah."

"Want me to get her number for you?" I teased.

"Ma, already you're trying to marry me off."

"Oh, trust, the only aisle I want to see you walk across is the one that leads you to getting your college degree. What have I told you, Emjay?"

"A degree is something no one can take away from you."

"That's right. You got plenty of time for girls, baby boy, but right now, you keep your head in those books."

Emjay slouched in his chair, waiting for Zandra to come back with the shoes.

"I don't want you to end up like me."

"What are you talking about? You own your own hair salon."

"And I had to work my butt off to get everything I have. No one is going to hand you anything, especially being black."

"It's never too late to live your dream, right?"

"Who told you that?"

"You did," he said. I took a long look at my son realizing I had taught him well. Zandra came back with a shoebox that was the same color as the pricey sneakers.

"This is the last size thirteen we have in back." She stooped down to his feet I prayed weren't funky once he pushed off his boots.

Zandra took out the stuffing in one of the shoes and started stringing them up. I looked at Emjay and couldn't be prouder of the man he had become. I was hell-bent on making sure he didn't end up like his daddy.

Fifteen, that's how old I was when I got pregnant with Emjay. For weeks, I didn't tell anybody, not even Rick, Emjay's daddy. Mrs. Boyd, the guidance counselor at my old high school, was the only person I had let in on my secret, God rest her soul. She was the only mother in my life as far as I was concerned being that my biological didn't give a fuck. She was home long enough to shove a bowl of SpaghettiOs in front of me, and then was back out on the street, selling her ass and food stamps for twenty dollars when she wasn't running off to wherever with her loser boyfriend of the month. I grew up fast, realizing no one was going to look out for Leandra Fox but Leandra Fox. I had stopped calling her Ma. She had lost that right the way she had fucked up my life and hers. When *Sherilyn* bothered to come home, I would steal money out of her purse for groceries while she slept off her high. I remember the track marks along her arm, these big, pea-sized holes that had gotten infected. I was ashamed to call her my mother, so I started calling her Sherilyn. When she was coherent enough, I was often met with insults. "I should have scraped you out of my pussy with a coat hanger when I found out I was pregnant with you. Ain't been nothin' but a nagging-ass crumb snatcher since I pushed you out of me. Mommy this and mommy that. Nag, nag, nag."

"Ma, are you all right?" Emjay asked.

"Huh? What?"

"Are you okay? You're crying."

"I am?" I wiped my face dry with my fingers.

"Happy tears, Emjay, happy tears," I said, resting my hand on my son's shoulder.

"Um...okay." Emjay gave me this puzzled look before he went back to watching Zandra string up the shoes.

"How do those fit?" Zandra asked.

"Good. They're comfortable."

"We'll take these," I said. Emjay smiled big when he saw that he was getting the shoes. Nothing's too good for my son.

"Great. You want to wear them out of the store?"

"Yeah. I want to work them in."

When I was a teenager, I used to wish my life was more like those white kids from *Beverly Hills, 90210.* I remember going to my school library and checking out every movie and music magazine I could get my hands on, and stare at hip-hop stars like Salt-N-Pepa, MC Lyte, Kool Moe Dee, Janet Jackson, Michael Jackson, and Notorious B.I.G. I live for Michael Jackson. I don't give a damn what anyone says. I'm a ride-or-die fan, and don't believe none of the rumors about him. I would pretend that I was one of the Jacksons, living in a big mansion in Hollywood, doing tours and videos, but reality hit me like a drive-by when I met Rick who was five years older than me, and had dreams of his own of wanting to be a big-time drug kingpin. The two of us were statistics of Holyfield Projects. Rick was always sweet-talking me, telling me how pretty I was.

"That oughta be you in those magazines. You prettier than those girls."

"You think so?"

"I wouldn't say it if I didn't think so. You should be walkin' the runways of New York and Paris."

Rick and I started seeing more and more of each other. There was nothing he wouldn't do for me. He moved up quickly in the game, gaining respect on the streets. Everyone called him Al. When I told him about my rocky relationship with Sherilyn, he wanted me to move into a one-bedroom apartment he got for us that was on the other side of town. I jumped at the chance to get away from my crack whore of a mother, and Holyfield Projects. I threw everything that mattered in two trash bags. Six weeks later, I found out I was pregnant. Fearing that Rick would leave me, I kept it from him. I considered getting an abortion but then thought of all the great things my baby could be: a lawyer, doctor, a great athlete or maybe a famous Hollywood actor. I decided to have my baby.

I wore baggy T-shirts and sweats so Rick wouldn't notice that I was putting on weight. I found out later that I was just another notch on Rick's bedpost. He had three baby mamas, all nibbling at his feet for child support. People warned me about him, that he fucked anything walking, but I wasn't trying to hear it until this ghetto-ass bitch, Marquise Chambers, came banging on my door.

"Who is you?" her illiterate ass had the nerve to ask.

"Who the fuck are you?"

"I'm Al's baby mama, bitch. Where he at?"

"I gotcho bitch, bitch, and not that it's any of your business, but Rick *isn't* home."

"You tell him his ass is two months' late paying me my money, and if he doesn't want me to go to court, he needs to pay me my shit. His daughter needs clothes and shoes."

That was messed up about her little girl, but I told this busted-ass heifer, "That's not my problem. He's with me now, and I ain't telling *my* man a goddamn thing. Now get the fuck off my porch before I beat the brakes off your ass."

"Bitch, who the fuck you—"

I said what I had to say and slammed the door in her face. Ain't nobody have time for her, least of all me. I let her yell at my door like the dizzy bitch she was. I was getting big. I couldn't go too much longer with all the weight I was putting on. Mrs. Boyd told me about getting proper prenatal care. She gave me a few numbers of some places to call knowing that it was against school policy to give out personal information. I knew I couldn't do this alone. I needed Rick's help. The night I decided to tell him, I cooked him a nice dinner, his favorites: baked chicken, yellow rice, black-eyed peas and sweet cornbread. He knew something was up being that I didn't cook that often. We ate, I sat him down on the sofa that was still on loan from Rent-A-Center, stuck a beer in his hand and told him.

"Rick, I'm pregnant." At first, he just stared at me like he was putting what he wanted to say together in his head as if they were puzzle pieces.

"Are you serious?" he said, smiling.

"Are you mad?"

"I'm going to be a father?"

"It looks like it, yeah."

Rick caressed my stomach, smiling from ear to ear to the news of the life that was growing inside of me. "You've made me the happiest black man on the planet, right now, Lee."

"I didn't think you wanted a kid right now with everything that's going on."

"That doesn't matter. We're having a baby. MY BABY'S HAVIN' A BABY!" he hollered.

"You so crazy," I said, laughing. Rick pressed his head against my stomach like it was a seashell.

"What do you want to name him?"

"How do you know it's going to be a boy? It might be a girl."

"I don't care as long as it's healthy."

"If it's a girl, I was thinking Kimberlyn, and if it's a boy, Emjay, after Michael Jackson but spelled E-m-j-a-y."

"I like that. That's a tough, take-no-shit kind of name." That night, Rick slept with his head laid sweetly on my stomach.

It was 6 a.m. on a Friday morning when I had pushed Emjay Landon Fox into this world on March 7, 1994. I had gone into labor Thursday night. My bed was soaked from my water breaking. Rick had been out all night, calling every hour on the hour to let me now that he was okay. This was something I insisted on, being that I worried about him 24/7. I called 9-1-1 and Mrs. Boyd soon afterward. She was the only one who gave a damn about me since I couldn't get a hold of Rick's ass. I would call only to have my call go to voicemail. The baby was coming whether I was ready or not. The paramedics had reached me before Mrs. Boyd got there. I told her that I was trying to reach Rick, but he wasn't answering his cell phone. "Will you keep calling until he answers?" I pleaded, as the paramedics lifted me into the ambulance.

I screamed for hours in pain like a hot, molten ball was trying to come out of me. No matter how much I hollered for Rick, wishing he was there, he never showed. I was in labor for six damn hours and no sign of him. I got a bad feeling that something was wrong seeing as how he stopped calling after midnight. Mrs. Boyd kept trying, but no Rick. I didn't have a clue where he was, and knew that he would have crawled through a ditch of snot and glass to get to me and the birth of our child.

After almost nine hours of being in labor, I gave birth to a seven-pound, three-ounce baby boy. My heart melted when I heard Emjay's first cries. The nurse wrapped him in a blue blanket Mrs. Boyd had given me and put him in my arms. Emjay was officially my son and I his mother. My love for him was sealed. The next day, I got a visit from some detective who informed me that Rick's SUV was found parked at Lake Jackson. He had been killed; shot execution style, the detective informed me. "No! No! No, God, Jesus, no!" I hollered so I must have waked up the entire hospital. "I told him to stay with me. I told him."

My worst fear of Emjay having to grow up without a father like I did, had come true. Rick never listened to me and did what he wanted without giving me or our son a second thought. He cared more about dealing than me. I buried Rick and got myself emancipated from Sherilyn in the same month. I couldn't believe she had managed to pull her ass together long enough to make it to court. She was a hot, whorish mess, barely able to stand. I watched her as she looked at Emjay cradled in my arms. Mrs. Boyd took me in, making sure I finished school and took proper care of Emjay. I took night classes in Cosmetology at the vo-tech school while she volunteered to babysit Emjay. She lived long enough to see me graduate. I was applying for jobs at beauty salons when I got the news that Mrs. Boyd died suddenly of a massive heart attack. Her doctor said she must have gone in her sleep. Seemed like everyone I cared about was dropping like flies. Her lawyer informed me that since she didn't have any family, she had left everything to me including her house.

I was sitting here and thinking of her, and how if it wasn't for her generosity, I would probably be on the street or worse. I look at Emjay sometimes and think, *you did good, lady. You barely made it, but you did it.* Emjay started asking about his daddy around the age of ten. I thought to lie to protect him, but lies eventually catch up with you. I thought if he was strong enough to ask, he was strong enough to know the truth. I swore that when he was born, I would never keep anything from him, which is why I wanted to tell him about Taj.

"How do they feel; they don't hurt your feet, do they?" We walked down the mall to the food court. A mixture of fried shrimp, Cajun barbecue pork, egg rolls and cinnabons infiltrated my senses.

"What do you want to eat?" Emjay asked.

I studied the menus of the adjoining eateries. There was nothing on any of them that advertised anything healthy.

"I think I'll have a pineapple punch from Orange Julius. I'm not really that hungry. Shariece would kill me if she knew I cheated on my diet."

"I want two slices from Sbarro," Emjay said, holding his hand out expecting me to put some money in it.

I looked at him, rolled my eyes and reached inside my purse. "I spoil you too much." I handed him a twenty. "You better bring my change back, Jay. I'm not playing with you."

As Emjay stood in line to order his food, I was jealous that his young behind could eat whatever he wanted and not gain a pound. Tall just like his daddy. I walked over to Orange Julius and got a pineapple fruit punch. The aroma of fresh baked cinnabons was calling my name, but I managed to fight temptation and walked away from the smell of cinnamon and gooey icing. I managed to get us a table that was over by the large fountain in the center of the mall. Emjay walked over with a paper plate of two slices of pepperoni pizza. You would think he hadn't eaten in days the way he wolfed down the junk food. His insatiable appetite was another thing he had inherited from Rick. "Boy, slow down eating that stuff, goodness alive." I took a few sips from my pineapple punch to calm the butterflies that were fluttering in my stomach when I thought how Emjay would react when I thought to tell him about Taj.

"Oh, so what did you want to talk to me about?" Emjay asked, as he wiped his mouth clean from greasy pizza.

"Well, I've been seeing someone."

"What, like a man?" he asked before biting into the second slice of pizza.

"No, a space alien, smart ass. Of course, a man."

"He's a photographer at *Tallahassee Magazine*."

"Is this the guy you're always laughing on the phone with?"

"Yes." I smiled. And he's a good man."

"Well, as long as he treats you good, I don't have a problem with him."

"I invited him over for dinner tomorrow night, and I want you to join us."

"Ma, I don't know. I got a lot of schoolwork I need to catch up on."

"Emjay, this is important. I want you to meet him. You can leave after dinner if you want."

He sat back in his chair. I could sense he was thinking about it. "What's this guy's name anyway?"

"Taj Bowman."

"That sounds like a fake name."

"Emjay?"

"Okay, okay, what time do you want me to be at the house?"

"Around seven."

"Fine if it means that much to you." I was happy that Emjay had taken the news of a new man in my life so well.

"Thank you, baby. I know you're going to love him."

"I want you to be happy, that's all, and if this guy makes you happy, then I'm good."

"I thank the Lord every day for giving me you. I was crying back in the shoe store 'cause I was thinking about your daddy and how proud he would be of you."

"You think so?" Emjay asked.

"He would have been proud to call you his son."

Emjay finished devouring his last slice of pizza.

"So Shariece tells me that you're doing well in her class."

"Yeah, I mean, so far so good."

"I hope you don't think you're going to coast through her class just because she's your godmama." Emjay took a long sip from the large Coke he'd bought.

"Oh, I'm working for it, trust me."

"I invited Shariece over for dinner as well to meet Taj."

Emjay started coughing like something had suddenly got stuck in his throat.

"See there. What did I tell you about chewing your food?" Emjay held a fist up to his mouth, damn near about to cough a lung up.

"Goodness, boy, are you okay? Over there sounding like you're about to cough up a lung."

"Yeah, um…you ready to go?"

"I need to go pick some stuff up at the grocery store for tomorrow night's dinner, then I can drop you off."

"That's cool. Whatever you need to do."

The drive back to Emjay's was so quiet I could hear my heart beating in my throat.

"What's wrong?"

"Nothing. I'm just thinking about this project I need to do for my Oceanography class."

I fever of relief passed over me after telling Emjay about Taj. "We should all be sitting down for dinner around seven-ish."

"I'll be there, Ma, I promise."

"Thank you, baby," I said before I gave him a kiss on the cheek. "This means so much to me."

FIVE
SHARIECE

had gotten to the door of my house when I heard my iPhone ring in my purse. My arms were full with groceries and school-work. Thankfully, I had my keys in my hand already. I pushed the key through the hole and turned the knob until it clicked open. I set my groceries and green folder of ungraded papers on the kitchen table. "Hold on, I'm coming, I'm coming." I fished out my phone that read: *Emjay calling, 570-8623.*

"Hey."

"I just left Ma and she told me about this guy she's seeing. She wants us to come to dinner to meet him tomorrow night. Please, please, please tell me that you're not going."

"I already promised her I would."

"When were you going to tell me that she invited you?" Emjay asked.

"I tried calling you, and left a text, but you never answered."

"You have to tell her that you got sick, that you came down with the stomach flu or something."

"Jay, she's pretty excited about us meeting this new man in her life. I told her I would support her."

"And you don't think it's going to be weird with me and you sitting there together?"

"What are you talking about? It's not going to *look* like anything."

"I don't think I can do this."

"Emjay, it'll be fine. It's only dinner."

"What do you know about this Taj guy, anyway?"

"No more than you know. Sounds like she's really into him, so I guess we'll see what all the fuss is about tomorrow night."

I sat on the barstool of the island in the middle of the kitchen. "Trust me. It won't be as bad as you're making it out to be."

"I guess. So what are you doing?"

"I just got in, why?"

"I've been walking around with a hard-on all day thinking about your sexy ass."

"I bet you have."

"Come over."

"I can't. I have a lot of work to catch up on."

"You know what they say about all work and no play."

"Yeah, there's always more work and hardly any play."

"Let's have phone sex?"

"What? I swear I think you blurt this stuff out to see if you can get a rise out of me."

"You know you like it when I talk dirty to you."

"Oh, I'm not denying that." I smiled.

"Come on, let's play."

I walked over to the sofa and made myself comfortable. I could barely focus on work for thinking about Emjay.

I pulled my skirt up my thighs and over my ass.

"Okay, now what?"

"Take your stockings off."

I gently rolled off my black silk hose from my butt, down my thighs to my ankles.

"Are you doing it?"

"Yes."

"Now slide your hand between your legs." I did what Emjay wanted.

"You doing it?"

"Yes."

"Play with your pussy."

I slowly inserted my middle finger past the wet lips of my pussy. I moaned, so Emjay could hear how hot he was making me. "Are you wet?"

"Always."

"Guess what I'm doing right now."

I heard the acute reverberation of a zipper being tugged down.

"Being nasty."

"My dick is rock-hard right now."

"Is it?"

"Hell yeah. Hold on for a minute."

"What is it?"

"I just sent something to your phone." I opened the pic on my cell to find a picture of Emjay's dick staring back at me.

"What do you want me to do to it?" I asked as I fingered my pussy.

"I wish your fine ass was here, so I could fuck you."

"You're crazy, you know that? How did I end up with such a kinky boyfriend?"

"How's that pussy doing?"

"Dripping. It needs some dick."

"Damn, that's what's up. Taste it for me." I stuck my finger tinged with my juices, into my mouth and sucked it clean.

"How does it taste?"

"You should know," I said.

"Is it hungry for my dick?"

"You better believe it."

"Damn, woman, you got me hard as hell."

"Jack that dick."

"I wish you were here."

"Tell me."

"What?"

"Tell me what you want me to do with that dick."

"I wish you were here to suck it."

"You want my big, juicy lips around that dick?"

"Fuck yeah."

"Slide it past my lips, down my throat."

Emjay moaned, sucking his teeth over the phone. "You're going to make me nut up in here."

"No, not until I tell you."

"I want to fuck you."

"I want you to fuck a hole through me, Emjay."

"Fuck, I wish I could come over there."

"I'm running that deep throat head on you, those big balls banging against my chin."

"Sucking my big dick," he moaned.

"What do you want to do to me right now?"

"Lay you on your back."

"Mmm…"

"Spread you open."

"You got me wet."

"I want to lick it, suck on your pussy lips, have your ass speaking in tongues." It took everything in me to keep from laughing when Emjay said that.

"Damn, baby."

"Tongue-fuck you 'til you can't take it anymore."

"I'm about to come," I said.

"Come with me."

"Oh fuck."

"Come with me, baby." I played with my pussy until I felt myself close to climax.

"I'm coming, Jay. Fuck, I'm coming!"

"Damn, me too. Do it, baby, do it."

I kept on until I oozed, juices trickling down my thigh.

"I just came all over my stomach and chest," Emjay said.

"Good."

"We need to get up and soon."

"So I'll see you at the dinner tomorrow?" I asked.

"I guess so."

"With everything Leandra's been through, I'm happy that she's found someone. She deserves that."

"I agree."

"I sense a *but* in that sentence."

"I just don't want her to get hurt, that's all. I'll be interested to find out what this guy's story is."

"We'll both find out tomorrow."

"So are you sure you don't want me to come over tonight?"

"It's not that. I'm tired and I have a ton of grading to do."

"I can come over and um…tuck you in."

"If you do, I won't get anything done."

"Probably not, but you'll be sexually satisfied."

"You're so silly. Goodnight, Emjay."

"Goodnight, baby."

SIX

SHARIECE

I ransacked my closet trying to find something fly-ass gorgeous to wear. Everything was either for work, or church. I didn't realize how badly in need I was of a wardrobe. With teaching taking up a large part of my free time, shopping for new clothes wasn't exactly at the top of my list of priorities. I finally settled on a pair of jeans that hugged me in all the right places and a silk, red, off-the shoulder top. By the time I had decided on something, most of my wardrobe was on the bedroom floor. You would have thought I was going on my first date, the way my room looked with clothes, shoes and jewelry everywhere. I called Leandra to see if she needed anything before I left.

"Girl, please tell me you're not canceling."

I could hear the commotion of pots and pans in the background.

"Not at all. I'm on my way over. I wanted to know if you needed me to bring anything."

"Just your diva self. Dinner is almost ready. Emjay called and said that he's on his way."

"You sound nervous," I said.

"Girl, I'm climbing the walls right now. I want everything to be perfect. I'm on edge about Emjay meeting Taj."

"Everything will be fine. Stop worrying."

I sprayed on some Chanel No. 5 and added a touch of strawberry lip gloss as a final touch.

"So what did you decide to make for dinner?"

"I wanted to try this new low-calorie lasagna recipe I got out of *Southern Living* magazine. I hope it comes out right. I followed the directions to the letter."

"Child, you worry too much. I'm sure it'll be delicious."

"That's why you need to hurry up, so you can taste it. You know how much I value your opinion."

"I'm walking out the door now."

"Okay, see you when you get here."

Just when I was about to hang up, Leandra said, "And Shariece?"

"Yeah?"

"Thank you for doing this. It means so much."

"Anything for my best friend."

SEVEN
EMJAY

"**D**amn, she ain't here yet," I said, pulling up behind Mama's jet-black BMW. There was a red M5 Spyder parked alongside the curb. The outside of the house looked good with the new white paint job and the red shutters. The grass was thick and emerald-green while the red tops that lined the perimeter of the house were newly trimmed. My heart was beating crazy matched by my sweaty palms that I dried against my jeans. I was about to ring the doorbell until I realized that I didn't have to; I grew up in this house.

"Ma, I'm home," I joked, letting myself in. Whatever she was cooking smelled good. "Is that my baby boy?" I heard Ma coming from the direction of the kitchen. Ma appeared in a red dress with black high-heel shoes. This brother who looked to be about twenty-one, six-three with pecan-brown skin walked toward us from the living room with a glass of wine and a dumb-looking smile.

"Taj, I would like you to meet my handsome and smart son, Emjay. Emjay, this is Taj Bowman."

What the fuck? This is him? This is the brother she's been laughing on the phone with? I sized him up. "Hey, what's up?" I said, giving this man who could have been my younger brother some dap.

"What's up, Taj, good to meet you."

He wore dark-blue jeans, black Kenneth Coles and a white dress shirt. Taj's hair was cut short like mine with rows of waves brushed in. I couldn't believe that this was the dude Ma was seeing. I was in for a long night.

"Leandra has told me a lot about you."

He sounded fake as hell. "Well, I just heard about you yesterday, and I don't know much."

"Emjay," Ma said with a tone of protest.

Ma eyed at me like she wanted to choke me. What the hell was she doing robbing the cradle at her age?

"Why don't you two have a seat in the living room and get acquainted while I go check on dinner." I stuck my hands down into the pockets of my jeans as I followed Taj into the living room.

"You want something to drink, Emjay?"

Okay, why the fuck was he acting like he was the man of the house already? Last I checked, Ma was paying the bills.

"A beer is cool."

Taj sauntered back behind the bar, pulled out a cold bud like he had pulled a rabbit out of his ass, popped off the top and handed it to me.

"So your mother tells me you're in school." All of his talking-proper bullshit was starting to wear thin. "What are you studying?"

I wanted to tell him that it was none of his business, and to get out of my house but instead… "I haven't really decided yet. I'm trying to get my gen-reqs out of the way."

"Gen-reqs?"

"General requirements. Math, history, English, science."

"Okay, gotcha," he said, sipping wine from his glass. The more I gawked at the guy that was fucking my mama, the madder I became. *You really know how to pick 'em, don't you, Mama?*

"Ma tells me you're a photographer."

"Yeah, catalog stuff mostly. I've done a few runway gigs in New York."

"Do you know Tyra Banks?"

"I've met her a couple times, but we've never worked together."

As we continued on with our conversation, the bell rang. I knew it was Shariece. Ma answered the door.

She walked in with a bouquet of flowers looking fine as hell in tight black jeans.

"I know you said that I didn't have to bring anything, but I saw these on the way here and thought they would make a beautiful centerpiece."

The flowers were better than that bowl of fake, dusty fruit I thought Ma would have sense enough to take off the table by now.

"Girl, you are too much; come on in."

Taj stood off waiting to be introduced. "You must be Shariece."

An expression of shock ran across her face. Surprised at how old Taj looked—no doubt. "Hello, it's nice to meet you finally."

"Would you like something to drink?" Taj asked.

This phony brother seemed like Ma's hired hand than someone she was fucking.

"A glass of Merlot would be great."

Taj disappeared behind the bar and poured Shariece a glass of wine.

"Leandra, the house looks terrific."

"That's right; it's been a while since you were last here. You haven't seen all of the remodeling." The living room consisted of an Afrocentric theme where masks and pictures of African kings and queens lined the gold-painted walls but looked more like a beige tone. A long, white leather sofa sat against the wall facing the entertainment center chock-full of figurines, pictures of me when I was little and rows of DVDs. The fifty-inch LG TV took up much of the space. There were two white leather love seats and a rocking chair that didn't match with anything Ma had. They belonged to some lady named Mrs. Boyd, who had left her the house when she'd died, so Ma wanted to hold on to them. A long dining room glass table sat in the center with gold placemats.

"I like the beige in here. It's cute."

"See there, Ma, I told you it looks more beige than gold."

"It's not beige?" Shariece asked.

"No, it's gold," Ma said.

"It doesn't look like gold," I said.

"It doesn't have to look like gold when it is gold, Emjay."

"Why don't you have gold furniture in here then?"

"Boy, where would I find gold furniture?"

"I don't know, maybe in a James Bond movie." I knew I was being a smart ass, but I didn't care. I was over this dinner bullshit.

EIGHT
LEANDRA

"I'm going to go check on dinner. Shariece, can you give me a hand in the kitchen, please?"

"Girl, I swear, I'm about to slap the shit out of that boy."

I slid on my pair of flower-print oven mitts, opened the oven, and pulled out the platter of vegetarian lasagna and set it on the kitchen counter to cool. "Has he been like this all night?"

"He's been salty ever since he walked in the door. It's not like him to be so rude. He might be too grown for me to spank, but he ain't grown enough to be kicked out of my house."

"Don't worry about Emjay. Him seeing you with someone will just take some getting used to."

"So what do you think of Taj? He's cute, right?"

"He's so…"

"Young I know, but he's good to me, Shariece, and girl, he can fuck like a bull."

"If nothing else, it's good that he can screw," Shariece said.

"Can you believe how successful he is at the ripe age of twenty-six?"

"Twenty-six? Damn."

"Did you see his Spyder outside? It's nice, right? He let me drive it the other day."

"It looks like the lasagna turned out all right."

"I only hope it tastes as good as it looks. I want to impress Taj, so I hope he likes it. He told me the other day, 'I'll eat anything you cook. I don't care if it's a mud pie.' Isn't he sweet?"

I took the flowers Shariece brought and set them in a crystal vase with water.

"Girl, these are so pretty, thank you."

"I know how much you love lilacs." I took a vase from under the sink, filled it with water, and arranged the long-stemmed flowers in the vase.

"They're beautiful."

"So what did you make for dessert?"

"Don't kill me for this, but I made cherry cheesecake with bits of walnuts on top. It's Emjay's favorite. And yeah, I know it's fattening, but I figure we can indulge for tonight and then hit the treadmill tomorrow."

"I don't think we'll blow up to blimps after one piece of cheesecake."

A bowl of Caesar salad sat off on the side of the counter next to the cheesecake.

"It looks like we're ready to eat."

I couldn't imagine what Taj and Emjay were discussing. I didn't hear yelling or anything breaking, so I figured everything was fine. I walked out to the dining room armed with lasagna while Shariece followed me out with the Caesar salad.

"Dinner is served."

Taj and Emjay joined us in the dining room.

"This looks delicious, baby," Taj said, giving me a kiss on the cheek.

"Thank you." I smiled.

"Lee, you really outdid yourself."

Emjay still had this look on his face that I had no problem slapping off if he didn't straighten his ass up and fly right. He is too big to be acting like a baby. He sat down at the dinner table and didn't utter a word. "Ya'll make sure you save room for some cherry cheesecake." I glanced over at Emjay when I announced that I had made his favorite, but still, there was no sign of cheer on his face. If he was going to continue to act stupid, I knew that before long, I was going to have to snatch his ass up. He's my son, and I love him, but nobody's going to disrespect me in my own house.

NINE
EMJAY

thought I was going to throw up when this brother kissed Ma.
I poured myself a glass of wine. The only way I was going to
get through this night was getting shit-drunk.

"Taj, you sit next to me, and Emjay, you're next to Shariece.
And Emjay get your elbows off the table." *There she goes again, talking
to me like I'm a child.* Shariece gawked at me like I was a misbehaving
child she couldn't wait to pull aside to spank.

"This is a new recipe, so I want ya'll to tell me how it tastes." All
of us were seated, ready to eat. I was starving.

"Who would like to say grace?"

"How about our esteemed guest," Emjay said.

Mama gave me this long, mean-mugging stare, but I was like,
whatever.

"Sure. I would love to."

Fake ass. I thought.

We all bowed our heads as this fool started to say grace.

"God, thank you for this food we are about to eat. Thank you for good health, life and the gift to love. Thank you for bringing Leandra Fox into my life when I had given up on ever finding love again."

Again? That would imply that he was with someone else before Mama. Probably some hood rat with ten kids.

"Amen."

Finally, he was done kissing Ma's ass. I couldn't stand the sound of this poser's voice. "So fake," I mumbled.

"Emjay, you got something you want to add?"

"What?"

"No, I thought I heard you say something. Speak up if you got something you want to say."

"I'm good," I told her.

With the way Ma was looking at me, I was sure she wanted to snatch me across the table. We passed the salad around while Ma cut into the lasagna.

"Taj, baby, hand me your plate."

Shariece acted like I had cooties, or some shit. I guess I was alone in thinking that Ma looked ridiculous with this dude. I mean, were they actually going out in public together? "So Ma, where did you and Taj meet?"

"We met on Blackpeople.com," she said, spooning salad onto her plate.

I started laughing. "What's so funny, Emjay?"

"Are you serious?"

"Yes. We talked for a couple of weeks before we decided to meet for coffee."

"Ma, come on, you don't think that's a little dangerous? Look what happened to that girl that met that guy on Craigslist. He turned out to be a serial killer. Not that I'm saying you're a serial killer, man, but..."

"That was one incident. Besides, I insisted on meeting him at a public place."

"Ma, you don't know. These guys could be anybody."

"Emjay, that's enough," Shariece said. There she was playing up the role of godmama. Out of everyone, I thought she would get where I was coming from being that her ex-boyfriend tried to kill her.

"Emjay, I understand the concern you have for your mother, but man, I'm not one of these crazies out here. Your mother is a pretty special lady, and I would never do anything to hurt her."

I know you're not going to hurt her unless you want to be sucking food through a straw for the rest of your fake-ass life, I thought.

"Man, how old are you, anyway?"

"Emjay!" Ma protested. "I'm just asking."

"I'm twenty-six."

"Damn, so you into cougars?"

"Emjay, you better watch how you speak to my guest."

"Ma, don't you think you look a little ridiculous walking around town with a guy this young on your arm?" I ran my mouth like Taj wasn't in the room.

"Let's get something straight right now. You don't have any say-so in how I live my life, and who I date ain't none of your damn business. Taj is a good man. Maybe if you would stop being such a spoiled brat, and took the time to get to know him, you would see what I see. This is my house, and if you can't respect me in it, you can get the hell out."

"Sounds good to me. I'm out of here."

"Emjay, wait," Shariece said.

"No, let him go. Until he can learn to respect me and respect Taj, he can show his ass to the door."

I hauled ass out of there, slamming the door behind me. I jumped in my car and sped off, kicking a fat body of white exhaust behind me.

"Fuck this."

TEN
SHARIECE

"Answer the damn phone." I redialed Emjay's number only to continue to be sent to voicemail, which aggravated the hell out of me. I stopped by his apartment first, but his car wasn't in the parking lot of the complex. I racked my brain trying to figure out where he could be. I thought of a place. "Emjay might not be there, but I figure it is worth a try."

I walked into Mockingbird Lounge and sure enough, there was Emjay, sitting idle at the bar. Other than a few patrons peppered throughout, the place wasn't packed for a Friday night. I sat next to him as he nursed on a Heineken.

"So what the hell was that back at the house?" Shariece asked.

A thin, young white guy dressed from head to toenail in a black T-shirt and black low-waist jeans came to greet me. There wasn't an inch of skin left that wasn't covered in tattoos. He had short, dark-brown hair that was buzzed on the sides and combed over to one side and a well-trimmed beard.

"Hi. Can I get you something to drink?"

"Vodka cranberry with lime," I said sternly.

"What is she doing? She looked ridiculous. Is she serious with that guy?"

"Whatever happened to you wanting Leandra to be happy?"

"I know him."

"What do you mean you know him?"

The bartender came back with my vodka cranberry. I handed him my debit card. "Ma'am, would you like me to start a tab?"

"No, just this, thank you."

He swiped my card and handed it back to me.

"I've seen him before. He plays basketball over at the Walker-Ford Center."

"So what does that have to do with how you acted in front of Taj and Leandra?"

"Why didn't you have my back? You both treated me like a child."

"I'm sorry to tell you this, Emjay, but that's exactly how you were acting."

"What?"

"You embarrassed me with your behavior tonight."

"I guess I know whose side you're on."

"You know what? You need to grow the fuck up. You're not a kid anymore. I can't believe the level of disrespect you showed Leandra and Taj tonight."

"I never would have agreed to this dinner had I known how old dude was."

I took a sip from my drink. "If you have such a stick up your ass about her seeing a younger man, how do you really feel about the two of us being together?"

"It's not like that."

"It's exactly like that."

"This is my mama we're talking about. I mean, damn, picking up men on a dating site?"

"It's no more dangerous than meeting someone at a bar, a party, a club or anywhere. And it shouldn't matter that he's a younger man. You're the one who said age ain't nothing but a number."

"Did he tell you how old he is?"

Emjay failed to grasp my point. "I can't do this."

"What?"

"What are we doing? We fuck around once a week, but outside of sex, what is this, really? I'm your teacher, for God's sake."

"What are you saying?"

I reached inside my purse and left Warren a generous ten-dollar tip for serving me. "I think whatever *this* is; we need to reexamine our relationship."

"Just like that?" Emjay asked.

"What do you want me to say, Emjay?"

"This is what you've always wanted, isn't it? You never wanted to be with me. I'm just a fuck-toy for you. Am I the first student you've seduced?"

"Fuck you."

"Me and who else?"

In a fit of rage, I threw my vodka cranberry in his face.

People at the bar turned their attention to the drama that had ensued. "Let me know when you decide to grow the hell up."

I exited through the double-glass tinted doors to the parking lot. "Shariece, wait!" I kept walking until I felt Emjay tug my arm.

"I'm sorry. You know I didn't mean that. It's just a messed-up night."

"I risked my job, my reputation, my friendship with Leandra, and all for what?" When I started for my car again, Emjay yanked at my arm.

"Let go of my arm."

"Babe, come on, don't leave; let's talk about this."

"I said let go of me."

"Hey, the lady said let her go." A deep, brawny voice reverberated out of nowhere. A heavy-set white man with a football player build, who was the size of a refrigerator, walked toward us. He had broad shoulders, huge arms with his chest puffed out. He looked like a villain out of a David Statham movie. "Is this boy bothering you, miss?"

"The fuck you callin' a boy. Look, man, this is none of your business, so keep walkin'."

"The lady can talk for herself."

Emjay and the man stood head to head until their chests almost touched. Emjay wanted to prove that he was no punk even though he knew that the giant of a man would probably wipe the parking lot with him.

"Sir, thank you, but we're fine. We were just talking, that's all," I said.

He looked at me and asked, "Are you sure you're all right?"

"You heard the lady, big foot. Step the fuck off."

The brute looked at Emjay wanting to fuck him up so bad, but he did what I asked and walked away. As he continued to beg me to hear him out, I got in my car and drove away. I was done. There was nothing else to say.

ELEVEN
SHARIECE

t had been two weeks since the incident at Leandra's—the last time I laid eyes on Emjay. He called me five, six times a day, texting me, leaving apologies on my voicemail. No lie; I missed him, especially when I would wake up from one of my sex dreams of him giving me one of his state-of-the-art, heart-pounding, toe-curling fuck sessions. I get wet every time I think back to that day in my office when he had his head buried between my thighs, fingering and tongue-fucking my honey spot. Fortunately, Leandra and Taj's relationship was getting stronger with each day they spent together. She was quick to fill me in on how good the sex was. "Girl, that man had me seeing stars after he fucked me."

We did lunch at Crispers last week where I asked her if she had heard from, or seen Emjay.

"No, not since he showed his ass in front of me and Taj at dinner. I've gone by his apartment a few times, but he's never home, or maybe he is, and just won't answer the door. Emjay needs to get over it. I'm too old for children's games, Sha. I love him, but I don't want to have to choose between my son and my man. It's like I say: when love comes knocking, you either answer the door, or sit on your ass. I have to do *Leandra Fox*, and if that makes me a selfish bitch, then I'll take it." Leandra knew Taj all of two weeks, and now she was talking about love? Seriously?

The day I saw Emjay, I was catching up on some much needed house cleaning that I couldn't find time to do due to my busy school week. I was doing a thorough cleaning of my closet, throwing some things in a pile for Goodwill, when I heard a boisterous knock on my door. My bedroom was a mess. The bed and floor was strewn with clothes, shoes and belts. I trudged past the mounds of discarded shirts, dresses, jeans, shorts and shoes, to go see who the hell was banging on my door like they were crazy. I peeked through the key hole and sure enough: Emjay.

"Shariece, please, can we talk?"

I started not to let him in, but figured he had seen my car out front and wasn't going to leave until he had his say.

"What do you want?"

"I've been texting and calling you. Didn't you get my voicemails?"

"Yes. I stopped hearing what you had to say after the eleventh message. Do I need to remind you that I was in a relationship with a man that started out exactly like this mess you're doing now?"

"That's pretty low to go comparing me to that psycho."

"I thought the same thing about Myrick until he broke into my house threatening to kill me."

I honestly had not moved past what Myrick had done to me. I thought after seeing him being taken away where he couldn't hurt me or anyone else, the nightmare was over, yet at times I wake up in a cold sweat after the bad dreams I've had of that night.

"Can we talk inside? I don't want your nosey neighbors to call the cops on me."

I looked at Emjay with hesitation, and then let him in. He looked good in a white Aeropostale T-shirt that was tight around his biceps. His ass was snug in a pair of light-blue jeans.

"So talk."

"I want to say that you were right. I was an asshole and a hypocrite, but I don't want my stupidity to be the end of us. I'm not trying to mess up what we have."

I was weakening to Emjay's pleas and heartfelt apologies. "Yeah, you were an asshole, but I'm not the only one you need to apologize to."

"I know; I'm going to call Mama to say I'm sorry."

"No, you need to go see Leandra. She says she hasn't heard or seen you since that night at the dinner. You need to talk to her face to face."

"Look, I've been thinking…"

"About what?"

"How do you feel about me telling her about us?" My heart froze when Emjay said he wanted to be forthcoming about our relationship. "It's not fair to you; it's not fair to us that we have to keep our relationship hidden from Ma like it's some dirty secret."

"Emjay, I don't know. I don't think she's ready for that."

He wrapped me into his strong arms, looked into my eyes and said, "She has no choice but to be ready, and besides, I love you."

Did he just say what I thought he said?

"Say again?"

"You heard me. I'm in love with you. Hell, I've been in love with you since I was fifteen."

"And you never said anything."

"I was a kid. You wouldn't have taken me seriously."

Emjay had a point. I probably wouldn't have.

"You would have thought it was some cute crush or something."

"You're serious, aren't you?" I asked.

"What, about loving you? Hell yeah."

I threw my arms around his neck, pulling him to me until we came together in a deep, passionate kiss that seemed long overdue. I could feel his erection nudging my thigh. "I've missed you. You're all I've thought about." I took Emjay by the hand and led him into the bedroom where we started making out. He kissed along my neck and my cleavage, slipping the muscle T-shirt off, causing my breasts to pop free from the snug, ribbed cotton. He knew all the right buttons to push, traipsing his fingers along my perky nipples. Damn, he felt good. Emjay practically smeared me on the bed strewn with clothes and belts that I pushed from under me to the floor as he peeled off my low-waist jeans like they were a second skin. My white, cherry-printed panties were next to go. My pussy was soaking wet. I reached up and undid his jeans as he slid off his shirt. I noticed the tent his dick made behind the light-blue faded denim. I was anxious to release that baby's arm from its prison. I unzipped him, pulled at the elastic band of his drawers, reached in and pulled Emjay's dick free. The shaft was smooth; the head full and plump with a teardrop piss-slit that glistened with precum that I licked clear. That dick was hungry for some attention. I threw my lips around the tip of Emjay's piece.

Sucking dick, I have to admit, has always been my favorite thing to do sexually. Dontavious Marks was my first at fifteen, who I used to blow under the baseball bleachers after school. He had a big dick for someone who was fifteen.

I kept at him until that fat appendage filled my mouth. I slipped until his pubes grazed against my nose. "You keep that shit up and I'm gonna blow." After a few strokes, I stopped. I wanted Emjay inside me. I lay back, legs agape, pussy clad and dripping. I was down for whatever. Emjay folded into me, our skin tender. Our eyes met like star-crossed lovers as he maneuvered his dick inside me. I sighed when I felt him spreading me. I roped my legs tight around him as he began to thrust, pinching my nipples between thumb and index finger. "Fuuuck!"

TWELVE
LEANDRA

When I saw Shariece's door hanging open, I started to think the worst. As I eased in with caution, I heard sounds of sex coming from the direction of her bedroom. I walked hesitantly down the narrow hall until I got to her bedroom door that was cracked open. When I saw Emjay bare-ass naked on top of her, I started to boil with rage.

"What the fuck?" Emjay pushed himself frantically off of Shariece. "Oh, my God, Leandra, I can explain." I was knocked on my ass when I saw my best friend in bed with my boy.

"You bitch!" I lunged for Shariece, catching her by her throat, my fire engine-red nails digging into her throat. I tried to kill this bitch.

"Ma, get off of her," Emjay yelled, struggling to pull me off Shariece.

"What was that shit about doing what makes you happy? More like doing *who* makes you happy."

"Ma, goddamn it, get off her!" Emjay pushed me damn near off the bed, causing me to free my grip from around Shariece's throat. She started coughing to catch her breath.

"I don't believe this shit. You and her?"

"We were going to tell you."

"We? How long has this been....boy, put some damn clothes on. I don't want to look at your little-ass dick," I said, turning away. Shariece had bed covers wrapped around her body, her titties bunched in Emjay's comforter. He covered up with a pair of boxers.

"A few months," Emjay said.

"We were going to tell you, Lee." Shariece was coughing, rubbing her throat.

"Shut up, bitch. I don't give a fuck what you have to say. Here you are supposed to be teaching my son something. Yeah, you're teaching him something all right."

"We weren't trying to hurt you."

"Don't talk to me. Don't even utter my motherfucking name, bitch."

"I love her, Ma."

"You what? What the fuck do you know about love? You're only twenty-two years old. You're surrounded by bitches all day at school, but instead, you fuck my best friend? No, correction: *former* best friend."

"Ma, let's sit down and talk about this."

"Of all the men you've fucked, why did my son have to be a notch on your goddamn bed post?

"Don't call her a bitch, Ma."

"How many times, Shariece? How many damn times did you look in my face, sit across the fucking table from me in my house, and didn't mumble a word, not a single syllable about you and Jay."

"I… we were going to tell you."

"But you didn't tell me. An eleven-year friendship and you kept this away from me."

"Ma, we love you, but we don't have to report every detail of our lives to you."

I struggled to hold back tears.

"You're right, Leandra. Out of respect for our friendship, I should have said something, but at the same time, I'm a grown woman."

"And I'm not a little boy anymore," Emjay chimed in.

"All that shit you gave me about Taj when here ya'll are on some down-low shit. Do you know I was considering breaking up with him, to sacrifice *my* happiness because I knew how upset me and him being together made you?"

"I was wrong for those things I said to you and Taj. I acted like a spoiled asshole, and I know you raised me better than that, Mama. Here I am trying to prove to you that I'm a man, and all I did was disrespect you, and I'm sorry for that."

"You have to believe that we didn't set out to hurt you," Shariece said.

"You know, I admit that I had my issues with dating a younger man. I was concerned with how it would affect you. She'll tell you. Ever since I pushed you out into this world, I sacrificed everything for you. That's what a mother does for her child. But I'm done. You're right, you are becoming a man, and I'm not going to stand in the way of that." I looked at Shariece and said, "He's all yours." I stormed out of her townhouse, out the door. I couldn't wait to get out of there knowing that it was the last time I would stand under her roof.

"Ma, hold up," Emjay said, but I kept on. I was done talking.

It was pouring rain. "Damn, every day it rains." My umbrella was in the car so I made a run for it. I don't like getting my hair wet, but with the shit storm I had walked in on, I didn't give a damn. I wiped tears from my eyes like the wipers obliterating hard rain from my windshield. I sped down the sleek, pitch highway on my way home. I searched for my cell phone that was in the recesses of my purse. I needed Taj. I needed to hear a friendly voice; someone I knew would have my back always being that I just lost the two most important people I ever gave a damn about, whom I would have done anything in this sorry, sad-ass world for. I straddled the road as I scrolled down the list of numbers in search of Taj's. When I dialed, it rang and rang, going straight to voicemail. *Hey, you've reached Taj Bowman, you know what to do.*

"Damn it." I grew angrier and angrier as I thought of all the times Shariece could have told me about her relationship with Emjay. The rain was coming down so hard, I could barely see anything. I tried reaching Taj again only to get his voicemail. When a tree branch fell in front of my Beamer, I jerked my wheel to the right, causing my car to careen off the road into a tree. When I came to, my head was throbbing in searing pain like someone had plunged metal spikes through my head. Smoke spirited from under the crushed hood. The windshield was smashed. I felt something rolling down the side of my face. I reached up to touch it. It was blood. The last thing I remember was the sound of sirens.

THIRTEEN
SHARIECE

I was startled awake by the chime of my iPhone that sat on the bedside table next to Emjay's alarm clock. It was seven minutes after midnight. Emjay's arm slung over my waist. "Hello," I said, wondering who the hell was calling my phone that time of night.

"Hello, is there a Ms. Shariece Houston there, please?"

I grimaced to the directness of the white woman's voice.

"This is she."

"Ma'am, my name is Emilie Nash; I'm a nurse at Tallahassee Community Hospital."

"Hospital?"

I felt Emjay awaken.

I sat up in bed to attention.

"Yes, we have you listed as an emergency contact for a Ms. Leandra Fox."

"Yes, she's my friend; what's going on?"

"Who is it?" Emjay asked.

"I'm sorry to have to tell you this, but Ms. Fox was in a car accident."

"Oh my God."

"What is it; is it Mama?"

"She suffered a mild concussion, but she's going to be fine," the nurse said.

"Oh, thank the Lord," I said, holding my hand to my chest. "I'm on my way." I hung up the phone before the nurse could tell me anything else.

"What is it?" Emjay asked.

"Leandra was in a car accident."

"What? What the hell happened?"

"They say she suffered a concussion."

Emjay and I got dressed and rushed to the hospital.

We walked through the automatic sliding-glass doors of the emergency room to the nurse's station where a thin, brown-skinned nurse with long, thick braids sat behind the desk. *Vaniesha*, her name tag read.

"Excuse me, my mother was brought in. She was in a car crash."

"Shariece Mills?" a white woman interrupted.

"Yes."

"Hello. I'm Emilee Nash. I'm the one who phoned you. I'll page Dr. St. John. He'll come down and speak with you about your friend's condition."

We sat patiently in the waiting room. A white man with short, blond hair who looked like he was fresh out of medical school and a tall, brawny cop was speaking with the nurse, as they glanced over at Emjay and me.

"Are you Ms. Fox's son?" he asked, directing his question to Emjay.

"I am, and this is my mother's friend."

"I'm Dr. St. John and this is Officer Lewis. He was first on the scene."

"So what happened? Is my mother all right?"

"They found her car on the side of Woodville Highway. Apparently, she had run off the side of the road. Can you tell me if your mother had been drinking, Mr. Fox?"

"Not that I know of, no."

The officer looked at Emjay like he was lying, like cops always do.

"Look, will someone tell me what the hell is going on? Is my mother all right?"

"She was lucky, but she's going to be fine." We both breathed a sigh of relief.

"Can we see her?" I asked.

"I'm afraid she's asleep. We gave her a sedative, so she will be out of it until morning."

"Please doctor, I have to see my mother," Emjay asked with an expression of desperation across his face.

"Okay, but please make it brief. Go down the hall, make a left and she's in room 116."

"Thank you," I said. When we entered the room, Shariece was quiet; it looked as if she were dead as her hands were folded in front of her like she was lying in a casket. The left corner of her temple was bandaged. When Emjay saw Leandra lying there, he broke down crying, falling to his knees at her side. He took her left hand into his, and pressed it against her face.

"I'm sorry, Ma, this is all my fault." I looked at Leandra, my eyes glassed over with tears realizing how close I came to losing my best friend. She was more than that, like a big sister with which I shared everything, and who had been there when Myrick was wreaking havoc on my life. The two of us were so stricken with grief that we didn't notice Leandra's eyes flutter open.

"Ma, it's me, Emjay."

She tried to speak. "Don't, Ma, don't try to talk. You need to get some rest," but I more than anyone knew how stubborn she could be when she wanted to get something off her chest. Emjay leaned in close. He gawked at me as she spoke. "She doesn't want to see you."

I wiped away tears with my fingers. "Okay, I'll be outside if you need anything." I walked down the hall that smelled faintly of sickness and disinfectant, outside where I sat on a bench in the resting area. I noticed a man standing not far from where I was sitting, dressed from tip to tail in scrubs, smoking a cigarette.

"Hey, can I get one of those from you?"

"Yeah, sure," he said, plucking a pack of Pall Malls from one of the breast pockets of his shirt. Smoke seethed out of his nose and mouth as if he were a dragon. He was dark-skinned, with a kind of Brazil-nut hue and thick braids that dropped down his back and broad shoulders. He wore dark shades protecting his face from the sun, though the weather was a bit mild. He handed me his pack of cigarettes, and I took one from the pack. He flicked the green lighter until a flame burned hot. He lit the end until it burned orange. I noticed how his pecs pulled at the sleeves of his shirt. He looked to be about six feet tall, give or take.

"Nice night out," he said in a Jamaican accent. I could have guessed that's where he was from. "Good for watching the stars if we had some to watch." I took a drag from the cancer stick and nodded in agreement. I wasn't really a smoker, but like drinking, it was something I did on occasion, or if I was under a tremendous amount of stress.

"I know I shouldn't," he said, examining the cigarette between his boney fingers as if it was something new he was trying. "These things will kill you." It was a sad attempt at him trying to tell a joke, but I was nowhere in the vicinity of being in a good mood seeing as how Leandra almost died.

"So who's sick?" he asked.

"Excuse me?"

"I noticed you and your son in the emergency room earlier."

"Oh, a good friend of mine was brought in a few hours ago, car accident."

"Is she okay?"

"Luckily, yes. She walked away with just a scratch and a minor concussion. Her doctor says she'll be fine."

"I'm Quinton by the way," he said, holding out his big, wide hand for me to shake.

"Shariece."

"Nice to meet you, Shariece," Quinton said.

"So aren't you doctors supposed to be like the poster children for health or something? It's kind of ironic seeing one out here smoking."

"Well, even doctors have their vices. So do…nurses," he said, showing me his ID badge that read: *Quinton Roberts, RN.*

"Sorry, I saw you in scrubs, I just assumed."

"Don't sweat it. I get that all the time when I'm not wearing my ID badge."

"It's funny."

"What, my being a nurse?"

I took another long drag.

"No, taking so much for granted until we end up in a place like this. Some people walk in perfectly fine, but then something happens, and they don't walk back out."

"I always say, live it like it's your last, you know? Nothing is guaranteed."

"Where's your hospital chapel?"

"Over there in that wing of the hospital." Quinn pointed. Other than Easter, I've never been much of the church-going type. I always hated church when I was a little girl; the preacher getting up there doing all of that yelling and hollering. Institutionalized religion wasn't my gig. I've always believed that we should have our own, personal relationship with God outside of feeling like I needed to gather in a church like a bunch of hens. I took one last puff from my cigarette, tossed it to the ground, and snuffed it out under my shoe.

"Well, I think I'm going to pay the man upstairs a visit. It was nice meeting you, Quinn."

"Likewise. I'm glad to hear that your friend is all right."

"Thank you, me too."

I walked toward the wing of the hospital that held the chapel.

As I was about to enter Leandra's room, Emjay cut me off. "What's wrong?"

"She's good. She's asleep. Listen, I spoke with her doctor, and he said that it would be okay if I stayed the night with her."

"I'll stay too."

"No, you should go home, get some sleep."

"Emjay, you need me. I want to stay."

"Yeah, but…"

"But what?"

"Baby, look, I will give you a call in the morning."

Emjay couldn't look me in the eyes. I looked over his shoulder at Leandra sleeping peacefully.

"I'll bring you and Leandra some clean clothes in the morning."

"That sounds good."

When I reached in to give him a kiss goodnight, he gave me one on the forehead like I was some cute puppy dog newly purchased from the pound. It was as clear as my hand in front of my face. Emjay blamed me for Shariece's accident.

FOURTEEN
SHARIECE

Three weeks had passed after Leandra's accident. She had been released two days after getting a clean bill of health. I hadn't talked to Emjay much when he decided to stay with Leandra for a while to make sure that she was doing well. Our relationship was nonexistent. I thought about calling him, but I felt it best to give him his space. He'd almost lost his mother. I thought about Leandra often. I stopped eating at our favorite restaurants like Crispers and Bella Bella because it was too painful. I still care a great deal about them both, but I couldn't put my own life on hold. I had a career, students that depended on me. I drowned myself in school work, catching up on grading and planning, tasks that had fallen by the wayside before all this high-octane drama ensued with me, Leandra and Emjay. A few weeks ago, Rochelle had offered me a full-time position with a pay increase. I had happily accepted. With everything that had happened, I needed a touch of good news.

I longed for Emjay's touch, those firm, muscular arms holding me, his lips pressed against mine. I would pull out my vibrator from the nightstand; shut my eyes and think of Emjay. I would touch myself under a desk piled with papers, thinking of his head between my thighs.

I was grading papers when I got a knock on my door. I had a ten o'clock appointment to speak with a student about an idea he had for a short story, so I figured it was her. When I'd opened the door to find Emjay standing there, I was in complete awe. He was dressed in a black and gray Coogi sweat suit.

"Hey, can we talk?"

I didn't say a word, but just invited him in. I was ecstatic to see him, but I wasn't going to show my behind just yet. I walked around my cluttered desk and sat down like Emjay was simply another student. I was curious to know the meaning behind his visits. I continued grading, failing to give him eye contact.

"How have you been?" he asked, as if to assume I was a mess without him.

"Just trying to get some work completed here before Thanksgiving break."

"I saw on my essay that you gave me an A."

"It was a good, well-written essay. You deserve it." I paused. "How's Leandra doing?"

"Good. She went back to work a week ago. Said she couldn't stand all the sitting around at home. Taj picked her up from the hospital. He takes care of her, gives her what she needs. I'm just glad I'm not at her beck and call anymore." He grinned.

"You know how Leandra is. High maintenance."

"That's true."

"I thought that you blamed me for what happened at your place that night."

"No, of course not."

"The night of the accident, when I tried to console you, you jerked away. Why?"

"Shariece, that was a crazy night; emotions were high. I completely shut down when I saw her lying in that hospital bed. Everything flashed before my eyes. I heard 'accident' and 'hospital,' and freaked out."

"I was upset, too, Emjay. It wasn't easy for me to see my best friend of eleven years lying there like that. This situation with Leandra made me think how much we take for granted, how we lose sight of what matters most, like family and friends. If she came to me and said that she didn't want anything to do with me, I would be upset, but I would have to live with her decision. This might sound selfish, and right now, I don't care, but I'm not going to put my life and my happiness on hold for anyone."

"Well, Mama is who I came here to talk to you about. I talked with the officer the day after the accident, and he told me that he did an investigation. He told me that Ma may have purposely run off the road that night."

I got up and began pacing my office. "What? Why would she do something that crazy?"

"She was pretty upset when she left my apartment that night. When I confronted her with the cop's findings, she said she would rather be dead than to see me with you."

I knew how cruel Leandra could be when she didn't get her way. A high-riding witch in a hurricane.

"Jesus, what the hell was she thinking?"

"She told me that she'll cut me off, that she won't pay my rent or tuition and close my bank account if I didn't stop seeing you."

"Emjay, this whole thing has gotten out of control. I don't want to stand in the way of you and Leandra rebuilding your relationship."

"I told her no, I'm not giving up on you. I meant what I said that night. I love you, Shariece, and that hasn't changed."

"What if she goes to my boss and tells her about us?"

"She won't if she doesn't want to lose me."

"You shouldn't underestimate Leandra."

"She can't hurt us as long as we stick together."

He slid those arms around me, hugging me close. I missed Emjay's touch. He kissed along the nape of my neck, licking me, driving me crazy with his touch. I could feel his erection against my ass. When I turned to face him, he pressed his lips against mine.

"Wait." I went to lock the office door. Emjay slid the papers off the desk and sat me on top. "You're crazy, you know that?"

Emjay slipped off my panties. We laughed as he tugged on the heel of my black platforms. I undid my blouse. I didn't want him busting off the buttons. My nipples were hard in my black bra that was off in two seconds flat. Emjay swirled his tongue around my nipples, sucking them past his juicy lips. My pussy was wet due to his advances, hungering for something more than my fingers or some sex toy that required batteries. I reached inside his Coogi sweat pants and fisted out his dick that throbbed hard in my hand. He fell into me, maneuvering his dick past the lips of my sweet center. My pussy devoured his dick like she had a mind of her own. I felt him stretching me, thrusting deep, sending shockwaves of ecstasy through my body. Damn! Two weeks of sexual frustration was literally being fucked out of me.

"Tell me you love me," Emjay said.

"I love you."

"Do you love me?"

"I love you."

Emjay moaned and grunted until we both came in a synchronized orgasm.

"I love you," Emjay said breathlessly.

"I love you, too."

FIFTEEN
DEANDRE

My dick was brick-hard watching Ms. Mills and Emjay fuck. I stroked the bulge that tinted my jeans as I captured every thrust and moan on my phone. And the whole damn time, they didn't see me standing there videotaping them in the act. *Ain't this a bitch!* Question now was how was I going to use this to my advantage? I knew something wasn't right between those two. I could tell by the way that pretty motherfucker looked at Ms. Mills in class, that something wasn't on the up and up. He sits there with his hand under the desk, grabbing at his shit as she paces across one side of the room to the next. I can't blame him though. Ms. Mills is all kinds of fine. I would be lying if I said I didn't want to hit that. I wonder how long they've been fucking? I pressed the button on my phone to stop recording and hauled ass before I was spotted.

I went to a bathroom that was directly outside of the building and walked into one of the larger stalls at the end. Still couldn't believe what I had just seen, and then to have the whole shit on camera, too? I wanted to play back what I had recorded. I walked into the bathroom that reeked of stale piss, but it wasn't enough to bother me. I sat on the toilet, took my phone out and started to play the scene back from the beginning. Damn, look at those titties. I could suck on those all day. I placed the phone on the end of the sink next to me, stood up, unzipped my jeans and whipped my dick out of my drawers. I was hard as fuck still. Eleven inches, the last time I measured. I be splittin' bitches in two with my shit. "Fuck yeah, take that dick," I whispered under my breath. She fuck with me, I'll have it coming out of the other end. Fuck her ass dizzy. I lapped up the precum that has pearled at the piss slit and wiped it off on my jeans. I don't like Emjay, but that brother be doing a damn thing with his dick. He's not as good as me, but he's all right.

Looking at Ms. Mills, I bet she's got that good refined pussy at her age. I bet it's tasty too. I could eat avenues through her, fucking with me. Comes to class wearing all that tight shit, knowing exactly what she's doing, having dudes on hard. She's a real woman, and not one of these dick-teasing chicks out here who act like they don't have the time of day for a brother. I'm officially done with college girls. Older women are established in their careers, they have money, a nice car and an actual house where they don't have to worry about roommate bullshit, and the pussy I bet is seasoned to perfection. Damn, look how high she's got her legs. Ms. Mills is flexible for a big girl. She looks smoking-hot smeared across her desk, playing with her titties, her mouth open, hungry to devour some dick. I'll give her something to suck on. Looks like a lady who knows her way around a dick.

I was about to pop off when I heard someone walk in. I quickly pressed the pause button on my phone. I massaged my dick as I heard the rustle of clothes, the ring of a belt loop and then the sizzle of piss hit urinal water. I peeked through the slit of my stall door at him wash his hands, checking himself in the mirror. *Hurry the fuck up*, I thought. He left. Finally, damn. I pressed play back on my phone and continued to work my dick, watching Emjay fuck Ms. Mills, sucking on those big, cantaloupe breasts. She looks like she would be into some freak-nasty shit too like titty-fucking. I worked my shit until I came, popping a load that shot across the sink only minutes before Emjay shot his seed. I snatched a few brown paper towels from the dispenser to wipe my dick clean before I tucked it back into my boxers and jeans.

Yeah, I got her ass now. Gonna use what I got, to get what I want. And other than an A, I want a taste of what Emjay's high-yellow, cornbread-ass is getting, 'cause it would be fucked up if this little amateur porn video I made ended up in the hands of the director of the English Department, or worse, on the desk of the dean's office.

SIXTEEN
LEANDRA

"I was lying in bed watching a *Real Housewives of New Jersey* marathon when my phone rang. "Damn, who is this?" I picked it up off the bedside table next to a bowl of milk from the Sugar Pops I had eaten to study the number. It read: *Unknown.* "Hello."

Oh my God, child, I'm so glad you picked up."

"Who is this?" I asked, irritated.

"Girl, it's me, Delora. I have a hair crisis of epic proportions."

How in the hell did she get my number?

"Hey, what's going on?"

"It's more like what's *not* going on. My damn hair. It has decided that it's going to act a fool today. I need an emergency do like yesterday ago."

"I'm sorry, but Sabrina is running the store today. I'm out sick." I wasn't really sick, but just needed one of my days where I could just veg out in front of the TV. I had one of those feelings that if I left my house, terrible luck would befall me, so I decided to stay in and take a lazy day. My head was killing me from the concussion

I had sustained. "Call the shop and make an appointment." *Just like everyone else.*

"I heard what happened. Are you OK? I was knocked on my behind when they told me at the shop that you were in a car accident."

That ain't nobody but Sabrina running and telling my business. I should fire her ass. She knows how I feel about gossiping in the salon. "Yeah, luckily, I just walked away with a mild concussion, that's all."

"Praise Jesus, girl. God is so good."

"Yes He is," I said, rolling my eyes.

"Child, I really need your help. I've tried to do something with this savage beast, but it's like she's got a mind of her own. I got a date tonight. Hook a sister up, just this once."

"Delora, any other time I would take care of you, but—"

"I understand that," she interrupted, "but I'm going crazy here. I can't go out looking a hot mess. You should see how I look. I don't think even a scarf could hold down this monstrosity that has taken over my head."

One thing I could say about Delora: she knew how to turn on the drama. If "drama queen" were in the dictionary, I wouldn't be surprised if a picture of her was right next to it. The last thing I wanted to do was put my hands up in somebody's head today, but I knew she wasn't going to take no for an answer.

"I'll pay you an extra forty dollars on to what you usually charge."

It wasn't about the money. I simply didn't feel like entertaining company. I sighed. "Okay, give me an hour and come on over."

"Leandra, girl, thank you. I knew you wouldn't let me down. I owe you one."

Damn right you do.

"Don't worry about it, just come on over. I'll hook ya up."

"I'm headed over there now."

Before I could say another word, Delora hung up. I was in and out of the shop really. I wasn't back to my full one hundred percent self. I would dip in, say hello to the girls, some of my regulars, and do a bank drop and stock inventory. That was stupid of me to run off the road like that. It hadn't been easy getting back on track after all this craziness with Emjay and Shariece. I loved them both, but I couldn't be looking up in their faces right now, pretending that I was fine with what they have going on. I had told Emjay that if he was going to continue to see Shariece, he was on his own and no longer welcome in my house. I have officially cut him off financially. I'm not paying his rent, tuition, none of that until he's come to his senses. No more babying him, and if Rick was here, he would probably agree. It burns my ass thinking about how Shariece had lied to me all this time, and here she was supposed to be my best friend. How do you keep something like sleeping with your best friend's son from somebody? I tell her everything under the sun, and she felt the need to keep the fact that she was fucking my son away from me. And then has the lady balls to tell me that who she fucks is none of my business. Bitch, please. I spent twenty-two years struggling to build a good life for myself and Emjay, to keep him on the straight and narrow, working two, sometimes three jobs to make sure he never wants for a damn thing. I didn't want him to have to struggle on the streets like I did. There is no way in hell I was going to have him turn out like his daddy did only to end up with a bullet in his head. The thought of going to the morgue and having to identify my baby—. God, I can't think about shit like that. No matter how old he gets, he'll always be my baby boy. If I hear anything about Shariece hurting Emjay, she will have Mama Bear to answer to.

I had forgotten what a mess the house was until I got out of bed and started straitening up. I didn't want Delora to think that I kept my house looking like a pigsty. There were dirty wineglasses from the drinks Taj and I'd had last night, along with files of sales receipts on the sofa and coffee table. I took the basket of dirty clothes I had sitting in the hallway to be washed, and set them in the linen closet until I had time to get to them. The kitchen was the worst. I took the garbage out to the trash bin in the backyard, and then loaded the dishwasher. My days of washing dishes by hand were over. Prune fingers is not a good look on me. I sprayed through the whole house with apple cinnamon air freshener, even the bedroom that smelled faintly of sex. I changed the bed sheets. There was no telling what kinds of stains were on them. I went to the bathroom to grab my tools for Delora's hair: comb, rollers and hot curlers. Everything was ready except for me. I spent a better part of the day walking around in nothing but sweat pants and a one-size-fits-all T-shirt. Any other time I wouldn't have cared, but since Drama Queen was coming over, I did. I pulled a pair of jeans out of the closet I had picked up from being lightly pressed at the cleaners. I threw on a T-shirt Emjay had made in one of his graphic design classes. He probably thinks that I don't have it anymore. It's one thing out of the many things he has given me I cherish. I laid my clothes and some clean panties and bra on the bed. I sauntered off to the bathroom wanting to soak in a bubble bath, but there was no time, so a shower had to do. When I turned the water on, my phone rang. I had hoped it was Delora calling to cancel, but it was Taj.

"Hey, baby."

"Hey, I called to let you know that this might be another shoot to run well into the night, so I might be a little late coming home."

I sighed. "How late is a little?"

"Sorry, baby. We're still out here trying to finish up the shoot, so who knows."

"Taj, this is the third time this week."

"I know. It's this photographer who's always showing up late on the set."

"I don't understand why the magazine won't fire him."

"I agree, but Travis Richardson has done shoots with big names like Halle Berry, Whitney Houston, Mariah Carey, Madonna, Rihanna, you name it. It's a pretty big deal. This could be huge for my career, for both of us."

The bathroom started to fog with steam from the shower, so I stepped out into the hallway. "I'm about to come down there and tell this Travis Richardson to get his shit together so my boo can come home." Taj burst out laughing. "You laughing because you know I'll do it."

"I know. That's why you need to stay home. I could get fired messing with you, woman."

"You want me to make us a nice dinner, then? I was going to thaw out some chicken wings and make those homemade hot wings of mine you love so much."

"That sounds good, but I don't know how late I'm going to be tonight."

"OK, well, call me to let me know that you're on your way home."

"I'm so sorry, baby; I promise I'll make it up to you."

"I know you will."

"I'll call you if we get out of here early, but I doubt it with this guy."

"OK. I love you."

"Love you, too."

I pressed *end call* on my phone and threw it on the bed with my clothes. "Whatever," I said to myself. I slipped out of the clothes I had been lying in all day until I stood booty-naked in the steam-filled bathroom. I smeared my arm across the medicine cabinet mirror to clear away the cloak of fog. I studied the large bandage that was taped in the upper-right corner of my forehead. I picked at the adhesive, pulling it gently away. I squirmed as I peeled it back to examine the gash I had sustained from my *intentional* accident. It wasn't bad, but was healing quite nicely. *Dr. St. John says that it shouldn't leave a scar, but if it does, I'm heading straight to a plastic surgeon.* I flung the bandage into a small trash can that sat between the foot of the toilet and the sink. I looked at myself, gradually starting to see the weight melting off of me. I wanted to prove to myself that I could shed the pounds without Shariece there to be my drill sergeant. It's not easy saying no to strawberry cheesecake ice cream. I thought for sure with the anger and sadness I felt over being kept in the dark about Emjay and Shariece. I didn't know how strong my will power was until now. As long as I watch what I eat, I didn't see why I couldn't be down to a size twelve.

I stepped into the bathtub, the warm shower water pelted against my body. I pressed some cocoa butter body wash into my palm and rubbed my hands sensually along my breasts, down my stomach, between my legs and down my thighs. It's Thanksgiving I'm worried about, one of my favorite days next to Christmas and my birthday. I'm used to putting out a big ol' spread, but I think this year, I will prepare a small romantic dinner for me and Taj. I don't really feel like being around a lot of people this year anyway.

I love my ass though. Taj says he likes something he can hold onto and slap when I'm putting it on him. He can be so freaky. I can't wait until the summer so I can put on this new two-piece I bought. All eyes will be on me when I serve some *Baywatch* realness at the beach next summer. Cocoa butter lather trickled down my titties and thighs, between the crack of my booty, to the tips of my toes. I wish to God I hadn't walked in on my son and Shariece that night, but I have to move on for the sake of my own sanity.

I ran my fingers between my legs, gently along my pussy, pleasuring myself without really being conscious of what I was doing. I was about to do a damn thing when I thought I heard someone outside of the bathroom door. I switched off the shower.

"Hello," I said.

"Leandra, hey, girl, it's Delora."

Damn, oh so you just going to let yourself in my house? See, that's how motherfuckers get shot. She's got a big pair of lady balls to be walking up in somebody's crib. I grabbed a towel from the rack under the toilet and stepped out of the shower, cocoa butter suds running off my body onto the rug at the foot of the tub. Already I was getting annoyed. "Hey, I'm getting out of the shower. I will be out in a minute."

"Okay, am I too early?"

"No, you good. Just um…have a seat in the living room."

"Can I help myself to some of that wine you have sitting out there while I wait?"

Was this bitch serious? What the hell she thinks this is? A day spa?

"Yeah, girl, go 'head," I said with my lips twisted. I wrapped the towel around my body and scurried down the hall. I was almost to my bedroom when Delora's clumsy ass ran smack into me, causing my towel to drop. Before I could regain my composure, I was ass-naked in front of her.

"Oh, girl, I'm sorry," Delora said, cloaking her eyes with her left hand as if she had just witnessed an unspeakable horror. She made a beeline back to the living room where I had told her to wait instead of taking her own personal tour of my house.

"It's fine. I need to get dressed, and I will be out there to do your hair."

I got to my bedroom, finished drying off and slipped on a pair of lavender panties.

Why in the hell did I agree to do this again? When I find out who gave Delora my phone number, I'm going to skin a bitch back to the white meat. I finished getting dressed and threw my hair back in a ponytail. With what had just happened, I wanted to kick Delora out of my house, tell her ass to make an appointment like everyone else. I checked my attitude at the door before I went out to see what else she had helped herself to.

Delora was sitting on the sofa, flipping through a hair magazine she had brought. She was one of these women who always came to the shop with a folded-up page out of *Hair* magazine going on about how they wanted to look like Rihanna or somebody with hair no longer than my pinky finger. I'm not a miracle worker.

"Hey, you ready?" I said, walking to the kitchen acting like her seeing me naked didn't happen. Delora wore a scarf, so I didn't know what to expect. I could see damaged bits of hair sprouting from an exposed part of the scarf. Delora plopped down in one of the kitchen chairs.

"So you said you want to get a wash and set, right?"

"Yes. I will kiss your feet if you can do something with this mess on top of my head."

"Well, let me see what you've done to it." I untied the knot from the back to unveil what she had been bitching and moaning about on the phone. "Damn, what happened?"

"It's a mess, ain't it?"

There was an assortment of colors and dyes in Delora's hair along with split ends and dryness caused by a flat iron, I bet. Hell, you might as well light your hair on fire messing with that shit.

"Believe it or not, I've seen worse." I ran my fingers through the rat nest of a mess that was her hair.

"So do you think you can do something with this?"

"Child, if I can't hook you up, nobody can."

"That's why I called you. I knew you would be able to work your magic."

"You're going to walk out of here looking red carpet gorgeous."

"You don't know how relieved I am to hear you say that. I was scared you were going to tell me that you had no choice but to hack all my hair off."

"No, it's not that serious, girl, but if you keep putting all these dyes and stuff in it, and using a flat iron, you won't have a choice but to cut it all off. Walk around here looking like a black Sinead O'Connor." We both grinned.

"Men don't like bald women. They like hair they can grab onto, if you know what I'm saying."

"You ain't never lied." I laughed.

Looking at Delora's hair took me back to how we had met. She was my first client before I even had a shop. After making it through high school by the skin of my teeth, and a baby nibbling at my heels, I'd needed to make some serious cake, and working at Church's Chicken, wasn't going to cut it. Rick's funeral was sad. The funeral director told me that due to half his face being blown off, it had to be a closed casket. I was determined to carve out a better life for me and Emjay, a life Rick would have wanted me and his son to have. I couldn't see myself doing the whole college thing. I had no patience to stick with that higher education shit for four years. I needed to do something that was going to get me in and out and employed, so I decided to take up Cosmetology at Lively Technical.

Before Sherilyn started fucking around with dope, she used to do hair for extra money. She knew how to do weaves, wash and sets, blowouts, all that. I would sit and watch her for hours do one head after the next, and these bitches would come through looking a hot project mess, but walked out giving housewife divadom.

Half the money she made she put up her nose. She would show me all of her tricks of the hair trade and before long, I was as good as her, if not better. While she was out doing God knows what, I was hooking girls up with fresh dos for everything from proms to weddings. What WIC couldn't cover, I used to keep diapers on Emjay's behind and food in his mouth. Whatever I had that was extra, I would put away.

I remember going to school with people who had all this talent: artists, singers, brainiacs, but never had sense enough to do a damn thing with the gift they had been given, but not me. I had a thing for hair, to turn trifling into triumphant. I wasn't about to waste this gift because I had a kid to raise. Mrs. Boyd had helped me pay half the tuition, which wasn't much, being that it was a short program. I finished in two semesters, got licensed and was ready to go to work. I got a job at Snazzy Cuts, one of the hottest salons in Tallahassee while I kept my regulars from the projects who continued coming over to get their dos done. It wasn't long before I got a following and gained a rep for being one of the best stylists at Snazzy Cuts. The day Delora came into the shop, her hair looked wild and crazy much like it does today. No stylist wanted her, so I took her to see what I could do. By the time I was done, I had her looking like royalty. She spread the word to all her friends and coworkers that I was the one to see. I was hooking up teachers, doctors, and wives of important local political figures. The girls at the shop were crazy jealous, but Diane, the owner of Snazzy Cuts, didn't care with all the cake I was pulling in.

Delora was the one who had recommended that I open up my own shop, but I was way ahead of her on that. I would plan out in my head how my own salon would look. When Diane found out that I was doing hair at my crib on the side, she didn't take too kindly to it, and fired me. I figured one of the jealous, brown-nose, ass-kissing bitches at the shop must have snitched. Shit didn't matter no way. Diane had gotten enough blood, sweat and hair grease out of me in the three years I'd worked for her. I had the clientele anyway, so I was ready to strike out on my own. I used the ten grand Mrs. Boyd left me in her will to open my own shop on Orange Avenue. Leandra's Hair and Beauty. I hired three girls fresh out of Aveda: Nishelle, Sabrina and Javonte, whom all had an assortment of talents. I was slam-packed busy that whole week of the grand opening and weeks and months after that. I even started to notice some of Diane's customers frequenting my salon. I was at my busiest during Florida A&M homecoming games and Demp Week. I was making money hand over fist, treating myself and Emjay to new outfits and shoes. A year later, I bought myself a black BMW with cream-leather seats. I had gone from living in a low-income, one-bedroom house to a three-bedroom home and making enough cake to buy my dream Beamer.

"So what kind of style are you talking about getting?" I asked Delora.

"Okay, you remember the third season of *Real Housewives of Atlanta* when Kandi was working that red, curly do?"

"You mean the one that made her look like Bozo the Clown?" I said, picking Delora's hair out with a pick.

Delora laughed. "Yeah, I want that, but without the red. Can you hook a sister up?"

"I think I can do that."

"I want something real simple, you feel me?"

"How about I cut it short; turn you into a blonde like Nene Leakes?"

"I love me some Nene, and I'm not knocking my girl's look, but that's too short. I want it to come to my shoulders at least."

These women tickle me wanting to look like celebs. They don't understand when I try to tell them that what looks good on celebrities isn't necessarily going to work for them, but it's like talking to a wall.

"If I can't get you there, I will get you as close as I can to what you want."

"I have faith in you, girl."

"Come over here to the sink and let me get you washed up." I slid the chair against the counter. Delora sat down and positioned her head into the kitchen sink. I ran warm water over her crinkled, unruly locks.

"So what's up, chil'? Everybody at the shop's been asking about you. Where you been?"

Delora was known to be nosey, always trying to get up in other people's business, so I was always careful about what I let her in on or it would be all over the shop in two seconds flat.

"Girl, since the accident I've just been laying low, trying to get back to being one hundred."

"Girl, everybody at the salon was talking about that. What happened?"

I figured somebody at the shop must have opened their mouth about the accident. It was probably Sabrina and Javonte, the way they run their damn mouths after I'd told them about how I feel about gossiping in the workplace. I'm a pussy hair close to firing both of them.

"I was um…driving home from Emjay's in that rainstorm. I think on it now and wish I had spent the night at his apartment as it was raining so hard."

"Chil', I was so scared that night, I thought a tree was going to fall on my house, the way it was knocking and banging everything around. All it did though was knock up some shingles on the roof," Delora said.

"I couldn't see a damn thing in front of me. I must have been driving on the wrong side of the road, because before I knew anything, I damn near got T-boned by a semi."

"Oh Lord."

"To keep from getting hit, I veered off the road and ended up hitting a tree."

"Girl, the Lord was with you that night."

I wasn't about to tell Delora of all people that I purposely ran off the road for the fact that I had just caught my son and my best friend in bed fucking. Not if I wanted all of South Side knowing my business. "Next thing I knew, I woke up in the hospital."

I took a bottle of Pantene that was sitting off to the side of the kitchen counter, flipped the lavender top open and poured some the size of a quarter in the palm of my hand and massaged the shampoo into Delora's scalp. I could tell that it felt good the way her eyes rolled back and forth into her head like she was about to fall asleep.

"I can't imagine how Emjay was feeling when he saw you lying in a hospital bed."

"He was actually okay once he saw that I was all right," I lied. "He helped to nurse me back to health for about a week—cooking, cleaning, filling my prescriptions and stuff. I don't know what I would do without him."

"Sons will do anything for their mamas. That's how Jermaine and Dontavius are. There's nothing they won't do for me. I think it would have been different had I had girls. You know how hot in the ass they can be. Wouldn't give me a second thought, but sons will stick by you no matter what. I've always been fond of boy-children."

I wanted to tell Delora that what she was saying wasn't true, that some sons, once they've sunk their teeth into something they like, won't turn it loose, and will leave your ass high and dry after all you've done to try and raise them up right, to try and teach them about respect and right from wrong, teach them not to lie and keep secrets. But what came out of my mouth instead was, "Yeah, Emjay has been good. I don't doubt that there ain't nothing he won't do for me."

"So, what's up? I've seen you walking around here with that fine-ass man on your arms."

Damn, that's random. We go from talking about our children to whom I've been stepping out with. Delora was putting a bitch on the spot.

"You better work, cougar."

When she uttered the *other* C word, I wanted to snatch her tender-headed behind back. No she did not just call me a cougar. I'm only forty-one and fabulous, I might add. "He's doing some stuff for *Break Entertainment Magazine* for their July issue."

"Girl, he is the definition of *fine*, mama. How did ya'll meet?"

"We um…met at Publix," I lied. "We were standing in the same checkout line and we struck up a conversation, and the rest is history. We exchanged phone numbers and he asked me out."

"So when are you going to bring him by the salon for everyone to meet?"

"Don't you mean for all ya'll to salivate over like a bunch of hungry lionesses." We both laughed.

"The only man I'll be drooling over is the one who's taking me out to dinner tonight."

"No, but he's busy on a shoot right now. As soon as Taj can free up some time in his schedule, I'll bring him over for everyone to meet," I said.

"Taj. That's a sexy name."

"And if I ever see any of you thirsty bitches put a hand on him, you'll be drawing back a nub."

"Hey, you ain't gotta worry about me. You know I'm not that kind of woman to go after somebody else's man."

I massaged the shampoo deep into Delora's scalp, making sure to get her back there in her kitchen.

"So is Emjay still in school?"

"He's about to finish up his freshman year actually."

"What is he studying again?"

"He's still undecided, so right now he's trying to get his basics out of the way: math, English, science, history."

"Did I tell you that Jermaine got a job working for the state?"

That's Delora. Always feeling like she has to one-up somebody like it's a competition. I tell her Emjay is in college, she tells me that her dirty-ass boy got a job working for the state like that shit is something to be proud of. From what I hear, people who have state jobs are in a constant state of panic, scared Rick Scott is going to pink slip their asses any day.

"Oh, did he? That's good. When did he get that job?" *Like I gave a damn to know.*

"Last month. He works downtown in the Capitol as a staff assistant for the mayor."

He's a damn secretary? I thought. When I was done, I rinsed all the soap out of Delora's hair, and sat her up out of the sink to towel her hair dry.

"Oh, girl, I almost forgot to tell you. Did you hear what happened to Katonia's boy?" Delora asked.

"He got shot."

"What?"

"He's alive, though. That crazy-ass boy shot at some police over on Bronough Street. They claiming that he shot first, but I don't believe that. You know how trigger-happy these cops can be out here. Shoot first, ask questions never, especially if you black."

"Where did they shoot him at?" Delora started grinning.

"What's so funny about somebody's child getting shot, Delora?"

"The damn cop shot him in the ass."

"Where?" I grinned.

"In his ass. I forgot to um…ask Katonia which ass cheek it was."
Delora and I both filled the kitchen with roaring laughter.

"Katonia says he has all this gauze wrapped around his ass,
looking like he has a diaper on." I laughed so hard, the muscles in
my stomach started to tighten. Katonia and I went to cosmetology school together. Her specialty is braids, coloring and weave.
I wanted her to come work for me at the shop, but she wanted to
venture off and do her own thing. Everyone knew that Tarell was
a member of the Pepper Street Posse. So if he got shot by a cop
or anyone else, it was because he was out here doing something
he didn't have any business doing.

"Girl, you know ever since he was a little boy, he was always
into something."

"Uh-huh," Delora uttered as I blow-dried her hair.

"He tried to steal Emjay's bike one time, I remember. He was
nine and Tarell was ten, I think. Me and Emjay walked to Katonia's,
'cause she only lived up the street from me back then."

"Yeah."

"I told Emjay that fighting was not the answer to nothing, that
it just makes things worse than better, but at the same time, I
wasn't raising him to be no punk, either. I told him if someone
wanted to try him, to lay his ass out. Emjay came home just crying,
saying that Tarell had stolen his bike."

"Aww, poor baby. So what happened when ya'll got to Katonia's
house?"

"She was there. She came to the door. I think she had gotten
home from work. She was working for the Department of Children
and Families at the time."

"Where she work at now?"

"I think she manages a Dollar Tree on South Magnolia."

Katonia was on welfare like a lot of us until she had to get out and get a damn j-o-b after they cut her check off. She thought she was all that just because they gave her an office.

"When we got to her house, Emjay's bike was sitting there on the porch. Tarell's bad ass was sitting in the living room watching cartoons. When I knocked on the door, I scared the hell out of that boy. He knew his behind was in some serious trouble."

"Where was Katonia?"

"In the kitchen cooking, I think. I yelled in at her. She didn't have a clue that Tarell had taken Emjay's bike. When she saw the bike on the porch, she hollered out to him. His fat behind bucked up out of the chair."

"Yeah, that sounds like Tarell's ass."

"'Did you take Emjay's bike?' she asked him. He claimed he was just borrowing the bike, but Emjay said he took it and didn't ask. He was talking all big and bad with me standing up there. Girl, when Katonia started knocking Tarell upside his head for taking Emjay's bike, it took everything in me to keep from laughing. I felt so sorry for him, and Katonia was cursing like a sailor at him the whole time. 'How many times have I told your bad ass not to touch nothing that don't belong to you?'"

"That's how you gotta do them boys; raise them hard," Delora said.

"Katonia made Tarell give Emjay his bike back and say he was sorry. Him and Emjay both gave each other these mean-mugging looks. She apologized to me for what Tarell had done. I was sure that it wouldn't be the last time that the two of them would bump heads again. Chil', a week after, they were at it again. He was always trying to punk Emjay, so I told him that he was going to have to stand up for himself."

"Uh-huh. The only thing boys like Tarell know is an old-fashioned ass whippin'," Delora said.

"I know, and that's what I told Emjay. They were playing stickball on the street in front of the house when they started fussing. Girl, I didn't know over what, kid stuff, I figured. I watched the whole thing from my door. I guess they didn't know I was standing there because Emjay and Tarell both was cursing and hollering. The mama in me wanted to march out there and bust Emjay's behind for cursing."

"But you knew that was just part of him learning how to stand up for himself."

"Right, so I just stood there and watched. I knew I would just embarrass him, his mama running to save him from that he had no control over, so I watched."

"You watched?"

"I watched to see what was going to happen, because had he walked away from a fight, I was going to beat his ass myself. Tarell punched him in the nose hard enough to make it bleed. All the kids were oohing and going on. I wanted to run out, but I wanted to see what Emjay was going to do."

"You were better than me, 'cause I would have slapped the shit out of that Tarell boy."

"Before I could bat an eyelash, Emjay charged at Tarell like a bull, girl, whose eyes were filled with red, and tackled him to the ground. He was just punching and punching him in the ribs and stomach."

"Goodness."

"He tore Tarell's behind up that day. The other kids stood around, cheering Emjay on. I don't think they liked him anyway."

"You let Emjay keep beating on him like that?"

"When I felt like his bad behind had enough, I ran out and pulled Emjay up off of him. He was still punching at the air like he wasn't done with Tarell. I thought he was going to take a swipe at me, but he calmed down. Girl, he was so mad that day. When I took him into the house, he started crying thinking that I was going to beat him, but as I wiped his nose clean of blood with my shirt, I told him how proud of him I was. He was even scared that Katonia was going to 'beat me up' because he beat Tarell up."

"Aww, that's so cute."

"I told him not to worry about Katonia. I was waiting on her to come to the house and raise hell, but she never did."

"That's because she knew that he was in need of an ass-whipping."

"And he got one that day. A few days later, they were back playing ball. They were friends until Tarell started skipping, hanging out on the street corner with that Pepper Street mess. There was no damn way I was going to let that happen to Emjay. The minute he started acting a fool, I straightened his ass up quick."

"That makes two of us. It's hard keeping them off the streets. I see these gangbangers out here now with the money and cars and shit, trying to recruit these kids as early as eight years old. It's a shame," Delora said. It was my turn to change the subject. All this talk about gangs was fucking with me.

"All right, enough talk about all that. You're going to have me crying up in here in a minute. Let me freshen up your drink."

"Girl, you ain't lying; next subject."

"I think I'm going to pour myself a glass." I took a bottle of Slovenia Vodka out of the refrigerator, and a glass from one of the cabinets above the kitchen counter.

"I don't want to get too fucked up. I gotta go pick Jermaine up from work at four-thirty."

"Delora, hush, I'm not going to let you drive nowhere drunk. We are going to get fucked up responsibly." We both cracked up with laughter. Delora was exactly what I needed to take my mind off of Emjay and Shariece.

"So what do you want? You want waves, you want curls, what?" I asked as I combed my fingers through her black, flaxen strands.

"Glam it up, girl. Make it big. The bigger the hair, the closer to Jesus."

"Amen."

It didn't take me long to do her up. By the time I was done, I had given her red carpet diva. I handed her the mirror. She smiled so big, I thought the child's face was going to crack.

"Leandra, you outdid yourself this time. The other girls are good, but lady, you are the queen bee of this shit right here."

"So you like?"

"Like? Girl, I love it. I have a LBD and some leopard-print red bottoms that's going to make Xavier's dick stand on end tonight."

"That's your new man?"

Delora was known to have a new man for every month. She would go on and on, saying how good they were for like three months, and then something would happen and she would go from saying how sweet a man was to saying he wasn't shit.

"Leandra, he is sex on a stick. He's six-two, brown eyes with a juicy, baseball player ass, and lips sexy that would put Dmitri Vance to shame."

It was my turn to be nosey. "So where did ya'll meet?"

"On Blackpeople.com. When he responded to my ad, I didn't believe that it was him. He looked like somebody out of a magazine or something, so I thought the picture was fake until we decided to meet up."

"Watch yourself. You never know what you're gonna get with these guys you meet online."

"Oh, I'm not worried, trust. If I find out he's some kind of sicko,

I got the remedy right here for his ass." Delora grabbed her purse off the kitchen table next to a bowl of tangerines I had sitting in the center. She opened it to show me what she had inside. This bitch had a gun.

"Bitch, are you crazy? What the hell are you doing with that?"

She took it and held it like it was some prize she had won. "Jermaine gave it to me to protect myself a few days after I got mugged in the parking lot of Harveys."

"That shit ain't loaded, is it?"

"Hell yeah, it's loaded. What's the point of me walking around with an unloaded gun? They'll think twice about fucking with me when I pull this .38 on their asses."

"Damn, girl, you couldn't get like some pepper spray or something?"

"Fuck that noise. I'm not trying to blind his ass. I'm gonna show them that I'm not the bitch to be trifled with."

"What if the gun goes off by mistake while you're in the mall somewhere or someone breaks into your house and steals it?"

"Leandra, you so silly." Delora laughed. "I doubt that will happen, and I have it on safety for the most part."

As usual, she had an answer for everything. "Well, I guess there's no talking you out of carrying that thing around then. You better watch your back with that."

"I understand your concern, girl, but don't worry. I got this. Jermaine showed me how to use it and all that. I got it all under control."

If I had a nickel for every time I heard that, but Delora was a grown-ass woman, and I wasn't going to keep pressing her about the gun. I've had disgust for guns ever since I found out how Rick died. There was a mix of emotions that night with the birth of Emjay and the loss of my man. I wasn't sure how to feel. In twenty years, a day hasn't gone by that I don't think about that night, someone shooting Rick like he was a dog in the street. I wonder if he thought about me and his unborn that night.

"Leandra, you're crying; are you all right?"

"Yeah, I'm just thinking about Rick."

Delora put the gun back into her purse. "I'm sorry. I didn't mean to upset you."

"No, it's nothing you did. It's just that I miss him so much, you know? He would be so proud of Emjay. I would give anything for him to see how his son turned out."

Delora got up and gave me a hug, something I desperately needed. "Leandra, you know how proud he would be of Emjay and what a great job you've done raising his boy. He's looking down on the both of ya'll from God's kingdom."

"I know. I wish he could see what a man he's become and how talented he is."

"He sees. Trust me, girl, he's seeing everything."

"Yeah, you're right. I hope he's getting that peace in death that he didn't get in life, you know?"

"He is. He's looking down on ya'll and he can't be prouder."

"I'm just going to think positive. All this crying isn't going to do me any good."

"Ain't a damn thing wrong with crying, baby girl, over the man you loved. Trust and believe, I know what that's like."

"Well, it's almost four, so you better get out of here," I said as I started to clean up.

"Shoot, I almost forgot. How much do I owe you?"

"Since you've been so sweet to me, just pay me forty."

Delora reached into her purse and pulled out two twenties and a ten and handed them to me. "All right, girl, I'm out. Are you going to be okay?" she asked, rubbing the side of my right arm.

"Are you okay to drive?" I asked.

"Yeah, I'm a little buzzed, that's about it."

As I walked Delora to the door, my phone rang. It was Taj. "Have fun on your date tonight. I want blow-by-blow details."

"Bye, girl, and thanks for hooking a sister up. Are you going to be in the shop tomorrow?"

"Yeah, I should be in for the rest of the week."

"Okay, then, maybe I will stop by."

"Well, take care and be safe."

SEVENTEEN
MYRICK

As I walked past Hardman and Leader, these two racist, ball-breaking prison guards who had given me shit in lockup, telling me when to sleep, shower and piss, I stared up into the sky, taking in the beams of sun that warmed my skin, the cool October breeze that kissed my face. I walked past the barbed-wire fence to freedom finally.

"You'll be back," Hardman said.

"You punks make sure you get a damn good look at my ass walking out of here, because it's the last time you see it."

As I eased past the gates, I turned around and shot my middle finger in the air. I proudly said, "Fuck you, motherfuckers," and spat in their direction like I was spitting in their lily-white faces.

"See you soon, nigger," Hardman said, as he shot me a sharp glance that had it been a shank, would have sliced my throat.

"Have fun fucking each other in the showers, faggots," I said, waving my middle finger at them from the other side of the walls that had held me prisoner for five years. Leader and Hardman were glad to see me go, but not as much as I was glad to be out of that shithole.

"You'll be back, boy. Your kind always comes back, and when you do, we're gonna give you the red carpet welcome."

"Take care of yourself, boys. Try not to miss me too much."

Two years were enough to last my black ass a lifetime. Krista stood in front of a black Ford Tempo smiling at me. She was just as happy to see me released as I was to be getting out of there. The first thing I noticed was her breasts that were the size of round watermelons spilling out of a white tank top. The pictures she had sent me didn't come anywhere close to doing her justice. The low-riding jeans she wore were so tight I wondered if she was getting proper circulation through that hot body of hers. Krista pulled her long ponytail that swirled with chocolate and blond highlights, around in front of her titties. Her hair hung past her waistline down to her ass damn-near. This white girl had some straight-up Rapunzel shit going on. She looked just as sexy in person. I would beat my meat twice, sometimes three times a day, thinking about her naked; fantasizing of slapping that juicy ass of hers while she gave me some of that good trailer trash pussy. Krista's letters and pics were the only thing keeping me from going cray-cray in the pin. I adjusted my dick that was twitching into a hard-on as I walked toward her.

"Hey, baby," she said, as she hugged me, wrapping her arms snug around my neck.

"Damn, you smell good," I said. Krista planted a sloppy, wet French kiss on me, a kiss I had been waiting to feel for two years. I came this close to throwing her fine ass over the hood of her Tempo, running my black mamba clear up through her—in front of Hardman, Leader, and the whole damn prison.

"You ready to get out of here, baby?"

"I've been ready," I said. The small bag of belongings I had was filled with shit I'd made in prison, along with the letters and half-naked pics Krista had sent to keep me company. I threw the bag in the backseat and got in. I couldn't get my ass out of there fast enough. Krista sped off, spitting dirt and gravel in her effort. As she drove, I rolled down the window to feel the air on my face.

"How does it feel to be out of there?"

I looked at Krista and smiled, running my hand along her thigh. "Damn good. No more telling me when to eat, when to shower, when to shit. I get to sleep in my own bed tonight."

"You hungry?" she asked.

"I'm starving."

"What are you in the mood for? Dinner is on me."

I often thought about fried chicken, burgers and pork chops instead of the pig shit that passed for food in the pen. "Well, a day didn't go by when I wasn't thinking about what I wanted to eat once I got released. I want a big T-bone steak with sweet potato fries and an ice-cold beer to wash it down with."

"That's what's up. You read my mind."

"Anyone tell you that you have the prettiest smile?"

"Well, now you can see it every day." Krista steered the car with her left hand while she reached between my legs with the right, running it up and down along the bulge in my jeans. I pinned my arms back behind the headrests of the seats and let Krista do her thing.

"Shit, somewhere," I said.

Krista looked around and said, "I know just the place." She veered behind a Best Buy and parked in a shady area under an oak tree. The second she killed the engine, Krista was pulling at my belt, fussing with the copper clasp of my jeans, anxious to get to my dick.

"Is it cool over here? Can't nobody see us, right?"

"It's cool. Just keep a lookout for anyone, baby."

I don't know who was more excited, me or her. When I wasn't beating off, I let this punk name Devante slob on my dick. I ain't gay, but shit, a mouth is a mouth. I was doing shit in the pen I never thought I would do.

Krista hooked her fingers over the edge of my drawers and pulled until she was in clear sight of her present. "Looks like Christmas came early for you this year, baby girl." Krista tugged at my underwear until my dick popped free like a jack-in-the-box. She started to play with it, massaging me with pedicured, fire engine-red nails. She threw her pretty, glitter-pink lips around the fat, mushroom tip of my dick. It was like a surge of electricity shot through my body when I felt her mouth on my dick. I rested my head against the seat as I kept a lookout. I spotted a Best Buy employee walking out to the Dumpster with some cardboard boxes, but it was nothing to get alarmed over, yet I kept a close eye on her as Krista sucked and slobbered on my ten-inch piece. "Take that dick, bitch," I said. Krista moaned, sucking air in through her nose as she went down on me. "Yeah, like that. Deep throat this dick." She was just as good as Devante, better even. I placed my hand on the back of Krista's head, easing her down on my dick as I watched the employee toss boxes in the Dumpster. I don't know, but it kind of turned me on doing this shit outside in the open. The rush of getting caught turned me on even more. I eased down into the seat as Krista sucked me.

Slurp.

Slurp.

Slurp.

The reverberation of her lips slapping against my meat echoed throughout the car. I looked at Krista, but suddenly saw Shariece's mouth stuffed with my dick instead. I thought of her often when I didn't have Krista's letters and pictures to keep me company. I thought about forgiveness, that it all was a big misunderstanding and that no matter what, I had to make it up to her in some way. I had to tell Shariece that I never meant to hurt her, that I hold no animosity and will be willing to take her back despite being locked in an eight-by-ten for three years with nothing but walls to stare at. But it made me realize that Shariece was the best thing to ever happen to my sorry ass. She was the only woman to see who I really was. I had to tell her that I was sorry for any pain I caused her. I gotta make her understand.

"Damn, you weren't lying in your letters when you said you give good head." Girl had my dick sprung and spit-soaked. I was close to popping my nut, but I didn't tell Krista that shit. I wanted her to taste me. She was sucking faster, never missing a beat as she wrapped her lips firmly around my dick. Her hair smelled like apples. "Come on, baby, make Daddy come." I held her down as she throated my juice. "Take that nut. Suck me dry." Krista drained me to completion. When she rose up off my piece, she wiped her mouth and smiled. I took my spent dick back into my drawers and jeans and zipped up.

"You like that, Myrick, baby?"

"Come here." I pulled her close to me and gave her a kiss to show just how much I approved of her blow job work. "Where did you learn to suck dick like that?"

"My stepdad," she said. I looked at Krista like she had said the craziest thing ever. And then she started laughing. "I'm fucking with you."

"Damn, ma, I was about to say, that's on a new level of fucked up."

Krista could suck a dick, yeah, but she couldn't hold a candle to Shariece.

EIGHTEEN
MYRICK

We headed across town to Outback Steakhouse. The last time I ate there was three weeks before I got locked up. I ordered the biggest T-bone they had with a mess of sweet potato fries. It was nice to be eating something other than bologna and mustard sandwiches on stale bread. That prison pig shit they called themselves trying to pass off as food did nothing but give me the bubble guts, had me shitting half the night. I savored every hearty bite of the meat, letting the juices run down my chin. I tore it up like it was my last meal.

"How's your steak?" Krista asked. "Or do I even need to ask the way you're scarfing it down?" She took a napkin and dabbed my chin clean of grease.

"It's funny what you take for granted when you're locked up," I said. "Something as simple as a steak. You don't know how good you got it 'til you lose it, you know?"

"Baby, stop, you don't have to worry about that anymore. I'm gonna take real good care of you for now on."

"Come here," I said, bending across the table. Krista met me in the middle with a kiss. "Don't know how I survived in that hell-hole if it wasn't for you. Your letters and cards got me through some rough, fucked-up days, Krista."

"With everything you told me about your last girlfriend and what she did to you, I knew you needed somebody to stand by you when you had nobody else."

I had gotten Krista's name and contact information from Craig, dude who was doing an eighteen-year bid for armed robbery. This brother was six-four, 278 pounds, whole. No one fucked with Craig knowing good and well it meant an ass whipping of Texas-sized proportions. He used to read me letters and poems Krista sent—real pretty poems that smelled of perfume with en-velopes sealed with lipstick kisses. When Craig showed me a pic-ture, her beautiful smile, long hair and big round titties, I had to holler at her, so I wrote her a letter introducing myself and what-not. I didn't tell her at first what I was locked up for. I wasn't try-ing to scare the girl. After several letters back and forth, I finally came out and told her what I was in for. I told her about Shariece and explained that it was all a misunderstanding. I told her how much I loved Shariece, that in return, she ripped my heart out and kicked my shit around like an empty soda can. After a week of not getting a letter from her, I figured she didn't want anything to do with a brother. Finally, I got this envelope decorated with hearts and silver stars, the address of the prison written in cute, cursive bubble letters. Krista explained that she understood, that she was in a bad way with her ex, when she was addicted to booze and meth.

I sympathized with her when she went on about how she grew up in a single-parent home, raised by a mother who did nothing but drink and beat on her. With the physical and sexual abuse I'd endured from my own mama, I sympathized.

I would get two letters a week from Krista, sometimes three, that smelled of perfume and smudged with lipstick kisses like the ones she had penned to Craig. There were other chicks that I corresponded with, but not as much as Krista. Most of them were prison groupies, but Krista was on a whole new level. I stopped writing this chick, Tanesha who lived in Boston who said I could come stay with her once I got out, but I didn't want to leave Florida, and Boston is too damn cold for this Southern boy. I took a job in New York once for six months and damn near froze my ass off. I ran back to Tallahassee after getting enough of the twenty-mile-per-hour wind chill and snow up to my balls. It was good to feel Florida sun on my face again.

Alexis, this cute waitress with sugar-brown skin and perky titties tight in a white Outback Steakhouse T-shirt, made her way back to our table. "Would you guys like some dessert? We have chocolate cheesecake, apple turnovers and peach cobbler, fresh and made from scratch." Alexis looked a little like Shariece. Seemed like every black woman I laid my eyes on resembled her in some way.

"You got room for some chocolate cheesecake?" I asked Krista.

"Sounds good," Krista said. She came off a little flippant to Alexis. I figured it was because she came off as a bit flirtatious. "Let me get two slices of chocolate cheesecake to go."

"Let me get those plates out of your way and I'll be right back with your dessert." I watched Alexis walk away, admiring her apple bottom booty taut in a pair of black shorts.

"So have you heard from your brother at all?" Krista asked.

"No, and I'm guessing that he doesn't want shit to do with me after finding out what I did to end up in prison. He's married with kids. I don't blame him for staying away."

"Have you tried contacting him at all?"

"Damn, what's with all the questions?"

"Sorry. I was just wondering if you had any family to come and see you."

"Look, I tried with Rashawn. Letters, phone calls, no word. I'm done. Far as I'm concerned, he's got his life and I got mines."

"I know, but baby, ya'll are family."

"Rashawn and I were always at each other's throats as kids. A lot of jealousy bullshit with me and him."

"When was the last time you talked to him?"

I stabbed a piece of gristle with my fork and forced it in my mouth. "Kris, look, I really don't want to talk about my brother. Like I said, he's got his shit and I got mine. Let's just...leave it at that for right now."

"Okay, baby, that's fine. No more talk about your brother."

Alexis's fine ass returned with two to-go desserts inside a bag. "Here you go and here is your check. You two enjoy your evening."

"Thank you, Alexis, 'preciate it." Krista rolled her eyes before she finished off the rest of her raspberry sweet tea. I can't stand jealous women, especially if it's over dumb shit like what Krista was doing. She was starting to grate on my nerves. First the twenty questions about Rashawn and now she's mean mugged because of some damn flirty waitress. Krista pulled forty dollars out of her purse and laid them on the table.

"Let's get out of here."

"Where to?" Krista asked.

"Back to my crib. There's a spare key I always leave under the doormat. I just hope it's still there." Krista and I walked out of the steakhouse with our chocolate cheesecake and full stomachs. "How 'bout I drive?" When we got to the car, Krista handed me the keys. It felt good to get behind the wheel of a car again. To feel all that steel under my ass. Krista's Tempo wasn't my Cadillac Escalade, by any means, and I couldn't wait to see my whip.

The driveway was strewn with leaves and pine needles, and the front yard was overgrown with weeds. "This is a beautiful house," Krista said.

"It could use a bit of work. It's all that's left of my mama. Surprised it's still here, really, and it hasn't been sold."

"It just needs a coat of paint, that's all."

We got out and walked along the overgrown lawn to the porch. I turned over the doormat. "Yep, right where I left it." I slid the gold-plated beak of the key into the slit of the doorknob and turned it open. The stench of mold and mildew bit my senses as we walked in. It felt damp.

"Myrick, it ain't that bad. Just needs a woman's touch is all. Once we get it cleaned up, it'll be livable again." I didn't recall asking for Krista's opinion about my house.

"I see that it needs cleaning. I'm looking right-the-fuck at it."

"I know. I'm just saying."

"Well, stop saying." Krista continued sizing up the house. Unfortunately, it was exactly like I had left it: dirty as hell. There were clothes folded over the back of the sofa and chairs; dirty plates and glasses filled the kitchen sink. I didn't realize that I had left the house in such a pigsty.

"Myrick, baby, what's wrong?"

"She would be so ashamed of me."

"Who?"

"Mama. Look at this place."

"Don't cry. You just need to straighten up a little, that's all."

"She was too sick to visit me in the pen 'cause of the cancer. She died and I wasn't there when she needed me the most. I let her down."

"No you didn't; don't talk like that. Your mama loved you."

I gave Krista an expression of disgust. "How the hell would you know? Did you know her?"

"What?"

"You didn't know her, so you don't know shit."

"I just think you're being too hard on yourself that's all," Krista said.

"Well, do me a favor. Don't think."

"Baby, I was only trying to—"

"Don't try, do. That's what Mama always used to say to me before she clocked me upside the head with a bedroom shoe. Don't try, do."

"Sounds like a wise woman."

"She was always on my ass for every little thing. Tell me how worthless I was. You know she told me once that she wished she had never had me."

"Oh my God, baby, I'm sorry." I pulled away when Krista placed her hand on my shoulder to comfort me.

"She used to beat me with anything she could find. One time, she gave me ten lashes across my back with an extension cord because I wet the bed."

"I'm so sorry. Was your dad ever around?"

"I never knew the man. Rashawn and I come from different daddies. Mama pointed him out to me once when we were in Publix, but I never met him. I never had anything to do with him. She made sure of that."

Krista wrapped her arms around me and gave me a hug. "All my daddy does is sit home and drink. He's probably fucked up right now. Why do they do it to us, Myrick? What did we ever do?" I looked about the house at all the work that needed to be done, knowing that there was no time for reminiscing.

"Okay, enough talking about our damaged childhoods. I just got out of prison and that calls for a celebration. I think I have a bottle of wine around here somewhere." I scavenged the cabinets, but nothing. When I opened the refrigerator, the rancid odor of cheese was like a pimp slap in the face. I slammed it shut, but I had already gotten wind of the stench. "Like a damn biohazard in there." I looked in the cabinets above the refrigerator where I found a bottle of Cabernet. I took two wineglasses, set them on the kitchen counter and poured. I couldn't keep my eyes off Krista's breasts. They were so big you could float out to sea for days on her titties. "I hope you like red wine."

"I like anything with alcohol. I heard that red is good for the heart or something," Krista said.

"That's true. It has antioxidants in it that help to prevent against artery damage." I handed Krista a glass.

"My sister and I took a wine-tasting class last year and we learned all about how healthy red wine is."

"In moderation, though. You can't go drinking the shit like it's Kool-Aid."

Krista inhaled the aroma of the wine before she took a sip. "That's pretty good."

"We'll clean up later. Let's take our wine up to the bedroom." The thought of smothering my face between Krista's tits, got my dick hard. My bedroom was slightly cleaner than the rest of the house. Every table, lamp and chair was covered with dust.

"This is my bedroom," I said, taking a seat on the edge of the king-size bed. Krista gave a sinister smile as she came over and sat next to me, knowing full damn well where it would lead. She placed her glass on the bedside table and began to rub my dick through my jeans again. I was already bone-hard. "Damn, girl, you fine." I roped my arms around Krista and pulled her down on top of me, her large titties pressing against my chest, the tent of my dick grazing against her camel toe. We came together with sloppy kisses, shoving our tongues mutually in each other's mouths. I pulled at Krista's white tank top until her breasts flopped out of the ribbed cotton. I tongue-teased her nipples, sucking them past my lips as I pushed my hand down into her low-riding jeans, past her panties until I felt her pussy slick with her juices. *How in the hell did I go without this so long?* I thought. Krista ran her fingers along my hair as I toyed with her nips. "Let's get you out of these clothes." I peeled off her cutoffs as she released her titties from the confines of her tank top.

I kicked off my Timbs as I tugged my shirt off. I had lost thirty pounds in the pin from lifting weights, building a nice six-pack. Taking the anger out on free weights was better than sitting in a cell to stew for five years.

My dick popped free from the cage of denim and underwear when I pulled them down to my ankles, pushing them from my feet. I pulled Krista to me, the mushroom head of my dick grazing against her pussy. She sighed when I sank my dick in past the lips of her vagina. Her skin was powder-white and soft as cream. Her pussy was as warm as apple pie as I stirred her insides with my double chocolate dip stick. "Fuck, don't stop," she said, as she clawed at my back, locking her legs around mine as I thrusted. When I looked at Krista, all I could see was Shariece's face again. I kissed her hard, sucking her tongue and lips, squeezing Shariece's round, brown breasts. "Baby, you're hurting me."

I glanced to find that it wasn't Shariece, but Krista's freckled, pasty-white face staring back at me. *Fuck!* "My bad," I said. I dropped my face off to the side. I couldn't stand to look at Krista. She wasn't who I desired. Shariece was who I wanted, not this trailer-trash, stringy-haired bitch. This wasn't me. I wasn't the type who slummed.

I fucked until I popped my load. I couldn't stomach being with Krista another minute. I wanted her out of my bed, out of my house and the fuck out of my life. I couldn't have been more disgusted with myself when my dick slipped out of her stank-ass cooch.

"You lasted a lot longer in the car," she said, as she caressed my chest. I almost cringed to this bitch putting her hands on me, the sound of her trashy Southern twang. I wanted to cut out her tongue for even fixing her mouth to speak to me. This skank couldn't hold a matchstick to my Shariece. I needed to get what I needed out of Krista before I got rid of her.

"So did you get the information I asked you to get for me?"

"Shariece just got hired at the community college teaching English on Mondays, Wednesdays and Fridays, and she has a Tuesday night class from six-thirty to nine forty-five. She lives on Sixth Street in midtown. She usually gets home a little after six on Mondays, Wednesdays and Fridays and around ten-thirty on Tuesdays and Thursdays."

"Did you get the other thing?"

"Oh yeah, I almost forgot." Krista took her shorts and pulled a key out of the back pocket. "It was tough for me to get this, but I managed."

"What would I ever do without you?"

"You know I would do anything for you." I kissed Krista, pressing her back down into bed. I ran my hands up along her stomach, in between her cleavage, stretching my hand across her throat. I looked into her eyes as I started to apply pressure. She started to cough, gawking at me as fear took her over. Krista clawed at my hand, pushing to get loose, but she couldn't free herself from under my weight. I straddled her, taking her by the throat with both hands now, squeezing, pushing, choking her. Krista tried to scream, but my hands were like a vise grip. I thought of Shariece. The more she fought, the more I tightened my hands around her throat. Krista stopped struggling. I could see the life fading from her ocean-blue eyes. Her body went limp, felt light. She was gone. The back of my hand was on fire from all her scratches. Her arms flopped lifeless over the edge of the bed. I eased off of her and watched her for a short while. "You do have some beautiful titties." I groped and sucked on her titties for what would be the last time. I stared at myself in the mirror, my dick dry with Krista's pussy juices.

NINETEEN
TAJ

It was five in the morning when I got home. I slowly pushed the key Leandra gave me into the lock of the front door, careful not to wake her. I twisted until the lock clicked open. I grimaced to the sound of the rusty hinges screaming to my advance. The house was dark and quiet. I set my gym bag in one of the love seats that sat against the wall facing the entertainment center. The bedroom door was slightly ajar. Leandra was asleep, but not soundly with all the snoring she was doing. It was one out of many things I found adorable about her.

I was so tired I thought I was going to drop dead right there in the hallway on my way to the bathroom. My body was sticky with sweat and cum. All I wanted to do was peel myself out of my gray sweats and T-shirt and scrub my skin clean. But in my line of work, could I ever be completely clean? I switched the bathroom light on, brushed back the plastic, flower-printed shower curtain and flipped on the faucet. The mere reverberation of the water had already started to relax me. I peeled the sweats off like they were scaly layers of skin. I grimaced to the faint scent of someone's cum that was permeating from my chest. I would have doused my clothes in kerosene if I could, but buried them deep in the rose-pink, wicker hamper. I lifted the lid on the toilet and plopped down on the porcelain throne. I pointed my spit-sticky dick down in the commode and pissed. Airy farts escaped my asshole as I pissed. I wanted to shit, but it wouldn't come no matter how hard I squeezed and strained. My shit was backed up. My eyes watered as I struggled to push out the waste. "Fuuuuuck," I swore until I felt myself pushing it out of my asshole. The shit plopped into the pissy toilet water. "Damn, my asshole is on fire." My eyes were bloodshot, every muscle in my body ached for relaxation. I wiped, and then flushed down the shit, piss and paper. Felt like I had been holding that log in all day. My body was working against me as I placed one leg and then the other into the tub. The warm shower water pelted my sore limbs. I ran the bar of soap along my arms and chest; lather trickled into my nest of pubes as I scrubbed my dick and balls clean of spit and ass. "Fifteen. Fifteen fucking hours on the set." I made sure every arm, leg, finger, foot and toe was clean from the filth of a long day. I killed the shower before I grabbed a towel to dry off. My feet were killing me. I slipped in quiet under the covers so not to wake Leandra, but I failed.

"Hey, baby, you just getting home?" Leandra asked.

"Yeah. Sorry I didn't call you."

"It's okay. How did the photo shoot go?"

I kissed her softly behind her left ear before I dropped a lie like poison into it. "One of the models was late. This fashion designer is a bitch on wheels. I came this close to walking off the set today."

"You kept your cool, though, right?"

"Um…yeah. It's a big account. I didn't storm off like some spoiled brat. Boo, at this point, I simply want to finish this project up and move on to something else. I'm over it, to tell you the truth."

"You hungry? You want me to make you some breakfast?" Leandra rubbed sleep out of her eyes.

"That's sweet of you, baby, but I'm not hungry. Glad I finally made it home to my lady." I took Leandra into my arms, spooning her. My dick began to go hard when it grazed against her booty. "How was your day?" I asked, as I slid my hands under her all size-fits-all T-shirt with a teddy bear on the front.

"It was okay. I had a client come over and I did her hair, but other than that, it was pretty quiet." I played with Leandra's nipples knowing how crazy horny that drives her. Wasn't long before she began moaning to my advances. I felt her backing her ass up against my twitching dick. I slipped her panties down off her ass, around her plump thighs. Leandra placed her hand on top of mine that massaged her breasts. I reached over to find that her pussy was sopping wet.

"Already, you worked up, huh?" I asked.

"I'm always ready. You know what you do to me."

I spat on my hand, slathered my dick, circled her knobs easy, pinching them between my fingers. Leandra turned to face me. Her lips were supple against mine. Her tongue tasted of strawberries. "Damn, baby, you turn me on," I whispered. Leandra slid on top of me, her breasts warm against my chest as we kissed. She maneuvered her body until my dick slipped like a hot secret inside her.

Leandra whimpered to the sensation of me plowing her sweet spot. "Fuck me, baby, fuck me."

"Whose pussy is this?"

"Yours," Leandra moaned.

"What?"

"Yours. This pussy's yours."

I don't know what happened, but as soon as I slapped Leandra's right ass cheek, the images of naked men began to dance in my head again. I tried to extinguish the images free from my mind by shutting my eyes, but that only made them more acute. It was Kurt Kameron this time—this porn actor wannabe Jimi discovered on Craigslist of all places. He has the dick to get the job done, but he leaves much to be desired in the looks department. First time I laid eyes on him, I thought he still needed to do some more work on his body if he really wanted to make it in the business.

I prayed that my dick wouldn't soften in the middle of fucking Leandra as I thought of Kurt sucking me off.

"Baby, are you okay?" Leandra asked.

"Yeah, why, what's up?"

"You just seem a little distant, that's all."

"No, I'm right here with you, baby." Leandra tightened her pussy around my dick yet I couldn't shake the images of Kurt blowing me. I only hoped that I wouldn't call his name out instead of Leandra's. *Why the hell am I thinking about him and now of all times?* It was one thing to be in this frame of mind on set, because it's work, but to bring this shit home with me? Leandra was putting it on me, which was understandable. The last time we'd had sex, was the night before the dinner with Emjay and Shariece. I focused on Leandra, groping her ass as she fucked me.

"Oh fuck, I'm gonna come," Leandra cried out, and within seconds, we both came to a mind-blowing, toe-curling orgasm. She collapsed on top of me, my dick still fat and hard inside of her. I braced myself as she rolled off of me.

"Damn, we haven't done that in a while," Leandra said.

"I know. With this project and you getting back on your feet after the accident, it's been a hot minute."

Leandra placed her hand on her brow from exhaustion. "You okay, you seemed like you were in deep thought somewhere."

"Sorry, Lee. I'm just stressed out with this project, that's all."

"You know what you need?"

"What?"

"A nice big breakfast. I know you said you weren't hungry, but I'm starving. I betcha they didn't feed ya'll nothing but junk food. You need you a meal of something to eat, not snacks."

"True. Maybe some bacon and eggs will get my mind off work."

"That's the spirit." Leandra got up and grabbed her robe from a white chair that was sitting on the other side of the bedside table. "How does, pancakes, eggs, grits and ham steak sound?"

"That's fine, pumpkin bear, whatever you want." The last thing my mind was on was food, but Leandra insisted.

"You just rest up while I go cook something up. It won't take me long. You need to get something in you other than honey buns."

I lay there thinking about the images I was having of Kurt and why I couldn't turn that shit off when I walked in the door. There was no way I was ready to tell Leandra what was really going on, that I wasn't a fashion photographer, but an actor in the porn industry—if you can call fake moans and groans acting.

With all the mess with Emjay, Shariece and the accident, the last thing she needed was to find out that I do porn for a living.

Slinging greasy pizza at Sbarro in the mall was the last job I had and lost after getting fired for coming to work late too many times. The last thing I wanted was to stand in another unemployment line, or sit around on my laptop applying for one piece-of-shit job after the next only to get emails telling me that the job had been given to a more *qualified* applicant. I applied for everything from bank teller to delivering phone books, spending all day in a Barnes & Noble Café typing up cover letters and honing my resume, until I developed carpal tunnel. I was hopeless about finding work until I decided to see what was up in the job section of Craigslist.

Most of them were bullshit fakes, or jobs that didn't lead to much of nothing. Last year, I went to check out this job in Kerry Forrest, which was thirty minutes across town. My ride was in the shop, so I had to catch the bus, something I'm not used to doing. The job was as a part-time security guard at Stein Mart. I get there and they tell me that the position had been filled. I lost my shit.

"Well, someone here told me that the position was still available and that I can come in and talk to a manager," I'd said to this old, short woman with short, curly, brunette hair, wearing wire-frame glasses that hung off the end of her big-ass nose. I was pouring with sweat by the time I got to the store as it was five store blocks from where the bus dropped me. My shirt and everything was soiled with sweat. "Sir, who told you that—"

"I don't know, some lady. I didn't get her name." I didn't even let the old bitch finish her question. She went on and on about how sorry she was for the inconvenience, but I think she was lying about the position being filled. When I told her about the security job ad, she looked me up and down like I was the filthiest thing that walked through their door, like I had some nerve for walking into their pricey-ass store inquiring about a job. I wanted to curse her out, but I kept my cool and hauled my ass out of there. But I didn't let my new clothes go to waste. I applied to every place after Stein Mart: Applebee's, Dollar Tree, Old Navy, Shoe Station, Books-A-Million. I needed a j-o-b bad. My rent was due and I was already two car notes behind on my TrailBlazer. The thought of being out on the street was freaking the fuck out of me. My back was officially against the wall. Funny what you will do when you have no money, when you stand to lose everything.

After I cooled my wing tips from taking that wild goose chase out to Kerry Forrest, I went back to Craigslist to check out the job site. I was hard up and I wasn't about to lose my car. Getting kicked out of my roach motel of an apartment wouldn't have been such a loss. I would apply for twenty jobs a day, spending hours on my laptop sometimes until 3 a.m. There was one ad I came across in the TV/film/video section of Craigslist. This new production company was looking for local talent, actors and extras for some film and they would pay thirty dollars an hour. Jimi Bryan Productions was what it was called. The shit seemed fishy to me, but after weeks of looking for work, I was down for anything. It was located on the East Side of town, nowhere near as far as Stein Mart. When I called to see if the job was still available, this lady answered. Well, she sounded more like a sorority chick slash Valley girl. I asked if I could speak with Jimi.

"Mr. Bryan is in auditions at the moment. Would you like to leave a message?"

"I saw the ad on Craigslist about the acting job, and I wanted to stop by and talk to him about auditioning."

She informed me that this Jimi guy was still looking for actors and that I should come in with a headshot and a bio. The only recent picture I had of myself was the one nigga, Deshawn took of me at a block party. It was the only pic I could get a hold of on such short notice. I didn't bother with dress attire for this one, being that it was an audition. I wore jeans and a muscle T-shirt to show off my muscles. People in the movie business like that kind of shit. I asked for Valley girl's name in case this guy, Jimi, wanted to pull that same shit that old wench at Stein Mart had pulled.

"My name's Cherri," she said.

"That's nice, like the fruit?" I asked.

"Yes, but spelled with an 'I' instead of a 'Y.'"

"All right, Cherri. I'll see you in a few."

I did an Internet search for Jimi Bryan Productions, but nothing came up. That's when a red flag went up in my head. I had a bad feeling, but wanted to see what was up anyway. I followed the directions to the letter that led me way out on North Monroe near I-10 that led me to this old building that used to be Skate-in East, this rink I used to go to when I was a kid. There were four large windows that were pitch-black with tint. You couldn't see anything inside from the parking lot.

"I don't know about this shit," I said to myself, but I figured thirty dollars an hour was worth it. When I walked through the double-glass tinted doors, a hint of feet and Fritos filled my senses. Thumbtacked along the wall were posters of some of the most famous movies ever made: *Close Encounters of the Third Kind, Jaws, E.T., Scarface, Blade Runner,* all of my favorite movies. My doubts had waned when I realized that this place was on the up and up.

This white girl with long, black hair pulled back high in a ponytail was sitting at a desk at the end of the hall. *That must be Cherri.* She looked as fine as she sounded on the phone looking like she wanted to be anywhere but in a place that smelled like toe jam and Tostito chips.

"How you doin'? Are you Cherri?"

"Yes," she said, gawking at me suspiciously, chewing her gum like a cow munching on field grass.

"What's up, shorty? I'm Taj Bowman. We spoke on the phone about the audition."

"Hello. Mr. Bryan is in with an actor. Have a seat. I'll let him know you're here."

I sat in one of the seven pleather black chairs that aligned the wall. Cherri had to be in her early twenties. Why was someone as cute as her working as a receptionist? She had the face that warranted being on the cover of *Essence, Ebony, Jet* magazine. I studied the movie posters wishing they were hanging on the walls back at my apartment, especially the *Scarface* poster. Those damn things are hard to find. Cherri kept looking at me, but would look away when I caught her eye. *Don't front. You know you want some.*

I waited near an hour before Cherri told me that it was cool to go into Jimi's office. This white guy with dark, wavy hair came out of the office wearing a faded, red Dr. Pepper T-shirt and jeans. He cut me this look like I didn't stand a chance. Had anyone told me I would be having sex for money, I would have popped them in the mouth.

"Mr. Bryan will see you now," she said, chewing on that same piece of gum like it would be the last piece she would ever have. *I got something for you to chew on*, I thought to myself.

Jimi Bryan Productions was emblazoned on a gold-plated tag screwed on the door. When I walked in, a white guy with short, curly, sandy-blond hair, wearing glasses was sitting on a sofa facing a desk with shelves that housed hundreds, hell, probably thousands of DVDs. They were not movies that could be seen in a theater, not anymore anyway, but the kind you could only find in adult video stores. I came close to turning around and walking out of the office, but the thought of the repo man coming at 3 a.m. to take my TrailBlazer, kept my feet planted in Jimi's office.

"Hey, you must be Taj." Jimi stood up from the black leather couch to shake my hand. His felt cold, kind of clammy.

"Hey, how you doin'? I'm here about the ad I saw on Craigslist." As soon as I had seen all the porn, I knew what kind of business Jimi was running.

"Great. Did you bring a headshot?"

"Um…all I could get ahold of was this pic my friend took." I handed it to him. There wasn't any time to have anything professional made up. Didn't know I was going to be coming out somewhere like this." I could feel Jimi's eyes scanning my body, over every inch of me, zeroing in on my dick.

Jimi glanced at the picture for all of two seconds before he switched his glance back to me like I was a slab of meat.

"It's not what I'm used to, but a headshot is a headshot, right?" A set of butter-yellow teeth were exposed when he smiled. "Have a seat, Taj. Tell me a little about yourself."

"Not much to tell. I came to Tallahassee by way of Celebration, Florida when I was eighteen. I've worked a few odd-and-end jobs ever since, staying on this grind, you know?"

"You a college boy?"

"I was taking some classes at the community college, but I had to drop out because I couldn't afford it, so I'm trying to save up some money to go back."

"That's great. What are you studying?"

Damn, this dude was nosey as hell. All up in a black man's business. I had to pull something out of my ass and quick.

"Graphic design," I lied.

"Oh, that's cool. I need someone to get my website up and running, so I may be in need of your…services." I felt Jimi's devil-blue eyeballs on my crotch again like it was a birthday gift he couldn't wait to unwrap. "So, have you done any acting?"

"I played Santa Claus in my third-grade Christmas play. Does that count?"

Jimi laughed, branding those cornbread-yellow teeth of his. "Well, let me give you a little information on what I do here." Jimi sauntered across the office behind his desk. "Just so there are no misunderstandings, this…is what I do." He held his arms out like a model from *The Price is Right* in front of the shelves of porn movies as if they were a washer and dryer and a new car sitting idle behind him. "GAY ADULT ENTERTAINMENT!" he announced.

"Porn," I said.

"Shhh, we don't like to use the p-word around here. *Adult entertainment* is more of a sophisticated term."

"Okay, I feel you."

"Now before I go on, because I don't want to waste your time or mine, would you have a problem working in this industry?"

"No, not at all."

"You sure? Because people get into this, work on one film and decide that it's not for them, so I need you to be absolutely sure that this is the right place for you."

"Look, Mr. Bryan."

"Call me Jimi," he interrupted.

"I'm about to get evicted out of my apartment, and my car is about to get repossessed. I've applied for job after job, and they either tell me that the position has been filled or I don't hear back from anybody. Unemployment only pays me ninety-five dollars a week. I'm pretty much eating Ramen for breakfast, lunch and dinner. I'm an ass hair away from being on the streets." I hadn't planned on telling my sob story to Jimi, but that shit was the t-r-u truth.

"Good. I'm glad we're on the same page. My next question is, have you ever done adult movies?"

"No. Never thought about it, really."

"Taj, here I run a clean operation. My actors go through mandatory drug testing for STDs and drugs. If you test positive for either, you can't work. I can't hire you. When was the last time you were tested for STDs?"

"It's been about a year ago."

"Would you have a problem taking a test for STDs?"

"I'm pretty clean, so no, not at all." I smoked weed every now and then, but out of fear of not getting the gig, I kept my mouth shut on that one.

"Now my next question is, do you have issues with homosexual men at all?"

I knew exactly the direction this was going in. "No. I've got gay cousins, so I'm cool."

The only person in my family that I know is gay for sure is my cousin, Darnell. I don't think anyone in the family knew until my aunt found some explicit shit of his he had put on the Internet. After that, Darnell's secret was front and center and the talk of Celebration. And being that my mama doesn't get along with my Aunt Layla, Aunt Tilly and Uncle Marcus, all had a field day with the news. When Uncle Marcus called Darnell a faggot at a Christmas gathering last year, a fight broke out that ended with Darnell holding a steak knife to Uncle Marcus's throat. Not another word was said about Darnell being gay after that. At least not from Uncle Marcus anyway. I'm the only one in the family he's cool with.

"Great, because I not only do straight films here, but I also do gay films, and I'm casting right now for my next film, *Hot Cops with Hard Cocks*, and you would be perfect for the role of Digger Hardman. Think you're up for it?"

It took everything in me to keep from laughing my ass off at the name Jimi came up with. "I think I can handle it."

"Good," Jimi smiled, "that's what I like to hear. Now, let me see what you're working with."

"What?"

"Your cock size, let's see it."

"Um…"

"Look, Taj, I need to see what you're working with. I can't have someone with baby dick on my set; now let's see the goods."

I stood up and reluctantly unfastened my jeans. Jimi stood in front of his shelves of porn, waiting with baited breath to see my dick. I reached inside my briefs and eased it out. "Christ, man, you got a battering ram between your legs." I looked off embarrassed standing in the middle of this guy's office with my dip stick hanging out. "Do you jack off?"

"Excuse me?"

"You know, masturbate?"

"We all do."

"You shoot big loads?"

Jimi was on a new level of none of your damn business, which was what I started to tell him. "I guess; I don't know. I never really noticed how much I squirt when I nut."

"Stroke your dick for me?"

"What?"

"I'm kidding." Jimi laughed out loud, but I didn't think that shit was funny. "Do you work out? Lift your shirt up for me."

"Six days a week."

"And it shows, my friend, it shows." This guy was coming off like a total damn grease ball.

"All right, you got the job."

"I got the job?"

"Can you come in tomorrow morning? The guy that came in before you is going to be playing a robber, and in the scene I've set up for you guys is where you unleash your own brand of justice, if you know what I mean."

"You talking about the Italian-looking guy that just left?"

"Yes, his name is Vance Rich. He's playing a guy by the name of Kurt Kameron. I've worked with him before, back when I was doing films in Miami. He's a huge power bottom and loves black cock. You two are going to be great. So tomorrow morning, eight a.m. Sharp. Do not be late. I can't stand tardiness."

"So how much are you paying for this?"

"I pay a grand for two hours and it's all under the table. I think it's easier that way for everyone."

"That's cool. It beats the hell out of having to deal with taxes and IRS bullshit."

"I like you, Taj. You and I are going to get along real good," he said, slapping me on the back, as we headed toward the door. "So come by tomorrow so my nurse can give you a piss test and take blood, and then we can get rolling."

"I was wondering if I could ask you a small favor."

"Sure."

"Is it possible that I could get a small advance until we start filming?"

Jimi looked at me like he was trying to find the answer to my question. "Say no more." Jimi took out his wallet that was chock-full of crisp one hundred-dollar bills. He counted out eight and handed me the money.

"I just need something to cover my rent this month. I owe you one."

"Forget about it. You're part of the team now." When I took the money, I felt like I had just taken cash from the Devil himself.

"I promise I'll pay you back."

"I'm sure we can work something out," Jimi said.

Cherri was sitting at the desk typing on the computer pretending to look busy. By the time we were done, three more losers sat in the hall with their headshots. I smiled at them and thought to myself, *bunch of chumps*. Little did I know that I was going to be the one looking like the chump when it was all said and done.

TWENTY
EMJAY

Dash had been mugging me for weeks about getting together. I'd been so busy with school and all this craziness going on with me and Mama, I hadn't exactly been best friend of the year to Dash. So when I called to ask if he wanted to go for beers and wings, he was all too happy to jump at the opportunity. I owed him one for being such an asshole. I needed to bounce my troubles off somebody, and Dash, who has been my best friend since fifth grade, I knew would give me some advice on what to do without telling me what I wanted to hear. Dash was the only one I can confide in and not worry about him blowing my shit up.

It was after two in the afternoon, according to the clock on my car stereo, when I pulled in front of Wing Stop. When I do have time for that thing they call lunch, I prefer to eat after two when the lunch crowd has died down. I didn't see Dash's Saturn, so I figured he hadn't arrived yet.

"His ass is going to be late to his own funeral," I said, as I addressed a text message to him. *I'm here; hurry your narrow ass up.* The spicy scent of buffalo sauce that met me when I walked in sent my stomach rumbling. The dining area was vacant, while the bar occupied a few patrons who sipped slowly on cheap beer. I sat at the bar where this girl with slick, brunette swimmer's hair pulled back tight into a ponytail, stood behind the bar. She wore black short-shorts and a black T-shirt with the Wing Stop logo emblazoned on the front. She had these tiny apple tits that came nowhere near filling out the T-shirt.

"Hello, welcome to Wing Stop."

"Hey," was all I said, as I sat in the middle of the bar. I could tell by her tone that she was the bubbly, cheerleader type. Give her a set of pom-poms and she'd break out with a cheer for a tip. One of them corny-ass white girls. Cute to look at, but cornball fuck.

"Can I get you anything to drink?" I made out her name scribbled in black marker on a plastic white name tag. *Kayla*, it read. Kayla had big, brown eyes and a cute smile.

"Do you all serve Shock Top here?"

"Yes we do."

"Can I get that?"

"Do you have ID?" I tugged my wallet out of the left-front pocket of my shorts and showed her my license. "Cool," she said, smiling. "Would you like bottle or draft?"

"Draft." I never seem to finish beer for some reason when I drink it out of the bottle. I was like that as a kid, too. Mama would give me soda, and I could never drink it out of the can. It had to be in a glass. Kayla took a mug from the back counter and filled it with Shock Top. I didn't know how thirsty I was until I watched her fill the mug up with the thick, cold beer. Since Mama had cut me off, I paid for the beer with cash I got from selling a few books back at the Paperback Rack. I didn't get nearly as much as I hoped, so I sold off some CDs at Vinyl Fever, making a total sum of thirty dollars. I hope I get a job soon because I'm getting down to the bare essentials. "That will be two dollars," Kayla said.

I handed her a ten and left her a two-dollar tip. I was trying to scratch up every penny, especially with Christmas around the corner.

Shariece said she would take care of whatever I need, but I don't want my girlfriend treating me like a kid. It only makes me feel like less of a man if I can't provide for us.

This is Ma trying to teach me a lesson because she can't stand the idea of Shariece and I being together. Damn, I can't help who I fall in love with. I'm not even going to play into her hate game. I love her, but she can think again if she thinks I'm going to pick the phone up and call her to apologize. I don't have anything to be sorry for. All I can do is live my life and hope that she comes around to my side of things, because Shariece isn't going anywhere. Everything will be everything once I get a job.

"Kayla, hey," I said, waving her over.

"Are ya'll um…hiring at all?"

"You know, I'm not sure. We might be. Brice, our general manager, just left. He would be the guy to talk to."

"When is he here?"

"Usually in the mornings, if you want to come by tomorrow and talk to him. He usually comes in around nine."

"That's what's up. I'll do that."

I was about to text Dash again when I felt someone slap me hard on the back of my neck. The sting was immediate and caused me to jerk up from the barstool. I turned around and it was Dash's ashy black ass playing too much.

"What up, Black?"

"Boyyyy, you was about to get punched in the throat." Dash was always doing sneaky shit like that. "Damn, dog, what have you been eating? You big as hell," I asked as he looked at me through a set of black-framed glasses. "Gimme some love." Dash gave me this big bear hug to the point I thought my lungs were going to collapse. "Dang, you trying to break a brother in half, shit." I laughed. At six-foot-three, two-hundred and ninety-five pounds, Dash didn't know his own strength.

Kayla stood with a smile on her pretty sorority girl face to take Dash's order. "Can I get you something to drink?"

Dash looked at my glass of beer and asked, "What is that swill you drinking?"

"Shock Top, baby boy, you know what's up."

Dash scrunched up his face like he had tasted something nasty.

"Let me get a Blue Moon. That's a real goddamn beer."

"Can I see some ID, please?" Kayla was smart and didn't let anything get past her. Dash pulled out his wallet and showed his ID. "Bottle or draft?"

"Draft is cool," Dash said.

"So I was surprised your ass called saying you wanted to have lunch. You know I've been trying to get you to hang out for a month now."

"Stop lying. It hasn't been that long."

"I thought you had forgotten about a brother."

"Yeah, my bad about that. Shit has been crazy with school and my mama pressuring me about keeping my grades up."

"Your mama's still on your ass, I see."

"Man, you have no idea. She makes a federal case out of every-thing. My grades, where I am, who I'm with, if I'm eating." Kayla set Dash's cold glass of Blue Moon in front of him. "She has to keep tabs on her only child, her baby boy."

"Would you guys like to see some menus?"

"Do ya'll still have the forty-cent all-you-can-eat wings?" I asked.

"We do. What flavor would you like?"

"You want to get a basket of twenty spicy Cajun and share it?" Dash asked.

"That's cool."

"Are they like mildly hot or real, real hot?" Dash asked.

"Oh, they're pretty hot," Kayla said in an almost cautious tone like she was warning us to eat the wings at our own risk.

Dash looked at me and I back at him. "Cool, let's do it. We'll get the spicy Cajun wings." Dash and I had stomachs like steel, so we didn't sweat it.

"You want plain or sweet potato fries with that?"

"Let me get a basket of sweet potato fries," Emjay said.

"Coming right up."

"You know she cut me off."

Dash took a long sip from his beer that oddly resembled stale piss. "Who?"

"My mama. She canceled my credit card, closed my checking account, all that."

"Damn, why?"

"It's a long story."

"Well, I got all day, so what did you do this time?" Dash joked.

"I fell in love."

"Who is it this time and do I know her?"

"Okay, before I say anything, you have to promise you won't say nothing to the guys."

"Jay, you know I love a good secret. What is it?"

"You gotta promise me. I'm serious."

"Jay, remember that time you told me in the fourth grade that you stole Mrs. Greene's glue out of her desk?"

"Yeah."

"Did I run and tell her that you took it? No. You know you can trust me, so what's up?"

"Pinky swear?" I said.

Dash playfully slapped my hand down. "Nigga, quit playing and tell me what's up."

I took a long drink from my beer before I let Dash in on what had been going on with me.

"The woman that I'm in love with is a little older."

"Like how old?" He smiled.

"About twenty years older."

"Oh shit."

"Man, keep your voice down, damn."

"Is she a student? How long has this been going on?"

I gawked at Dash as he took a swig of beer. "It's a teacher." Suddenly, he sprayed Blue Moon across the bar almost hitting Kayla. He howled out with laughter.

"WHAT!?!"

"I knew I shouldn't have told you. Kayla, did he spray you, did he get you?"

"Oh my bad, baby girl. I didn't spit on you, did I?"

"I'm fine. I think you missed me by a few inches." She laughed.

"You sure? I'm sorry."

"Yeah, guys, I'm fine."

One of the cooks came out with our order of sweet potato fries and hot wings. Kayla set our food in front of us and said, "Can I get you guys anything else? You want another beer?" she asked me.

"Please."

"Are you shittin' me, Jay?"

"Why don't you tell the whole bar?"

"Who is she? Do I know her?" Dash asked.

"It's Shariece."

"Shit, the chick that used to babysit you? Holy fuck! You did tell me that you've always had a crush on her. I didn't know she taught at TCC. Hell, I didn't know she was even a teacher." I plucked one of the wings from the basket and started to rip meat from the bone with my teeth. I quickly started to feel the spicy effects. "My boy's fucking a cougar."

"Man, shut up, damn."

Dash sucked chicken from one of the wings. "Hold up. Isn't she your mom's friend? Oh shit, does she know? Your moms, I mean?"

"Shariece and I tried to keep our relationship on the low, but she found out."

"And that's why she cut you off? How did your mama find out; did you tell her?"

I was only on my second wing and already my mouth was on fire. "Shariece and I were at my crib when she caught us."

Dash started laughing as he sucked wing sauce off his fingers. "She caught ya'll fuckin'."

I took a drink to cool off the four-alarm fire that was going on in my mouth.

"So your moms was pissed after walking in on her son fucking her best friend."

"We tried to talk to her, but you know how my mama gets when she's mad. You can't tell her anything when she gets like she does."

"I'm glad you called to catch up. That's some crazy shit for real. Have you tried to talk to your moms since then?"

"There's no point. She won't talk to me and I really don't have anything to say to her."

"So what are you doing for money?"

"Selling off shit. Books, CDs and whatnot until I can find a job."

"Shit, I'm sorry, bro."

"It is what it is. I need to do for myself anyway. I'll feel better when I start making my own money without her threatening to cut me off if I didn't live how she wanted. I'm relieved. It sucks the way everything went down 'cause I didn't want her to find out like she did, but I can't rewind back to that night and change it, so it's whatever."

Dash was wolfing down the wings faster than me, as if he wasn't affected by the fire from the meat. I took swigs from my Shock Top, but seemed like the beer only made the burn worse.

"Are you and Shariece careful?"

"What? Yeah. She's on the pill and I use rubbers just in case."

Dash laughed between devouring wings. "That's good to know, but I mean, no one at the school knows what ya'll are doing, right?"

"We messed around in her office a couple of times."

"Are you serious? Man, you gon' get caught; watch and see."

"We locked the door. Nobody saw us."

"Jay, someone always sees."

"We both agreed that if we were going to make this work that we weren't going to risk her career, so we make sure to keep it professional on campus. We've decided to maintain a professional teacher/student relationship at least until the end of the semester."

"Ya'll better hope the department doesn't find out about you two."

"We're careful."

"I'm just saying, you can never be too careful."

"Dude, I love her."

Dash shrugged. "I hope she's worth it."

He had put away ten wings while I had seven. "I can hear your moms now: 'She's a damn cradle robber.'" I laughed to his spot on interpretation. "Trust. I know how your moms can be. She wouldn't let you do anything when you were a kid. Remember that time you fell off the monkey bars? Your moms acted like you broke every bone in your body. All these cops and ambulances were at the playground. It was crazy."

"I know. I was so embarrassed that day. Everybody started calling me 'Mama's Boy' after that. You included."

"I'm surprised she let you hang with me knowing how she feels about gay people."

Kayla came and refilled our glasses with beer.

"But I almost forgot to tell you this. This goes to show how much of a hypocrite Mama is."

"Why? What's up?"

"This was before she found out about Shariece and me. She invited me to have dinner at the house, right. When I get there, she's got this dude who looks like he could be my big brother sitting in the living room sipping on wine and shit."

"Whaaaat?"

"She gave me all this shit about me and Shariece, but here she is playing shack-up with a man half *her* damn age."

"So what is so different from your relationship with the cou— I mean, Shariece, and…"

"Exactly. I guess the difference is that Shariece was her best friend."

"I can see how that would come as a shock, but she has no right to preach to you about who you see and how old somebody is when she's out here doing the same thing."

"I was mad pissed when I saw this dude in my mama's house sitting there like they're husband and wife."

"Well, you and your moms will work things out. She'll come around. I know Shariece is her bestie and everything, but she has to accept your choice like you have to accept hers."

"True, but I don't think that's going to happen anytime soon. She's never been this mad. I mean damn, I'm still her son."

"Just give her some space. The two of ya'll need to process what's going on."

"I guess."

I managed to steal the last wing while Dash stuffed his face with sweet potato fries.

"So when do we get to meet her?" he asked as he sucked chicken from the bone.

"I don't know if she's ready to meet my friends yet."

"She's not ready or you're not?"

"Do you really think that she can handle our group of friends? Nosey Chadae who you know likes to give everybody the third degree."

"Forget Chadae. You can handle her. Shariece sounds like a cool chick. I'm sure she can hold her own with our clique."

"Here I am running my mouth about my life and haven't asked you what's been up with you. You still holding it down at Black Dog Cafe, hosting Thursday night poetry readings?"

"You know it. We're trying to get a Tallahassee slam team together, if you're game."

"I don't know, man. I've been so busy with classes and looking for a job, that I've barely had time to put pen to paper."

"True, but we miss you. Cameron and Jalinda are always asking me about you, and you know Chadae is. Asad is back from New York."

"I haven't seen him in a year."

"Asad is back doing readings, and guess who works there now as a waitress?"

"Who?"

"Arielle."

"Arielle Mobley?"

"Yep. She's thick, but she still looks the same. She asks about you all the time."

"I don't know. I'll talk to Shariece about it."

"Jay, you know you my boy. All I want is for you to be happy, and if this sister is truly the one—"

"She is. I know she is."

"Then that's all that matters."

"Thanks, bro, that means a lot. Glad to know that someone's on my side."

"And don't stress about your moms. She'll come around."

"I hope so. Well, enough about me, what's up with you? You still dating that same guy you met on Grindr?"

"I didn't tell you? I kicked Montez's cheating, lying ass to the curve when I caught him with his dick in the ass of a pizza delivery boy."

I laughed through tearing meat off a hot wing to Dash's ballsy confession. "I thought Montez was the one?"

"Oh, me too, but apparently he had other ideas. I should have known when he started talking about having an *open* relationship, something was up. You know I've never believed in no shit like that, Jay. These dudes out here want to have their cake and cat that shit too. Even the ones that are supposed to be in relationships are out here creeping on Grindr, *and* who knows where else. I kicked him and his pizza boy bottom out of my crib, booty-naked and all."

"Aww, shit, son, no you didn't, not ass-naked."

"Ass… naked, both of them, and I tossed Montez's clothes out the window. You know I don't cosign on some shit like that. If this double-bubble chocolate ass ain't enough for you, then we don't need to be together."

"Well, I never liked Montez anyway."

"Maybe I need to take a page out of your book, get me a sugar daddy. A big ol' Santa Claus-looking motherfucker with some coin. I'm sick of these baby gays wanting to stick their dicks in every ass they see. Get me a prime-timer, a man with sophistication, class, and a fuck load of Obamacare."

I laughed so hard to Dash's rant, I damn near choked. "I've never pegged you as the gold-digging type."

"I'm just over being taken for a ride by these…garbage pail kids. So, yeah, I'm back on the meet market. I hope Montez and his pizza boy are real happy together because I'm in a whole new area code of over it."

I was knocked on my ass when Dash had told me he was into guys. As early as middle school, he had girls on his jock 24/7, so when he came out to me in the tenth grade, I honestly didn't believe him. He played sports, had cheerleaders giving him head behind the gym, so *he* said. It wasn't like I actually saw him fuck females. When he had told me that he fucked Craig Lawson at his house after school one day in his parents' basement, I almost shit a car. "Hold up. You and Craig Lawson? The same Rickards Raiders quarterback who got a full ride at Florida State who went on to play ball for the Baltimore Ravens?"

"The very one, and baby, he can take dick like a porn star."

I grimaced to the thought of this big, muscle-bound dude taking it up the ass by my best friend. "Please. I don't need that image running around in my innocent fifteen-year-old mind."

I wasn't sure I could deal with having a gay guy as a friend and started to end the friendship, but Dash and I had been boys since grade school. He made me popular. If it wasn't for him, I would have spent the next four years as some comic book geek, hermit crabbing it in the school library with the rest of the Dungeons & Dragons geeks. I got enough of that in grade school. I was not about to be one of those statistic kids left to be bullied and punked.

"So what's up? You and Shariece coming out to the poetry reading on Thursday or what?"

"I can't give you a definite answer on that yet."

"In other words that means no."

"That means I will call you and let you know. I gotta talk to Shariece about it. I told you we're trying to keep a low profile until the semester is over."

"Well, I'll tell the gang that you *might* make a special appearance. They'll be glad to see you. Maybe we can get your high-yellow-ass up on the stage and spit something."

Kayla came over and cleared away our basket of bones. "You guys want another beer?"

"You want another one?" Dash asked.

"No, I'm good. I'm not trying to get a DUI in the middle of the day."

"We'll get the check, Kayla," he said.

"Is it on one check or separate checks?"

"One check,," Emjay said.

"Man, I got this," I told him.

"No, let me take care of it. You can get the next one when we go out again."

Kayla returned with the check., "Have a good afternoon, guys."

Dash pulled out his wallet and handed Kayla forty bucks. "Keep the change, baby girl."

Dash asked, "So have you been writing?"

"I'm working on some new stuff I'm still polishing."

"I'm sure Shariece would like to see you in your element."

Dash was bad about taking no or even maybe for an answer. If you didn't give him a solid yes, he would nag and nag until he got one. We walked out into the parking lot to our cars where we continued talking. "I will say this right here. If Shariece can't make Black Dog, then I'll come out. I might even read something new."

"Can I get that in blood?" Dash joked. "I'll let the group know."

"Remember what we talked about. Not a word."

"I won't say nothing, Jay. Scout's honor." Dash held up two fingers.

"Scout's honor is three fingers, dumb ass."

"You know what I mean. I'm excited already. Show me some love." Dash held his arms out for another one of his rib-cracking bear hugs. I was still feeling the love he gave when he walked into Wing Stop. I braced myself. "Come on, take it like a man, bro, come on." His hug was like a thousand and one kung fu grips around me.

"See you Thursday."

I was on my way to the library to catch up on some homework for my Western Civilization class when my cell rang. I recognized the first three digits. It was from Capital City Movie Theatre, where I had applied three weeks ago.

TWENTY-ONE
SHARIECE

I was sitting in my office milling over essays from my 11:15 freshman composition class, but I could barely concentrate on the task at hand for staring at my cell phone. I picked it up and strolled along a list of text messages that were from Emjay mostly, a few from Leandra, but nothing recent. It's fucked up how we went from laughing over Chinese mall food to her throwing her hands around my throat wanting to kill me. I've been thinking, and the truth is, I don't blame her for how she reacted when she found out about Emjay and me. I can't sit here and say that I wouldn't have gone ape shit-crazy too had I caught my best friend in bed with my own son, but damn, it's not like I planned to fall in love with Emjay. Leandra and I have always been able to talk about anything and everything. This silent treatment shit is a fate worse than death. I supposed I could call her, but why couldn't she pick the phone up and call me? Ma Bell runs both ways. Leandra had always been like a sister to me, and I love her like a sister, but damn, I wasn't going to beg her to forgive me. I didn't plan on crawling on my knees to her doorstep anytime soon. Most people would think that I robbed the cradle; well, I'm here to tell you I don't give two shits about *most* people. Emjay is a grown man who is perfectly capable of making his own decisions. My head is still swimming over the fact that he told me that he loves me, that he's *in love* with me.

I was about to get my head back in the game of grading when my phone rang. Emjay's name appeared in big, white letters on the flat screen of my phone.

"Wow, you must be able to read minds," I said when I answered.

"Why do you say that?"

"I was just thinking about you."

"Oh really? Am I wearing clothes in these thoughts of yours?" I asked.

"You so silly. So what's up?"

"What are you doing right now?"

I could sense a hint of excitement in Emjay's tone.

"I was catching up on some grading. Why? Is everything okay?"

"It's better than okay. I just got off the phone with the manager at Capital City Movie Theatre. He wants me to come in for an interview tomorrow."

"Baby, that's fantastic, congratulations."

"I'm hoping I get it. I really need this job. I don't care what kind of job it is."

"That's the right attitude to have. Baby, I'm so proud of you."

"And you know how much I love movies."

"When you get the job, we'll go out and celebrate, have a special dinner."

"Don't you mean *if* I get it?"

"No, just like I said, *when* you get it. You just need to stay positive."

"Baby, you should do a tea reading or something," Emjay said, laughing.

"Let's call it a hunch."

"So you want to have dinner at my place tonight?" Emjay asked.

"I don't know. We need to be careful, especially now."

"I know, but I'm feeling too good over this job interview right now. Besides, I miss you."

"I miss you too, but we need to keep a low profile. We can't risk getting caught."

"There's something else I want to talk to you about," Emjay said.

"What is it?"

"Have dinner with me tonight and I'll tell you."

"Emjay, you know I'm not the biggest fan of surprises."

"Have dinner with me and I'll tell you what's up."

I knew Emjay was not going to take no for an answer. "What time?"

"Around seven."

"Okay. I have a class at six, but I should be done before seven."

"Cool. I'll pick up some take-out from El Jalisco."

"Sounds good. I need to finish grading and answering some emails before my next class. I'll see you tonight for dinner then."

"I love you."

Damn, he said it again. "I love you too."

After I hung up the phone, the first question that came to mind was, *woman, what the hell did you just say?*

I was going through the rest of my emails, most of them junk, until I came across one that had *Teacher's Pet* as the title in the subject line. I opened the email to find that there was an attachment enclosed. I was hesitant about opening it, thinking that it might be some kind of computer virus someone had sent, but my curiosity had gotten the best of me. When I opened the attachment, my heart sank to my ass. It was a video of Emjay and I having sex in my office. "What the hell is this?" Someone had seen us. We had not only been seen, but fucking videotaped. I looked at the email, but didn't recognize it. "Damn it!" Who would think to do this? More importantly, is this shit on the Internet? As I tried to figure out who may have sent the video, I got a knock on my office door. Startled, I slammed the monitor of my laptop shut. It was Rochelle.

"Hey, am I disturbing you?"

What the hell do you want now? "No, not at all. What's up?"

Rochelle walked into my office wearing a black-and-white tweed Chanel suit. The only person who loves tweed more is Leandra. The two of them would have fun raiding each other's closets.

"Where are you going all dressed up?"

Rochelle looked down at herself, studying the suit that probably cost more than my rent. "Oh, this old thing? It was just something I had sitting in the back of my closet."

Yeah, right, I thought.

"Would you believe that the price tag was still on this suit? Girl, I almost forgot that it was in my closet."

Rochelle's words were going into one ear and coming out of the other. I was sitting there watching her chatty lips move as I thought about the video, wondering who could have taken it.

"Some girlfriends and I are going to the Mockingbird for drinks later; would you like to join us?"

"I really wish I could, Rochelle, but I still have a ton of work I need to catch up on. And I have my six o'clock class, and then I have dinner plans with a *friend* after, but how about a rain check?"

"I'm going to hold you to that."

"Oh, I know."

"So how have you been doing? I haven't seen you much around the office," Rochelle said.

"I've just been busy with classes and grading, trying to finish up some things before the Thanksgiving break."

"Girl, if you keep this up, you might have my job," Rochelle said, grinning.

I glanced out of the window thinking of the pervert who had caught Emjay and I fucking on camera. It could have been anyone.

"After the faculty/student horror stories you've shared with me, I highly doubt it." I figured if Rochelle knew about the video, it would have been the first thing she would've blurted out, and I would be packing all of my things in a filing box by now. I wondered if the same email was sent to Emjay or worse: Leandra. I had a million questions, obviously, and the last thing I wanted to do was sit with Rochelle talking my ear off about trivial shit. Here she was the director of the English Department, and she had nothing better to do but waste my valuable office time. I was sure she had a stack of paper work on her desk that required her attention, but she was running her mouth to me.

"Earth to Shariece."

"Huh, what? Girl, I'm sorry. My mind is on a million things right now. What were you saying?"

"I was asking if you have any plans for Thanksgiving."

"I haven't made any plans yet, really. I may go to Orlando to see my sister and her kids."

"That sounds nice. How old is your sister?"

"She's thirty-six, four years younger than me."

"So it's just her and her kids down there?"

What is this, Twenty Questions? "She's married. Her husband works in real estate."

"Are ya'll close?"

"As close as sisters could ever be," I said, wishing Rochelle would get out of my office.

"That's nice. I wish my brother and I were like that. He and I go together like oil and water."

"The best way to deal with family sometimes is to love them from a distance."

"I can definitely relate."

"Well, Rochelle, I hate to rush you off, but I have to get back to work."

"Oh, girl, no problem. I'll let you go. We'll talk later in the week."

"And we'll get together for a drink one night when things are not so crazy," I said.

I thought Rochelle would never leave. How in the hell could I have been so stupid and careless? I knew this with Emjay and me was a mistake, yet my selfish ass allowed it to go on. Of all the men to fall for, I had to fall for a student, my best friend's son. I had to stop this before it got out of hand. That's if it hadn't already.

TWENTY-TWO
DEANDRE

would have given my right nut to see the look on Shariece's face when she opened up that attachment of the video of her and Emjay fucking. I wasn't going to let her know who I was yet. I was having too much fun toying with her ass. I was going to keep her on her toes, teach the bitch a lesson she would not soon forget. I actually had not planned on videotaping them. I was getting some footage for an experimental film I was doing for my intro to filmmaking class. The assignment was to get comfortable with the camera by capturing and observing. Most of what I caught was birds and squirrels scurrying across my feet, and Mrs. Laws, a music appreciation teacher cheating on her diet by pigging out on Popeyes. I had stumbled on Shariece and Emjay by mistake. At first, I just had watched them without filming them, but I had the camera in my hand, so I couldn't resist. I can't stand Shariece, how she flirts her ass around class, coming off like she doesn't have a clue as to what she's doing, prancing around in class wearing those tight skirts and blouses. She ain't fooling nobody, least of all me. I see how Emjay looks at her. I should have known something was up by the way he sits there with that shit-eating grin on his mug like there's something he's in on that no one else knows about. Yeah, he's *in* on some shit all right. In on that pussy. Who knows how long it's been going on. Weeks, shit, months probably. And I will bet any amount of money, he's getting an A in her class. An A for having good dick. Well, their shit is out now. I could do whatever I want with the information I had, but like I said, I was going to let the dick-teasing bitch stew. Trust and believe, she's going to get exactly what she deserves.

TWENTY-THREE
LEANDRA

"Who in the hell parked that ugly-ass PT Cruiser in my space?" See, someone is already getting on my last nerve and the day has barely started. You would have to be deemed legally damn blind not to see the sign that clearly reads *Reserved for Leandra Fox.* Whoever parked in a reserved space is either stupid or just…stupid. I pulled into an empty space, two cars down, grabbed a bag of supplies I'd brought from home and my pumpkin spice Frappuccino and got out. I could hear roars of laughter from outside the shop before I got near the entrance. "That sounds like Devonte's big mouth."

"Ya'll hush all that fuss in here," I said jokingly.

"Hey, ma," Sabrina said, as she approached me to give me a hug. She had on enough perfume to choke a barn of horses. "You didn't say anything about coming in today."

"Girl, I have a business to run. If I knew that sitting around on my behind all day, would make me money, I would never leave my house. Besides, you know I don't announce when I'm coming in. I won't catch ya'll off your job that way."

"Hey, Leandra, I'm glad you're back," Nishelle said, giving me a hug.

"Me too, baby girl. I came in to see how ya'll are holding it down."

"You know how we do. Ms. Lady. Working just like you're in the shop," Devonte said. "How you feeling?"

"Hell of a lot better than a few weeks ago. It feels damn good, though, to get back on my feet."

"Girl, when I heard what happened, I had a fit. I was telling Sabrina. I said we need to go see how she's doing." If it was one thing Devonte was good at, it was licking people's asses to get what he wanted. He would pucker up in front of my ass every chance he got if he wanted a certain day off, so he could go out of town for some gay Pride thing.

"That's funny that you should mention that, Devonte, 'cuz I don't remember you coming to the hospital to visit me."

Sabrina and Nishelle cleared their throats and looked off knowing that Devonte had been read.

"Every time I came through, you were dead to the world."

"Uh-huh," I mumbled, as I rolled my eyes. "So how is business?" I asked.

Everyone fussed over me like I was the queen of England.

"Business is good," Sabrina said. I barely recognized Ms. Girl with her new Chaka Khan do. "I'm feeling your new look, Sabrina. Who did it?"

"I did," Nishelle chimed in.

"I like the color and the volume. It's pretty."

"You think so?" Sabrina asked.

"I like how it frames your face." Sabrina had a pretty, light-brown skin complexion with a figure I would kill for. She was one of those women who could eat whatever she wanted, and didn't gain a damn kilogram. And Sabrina could put food down like a grown-ass man. She had her plate piled with chicken, potato salad, baked beans and ribs at the housewarming cookout I'd had last year. We all just watched her as she practically licked the plate clean. Me, Nishelle and Devonte placed bets that she was taking something to keep the weight off. "I think she's on that cocaine diet," Devonte said while Nishelle and I bet that it was laxatives. Sabrina was always going on modeling auditions. Whenever the *America's Next Top Model* crew blew into Tally, she would ask for two days off all, so she could stand in a line that ran from Tallahassee to Quincy and didn't even make the semifinals. And when the crew doesn't make it to Tallahassee, Sabrina will drive to wherever they are. Orlando, Atlanta, Tennessee, wherever, she's there standing in line. Tyra Banks oughta be sick of looking at her face by now. At this point, I would put her on the show just so she would stop coming to auditions.

"So how are you feeling? Did you get the flowers and cards I brought by?" Nishelle asked.

"The lilacs? Yes I did, baby, and thank you. I still have them sitting in a vase on my coffee table at the house. They're beautiful."

Nishelle smiled like she had been waiting to get my approval. "I remember you saying something about lilacs being your favorite flower."

Sabrina and Devonte looked at one another and rolled their eyes as Nishelle kissed up to me. Nishelle was the complete opposite of Sabrina. She was thick and damn proud of her big bust and booty. The girl ate like a bird, though when she was up around people. She would plop a spoon of potato salad and one chicken drumstick on her plate, acting like she was watching her weight or whatever, but we all knew when she got home or hid herself off in the office with Popeyes, she would scarf chicken and mashed potatoes down like she was in a chicken-eating contest. I knew with a big ass like hers, she was doing a lot more than picking at her food. Nishelle had a kind of pecan-brown hue to her skin with voluptuous lips and dark-brown eyes. Well, today anyway. Most days they were either hazel or hunter-green, depending on her mood or the outfit she wore. Everybody thought she was a softie, but I knew if you pushed her enough, she would be quick to put a bitch together if you came at her sideways.

"You need me to get you anything?" Sabrina asked.

"I think there's still a McGriddles left in the microwave," Devonte said. Sabrina slapped him on the arm. "What, I'm just saying."

"I'm good. I came in to catch up on some of these bills anyway."

"Are you sure you should be here and not home resting?" Sabrina asked.

"Trust me. If I sit home another day, I'm going to rub a hole in my sofa. I need to get back to some sense of normalcy."

"I feel you," Sabrina said

"So is it true?" Devonte asked.

"Is what true?"

He looked at Sabrina and Nishelle like he wanted to get approval to ask me something he knew would be inappropriate to ask.

"People are saying that you drove your car off the road."

Sabrina nudged Devonte in the ribs with her elbow.

"I can't believe you just asked her that. Ignore him, Leandra. He must have left his brain at the house of his latest one-night stand last night."

Devonte glanced around, looking at Sabrina's back. "What are you looking at?"

"I'm just trying to see if you still have that mattress strapped to your back," Devonte said with his lips tight and arms folded in front of his shoulders.

I snickered under my breath to Devonte's smart-ass comeback. When it came down to reading somebody, he was the head librarian in charge.

"Do you always believe what you hear?" Nishelle looked at Devonte and asked.

Before they could start in with all of their fussing and fighting, I cut them off. "Where did you hear that?"

"Leandra, you know how people around here run their mouth."

"I know how you run yours," I said to Devonte.

"All I'm saying is, you know how people around here talk. Tallahassee is big but not that big."

"Well, the answer to that question is no," I lied. "What's important is that I'm better now and I want to thank ya'll for taking care of the shop and making sure the place continued to run like a well-oiled machine while I was laid up."

"That's what we're here for, boss lady," Sabrina said.

"So my next question is this: who's the dumb ass that parked in my space?"

"We were trying to figure that out," Sabrina said. "That car was there when I opened up this morning. I was going to ask whatshername at The Golden Dragon if she knew whose car it was, but I got busy and never got around to finding out."

"Oh, I bet I'll find out who it is. No, you know what, fuck that. I'm going to have that ugly shit towed from in front of my shop. I don't have time to be walking from store to store asking about somebody's car."

"I'm already ahead of you, Leandra," Nishelle said. "I called the tow truck twenty minutes ago. Here they come turning into the parking lot now."

I went outside to greet the fat, greasy, slouchy driver. "You the one who called a tow, ma'am."

"Yes. I don't know who this is, but as you can see, they parked in my parking space, and I want this ugly, little bug gone."

"Your wish is my command," he said, laughing sarcastically. Tow truckers live for this kind of shit. I made out the embroidered name stitched onto the top left corner of his white shirt smudged with grease and dirt.

Gus, it read. Yeah, he looked like a Gus. I would have guessed Roy or Bubba. Just as he had hooked the cruiser onto the back, this guy came sprinting out of Gold's Gym. He looked to be Emjay's age, slightly older maybe, wearing a sweat-stained, red muscle T-shirt and black basketball shorts.

"I'm here, I'm here, wait, stop!" he came out yelling.

"Is this your car?" Gus asked.

"Yeah. I was just about to come out and move it."

"Sorry, man, but once I have it on the truck, it's a hundred bucks to release your ride."

"Oh my God, are you serious? Come on, bruh, give me a break."

"Talk to her. She's the one who called a tow."

"You didn't see the sign when you parked here?" I asked.

"I was in such a hurry; I didn't pay any attention to the sign."

"You had to have seen this sign."

"Come on, ma'am. I really didn't. I was going to run in, pay my membership and run out. Can you give me a break? I don't have a hundred dollars."

My heart was softening like a creamsicle left out in the heat too long. He reminded me a little of Emjay with those puppy dog-brown eyes of his, eyes Emjay would bat when he wanted to borrow the car or needed twenty dollars to go see some superhero movie. I thought of making an example of him and letting Greasy Gus tow his car.

"You're lucky that I'm in a good mood today."

"Oh man, thank you; I appreciate it."

"Let his car go," I told Gus.

"Are you sure?"

"Yeah, let it down."

"Thank you."

When I turned around, Sabrina, Nishelle and Devonte practically had their noses pressed to the store front window like kids outside of a candy store. Gus released the car. This blind fool jumped in his punk mobile and hauled ass, burning rubber across the lot. "Thanks, you old bitch!" he yelled, as he stuck his hand out of the window and flipped me off.

I looked at Gus and said, "See what happens when you try to be nice?"

I returned to my nosey hairstylists. "Damn, he was fine," were the first words that Devonte blurted out.

"D, is there anyone on God's green earth you're not attracted to?"

"Oh, whatchu trying to say, that I'm a slut?"

"If the shoe fits," Sabrina said, pointing at Devonte's seven-inch black platforms.

"Ya'll, hush. All this back-and-forth bickering is giving me a migraine. Who has appointments this afternoon?"

"I have Mrs. Mason coming in at three o'clock," Devonte said.

"And Mama Carter is coming in at two-fifteen for her usual wash and set," Sabrina said.

"And the rest are walk-ins," Nishelle said. "Good. What is it I always say, when the salon makes money…"

"We all make money," they said simultaneously.

"Preach it. I will be in my office catching up on some much needed paperwork, if anyone needs me."

I often thought how blessed I was that Mrs. Boyd left me some money for me and Emjay to live off. After I had buried Rick, I found myself a single mother, something I never imagined in a million years would happen. The last thing I wanted was to end up another statistic on welfare and food stamps, living in the projects like my auntie. I wanted more than that for Emjay.

It wasn't long before word got around that I had my own salon. Word of mouth is the best kind of advertisement. The women whose hair I was doing, soon followed me to the shop, and with them came new clients. Business was booming, so I had to hire two stylists. The money was coming in, so I could afford them. Shariece had helped me for a while by answering phones and setting up appointments until I hired Nishelle. I don't know what I would have done if it wasn't for Shariece. Nishelle came to me knocked up by this white boy, Reed, who attended Florida High who left her after finding out she was pregnant with his kid. He had a full scholarship to play basketball for Wake Forest, and couldn't have his rep tarnished with the label of baby daddy, not to mention have his parents find out that he had knocked up some black girl from the South Side. Delora told me all about how Nishelle's mama had disowned her and kicked her out of the house after she'd told her she was going to keep the baby, so Delora took her in until she had the baby. A beautiful baby girl she named Autumn because she was born October 13th on a cool Tuesday morning. The baby is a spitting image of her daddy too. He has soft, curly black hair, a good grade of hair like her mama, and cheeks so chubby, you want to just eat her up. Nishelle didn't have a lick of experience, but hell, what's so hard about answering phones and making appointments? I couldn't pay her much, but something was better than nothing. I told Nishelle she should drag Reed's white ass on Maury's show.

"Girl, he's a big-shot college basketball player. He's going all the way to the NBA. You better hit that fool up for child support."

She just dismissed me every time I mentioned hitting him up for money. "Suit yourself," I told her. "It's your life, baby girl."

A pancake-size stack of bills and papers were strewn along my desk. As soon as I saw all the work that needed to be sorted, I started to turn around, walk out of my office, get back in my Beamer and drive back home. Being back in the shop felt like I had never left. I never knew how much I missed the smell of burnt hair and chemicals and shop gossip about whom was caught sleeping with whose man. I was about to break into the first bill with the tortoise-shell letter opener Emjay had bought me from Kirkland's for my birthday, when Nishelle knocked on the door. "Hey, baby girl, what's up?" I said.

"Now that we're alone, we can talk."

"Okay," I said, looking at her inquisitively. Nishelle walked over and threw her arms around me. "I want to say that I'm happy that you're back. I got so scared when I heard about your accident. I prayed for you every day."

"Well, thank you, baby, for keeping me in your prayers. I'm sorry I scared you."

"You're like a mother to me. I don't know what I would have done had I lost you." I could sense Nishelle holding back tears, but they came anyway. "You've been so good to me."

I padded and rubbed Nishelle on her back. "Everything's all right, Shelle." I wiped away her tears with my finger that streaked her plump face. To be honest, Nishelle was like a daughter to me, and therefore, I was quite protective of her like she was my own.

"By the grace of God, I'm still here. He wasn't ready for me to come home yet."

"He gave you a second chance."

"Yes he did, praise Jesus."

A day doesn't go by that I don't think about that night. All I could think about was seeing Emjay and my best friend in bed, thinking how she had betrayed me. They'd called me and left messages on my phone, but honestly, I couldn't deal with those two right then. I needed my space from all that. Some might say that cutting him off was a little cold-hearted, but Emjay has to grow up sometime. Nishelle gawked at me like there was something dancing on her tongue that she was dying to tell me. "Is something else bothering you, sweetheart?"

"It's nothing."

"I know that look, Shelle. What is it, girl? Spit it out."

"I don't want you to think that I'm a snitch."

"Nishelle, you know I don't believe in none of that street law stuff when we're in my shop. Now tell me what is going on."

As soon as she was about to loosen her lips, Sabrina walked into the office. *We'll talk later*, she mouthed. Whatever she wanted to tell me, it had something to do with Sabrina.

TWENTY-FOUR
EMJAY

I was happier than flies on shit when the manager from the movie theater called me for an interview. I had seen countless movies there when I was a kid and even told Mama in the car on the way home that I would work there someday when I grew up. I was so psyched about the interview that I realized that I didn't have any job interview clothes. Most of what I had was back at Mama's house, but was old stuff that wasn't all that appropriate for an interview. I thought of these pair of khakis I had, but remembered I had ruined them with paint when I'd helped Mama remodel the bathroom in one of the upstairs bedrooms. The only shirts I owned were Polos and T-shirts. I still had close to two hundred dollars left to my name, money that I was holding on for food and rent. "Looks like I'll be eating ramen noodles for breakfast, lunch and dinner this week." If worse came to worse, I would head over to the blood bank and give plasma for a hundred bucks.

I stopped off to Marshalls to see what I could scrounge up. I hated Marshalls 'cuz the clothes looked picked over, dropped on the floor from hangers and torn out of the plastic. Burlington is where I buy most of my gear, but it was located all the way across town in Tallahassee Mall, and there was no time to take the drive over. I had to think outside the box of Coogi, Rocawear and that Sean John shit I was used to wearing. When I got to Marshalls, I rushed over to the men's section to see what I could find, but I wasn't getting my hopes up on finding anything that didn't make me look like Urkle from *Family Matters*. There were tables of dress shirts, racks and racks of dress pants and scores of ties, most of it ugly shit old white men wear. The one shirt that I thought was cool was like thirty-nine dollars, more than what I was willing to pay for a dress shirt I would probably only wear once. I scavenged through the clearance rack to find something cool, but nothing. I eventually settled on a white dress shirt and a pair of black pants. It wasn't like I was going to interview with Tyler Perry or somebody. "The manager is not going to care what I wear anyway." I was used to Mama buying me clothes for special occasions. She's the one with taste. With the shirt, the pants and a Bill Blass tie I picked out, I was content enough with what I had picked out. I was standing in line waiting to check out with my gear when I felt a tap on my shoulder. I turned around to find Chadae standing behind me. She smiled big when she saw how surprised I was to see her.

"Hey, baby girl, what's up?" I said, wrapping my arms around her. No lie, she still looked good. Big titties and a juicy booty holding snug in a pair of tight low riders.

"Hey, Jay, how long has it been?"

"A couple of years. I think the last time I saw you, you were at the senior party at Hilaman Golf Course."

"Oh my God. I almost forgot about that. That was a crazy night." Cha would know considering she spent most of it throwing up in the bushes after drinking too much punch Bobby Howard had spiked with vodka.

"So where have you been hiding?" she asked.

"Nothing, just going to school at Tallahassee Community College, trying to get this education. I've been crazy busy with classes. You know how that can be."

"That's great. I see you're buying some new clothes."

"It's for this thing I got, a job interview."

"Oh cool, where are you going to be working?"

"Capital City, the movie theater over off Thomasville Road. The manager called me today to set up an interview."

"That's great. I remember what a big movie fanatic you are. Remember how I used to quiz you on movies? You knew who made it, who starred in it, who wrote the script, the score, who did the sound, all that. I remember you telling me how you used to write personal letters to every manager at every movie theater in town once every other week and then follow up with a phone call."

"Yeah, that was kind of weird, I know."

"No, not at all," she said, caressing my arm. I forgot how affectionate Chadae could be, how just one touch from her was enough to send shivers through me. It took me back to how she and I used to make out in her daddy's truck.

"You were determined. I always thought you should be a movie director or something."

"So enough about me. What have you been up to? You look great."

Chadae glanced down shyly at the floor. "Thank you. I'm studying nursing over at Keiser University. Matter of fact, I'll be graduating in December."

"Wow, ma, a nurse? That's pretty awesome. I'm proud of you. Have you decided where you want to work, like in a hospital or private practice?"

"I was thinking about being a traveling nurse."

"You're talking about some serious money."

"True, but I don't do it for the money. You know I've always liked helping people."

"I remember in the mall when you gave CPR to that little girl's mama."

"That was pretty scary."

"Yeah, but that little girl probably would have been without her mama, if it wasn't for you. I had never seen someone act that brave."

"I had to put that CPR class to use for something. Everything changed after that. I guess that was when I knew I wanted to be a nurse."

I was next in line to be waited on. Chadae had a cart full of clothes from dresses, to blouses, to bras and perfume.

"Well, you can have it. I don't think I could be around blood and puke all day."

"Like everything, you get used to it."

I laid my shirt, pants and tie on the counter to be rung up by Kai'ja, this gum-smacking redbone with fat braids that draped down her back.

"Better you than me, then. I have never liked hospitals, or being around sick people."

"Yeah, remember that time you stepped on a nail? You didn't even want me to pull it out. 'Don't touch it; don't touch it, you kept yelling.'" Chadae laughed as we wandered down the road of memory lane.

"What? That shit hurt. I had to get like three shots that day."

"Oh, guess who I had lunch with the other day? Dash. I ran into him at Publix the other day. He told me about what happened with him and Montez."

"Your total is $22.36," Kai'ja told me, as she folded my clothes and put them in a plastic bag. I took out my wallet and gave her twenty-three dollars.

I waited at the end of the counter for Chadae to make her purchases. She had enough clothes to fill three bags. We continued our conversation outside as I walked her to her car.

"I laughed my ass off when he told me he caught Montez fucking the Chinese food delivery boy."

"He told me it was the pizza guy."

"Oh, it probably was. Either one, I don't know. Jay, you and I both know that Dash is no angel. We have seen him play grab ass with his share of men."

"That's what I thought about when he told me about Montez cheating on him. Dash had a different brother in his bed for every day of the week. Matt on Monday, Tyreese on Tuesday."

"Will on Wednesday," Chadae said. "And on the weekend, he would bring two guys home."

"Damn, I forgot that ya'll used to be roommates."

"And honey, the stuff I used to see is enough to fill a tell-all."

"I bet."

Chadae was one to talk, though. She had more than a few skeletons in that walk-in closet of hers. She was far from pure.

"Dash told me that ya'll still get up over at Black Dog to do poetry readings."

"Well, you know that's you, Dash and Brett's thing. I just tag along to support my guys."

This was true. Chadae was our one-woman pep squad when we performed on stage.

"Dash invited me to come out this upcoming Thursday to read."

"You should," she said, with a wide-eyed expression. "I love your poems. You should come out. I think people would love your stuff. Did Dash tell you that he's trying to start a Tallahassee poetry slam team? Emjay, you would be great for it."

"It's been a hot minute since I've read. I might be a little rusty."

"Man, whatever. You get up there on that stage and spit mad fire, people giving you standing ovations."

"Well, thank you, boo, for the vote of confidence. I told Dash that I would try to make it out, but not to hold me to it. School has been kicking my butt, and if I get this job…"

"Well, I'll definitely be there to cheer you on if you do decide to come."

"It would be cool to have everybody together. Dash was on my ass at lunch about how he never sees me around anymore."

"On your ass?" Chadae laughed.

"That's probably the wrong choice of words."

"Jay, I know you miss being up there, having people cheering for you."

"I admit I miss the adrenaline rush."

"Good, then it's settled. You're coming to the reading on Thursday, and you know how I am when it comes to taking no for an answer."

"You don't take no for an answer."

"Exactly. I recall that it was one of the many things you loved about me when we were together." Damn, she threw me for a loop on that one. "Do you ever think about those times?"

"Sometimes," I lied. The truth was, our relationship had sailed, hit an iceberg and sunk, and I was the only survivor.

"So are you seeing anyone?"

"Actually, I am."

An expression of disappointment set in when I told her I had someone.

"That's um…that's good. What's her name?"

"Shariece."

"Shariece. That's a pretty name."

"How about you?" I asked.

"Actually, yeah. He's a Pharmacy major at Florida A&M

University." I knew Chadae was lying. She don't give eye contact when she's bullshitting. "His name's Stefan." It sounded like a name she made up, but she was trying to save face, so I didn't have a choice but to believe her. "Well, I really need to get going. I have a class in an hour," Chadae said.

"Okay, well, it was good to see you, Cha."

"Yeah, it was fun, catching up. I look forward to seeing you at Black Dog on Thursday, and good luck on your interview. I hope you get the job."

"You and me both."

"Here, let me give you my number," Chadae said, as she reached down in her purse to pull out a pen. "This is my new number. I had to get a new phone after I dropped mine in the kitchen sink." She scribbled her digits on my palm. "Call me sometime. We'll have lunch or something."

"Cha, I have a girlfriend."

"Okay. And? We're still friends. What's wrong with just hanging out and chilling?"

"Nothing, I guess."

"Get over yourself, Jay. It's only lunch." I knew what was up, what game she was playing, and she doesn't do so well with strictly platonic relationships. "Give me a call next week."

"That's cool."

Cha surprised me when she gave me a kiss on the cheek.

"It's good to see you again."

"You too."

"Don't be a stranger, Jay. Come out on Thursday. We miss you."

Cha and I went our separate ways. Due to the erection in my jeans, I was surprised my ass could walk. I sat in five o'clock bumper-to-bumper traffic pressing my boner down with my left hand as I steered the car to Dragon Room, this Chinese restaurant, with my right.

When I got to my place, I noticed Shariece's ride parked in front of the apartment complex. Both of my hands were filled with bags stuffed with pork dumplings, General Tso's chicken, spring rolls, Moo Goo Gai Pan and newly purchased dress clothes. My stomach was growling crazy from the hearty aroma of brown rice coming from the white-and-red plastic bags. I set the food and clothes down as I fished my keys out of my front pocket. When I opened the door, there was Shariece sitting in the living room in the dark. I set the bags on the dining room table "Hey, baby, what's going on? Why is it so dark in here?" She didn't answer me, but simply sat there staring blankly at the TV. "Hey, are you okay?" I switched on one of the lamps on the nightstand. The illumination rattled Shariece out of whatever daze she was in.

"I was in my office today grading papers and answering emails, and I got this."

Shariece flipped up the monitor on her Acer laptop and typed in her email address. She strolled down to an email that read *Hot for Teacher*. When she opened it and it started to show a scene of us fucking, my heart dropped down into my ball sac. "What the fuck!" My first instinct was to take her laptop and hurl it across the room.

"Someone taped us, Jay. Someone fucking taped us!" Shariece got up and began to pace the floor.

"Who?"

"I don't know who, but you can look and tell that somebody was standing outside of my office window that day."

"But we were careful."

"If my boss sees this, I could lose my job. My God, this could be anywhere. YouTube, Facebook."

"Hold on. Is there an email address?"

"I sent a message, but it just bounced back to me. It doesn't look familiar."

"So you have no idea who could have videotaped us?"

"What, you think I'm lying?"

"Baby, no, I'm just—"

"I knew this was a mistake."

"What are you saying?"

"This, Jay, us!" Shariece kept pacing like she was trying to burn a hole in the carpet. "How in the hell could I have been so careless?"

"Don't blame yourself."

"Who else is there to blame? It was completely unprofessional of me to even allow this to happen." She pointed at the video on her computer as if it were the dirtiest sin imaginable.

"If you want to blame someone, blame me. I'm the one who put your career in jeopardy."

"I was a selfish bitch. What was I thinking? You're a student, for God's sake."

I don't know what I was pissed off about the most: the video or Shariece chalking me up as a low point in her life.

"Baby, we'll get through this. I'll find out who sent the video."

"And how are you going to do that?"

"I'll come up with something."

"Great, that's reassuring."

"What is this shit about this motherfucker wanting to meet you somewhere?"

"They say if I meet them, then they'll hand over all the copies of the video."

"Sha, you're not really serious about meeting whoever this is? Who knows who it could be? Could be a damn serial killer or somebody."

"I don't have much of a choice. They said if I don't meet them, they'll send a copy to my boss."

"Okay, well, I'm going with you."

"No you're not. I need to do this alone."

"No, fuck that. We don't know who this pervert is. He could be some student stalking you, for all you know. This could be dangerous, Shariece. We can take separate cars. That way he will know that you came alone."

"I don't know. My career is on the line here."

"I will make sure I stay out of the way, but close enough to where I can protect you. It says here that he wants you to meet him at the Wendy's on Pensacola and Appleyard."

"I still don't think this is such a good idea."

I took Shariece's hand in mine in an attempt to comfort her. I had never seen her so scared and tense. "We will get through this. Together. Everything is going to be all right."

"I so want to believe that."

"You should and you can."

Whoever this was, all I wanted to do was get my hands around their throat and break their neck. It was killing me to see Shariece so scared and vulnerable.

TWENTY-FIVE
TAJ

When I got home, I noticed a note stuck to the refrigerator from Leandra. *Hey, baby. I'm going to be at the salon late tonight to catch up on some paperwork. I have a stack of bills on my desk that I need to sift through. I'm not sure how late I'll be. If you're hungry, there's some leftover baked chicken, cabbage, yellow rice and squash in the refrigerator. Just put it in the microwave and heat it up. I will be home as soon as I can.*

Kisses,

L.

I was looking forward to chilling with some good food in front of the TV and watching the Chavez vs. Rios fight when my cell rang. "That's probably Leandra now."

I tugged my phone out of the front pocket of my jeans. "Fuck does he want?" It was Jimi. I started not to answer. I was hungry, tired and not in the mood for Jimi's sleazy ass.

"Hello," I said, coming off annoyed as fuck.

"Hey, what are you doing right now?"

"About to eat and veg my ass out in front of the TV. Why?"

"I know it's your day off."

"I'm glad you're aware of that shit, Jimi."

"I have a job for you."

"Not interested."

"Hold up. You're not even going to hear me out first?"

"I'm tired, Jimi. I need to sleep. You know what sleep is, don't you?"

"I don't have time to sleep when there's green to be made out here," Jimi said.

"I want to sleep, Jimi."

"There's a big payday in it for you."

"My dick is sore from jacking off."

"Well, ten g's can buy you a lot of ice packs for that sore cock of yours."

As much as I wanted to tell him to go fuck himself, the cash amount piqued my interest. "I'm listening."

"Now before you say anything, hear me out first. It's a gay film."

"Come on, man. I told you that I don't do gay shit."

"I know, but that fucker, Jax pulled another no-show, and I need someone for a couple of butt-fuck scenes I'm doing."

"Jimi, I don't know."

"Taj, do me this favor just this once. Come on, man, I need you."

"Ten grand, right?"

"Cash money, brother."

I was exhausted from doing two films last week, and all I wanted to do was relax at the house, but money was money. "What time do you need me to be there?"

"Can you make it here in twenty minutes?"

"Let me shower first and then I'll head over to the studio."

"Thanks, brother. I'll see you in twenty."

I ended the call. "Kiss my black ass," I said, as I slapped my phone on the coffee table.

I took a quick shower, put on a pair of basketball shorts and a tank, grabbed an apple from the fruit bowl that sat in the center of the kitchen table and rushed out the door.

My first day on the set of Jimi's movie was like being on a real Hollywood set except there was more ass and dick than what you would not normally see on a real movie set. I thought I would never get used to seeing dudes walking around with their oiled-up dicks wagging all over the place. It was like a strip club, but with gay men. I was grossed out when I saw Vance wrap his lips around Jax's dick in a scene Jimi was shooting. They both had big dicks. Not as big as mine, but big for a couple of white boys. Vance was like the king of gay porn and was a huge draw for Jimi and his production company selling thirty-thousand units in one week. And when it came down to sucking dick, Vance was a dick-sucking king. The superstar of dick suckers. He's a huge draw because he's versatile. He tops, bottoms, sucks, get sucks, you name it, Vance does it. If you ask him, he'll tell you that he likes to get fucked.

The first time I saw him get fucked by Jax, it was enough to make my own dick hard. I never thought I could get hard watching two dudes fuck. I spent a good month doing go-for shit for the actors and crew, including lug heavy camera equipment around. The set always smelled like poppers and ass. I had no idea what a popper was until I started working for Jimi.

Jimi was working on this new movie called *Hot Fuck Firemen* with Jax and Vance when Jax didn't show up on set. I wasn't surprised considering he was always high on and off set. I caught him in the bathroom once snorting coke off the counter. I didn't say shit to Jimi about it, figuring he wouldn't care being that he supplied the drugs most of the time anyway. Somebody is always high on set.

"That coked-out cocksucker is costing me money. I'm done. This is it. He's out."

Instead of Jimi wrapping for that night so he could find a replacement, he asked me if I would be interested in stepping in at the last minute.

"Jimi, I told you when I started that I wouldn't do none of that gay shit."

"Look, all you gotta do is let Vance blow you and you get two grand."

"I'm not gay. You hired me as a production assistant, to get food, go for coffee, help set up cameras."

"Have you ever let a guy blow you before?"

"It doesn't matter. I'm not doing it."

"Answer the damn question."

"When I was in high school."

"Dude, it's the same damn thing except with this right here, you'll get paid."

"Man, I don't know."

"You don't have to do nothing. You just stand there, and let Vance do the work."

"I don't know if I can stay hard with all these people around."

"There's a trick to that. Picture yourself at home. No crew, no cameras, nothing. Only you and your lady. Picture her on her knees, sucking your dick instead of Vance. You simply tune the rest of us out."

"So all I have to do is let him blow me? I don't have to fuck him?"

"That's it, and you're done."

"'Cause, man, I'm not gay."

"I know, and that's cool. I just need you to loan your dick out to me for these last two shots."

"But only this one time, right?"

"Only this one time, and I'll pay you a thousand bucks."

"Fine. Let's do this shit then."

They took me to wardrobe where they put me in this fireman uniform. I looked goofy as hell wearing this big red fireman hat. They then rubbed my chest down with this oil that smelled like cocoa butter. I got a kick out of the V.I.P. pampering I was getting. Jimi was running around like a chicken with its head cut off due to all the cocaine he was high on. Vance was dressed in the same get-up except the ass part of the uniform was cut out.

"Jimi, you said no fucking."

"Don't worry about that. It's only for show."

I was so nervous, I couldn't get hard.

"You need a fluffer."

"A what?"

"A fluffer. Someone who can get your dick hard," Jimi yelled, "Cherri, I need you."

The cute receptionist who was sitting at the desk the day of my interview walked over. Jimi whispered into her ear. She gave me a sinister smile when he told her what was up like touching my dick was the moment she had been waiting for.

"Come on, big boy, let's go," she said.

"Go with Cherri. She'll take care of you."

We disappeared to the unisex bathroom that was located directly behind the lounge while Jimi prepped for the scene. When Cherri unbuttoned her blouse, she wasn't wearing a bra. My dick was twitching erect as I felt her up. My dick got harder as I traipsed her nipples with my fingers.

"Are you hard yet?"

"Why don't you feel it and find out."

Cherri ran her hand along the shaft that tinted the fireman fatigues. She moaned, licking her lips like she would love nothing more than to wrap those juicy, bubble burst-red lips around my dick. Hell, I would have preferred to see her fine ass dressed in firemen garb than Vance. Bet it would be a hell of a lot sexier than some greased-up dude prancing around with his dick bopping around in people's faces. Cherri unzipped the firemen bottoms, palmed my dick and eased it over the waistband. She ran her manicured thumb over the piss slit that had oozed a bit of pre-cum. She brought it to her mouth for a taste test.

"Mmm…you taste sweet," she said as she gave my dick a couple of strokes. "I've wanted to suck your dick the moment you walked in the office."

"Damn, that's what's up."

I wanted nothing more than to throw her down on the floor and fuck until her toes curled. That's the kind of shit Jimi should be filming instead of making this gay shit. Zoom in on me popping that pussy, medium shots of me eating Cherri out, that's what people want to see. As she caressed my dick, there was a knock at the door. *Shit.*

"Is everything okay in there? Let's go; time is money."

"He's ready," Cherri yelled.

She looked down at my dick that laid across her palm and said, "Glad I could be of service."

Cherri exited the bathroom before me. I walked out with a raging hard-on, ball sac swirling with cum.

"Are you good?" Jimi asked.

"I hope you're ready for one hell of a money shot."

"That's what I like to hear," Jimi said with an exuberate tone. "All right, so all you have to do is lean up against this fire truck like so, while you're playing with your dick. When Vance walks over, you say, 'Hey, you wanna hold my hose?'"

It was a typical cornball line that you would hear someone say in cheesy pornos like the one Jimi was making. It's why most people prefer to watch that shit with the sound down. But my opinion didn't matter. It was Jimi's picture, and he was putting in the money to make it happen.

"You're looking a bit dry. That's not going to look good on camera. Let's get Taj oiled up over here."

Tianna, one of the makeup girls, rushed over with a tube of cocoa butter oil and started slathering it on my face, chest and thighs. She had pretty, perky titties and more ass than Nicki Minaj. Too bad she was a dyke, but the way she was rubbing up on my body was enough to keep my dick bricked up. I glanced at everyone scurrying around the set and thought, *I need to have my damn head examined for doing this shit.*

Vance came out glistening with oil from his face to his chest. He looked over at me getting the oil put on and smiled like he couldn't wait to get his lips around my dick. Not that I'm queer or nothin', but Vance wasn't half bad-looking. I could see him turning heads up in the club, making more than a few mouths drop. Leandra would take one look at him and be like, "What a waste." I'm sure there was no shortage of men in his life, especially if you do porn, and the whole damn country has seen your dick and how good you fuck.

"Okay, Taj, let's get you back in position," Jimi said.

Kyle, this fresh-out-of-film school Martin Scorsese wannabe, toyed with the camera while I stood where Jimi wanted. There were a total of eleven crew members, not including me and Vance, so I was still a little nervous about doing this shit in front of a set of strangers.

"You ready to do this?" Jimi asked.

"Yeah, let's go before I lose my hard-on."

"Remember what I told you. Just pretend you're at home with your lady." Images of Leandra sucking my dick began to dance in my head, which helped to keep me hard for the shot Jimi needed. Vance walked over to me and dropped down on his hands and knees as makeup and hair people primped and preened us with brushes and combs like we were exotic peacocks.

"All right, that's enough makeup. I don't want them to look like drag queens," Jimi said.

"Taj and Vance, are you guys ready?"

Vance gave him a thumbs-up while I simply nodded my head anxious to get the shit over with. Kyle had the camera aimed at my crotch when Jimi yelled action.

I delivered the cheesy cornball line Jimi wanted. "I thought you would never ask," Vance said. As soon as he unzipped the pants of my fireman uniform, my dick popped free, slamming against Vance's chiseled chin. He gave a wide-eyed look at my dick. *Oh, I know damn well you've never sucked on anything this big.* He started with the head of my dick first, licking it and then he threw his lips around it, sucking, taking an inch here and big thick inch there until my dick filled his throat. Kyle was right up in that shit, capturing every second of Vance's blow job work on camera. He lay down on his back at one point, positioning the camera just so under Vance's chin, so he could get some shots of his lips sliding back and forth on my meat.

"That's great, Kyle, get in tight," Jimi said. Kyle massaged his own dick as he took mine throat-deep. I knew that if I looked over at the crew, I would risk losing wood. Vance's mouth was just as wet and warm as any pussy. White boy was giving some serious head game. It was true. Gay dudes give good-ass head. Kyle rose up and pointed the camera in my face, capturing every expression as Vance slurped on my dick.

"Taj, give me a little nip action."

I tugged gently at both my nipples that were sensitive to the touch, which sent pings of electricity straight down to my dick. Vance tilted my dick up like a lever on a slot machine, and commenced with licking along the shaft, sucking my hung nuts like a dick-sucking maniac. He sure as hell knew how to put on a show for the camera. I felt myself getting close to climax as Vance slid his tongue along the shaft of my piece to the bulbous mushroom head. I could damn near feel my semen boiling in my ball sac.

"Vance, play with your asshole," Jimi demanded. Kyle captured a shot of him running a few fingers inside his asshole, which from what I had seen on films he had done, was the size of a ping-pong ball. You could tell he had been stretched by who knows how many dicks—two, three or ten fingers was nothing. "Yeah, that's good," Jimi said.

I didn't think I could ever bring myself to fuck a man up the ass. Maybe I would if the price was right and a fuck load of fluffing was done, and I ain't doing shit without a rubber.

"Taj, are you ready to cum?"

I nodded my head, yes.

"Okay, Kyle, make sure you get in tight for the money shot."

"Got it, boss," Kyle said.

Vance sped up his dick sucking as he gripped my stick tighter, taking me to the far reaches of his throat.

"Let's see the cum shot," Jimi said.

Vance unclenched his cherry-red lips from around the shaft of my dick and started jacking me off. Within seconds, I exploded, cum skirted from my dick, landing across Vance's face. Kyle veered in, catching scenes of semen ooze over Vance's fingers and knuckles like white lava. My heart was pounding like a jackhammer in my chest as thick loads of spunk trickled out of the spout of my dick.

"And cut," Jimi yelled.

One of the production assistants swooped in with a hand towel where Vance cleaned his hands of semen. "You had a big load built up," he said.

"Yeah, I guess I did."

"Good job," said Vance. Someone threw a robe around him and ushered him away. It was nothing to Vance. Who knows how many dicks he had gotten off; how many times his face had been jizzed on?

"That was awesome," Jimi said.

"Did you get what you wanted?" I asked.

"That and then some. It's going to look fan-fucking-tastic on camera. I can't wait until we get it to the editing room."

Jimi paid me ten grand in cash like he said, and all I had to do was get a blow job. Easiest two grand I ever made without breaking my back. I quickly wanted more and knew what I had to do to get it. Later that week, Jimi asked me if I wanted to graduate from being a feeble production assistant to being in his films.

"I can start you off at ten thousand a picture."

I was starting to see dollar signs, images of checks with zeros behind them. "With my business savvy and your...well endowment, I can turn you into one of the top gross-selling adult stars in the business. You can make more money than you know what to do with. What do you say?"

"I don't know, Jimi, I gotta think about it."

"Sure, you think about it, let me know by tomorrow, but I definitely want you on board, here. You know me well enough by now that I don't take no for an answer, so go home, think about it, pray about it, meditate on that shit, whatever you have to do, but hit me up tomorrow to let me know what's up."

I could barely keep my eyes open on the way back to Leandra's. I didn't want to get into bed smelling like cum and cocoa butter, so I hopped in the shower. I scrubbed every part of my body, relishing at the thought of Vance's spit and cocoa butter oil swirling down into the shower drain.

I gave Jimi a call.

"Taj, hey, what's up?"

"I've thought about your offer."

"Okay."

"I will do it, but only on two conditions. I don't fuck without a rubber and I sure as hell don't get fucked."

"It's a deal. I was hoping you would say yes. Come to my office tomorrow and we'll discuss the contract. I have big plans for us, Taj; I'm going to take you all the way to the top."

"Good, well, we can discuss it tomorrow in your office."

"What is it, I always say? When I make money…"

"We all make money."

What the hell did I just agree to? I thought to myself.

I had no idea the trap I would soon find my ass caught in.

TWENTY-SIX
MYRICK

How can anybody sit here and say that Whataburger's hamburgers are only good when you're drunk? I'm going to have to call bull-shit on that one. They, by far, have the best burgers in Tallahassee, especially this one in midtown. All I thought about when I was locked up was a triple-meat, triple-cheese bacon burger with all the trimmings with thick sliced jalapenos. Next to Shariece, there are three things I can't live without in this fucked up-ass world: sex, ranch dressing and jalapenos. I'm probably the only man on the planet who eats them with ice cream. I'll eat a whole jar of them in one sitting. Fuck heartburn. When I die, I want to be buried with a jar of jalapenos tucked under my arm in the casket. Figure I'm going somewhere hot anyway, so I might as well snack on something on the trip there.

I usually watch what I eat, but tonight, I didn't give two opossum shits about high cholesterol or the extra onions I had them slap on my burger. I would end up with stank breath, yeah, but shit, that's what orange-flavored Altoids are for. I was finishing up the rest of my shoestring French fries when some college-aged kids from the bars across the street began filing in. I looked at the clock that hung on the wall above the grill in the kitchen. It read, *1:50*. The bars and nearby clubs were letting out. I almost forgot how crazy the midtown Whataburger gets between 1:30 and 2 a.m.

"All right, everybody, get your game faces on," Dalton, the assistant manager, yelled from the kitchen. I could tell they were college brats judging from the sun-bleached look they had about them like they had been sun-bathing on the beach all day. *It must be nice to have nothing better to do*, I thought. They were white kids mostly from Florida State, I gathered. There were a few black kids peppered in, all of them loud and disruptive, trampling in like wild zoo animals. Many had bloodshot eyes from all the drunken pomp and circumstance. Completely drunk off their spoiled asses. Some could barely stand, they were so sloshed. I took a sip from my cup of root beer when I zeroed in on this one black girl. She had a plump, apple-bottom ass wearing a red low-cut top that barely held in her double-D titties. She wore glasses making her look bookish and smart. *Pre-med, I bet. No, pre-law*, I thought. Because of her bifocals, she wasn't so to where she would be stiffening the dicks of frat boys, but once you looked past the bottle caps, she had pretty, light-brown eyes, a kind of honey-brown almost. My dick hardened as I gawked at her tight ass in the pair of low-cut jeans. I was so mesmerized by her ass that I didn't realize she had caught me staring. I looked off out of the window into the parking lot as I sipped on soda. I could see from the window's reflection at her staring back at me, smiling flirtatiously. She ordered her food and sat in the booth seat in front of the counter as she waited for her food. I thought about going over and introducing myself to the young honey, but I didn't want to freak the girl out.

The fast-food lobby soon brimmed with drunk, fucked-up students until a line of them began to form outside into the parking lot. It didn't take long for them to whip up her food. I stared down into wax paper and empty spicy ketchup condiments as she sauntered past me, leaving a faint scent of her perfume to comingle with the rancid smell of meat and grease. I watched from the window at her walk down Thomasville Road that glowed from the neon peach illumination the street lights gave off. I gave her a good ten minutes, trashed the paper from all that was left from the burger and fries I ate and went after her. "Time for dessert," I said, as I tossed my empty cup of root beer into a nearby trashcan. That big booty of hers was switching and bouncing as she strutted down the street. I can see how some would mistake her for a hooker, but shit, hoes ain't that fine on their best days. I eased my SUV alongside shorty, and let my window down. "How you doin'?" I startled her coming out of nowhere like I did. "My bad, I didn't mean to scare you."

"You almost gave me a heart attack," she said, holding her hand up to her chest.

"I saw you walking and I was wondering if you would like a ride?"

She looked into the SUV to see if she knew me. I could tell she had her reservations. "Um…no, I'm good. I don't live that far from here." She smiled.

"Come on now, are you sure? It's late, it's dark, and it's way too hot out here tonight for anyone to be walking, especially in those heels."

I could see contemplation in her cute and chubby face. She was the cautious type who said her prayers every night, who curled up with her teddy bear even though she was a grown woman—yeah, one of these daddy's girl kind of bitches.

"Think how many foot blisters I could save you from right now." When I cut her a smile, I could sense the reservations she had about me crumbling.

"Well, it is pretty late," she said.

"Good girl, hop in," I said as I pushed open the passenger side door. With her bag of greasy fast-food in tow, she got in.

"I'm Myrick, by the way."

"Deanne."

"Nice to meet you, Deanne. That's a pretty name."

"Thank you."

"So where to?" I asked, as I pulled off.

"I live on Meridian Road, not far from the mall."

"Cool. I think I'm familiar with the area."

She smelled so sweet, looked as pure as the driven fucking snow. My dick was throbbing like a percussion drum in my jeans. I was going to have fun with this one.

"So all those people back there, was there some kind of concert in town or something?"

"Oh no." She smiled, displaying a set of pretty white teeth. "The Seminoles beat the Miami Hurricanes 31 to 14, so in true college town form, everybody went and got drunk tonight."

"Oh, okay, that explains it. I don't really follow college football, but I'm glad the Seminoles won."

"Yeah, I think people would have partied even if they hadn't have won. Any excuse around here to drink."

"That's true. Partying is like a prerequisite at FSU."

"They don't call it the number one party school for nothing."

"So I gather you're a student there?"

"I am. A junior."

"Nice. What's your major?"

"Pre-law."

I knew it. I guessed right.

"That's great. You want to be a lawyer." *That's all the world needs.*

"Oh yeah. I come from a long line of lawyers. My mom's a lawyer, my dad's a court judge, and I have a brother in law school."

"Keepin' it in the family, I see."

"In the blood, I guess. Make a left here at the light."

"I can see you as a lawyer."

"You think so?"

"Absolutely. You seem like a smart girl, intelligent, well-spoken, good head on your shoulders."

"Well, tell that to my parents. I get a B in a class and they make a federal case out of it."

"I'm sure they're proud of you."

"They put so much pressure on me. I have to succeed at all costs, no matter what. Do you know my dad calls the school to have a copy of my grades sent to Tennessee?"

"Is that where you're from?"

"Yeah. I wanted to go to school in New York, but uh-uh, they wouldn't hear of that. I had to go to FSU; I had to study pre-law. It's like they have to control every single piece of my life. I would love to see the look on my dad's face if he ever caught me drinking in a sports bar. He would have shit a car probably." Deanne laughed at the thought.

"That's messed up that your parents are so hard on you."

"They claim that they love me and want the best for me. That's bullshit. They want to control me. Funny thing is, I don't even want to be a lawyer. I really want to be a nurse. My cousin is studying nursing at FAMU and she loves it."

"So study nursing," I said, staring at her breasts when I knew she didn't notice.

"My folks would have a conniption. Daddy would probably stop paying for me to go to school."

"If that's your dream, baby girl, you should pursue it. Life is too short not to do what you love."

"You know what, I'm sorry for laying all this on you. You don't even know me and here I am going on about my dominating parents."

"No, it's fine, really. I feel ya. I mean, if you ask me, you are way too pretty not to do what you want in life."

Deanne smiled again, showing those pretty teeth. "Thank you."

"So how um…does your boyfriend feel about all of this?"

"Oh God, I don't have a boyfriend."

"Now that's a damn shame. Someone as beautiful as you don't have a man waiting up for her?"

"No, no boyfriend. Too busy for all that."

"That's too bad. Any man would be lucky to have a fine girl like you on his arm."

"Turn here. It's the brick house on the left."

I pushed my SUV in front of her place. I didn't see any cars parked in the driveway, so I figured she lived alone; being that she had fancy, rich-ass lawyer parents, she probably had the place to herself.

"Well, thank you for the ride. What did you say your name was again?"

"Myrick."

"Thank you, Myrick."

I watched Deanne walk up to her front door, my high beams shining bright on that apple-bottom booty of hers. She waved goodnight as she made her way inside. I was familiar with the area; my old dentist office was located two blocks down from her crib. I parked into the lot of some old abandoned office spaces. It was dark and quiet. I looked around to make sure no was around: cops, late-night joggers, old bitches walking their dogs. I opened the door in back where my gym bag sat idle on the floor. I took out a pair of black gloves and worked each hand, each finger one after the other into the leather. I pushed my lock pick down in the back-right pocket of my jeans and a small bottle of chloroform in the back left. I snuck past driveways and backyards until I got to Deanne's apartment. I watched her undress from her bedroom window. I heard water running from the bathroom. My dick budged as she peeled jeans down around her booty and thighs like they were a second skin. Her titties bounced free when she released them from the cocoon of black nylon and lace. Deanne had a kind of hourglass shape. "Damn, you a fine-ass bitch." I pulled at my crotch in an attempt to make room for the growing muscle that was getting harder in my jeans by the second. I watched her until she disappeared out of sight into the bathroom in her bedroom. I made my way around to the rear of the house. I forked my pick lock out of my pocket and jimmied the lock open to the back door. In less than a minute, I was in. Her apartment felt warm and lived in. The greasy bag of food sat next to her purse and house keys. I could hear her humming in the bathroom as I cautiously made my way down the hall that led to her bedroom. I took her black panties, held them up to my face and took a deep whiff of the juices that soiled the nylon fabric.

A body of steam spirited out when I nudged the bathroom door open. I could barely make her out through the shower curtain that blurred her naked hourglass body. The minute I threw back the curtain, Deanne turned to me and screamed, but that stopped as soon as I punched her in the face. She stumbled back against the wall of the shower, sliding down unconsciously into the floor of the bathtub. She was knocked out cold. Blood trickled from her nose. I dropped to my knees, pushed her thighs apart and gently shoved my middle finger inside Deanne's pussy that was grown with a nest of black hair. "You like that, bitch, you like that?" I kept saying as I thrust my middle digit inside her cunt. "Filthy bitch." I took her by the arms and dragged her out of the shower back to her bedroom where I folded her over the bed. I took the box cutter and slashed her across the throat with it. Pools of blood soaked the bed sheets and mattress. I set the blade on one of the nightstands nearby before I undid my jeans, took my dick out that was rock-hard by now and started jacking off as I watched Deanne bleed. It turned me on even more to see the life drain out of her. I took a rubber from my front pocket and tore it open with my teeth. I grew frustrated in the attempt to roll it on with the gloves on my hands, so I pulled them off. I turned her over on her belly to expose her ass. I pushed my jeans and drawers down around my ankles and lay on top of her. I aimed my dick between the plump, mahogany-brown cheeks of her ass and pushed.

"Damn, girl, you tight."

The smell of blood thickened in the air as I fucked her, pressing her face into the pillows. I imagined it was Shariece I was fucking. "You like that, you dirty bitch; you like that dick up your ass, whore? This is what you get for leaving me." I thrust until I came inside the rubber, up Deanne's ass. I eased off of her, careful about getting any of her blood on me. I quickly got dressed as I watched the bed turn red with Deanne's blood. I went to the bathroom, pulled off the rubber with my spunk inside it, rolled it up in some tissue and rammed it down into my jean pocket, making sure to burn it later. A sweat-drenched face stared back at me when I looked at myself in Deanne's bathroom mirror. I put my gloves back on and made damn sure I didn't leave any fingerprints behind. When I got home, I scrubbed my skin damn-near raw with bleach. I took the tissue paper with the rubber inside it and burned it in the sink. You can never be too careful.

TWENTY-SEVEN
MYRICK

July, Summer, 1991

I t was one of the hottest days in Tallahassee that month. The air conditioner was broken, so Mama set two fans out in the living room to keep cool, but it didn't do a damn bit of good but blow hot air. I sat around trying to keep cool by running my head over the shower when I wasn't lying up with a cold washcloth of ice on my forehead trying to keep the heat at bay. One-hundred and ten degrees, I think it was. So hot I could have walked around booty-naked and still would have been hot. I remember old people and pets were dying from heat stroke and shit that summer. There was an incident where a lady left her baby in the car in the parking lot of Big Lots. The dumb bitch said she had the window cracked and was only going to be gone for a minute. It was all over the news, some poor hick from Crawfordville. Needless to say, they put her baby killing-ass under the jail. Should have done worse than that. They find out in prison that she killed her baby, they're going to shank that bitch.

"What kind of world is this we live in?" Mama had said.

"The kind where mothers leave their babies in hot cars." As soon as I said that, Mama backhanded me across the face. "Why'd you hit me?"

"For being slick at the mouth."

"I wasn't being slick."

"Don'tchu talk back to me, boy."

I attempted to rub the sting away with my hand. Mama was always hitting me for something. She didn't give a shit if it was my fault or not. Of course she never laid a finger on Rashawn. He used to piss in the bed, spill cereal on the table, step out of his nasty drawers and leave them on the bathroom floor; it didn't matter. It was all right by her, but if I did it, I got beat within an inch of my life. She would beat me with whatever she could get her hands on: a shoe, an extension cord, a fly swatter, a wire hanger. Even when she knew Rashawn was in the wrong, she would beat me for his fuck-ups. I knew a lot of that shit had something to do with the fact that Rashawn and I came from different daddies. Rashawn was always praised for his good looks, light skin and soft hair while I was shunned and picked on for being brown-skinned with nappy hair. Mama told me once that every time she looked at me, I reminded her of my daddy and how he ran out on her with a white woman after he found out Mama was pregnant with me. Rashawn's daddy got shot and killed over some money two years after he was born, but she never talked about that, but always went on about how good he was in bed. What mother tells her fifteen-year-old son that kind of shit?

I never knew my daddy, but I've seen pictures of him Mama used to keep in a shoebox that sat in the closet on the shelf above the water heater. I'm a splitting image of him. She constantly reminded me how no-good he was.

"Wasn't worth the skin his black ass was printed on," she would say. I understood why he'd left her for somebody else. Who the fuck would want to stay with a witch like her? She was a shitty mother and would have made an even shittier wife. I would have left her too. I think about him sometimes, wondering what kind of daddy he would have been had he stuck around to know me. I bet he would have done all kinds of things with me like taken me fishing, or to the park to play football. I betcha he would have been the best daddy ever and I would have been the son he would have been proud of. He wouldn't call me a black monkey, or an ugly ape either like Mama does. My daddy wouldn't have beat me with hangers or burned me with cigarettes 'cause he couldn't stand the sight of me. I thought about running away to find him. Some guys who knew him said he was living in Jacksonville somewhere. I used to think sometimes what I would say to the man if we came face to face. I would throw my arms around him probably. That, or kick his ass for leaving me with such a bitch of a mother. I thought about him all the time when I was locked up, about how different things might have been had he raised me over her. But what the fuck is the point of thinking about what might have been? That shit is just wasted emotion. I am where he is and he can stay wherever the hell he's at.

Rashawn and I aren't close now because of the wedge she drove in between us. He didn't write or come see me one single time the whole time I was locked up. Girls flocked around Rashawn like he pushed golden eggs out of his ass, while I was the darker-skinned, less attractive brother who often got called an African Booty Scratcher in school. Women wanted to fuck Rashawn because they thought he was mixed, while I repelled women, often called a black cockroach. I would hear her talk of how Rashawn was meant to do big things, change the world and shit, while I wouldn't amount to nothing because I hung out on the street with gangs.

He was the flower in Mama's hair while I was the shit stain in her underwear. I despised Rashawn about as much as Mama despised me. I was always thinking about killing Mama, thinking of creative ways to do it. Put a pillow over her head and smother her in her sleep, douse her with kerosene and set her on fire, maybe put a snake in her bed, but I was scared shitless.

The night that I finally got up the nerve to end her, Rashawn was spending the night over at Seandre's house. What kind of pussy-ass, faggot-ass name is Seandre anyway?

Me and Mama were the only ones home. I was dog-tired from running with my crew, so I showered, ate the cheeseburger Hamburger Helper, which was Rashawn's favorite, and conked out on the sofa. I had forgotten that I had left my dirty plate and glass on the kitchen table. I woke up just as Mama had come down on my head with a glass ashtray.

"Ow, what I do?"

"Get your ass in there and get your plate off that table."

My head instantly began to throb with pain. I felt blood run down the side of my face.

"Look at me, Ma; I'm bleeding."

"I don't give a damn. You better not get none of that blood on my floor. Here I am spent all day cleaning up and cooking, and you bring your black ass in here and start making a mess."

I had never been as mad as the day she hit me with that ashtray. She had graduated from hitting me with belts and fly swatters to hitting me in the head with ashtrays. I went in the kitchen and put my plate and glass in the sink. "Boy, where you goin'?"

"What?"

"Wash that goddamn plate and glass, and you had better not have ate up all the Hamburger Helper from Rashawn. That's his favorite and I want him to have some when he comes home."

I didn't say shit, but just washed the plate.

I was fed up; sick of her hitting me and treating me like I was dog shit under her shoe. It wasn't my fault Daddy ran off with someone else. If she didn't want me, then she should have kept her legs closed. Don't put it on me because you had a miserable, sorry-ass life.

"Boy, don't you eyeball me. I'll give you something to roll your damn eyes at. I have better shit to do than to clean up after your narrow ass. You just like your damn daddy. I should have sent you to Jacksonville to go live with him and his white bitch."

I dried the plate and glass and put them away. I took a paper towel and wiped the blood from my face.

"And cut off all these goddamn lights. That's why the light bill so high now. I'm going upstairs to take a bath. Don't bother me about nothing." I was too pissed to hear what she was saying. "You understand me, Myrick?"

"Yes."

"You know how I hate to be disturbed when I'm taking my bubble bath."

That was the last straw. I knew if she could hit her own child in the head with an ashtray, then she was capable of worse, capable of killing the child she never wanted. I was feeling slightly dizzy from the blow to my head. I stood at the bottom of the stairs, fists clenched tight, staring angrily up at the bedroom, pissed still. I stared angrily at the top of the stairs as beads of blood dripped onto my shirt. The stairs creaked to my weight as I made my way up. It was then that I had to kill her before she killed me.

I watched her as she pinned her hair up in the mirror of the medicine cabinet. She turned, faced the bathtub, undid her powder-pink satin robe, letting it drop to the bathroom floor to her feet. Mama was the first woman I had ever seen naked, but I had seen enough of her pudgy ass and sand bag-saggy titties, to last me a lifetime. Candles filled the bathroom: candles around the sink, and the perimeter of the tub. Mama eased herself into the water as she hummed. Without hesitation, I rushed in, grabbed Rashawn's radio, held it over my head and said, "Burn in hell, bitch," and dropped the radio into the tub of water. I watched her body shake and convulse uncontrollably, her eyes rolled back into her head and then silence. I thought after I did it, I would feel remorse, but instead, I was relieved like a ten-ton anvil had been lifted off my shoulders. Any love I had for her had shriveled up and died long ago. There was water everywhere. I stared at her for an hour before I walked downstairs and dialed 9-1-1.

"Help, please help me! Something's happened to my mama!"

The driveway was littered with cop cars, fire trucks and ambulances, blue, red and white lights illuminating the hot, July sky. Rashawn cried like a baby, screaming like a little bitch for his mama. The pathetic little fuck was upset he wouldn't be able to suckle from our mama's teat anymore. I cried, but not for her, but because I had watched the movie, *Steel Magnolias*, two nights before. I needed to show that I was upset. When the coroners rolled her out of the house, I put on an Oscar-winning performance that would have made Denzel Washington's ass look like a chump. I cried to keep from laughing, rejoiced that the evil bitch was out of my life. Mama was my first kill, and as I grew older, so did my hunger to kill more.

TWENTY-EIGHT
SHARIECE

I tossed and turned all night, sleeping for only an hour at a time. It wasn't fair to Emjay to allow my insomnia to keep him from losing sleep, so I got up, went to the kitchen and made myself some warm milk. I'm probably the only woman on the planet who drinks the stuff, but it's the only thing that helps me sleep. I sat down in front of the TV with chocolate chip cookies and watched a late-night, early-morning episode of *The Closer*. I hoped it would be enough to get my mind off that damn video, but all I did was worry even more, thinking about my job, my reputation. My life was suddenly spiraling out of control. The thought of Rochelle seeing that video, or worse, having my students see it, made me sick to my stomach. Emjay says I should remain positive, but how in the hell can he stay calm in a time like this? I stand to lose a hell of a lot more than him. I could get fired while he would be praised for fucking his English teacher. My hands perspired to the thought of meeting this sick fuck who had videotaped us. I went back to bed after drinking half a glass of the milk I had made. I had another four hours of sleep left before Emjay got up for class. I decided that I was going to call in, and have Kalisa, the receptionist, cancel my morning classes. There was no way in hell I would have been able to teach thinking about that video. I'd tell her I came down with something.

I glanced at the clock on the nightstand table that read *10:36*. The aroma of bacon stirred me awake. I managed to drag myself downstairs where Emjay stood over the stove in a pair of boxers, flipping pancakes. He looked so cute in his blue flannel boxers.

"Good morning," he said.

What was so good about the morning when my life was falling apart?

"Is there any coffee?"

"Yeah, I just made some."

Emjay could make the hell out of some coffee for someone who was all of twenty-two years old. I grabbed a coffee mug out of the cabinet above the counter and poured. "How did you sleep?"

Was he serious? "Is that a trick question? You didn't feel me tossing and turning all night?"

"Yeah, but I didn't want to bother you, knowing that you had to be up for class today."

Emjay forked bacon out of a frying pan and laid the crispy strips onto a paper towel onto a plate.

"I slept for maybe an hour at a time. My head was too busy swimming for me to get any real sleep."

"I heard you go downstairs last night," Emjay said as he placed a plate of pancakes in front of me. "Are you okay? Is there anything I can do?" he asked, caressing my elbow.

"Baby, I wish. I think once I get through this semester, the holidays will give me a chance to rest up from everything."

I desperately wanted to tell Emjay what was going on, but knew that I would only make things worse for both of us if I got him involved in my mess. Whoever this person was, I had to deal with him on my own.

"So I had lunch with an old friend of mine at lunch yesterday."

"Really? Who?"

"My boy, Dash. I hadn't seen him in months and we talked, caught up on stuff. I told him that I met somebody."

"Did you tell him about us?" I asked, wiping sleep out of my eyes. I could tell by the sly, giddy look on Emjay's face that he had talked about me.

"Jesus, Jay, I thought we both agreed that we would talk first before telling other people about our relationship."

"Baby, Dash has been a good friend of mine since high school. Trust me when I tell you he can keep a secret. He's not going to tell anyone."

The smell of eggs was making me sick to my stomach. "It's tough enough to deal with Leandra knowing, and we still don't know if she will say anything to Rochelle."

"If Mama was going to do anything to us, she would have done it already. She knows that she would risk losing me if she tried something against you."

I had quit smoking a year ago, but I was in dire need of a cigarette.

"So Dash wants me to come to Black Dog Cafe and read some of my poems. He said he would love to meet you, and I would love to show you off."

"What do I look like, a prize pony you won at the fair?" I regretted my words as soon as I let the last word tumble from my lips. "I'm sorry. I didn't mean that."

"Are you sure everything is okay?"

"I told you I just have a lot of stuff going on at work."

"We don't have to go if you don't want."

"No, you haven't seen your friends in a while; you should go, have fun." Emjay sighed, disappointed that he couldn't show me off as he put it.

"Rain check then, I guess."

"Absolutely. You know I'll make it up to you."

"I can think of a few ways you can make it up to me right now." Emjay pulled me close to kiss me, pushing his tongue past my lips. "Jay, as much as I want to, I have a class in an hour."

"An hour is all I need." He slid two fingers along my nipples that were enough to get me wet. He fingered the spaghetti straps of my nightgown off my shoulders, powder-pink satin grazed against my breasts. The moment he slid a finger past the lips of my pussy, I was officially caught in Emjay's rapture. My gown collapsed off my shoulders, past my thighs to my feet. Emjay cleared the kitchen table of half-eaten plates of pancakes and set them in the kitchen sink before he smeared me onto the table. He yanked his flannel boxers down around his bubble butt, exposing nine, thick hung inches that was more than anxious to explore my sweet spot. I let loose a soft gasp as he slid his dick inside me. Being so busy with school, and all the crazy-ass drama with Leandra and this video, I forgot how good Emjay's dick felt. Sometimes some good dick is all a girl needs to take her mind off things. Emjay kissed me with a sweet passion that only he could commence as he thrust inside me, filling me with inch after hard, tender inch. From sucking the lobes of my ears to my chocolate chip nipples, it was like Emjay knew all the right buttons to push on a woman to make her toes curl. The kind of head game he put on my clit, was enough to give me pussy spasms. Yeah, I've had my share of deep-dick love-making, but Emjay is the first to ever tap my pussy right from front to back. He fucked me like a porn star. I figured it was what I deserved for leaving him sex starved for days on end. Men like Emjay needed to get a nut at least three days a week and Emjay's dick was looking a bit ashy. He dicked me until we both came in an earth-shattering orgasm. The best kind of sex was the kind that always took place outside of the bedroom. The kitchen table, the kitchen floor, the shower, giving him car head every now and again while he drove home.

We lay there for a while in our own juices before we managed to pry our buck-naked bodies off the kitchen table to head upstairs to shower.

"What class do you have today?"

"Western Civilization, Algebra 2 and this bullshit Positive Living class. The easiest class I have this semester."

"So what's the story with your friend, Dash?"

"We've been boys since elementary school. We lost touch for a couple of years when his moms moved on the North Side of town, so he could go to Godby High School, 'cause she didn't want him going to Rickards on the South Side."

"Rickards though, has gone from a D-list school to A-List. It's nowhere near as bad as it was back in the nineties."

"Tell Dash's mom that, but it was cool, 'cuz we kept in touch through e-mails and Facebook. You'll get a chance to meet him. He's a cool guy and an amazing poet."

"Speaking of that, have you been working on any new material?" I asked.

"I've had a few ideas, but nothing solid. I have a couple of things going, which is what I wanted to ask you. Do you think you could maybe read over some of what I have? I'd like your opinion on what I have so far."

"Sure, baby. I would be honored."

"Dash wouldn't let me leave yesterday until I told him that I would come out and hang."

I thought about what Emjay said about getting me to come out.

"You know what, I see how important this is to you, so let me see how my workload is looking at the college. I think I may be able to free myself up to attend the reading."

"Really? What about what you said about us being careful and us being seen in public together?"

"Well, I see how much this means to you. Besides, I would love to hear you read."

"You'll get a kick out of Dash. The two of you have a lot in common."

"The way you talk about him, I like him already. What time is the poetry reading?"

"Dash told me that it starts at like eight o'clock, but you know those things never start on time, so how about I meet you there a little before eight—that way you can meet Dash, Brent and Chadae."

"We can grab something to eat before the reading if you want."

"I'm down for whatever as long as you're there," Emjay said before he kissed me.

"I know this might be an uncomfortable subject right now for you, but have you thought about maybe inviting Leandra?"

"I have, but I don't know. I mean, I've tried calling Mama, but she never answers the phone. I leave messages, but she doesn't return my calls, so I don't know what else I can do. I doubt she would show up anyway."

"I don't know, Jay. Sometimes people will surprise you." Emjay sighed like he wasn't sure what to do about the state their relationship was in. "At the end of the day, it's up to you."

"I'll think about it. Honestly, I would like it if it was just you and me, you know? I would like the night to go off without a hitch, and not have to worry about Mama kicking up drama."

"I don't blame you on that. Whatever you decide to do, I support your decision."

Emjay and I kissed each other before we divided off to get in our cars.

"Don't work too hard," Emjay said.

"Give them hell in that Positive Living class." I smiled.

As I drove off, my palms started to sweat to the thought of meeting the person who had caught Emjay and me on camera.

TWENTY-NINE
DEANDRE

I sat anxiously in the parking lot of Wendy's for what seemed like damn hours for Shariece to show up. She must have thought I was playing when I'd told her ass that I would show the video to the director of the English Department. If she didn't give me what I wanted, I would run that shit all the way up to the dean if I had to. She wouldn't be able to get a job changing diapers after I was done dragging her cradle-robbing ass through the mud. She'd better show if she didn't want me to fuck her shit up. I knew if I saw Emjay's high-yellow ass, all fuckin' bets are off. I would like to think that someone who's as educated as her ain't that damn stupid. I hadn't stopped watching the video since I got it home to watch it the day I took it. I'd jacked off twice to the bitch before even coming to meet her. I was sitting in my Xterra chilling, tearing up the twenty-piece nuggets as I waited on Shariece. Since I skipped lunch, a sausage McGriddle from Mickey D's was all I had to eat the whole day. Ain't nothing more embarrassing than sitting in a lecture course of three hundred people, elbow to damn elbow, and have your stomach growling.

I had to play this shit right if I wanted to get what I wanted out of Shariece. It would be some shit she couldn't and wouldn't refuse unless she wanted the video to be sent to her higher-up. I tossed the last sweet n' sour-dipped nugget in my mouth when I noticed a silver Sequoia pull into the Wendy's parking lot. "It's her." I sank into the front seat of my SUV to make sure Shariece didn't see me. "Damn, she's fine."

She was wearing a black skirt with a gray blouse. I adjusted my dick in my baggy denim, Southpole shorts as I watched her slink her fine ass through the double-glass tinted doors. Those were the very titties that Emjay was sucking on, the same sexy legs he had hiked on his shoulders as he fucked her on her desk in her office. Hell, I thought I was going to pop off right there in the car. It wouldn't be the first time. I bet she could make a brother blow his nut by just the bat of her eyelashes. It oughta be a capital offense for a woman to look that good. It was bad enough she had me brick-hard three days a week when I could barely walk out of her class without my dick busting through my shorts. I haven't kept my hand off my dick all semester because of Shariece. I betcha her and Emjay fuck every night. The way they were fucking in her office, she looked like one of these women who has several orgasms. I would gorilla-fuck that bitch to the floor, split her ass in two if she fucked with me. They don't come no finer than Shariece.

I should have known something was up with the two of them. I sat across the class from Emjay, and noticed how he looked at her, licking his lips and shit whenever she walked past, grabbing at his dick under the desk.

I put the paper and sweet n' sour condiments in the empty Wendy's bag got out and locked the door. I pulled at my crotch to free up some room for my dick to hang. I couldn't wait to see the look on her pretty face when I told her it was me that had put her and

Emjay on some *Candid Camera* shit. Shariece didn't peg me as the kind of woman who didn't like to be kept waiting. I looked over at her sitting in one of the booth seats at the rear of the dining room, nervously checking her watch. As I walked toward her, she noticed me instantly. "Hey, Ms. Mills."

"Deandre, hey, how you doin'?" She looked out of the window like she was waiting on someone else; not knowing that I was the one she was waiting on so impatiently.

"Would you mind if I sat down?"

"Um…actually—."

"Thank you. My feet are killing me. I just walked all the way over here from Lake Bradford."

"So how are you?" Shariece asked.

"I can't complain. I'm ready for this semester to be over, so I can go home for the holidays."

"Are you from Tallahassee?"

"God, no. I'm from Jersey. Most of my family's from up there. I have family scattered all over, though."

"Any plans for Thanksgiving?"

"I'll most likely head up to Jersey to spend a few weeks with the fam."

"Sounds like fun. How's your semester going so far?"

"Well, if I get my way, I should graduate with a 3.8 GPA."

"That's great. Do you know what school you want to transfer to, or do you plan to go to school in Tallahassee?"

"I've applied to a few film schools in California and New York, so I have my fingers crossed."

"Those are great schools. Any one of them would be lucky to have you."

I was falling for this act of her pretending to give a damn about me.

"Thank you, and yeah, I hope so. A couple of my teachers wrote me some great recommendation letters. The schools are hard to get into."

"You just need to be positive and it will happen."

"I try. I'll see what happens. Well, enough about me. What's up with you? I know you'll be glad the semester's over."

"You have no idea. I'm up to my neck in grading, teaching and faculty meetings."

"Got any plans yourself for Thanksgiving?"

"Not really. I think I'm going to have a nice, relaxing holiday at the house."

"Fucking Emjay?" I asked.

Shariece paused and looked at me with a shocked expression on her face. "Excuse me?"

"I see the way he looks at you in class."

I could tell that something was sinking in.

"I don't know what you're talking about, and you better be glad we're in this lobby and not in my classroom."

"You know what, you're right. That was out of line. I didn't mean to say that. Your business is your business."

"Thank you," she said.

"So does the director of the English Department know that you're fucking one of your students?"

Shariece stared at me with a kind of mean grimace. "This conversation is over."

When she got up, I grabbed her hard by her arm. "You might want to think about closing your blinds in your office."

As soon as I said that, her face turned stone white like all the blood had rushed from that pretty face of hers. She sat back down in front of me.

"It was you, wasn't it?"

"I gotta give it to you. You can suck a mean dick."

"You're disgusting."

"You didn't seem like such a prude when you were taking it up the ass over your desk in your office."

Shariece nervously began to twirl a ring around the finger of her right hand. "What the hell do you want?"

"That's good; I like a woman who cuts right to the point. Let's see. To start off, I want a glowing recommendation letter from you. I'm talking Ivy League good. I want that shit to sound like the president wrote it."

"Is that it?"

"I want a taste of what you gave Emjay."

"What the hell are you talking about?"

"You're an educated woman, so when you try to play dumb with me, it doesn't go over too well, so let's not play this game. I want some of that good pussy that your little boyfriend gets a taste of every night."

"You must have me mistaken for somebody else, because I'm not the one who responds to threats."

I tugged my phone out of the front pocket of my shorts, and opened the attachment of the video I had sent to Shariece. "Suit yourself." I showed her the video. "Now can you imagine the look on the director's face and on the faces of your colleagues when they see you spread eagle on your desk in the office, getting rimmed by a student? Your career—hell, your life in Tallahassee—would be over. And once I release it on the Internet, this will follow you for the rest of your life."

"Cut it off."

"Are you sure? I love the part where you—"

"I said cut it off."

"You're really flexible. What, are you a gymnast as a pastime?"

"So if I do what you want, you'll hand over the flash drive that the video is on?"

"Once I get the letter, and you give me the fuck of the century, I'll give you the flash drive the video is on."

"And how in the hell do I know that you'll keep your word?"

"Once we're done fucking like rabbits, you can watch me erase any copies."

"How do I know you haven't sent a copy of that video to my boss?"

"Damn, you have some serious trust issues, don't you, ma?"

Shariece looked at me like she wanted to rip my throat open. "You come here and blackmail me with a video you took of me and Emjay, tell me that if I don't sleep with you, you will send the video to my boss and colleagues. You're damn right, I don't trust you."

The bass in Shariece's tone was enough to make a few heads turn toward the direction of our table.

"Look, you wouldn't have a job right now had I sent the video to your boss."

"Fuck you."

"In due time, but let me give you my phone number to call me." I jotted it down on a napkin. "Once you've made your decision, holler at me. And I don't have to tell you to keep this on the low from Emjay. If I get wind that you have uttered so much as a syllable to him about our arrangement, I won't only make sure the director of the English Department gets this video, I'll put it all over the Internet. Hell, I'll throw a fucking film festival if I have to until everyone at the school knows what you two did."

"You're sick, you know that?"

"Think about it, and who knows, I might be a better fuck than Emjay."

"Tell you what, why don't you go fuck yourself." Shariece stormed off through the dining area through the double-glass tinted doors.

THIRTY
SHARIECE

had to pull off on the side of the road and throw up the pancakes and eggs I'd had for breakfast five hours earlier. "How in the hell could I have been so stupid?" I said to myself, as I wiped my mouth with the back of my hand. This is what I get for letting my pussy do the talking. I lose not only everything I have worked my ass off for, but will lose Emjay. If I decide to fuck Deandre, and Emjay finds out, he'll never forgive me. But I don't see where I have a choice. It's either fuck him, or lose everything. Damn, Deandre Knowles of all people. The thought of doing anything with him makes me sick to my stomach. This keeps getting worse by the day. I wish Leandra was here right now. Had it been her, she would have told Deandre to go to hell and kiss her ass on the way down. I miss my best friend, and if I could lay my hands on her to make her forget that night, I would if I thought it would do any good. I miss being able to talk to Leandra about anything: men, politics, religion, menstrual cycles. Everything that has happened is my fault. Leandra and I still would have a friendship if I hadn't slept with Emjay. I know that I have to make this right no matter the outcome. I don't trust Deandre as far as I can throw his ass. I knew there was something strange about him the day he walked into class. Most men undress you with their eyes, but the way he looked at me. I felt like he was practically ripping my clothes off. He sits in the back of the class, looking at me with those creepy-ass eyes skinning and grinning at me with those nasty gold teeth in his mouth. Deandre never asks any questions, so it's easier to ignore him. Being looked at like I'm a piece of meat by these college boys was something I was used to. Hell, they're really no different from the losers that try to hit on me at Grown Folks night at Blue Moon. My tits get more attention than me. I'm like, *excuse me, my eyes are up here.*

A few weeks ago, Deandre came by my office claiming that he wanted to run some ideas by me about a short story he was working on. With him, I made sure that I kept the door open. There had never been a man who made my skin crawl more than him. Like I said, creepy as hell. Wanting to talk about ideas for a short story was only an excuse he used to get me alone when he wanted to stick that big, ugly nose of his in my personal life.

"What do you like to do when you're not teaching?" "Do you ever go out to the club?" "What types of men do you go out with?" He sat there pulling at his dick through his shorts the entire time. At one point I thought he was going to take his dick out. I'm pretty sure he wanted to with his nasty ass.

"Well, if there aren't any more questions related to classwork, Mr. Knowles, I really need to prepare for my next class." I didn't really have a class, but simply used that as a reason to get him out of my office.

"I see how you be teasing dudes in class."

"Excuse me?"

"You think I don't notice how you look at me?"

It was clear that Deandre had me fucked up.

"Mr. Knowles, I'm your teacher and you're my student. You need to know right here and now that there will be no improper conduct going on. This is strictly a teacher/student relationship. Am I making myself clear?"

I could look at him and tell he was pissed if not embarrassed. I guess he expected me to drop to my knees and suck his little-ass dick. He hauled up, threw his backpack over his shoulder and walked out. "Stuck up-ass ho," I heard him whisper under his shit-stank breath. And then I heard him say something about my pussy and cobwebs. I shut my door and locked it behind him as he shuffled his baggy shorts-wearing ass out of my office. I just let what he said roll off my back even if I wanted to hurl my paperweight at his head. If I wasn't quick to spread my legs, then I was either stuck up, or a lesbian, anything to make themselves feel better about the fact that they got rejected. I can't stand these men out here who think they're God's gift to pussy, and Deandre was no exception.

I hoped that Deandre would be too embarrassed to return to class, but he showed up Wednesday afternoon with his tail tucked between those baseball bats he calls legs; my talk with him didn't slow him down. He sat in the back and continued gawking at me like I was a baby back rib. And now here I was being blackmailed by the one person who I wished would disappear off the face of the earth.

THIRTY
LEANDRA

When closing time came around, my feet were killing me. That's the price I pay for being born with flat feet. I called Taj to tell him to grab some Popeyes on the way home, but he said he would be spending another late night on the set of the magazine fashion shoot. With all the drama that high-maintenance fashion designer was giving him, he had better be getting a fat check from this job.

Nishelle volunteered to stay behind to help me clean up while Sabrina and Javonte were out of the door as soon as six o'clock hit. I preferred to close with her anyway. "I'm starting to think that it was a mistake making her manager of the place."

"Who, Sabrina?"

"She used to be so reliable. Now that I've made her manager, she's stopped pulling her weight."

"I never thought she was a good choice. I mean, Sabrina is cool and whatnot, but she plays and jokes around too much. "

Everybody thinks that Nishelle is this quiet, mousy girl, but when it's me and her in the shop, she's quick to tell me everything that's going on when I'm out.

"Yeah, I'm starting to see that. Oh, by the way, what was it that you wanted to tell me today?"

"When?"

"When you and I were in the office, before Sabrina walked in. It seemed like you wanted to tell me something."

"Oh it ain't nothing," she said as she swept cut hair off the floor.

"Nishelle, look at me. If it's about Sabrina or the salon, you need to tell me what's up."

"I don't want to get nobody in trouble."

"Stop acting like a teenager, and tell me what's going on."

"Well, you know Sabrina's boyfriend, Kier, right?"

"Yeah, I met him once when we had the fundraiser for cancer survivors last year. What about him?"

"Well, while you were out sick, he was hanging around the shop a lot, and sometimes he would bring in a few of his friends to get edged up."

"Okay, what's wrong with that?"

"It was nothing at first, but I was noticing that day after day, he started spending more and more time here, hanging out, smoking those stink Black and Milds, kicking his feet up like his ass was at his crib."

"Now Sabrina knows that I don't want nobody smoking in in my shop. What was he doing in here sitting up if he wasn't paying any money to get nothing done?"

"I have no idea, but Sabrina would just let him do whatever he wanted. Sometimes he and his boys would come here, smoke, drink and play cards until we closed. They would show up around two in the afternoon, and wouldn't be up out until five o'clock, leaving the salon in a mess for me and Javonte to clean up."

"Oh hell no, see Sabrina knows that I don't play that shit in my shop. I'm trying to run a business."

"That's what I told her. She said that I better not say nothing to you about Kier and his boys being here, or that I would be sorry."

"Her ass is the one that is going to be sorry," I said.

"So, it wasn't until a week before you came back, that I noticed that some stuff was missing from the salon."

"Missing? What's missing?"

"Some shampoo, hair grease and stuff."

"So you think that Sabrina and Kier been stealing shit out of here?"

"I don't know. I haven't seen them take nothing, but I've noticed that some supplies have been missing, and none of it was logged in, so I don't know."

I was livid to hear the news that Sabrina was using my shop like it was a goddamn Atlantic City casino, letting scrubs roll up in here and have the run of the place.

"Sabrina obviously thinks that she's fucking with a clueless bitch, but it's cool, 'cause I'm about to get her ass together. Somebody is about to be out of a job."

Nishelle swept and mopped the floor while I wiped down the seats and mirrors. "I'm going to have to have an employee meeting."

"Oh, and I don't know where Krista at."

"She hasn't called?"

"Not a phone call, email or text message. I called her moms, but she said she hasn't seen her in three weeks, so I don't know what's going on."

"Damn, why does everybody start actin' a fool every time I'm out? Sabrina's stealing shit, Krista pulls a no-show. Wherever she's at, she needs to keep her ass there because as far as I'm concerned, she is no longer employed at Radiance Salon. I don't know what these girls think I'm running. See, that's what I can't stand, you show a little bit of weakness and the hyenas pounce trying to rip a lioness's throat out. Well, not here. I'm the queen bitch of this jungle. This shit officially stops now."

"I tried to tell them, Leandra, but you know nobody listens to me around here. They all treat me like the annoying little sister. Nobody counts me around here and I can work some hair better than Sabrina, Javonte and Krista combined, but all I do is answer phones and sweep hair."

I knew the way she was going off, it was a dig at me, but I let Nishelle have her say since this was some shit she wanted to get off her chest.

"You know what, baby girl, you're right. I admit that I have taken advantage of you and how loyal and dedicated you are here at the shop. Nishelle, I do notice how hard you work around here."

"I'm sick of cleaning up Sabrina's messes. I'm not a maid."

"Well, trust I will talk to Sabrina and Javonte and that some changes *will* be made."

"So I don't want to keep bugging you about this, but I was wondering when you're going to give me my own chair. You already know how I do. I stay late, I clean; organize the supply closet, clean the bathrooms and I even play plumber in here sometimes when the drains get clogged with all that nasty hair."

"You're absolutely right. You have gone above and beyond the call of duty in proving yourself, and yes, I do think it's about time I turn you loose to do your own thing."

"Are you serious?" Nishelle gave a wide-eyed smile.

"Absolutely. Krista has been M.I.A. for weeks and her station is just going unused, so why not?" *Krista was a pain in my dick anyway.*

"She and Sabrina are tight. She's not going to like that."

"I don't give a damn what she likes. She doesn't write the checks, I do. If she doesn't like it, she can kick rocks."

"I'm so glad you're back." Nishelle smiled.

"You and me both, baby girl."

"So when can I start doing hair?" Nishelle asked.

"Well, I would need to hire a new receptionist, but I don't see why you can't start next week."

"Oh my God, Leandra. I promise I will not disappoint you." She roped her arms around me, giving me a hug.

"I know you'll make me proud."

"You've made my day, my week—hell, my whole year."

"Lying up in that hospital made me realize that life is too short for the devil's bullshit. I thought about all the things I wanted to do, but had not yet done. I thought about how it would kill Emjay if anything ever happened to me."

Nishelle looked at me with a serious expression on her face. "Can I ask you something? You can tell me to mind my own business if you think I'm being too nosey."

"Go 'head. What's up?"

"Did you really intentionally run your car off the road?"

I was unsure whether or not I should answer Nishelle's question, but since she had the lady balls to ask, then I had the lady balls to tell her what was up.

"I was going through a lot of pain at the time. Some family stuff that I don't really want to go into details about." I didn't feel comfortable telling her about my mess with Emjay and Shariece. I was close with Nishelle like she was my daughter, but I wasn't ready to go there with her yet.

"I totally understand," Nishelle said. "I want you to know that if you ever need to talk, holler, vent, have a damn pillow fight, I'm your girl. You can call me day or night."

"Thank you, baby girl. I could definitely use a friend."

"Well, you got one in me. I want you to know that I gotcha back."

"Good, so I don't have to tell you that what goes on in the shop, stays in the shop. What I told you and what you have discussed with me about Sabrina and Kier stays here within these four walls."

"Not a word," Nishelle assured me.

By the time we were done sweeping and mopping, it was ten minutes after seven. Nishelle and I grabbed our purses, mine with that day's deposits, and locked up. I made sure I had my keys in my hand that had a small thing of mace hanging from the key chain. You can't be too careful on the South Side. I walked Nishelle to her car that was parked under an oak tree that was in the center of the plaza. "So, I want you to continue to be my eyes and ears around here. If you see anything out of the ordinary, let me know immediately."

"Oh, absolutely."

"I'm trying to run a business here, and I have to have people around me that I can trust."

"And I'm your girl."

Nishelle unlocked the driver side door of her white Ford Focus, and slid in.

"What are you going to do about Sabrina?"

"Let me worry about her. You go home and break open a bottle of champagne with your man and celebrate your promotion."

"Oh my God. I'm so excited. I can't wait to get started, and I can't wait to break the news to Devondre and Sabrina. Now that drama princess can clean up after her own messes."

"Well, just remember what I said. What happens in Radiance stays at Radiance."

I was so tired; I could barely walk to my car. I ran a few errands and stopped off to Popeyes to pick up some chicken and red beans and rice for dinner. I made it home in time to watch *Scandal*. I live for some Kerry Washington. I'm going to punch somebody in the throat if my girl gets snubbed again for an Emmy.

I wish Taj was home waiting up for me for once. I miss our cuddle sessions on the sofa. I had a good mind to go to that photo shoot and tell that prissy fashion designer to stop breaking my man's balls and send him home, but I was too tired to even blink. I ate my dinner, and before long, I was nodding off on the sofa, barely able to stay awake to watch the last thirty minutes of *Scandal*.

THIRTY-ONE
TAJ

I was having my body slathered with baby oil by a couple of production assistants when Leandra called. "Okay, everyone, places," Jimi yelled. "Is that the ball buster you were telling me about?"

"No, it's um, the set manager," I lied, "but let me hit you up later. Don't wait up. The way this shit show is going, it looks like I might be pulling another all-nighter."

"It's been three weeks now," Leandra said.

"I know, baby. I promise after I wrap this project up, we will take a long vacation, just the two of us."

"I'm going to hold you to that."

"Oh, I know, but let me go. I think they're ready for me."

"I love you."

"Love you, too."

Lying to Leandra every time she asked me about my business was like my having to pull off a layer of my skin every time I told a lie. The production assistants Lara and Rachel were making my dick hard as their hands grazed across my nipples putting on the oil—Lara, especially, who knew exactly what she was doing. She had been on my jock ever since I'd started doing porn.

"All right, ladies, that's enough oil. Let's get this show on the road," Jimi said. I handed Montez, one of the new crew members, my phone, as Jimi ushered me onto the set. The movies were flying off the shelves in video stores and online sells doubled. Vance bought a new car, a black Maserati he had no problems showing off to the crew like he was some Hollywood movie star. Vance was straight up VIP wherever he went, but I thought he was cornier than my big toe, and fake. We were the highest-grossing porn actors in the business, but I knew the way Vance was headed with the drugs, drinking and partying every night, it would only be a matter of time before his golden boy image would start to tarnish. I was smart enough to know that nothing ever lasts. Being on top is cool, but staying there is the hard part. There's always somebody waiting to pull you down off that pedestal. Vance was slowly spiraling out of control, and dudes like him always hit rock bottom sooner than later. Jimi came up with this idea to do a movie about two landscapers fucking. *Morning Wood*, he called it. I didn't care what kind of movie he made. I stuck my dick in whoever he wanted, when he wanted as long as there was a fat check waiting for me after I came. I knew Leandra would never see the movies, considering she wasn't big into porn. "My imagination is all the porn this woman needs," she'd told me.

Jimi had been able to get permission to use his buddy Greg's house in Crawfordville to make the film, but not before he paid him a fat chunk of money. The house was like this country mansion out in the woods with five bedrooms, four bathrooms, a fireplace, a kitchen, a steam room, a Jacuzzi and a pool in back.

"Damn, man, I didn't know they built them this big in the sticks."

"I know, it's gorgeous, right? I come out here sometimes to get away from the craziness of the city from time to time. I like to relax and clear my head."

"So I'm assuming that this is not the first film you've done here."

"I've done five movies here. I made *Jack-Off Buddies*, *Attack of the Twelve-Inch Dick*, *Muscle Lust*, and *The Sweetest Ass* out here, and with the money I've paid Greg, I've practically helped him build this palace."

The living room area, which was the size of a bowling rink, was littered with cameras, light stands, tripods and cables that ran like snakes along the floor. The crew was scurrying around like ants making sure that everything was operational. I laughed watching them all run around shoeless, which was one of the things OCD Greg had on his list of what not to do. He didn't want anyone to scuff up his hardwood floors or to track dirt from outside on his fancy expensive carpeting, so all the crew people were walking around the house barefoot. Everybody's got their thing, I guess.

Jimi wanted to get some shots in one of the guest rooms, which he had to fork out an extra four hundred stacks for, and Greg had to be on set at all times to keep watch over everyone to make sure they didn't steal anything. If it was up to him, he would have the entire house covered in plastic.

"How do you put up with this guy?" I asked Jimi.

"Greg's not so bad. He's only like this when I want to make a movie here. You get enough drinks in him, he can be pretty chill."

"I would have shoved his rules and this no-shoes shit so far up his ass, he'd be shitting shoestrings."

Vance came out dressed in a white T-shirt and booger-green Dickies. He was oiled up and smeared with some kind of grease to give the impression he had been working outside in the heat all day. All I wore was a pair of blue, satin boxers. We started in the bedroom where Jimi and the cameraman, Kyle, stood.

"So the story begins where you're asleep, and you're woken up by the buzz of a leaf blower going outside of your window. Annoyed, you get up; look outside to find this hot, sweaty landscaper blowing leaves off your driveway. You walk downstairs and open the door to find shirtless Vance outside armed with his blower."

Since making porn, I've become quite the exhibitionist. Before I was nervous about showing my ass and dick in front of people, but seeing as how I work with the same people three times a day, I've gotten used to it. I don't give a fuck now who sees my dick. Cherri has two jobs these days. Pushing papers back at the office and making my dick hard. And if you can't get it hard and keep it hard, Jimi is quick to replace you with someone else who doesn't have that problem. Luckily for me, I don't have a limp dick issue. "Time is money," Jimi was always saying.

"I want you to lie on your back, Taj." The crew adjusted the bed covers just so, exposing a sliver of pubic hair.

"Okay, good, that's perfect. All right, positions everybody, let's go." The moment he yelled, "Action," I was no longer Taj, but Dillon Douglas, a name I came up with myself after watching *The Outsiders* on Netflix a few nights earlier. When I told Jimi of my porn screen name, he loved it.

"I knew you would."

Kyle was in position, holding the camera over me as I opened my eyes to the sound of the leaf blower. Kyle got a shot of my rock-hard dick pressing against the soft fabric of my boxers. I glanced out of the window to find golden boy Vance blowing fake leaves that had been peppered around the driveway for effect. Vance held the hose of the blower in front of his crotch as Jimi requested. He and Kyle followed me as I descended down the set of stairs. I turned the large, wide oak door open to find Vance glistening, shirtless from the baby oil. His bulge tented his booger-green Dickies, thanks to a dick ring he wore around his balls to stay hard. Maybe if he didn't snort so much fucking coke, he wouldn't need to wear one.

"Taj, caress your chest," Jimi demanded. I slowly moved my hands along my chest, tweaking my greased nipples. "That's good, exactly like that." Vance shut off the blower when he was directed to look in my direction at me standing half-nakedly in the door.

Vance and I began making out. Kissing a man seemed like something I never thought I could bring myself to do, but I reminded myself that it's a part of the job. As we kissed, I could taste the cherry-flavored Altoid on his breath. He stuck his tongue in my mouth, something he knows I can't stand. Not from a man anyway. "It needs to look as real as possible," Jimi was always saying, but ain't nobody tell Vance to stick his nasty-ass tongue in my mouth, however, it was all good. I got through it by pretending I was kissing Leandra. I was becoming damn good and faking it, which is what this business is about most of the time.

"Keep rolling," Jimi said. I took Vance by the hand and led him to the sectional in Greg's living room. My dick was still hard as I thought of eating Leandra's pussy, her thick, juicy lips around my dick. I sat slouched on the sofa as Vance positioned himself between my legs. He reached into the open slit of my boxers, and slowly tugged out my dick. Vance wasted no time and started sucking the head, cradling it with his tongue. With each suck, he slid down lower, devouring inch after brick-hard inch, taking my shit to the balls as he glanced up at me all wide-eyed with his mouth stuffed with my meat.

Vance hooked his fingers over the waistband of my boxers and eased them down over my ass until my spit-soaked dick popped from the satin fabric like a Jack from its box. Vance knew his way around a dick, how to apply the right amount of pressure. I moaned as he suckled the head, the most sensitive part of my dick.

I tried to keep my mind on Leandra, but Vance was making a

brother forget what he had at home. I liked how slow he was sucking me, how he took my shit to the back of his throat and then come up to the tip, hugging my dick tip with those talented, cherry-red lips. Kyle was all up in the action, catching every position, every moan, making sure he didn't get in the way. Vance knew he had me exactly where he wanted, and was hell-bent on getting this nut. I was told that gay men can suck dick better than women, but I didn't believe it until now. *Damn, get this dick, boy. Throat that shit.*

"Cut!" When Jimi yelled, "cut," it shook me out of the moment. *Fuck he hollered cut for? We could have kept going.*

My dick popped out of Vance's mouth as he got up off his knees. Lara threw a white robe over him like he was James Brown, and ushered him off to one of the bathrooms while another production assistant handed me a hand towel to wipe Vance's spit off my dick.

"Let's get set up for the anal scene." I secretly didn't want Vance to stop sucking my dick. "Are you okay?" Jimi asked.

"What? Yeah, I'm good. Can I get some water or something?" I asked as I dabbed my dick dry with tissues.

"Can we get Taj a bottle water over here!"

Lara came over and applied more oil. "Not too much this time. Where's Vance?"

"He's in the bathroom douching for the anal scene."

"Good. Lara, give us a minute."

"I'll go check on Vance."

"This is going to be one of my best films ever," Jimi said, but he said that about all the porn movies he made. "This fucking film is going to put me on the map in the industry."

"You mean us, right?"

"What?"

"Us, yeah, that's what I mean."

"Yeah, sure." Greg started fussing like a little bitch again. "Make sure there's something on the sofa before you start shooting. I don't want it smelling like ass."

"Greg, relax. I got it taken care of. Go have a doughnut or something."

"Vance, baby, are you ready?"

"We're doing hands and knees and on my back, right?" he asked Jimi, as he gawked at me with a sinister grin.

"Yeah, we're going to get some shots of you on your hands and knees first and then some of you getting fucked on your back."

"That works."

"Taj, are you good with that?" Jimi asked.

"Rubbers only. I don't do none of that bareback shit."

"Absolutely, of course."

Vance looked as if he wasn't too happy when I said I wanted to use protection, but I didn't give a fuck. I did it for two reasons. I don't want to get any STDs and I don't want to get shit on my dick. I didn't care how long or how many times that power bottom washed his asshole out.

"Okay, places, everybody!" Jimi yelled.

Vance went over to the sectional, took off his robe and handed it to Lara.

"Taj, do you need Cherri to take care of you or are you good? I don't want any limp noodles on my set."

Jimi tried my ass then. Just because I needed someone that one time to get my dick hard.

"Man, whatever, let's do this shit."

"Here's a rubber," Jimi said, as he slapped the rubber in my hand.

I tore open the cellophane with my teeth, took out the rubber and rolled it slowly onto my dick, making sure there was room at the tip to capture my cum. Vance took his position at one end of Greg's sectional with his oiled bubble butt sticking up in the air looking as if he was down for whatever. I took my place behind him. I could tell that his asshole had been stretched, which was not a surprise, considering that he told me that's he's done well over thirty movies. So imagine how many times he's been dicked on film, not including what he does when a camera isn't rolling. I can't see myself doing this shit in ten years, not the acting part of it anyway. I've thought about making porn films. I mean, how hard can it be? All you do is point the camera on someone's ass and shoot. I damn sho' wouldn't make gay porn films. Jimi says that his next film will be a straight one. Kyle told me that you make a shitload more money playing gay in a porn movie than playing straight, but I don't know if I believe that.

"Okay, are we ready?" Jimi asked.

Kyle stood with the camera up to his face, ready to shoot the moment Jimi yelled, "Action." Kyle was one of the most reliable cameramen Jimi had on his crew, if not the biggest kiss ass in the history of ass kissers. Jimi was always sending him off to go fetch something. If Jimi told him to lick the dog shit off his shoes, he would drop to his knees and do it. I suspected it wouldn't be long before Kyle would be making his own films someday at the rate he was going. He was always begging Jimi to give him a shot, but the only shots Jimi wanted him to have were of my dick going up Vance's ass.

"Okay, cameraman rolling, and action."

Kyle was hovered over Vance's ass as I grazed his slick-ass crack with the meaty tip of my latex-covered dick.

"Make sure you get in real close," Jimi told Kyle. I slipped the head of my dick up Vance's ass easily, which was much looser than pussy. Again, not a surprise. I teased his ass by sliding in to the head and then pulled out, then pushed in hard and deep, inch after black inch sinking into Vance's ass.

"Fuck me," he said. "Break that dick off in me." The dirty words that tumbled from his effeminate lips were turning me on. I fucked hard, but slow knowing that Jimi needed it to last until the final scene. Kyle positioned himself under my legs to get a shot of my balls slapping against Vance's ass. I gripped Vance's hips, pulling his ass onto my dick as I hit it from the back. We both began to work up a sweat as I pillaged Vance's hole. Vance moaned when I smacked his ass. Jimi didn't object, but secretly gave me the thumbs-up to keep it going. "Whose ass is this?"

"Yours," Vance answered, with a bitchy whimper.

"Whose ass is it?"

"Yours!" he shouted.

"Damn right."

Jimi gave us the signal to switch positions. Vance eased onto his back with his legs high in the air as Kyle stood over us to get a shot of my dick sliding inside Vance's booty, playing with his dick as I fucked him balls deep. I gave Jimi the signal that I was close to coming.

"Okay, cut!" he shouted. I gently pulled my dick out of Vance's ass, careful not to come in the rubber as I eased out of him.

"Three-minute break, people, before we get the money shot."

Lara rushed over with our robes. "Why don't you go freshen up a little while we get everything ready for the money shot?"

I went to one of the bathrooms upstairs and worked the rubber off the shaft of my dick. A reverberated slap echoed when I tugged it off the mushroom head of my piece. I wrapped it in tissue paper, threw it in the toilet and flushed. I soaped my palms up until I worked up a thick white lather to clean my dick free of lubricant from the latex.

"Taj, are you ready?" I heard Jimi yell.

I rushed back downstairs to the living room of crew, cameras and assorted colors of cable wire that ran across the floor.

"Okay, we're going back to the first scene where you're sitting on the sofa getting head from Vance. Except this time, I want you to be expressive, talk dirty to him more: 'Suck that big black dick,' 'go down on that dick,' or whatever you want to say."

"Not a problem."

"How are you feeling about the anal scenes we shot?"

"I would have to see in editing, but I think Kyle got some good shots."

"I saw the playbacks. It's some pretty good stuff."

"I would hope so being that he was all up under my legs with the camera on my nuts."

"That's show business, baby."

Vance and I took our positions back on the sofa with him parked between my legs.

The minute Jimi yelled, "Action," Vance went at my dick, taking the fat head past his cherry-red wet lips, staring up at me with a lustful gaze as he gagged on my dick.

"Suck that dick, slut," I said as I looked into a set of watery, red eyes.

I placed my hand behind Vance's head, slowly pushing him down on my ten-incher.

"Take that black dick." I could feel the tip-tap against his tonsils; soft, black wires of pubes tickled his nose.

"Fuck, I'm close," I said. Kyle got in to make sure he got the shot of me popping my load. Vance sucked hard, speeding up his blow job tempo, tightening those pretty lips around the shaft.

"Shit, I'm about to…"

When Vance eased off, a web of spit hung like a hammock from his bottom lip to the tip of my dick. He jacked me off until I shot thick streams of cum across his face and chest.

"Cut! Holy fuck, that was perfect," Jimi yelled enthusiastically. Lara handed Vance a towel to wipe my spunk off his face and chest. "Dude, I've done a lot of films, but that was one of the best cum shots I've seen on camera."

"I guess I had a lot pent up."

"You ain't lying. It sure as hell looked like Vance enjoyed it."

"Oh, no doubt. He's wanted to taste my dick the moment he saw me walk into your office." I took a tissue and wiped my dick dry of Vance's spit. "So you're done with me, right?"

"Yeah, I'm going to shoot the solo jack-off scene with Vance, but yeah, you're done for today."

"Better be, 'cuz you know I don't do reshoots."

"How do you feel about working with a new guy I have lined up for a new film idea I've been working on?"

"If the money is right, I'm down."

"Well, here's your cut, ten thousand, all cash." Jimi handed me a sealed manila envelope.

"I'm in the planning stages of it right now, but I hope to start shooting in two weeks. It's mostly vanilla, but I'm thinking about mixing in a little bondage."

"Are we talking about whips and cuffs and shit?"

"Yeah, are you cool with that?"

"As long as it doesn't get too crazy. This ain't no snuff film, is it?"

"Hell no, nothing that fucked up. Here, you know what, let me get you a copy of the script. You can take a look at it and tell me what you think."

This was a first for Jimi. "What is this about? You usually keep your scripts for new films under lock and key."

"Well, you're one of my top money-makers, so I want you to see what I have planned."

I was psyched to read the new script Jimi had written. "Cool. How about I give you a call next week, let you know what I think."

"Sounds good. I've hired two news guys I want you to meet. Demetri, this cute Italian twink from Miami, and the other guy, I think you know."

"Who?"

"Montez," Jimi shouted, as he waved him over. Jimi threw an arm around Montez's shoulders. "This guy has a huge cock and I can't wait to show it to the world."

"Welcome aboard."

"Oh man, this is an honor. I love your movies, Mr. Bowman."

"Call me Taj, young buck."

"Taj. That's cool."

"How old are you, man?" I asked.

"Nineteen. I'll be twenty in January."

He was a few years younger than me, but judging from his baby face, this lil' brother could have passed for twelve.

"All right, Montez, back to work."

"They get younger and younger with you. I hope he has all of his shots."

"I think I'm going to call him the blow job prince. He can suck the hell out of some dick, which you will soon find out." I had no doubt that Montez had fallen victim to Jimi's casting couch. "So read over the script and let me know what you think. Feel free to make notes if you want, add some suggestions."

"I appreciate you letting me read it."

"What are friends for?" Jimi said, as he gave me a stern slap on the back.

That night I drove home reeking of baby oil. Leandra was asleep on the sofa with an empty Popeyes box sitting on the coffee table. I switched off the TV and blanketed her with a fleece throw. I took a shower, letting the filth of the day wash away into the drain. I made a bologna sandwich, poured myself a glass of milk, sat at the kitchen table, and began reading Jimi's script.

"Where in the hell did he learn how to write a script? Kindergarten?" I took a pencil from one of the kitchen drawers and began to make notes in the margins to improve it, making sure I didn't step on Jimi's ego-tripping toes in the process.

THIRTY-TWO
EMJAY

I sat in the bookstore café with my composition notebook opened to the first wide-ruled page and stared at it for ten minutes. I sat there tapping my pen against the page, attempting to come up with the first line that would give birth to a poem. I had poetry books stacked on the small round table, from Langston Hughes' collected works to Alice Walker hoping they could light a fire under my ass. Nothing would come until I thought about Mama and Shariece, and that's when the words came. Before long, I was three pages in and kept on writing; each scribbled word and every short-hand sentence came from the heart. This poem was better than most poems I was considering for the reading. I wrote and wrote until the poem was finished.

I continued composing until I heard someone say, "What up, Emjay?" I glanced up from my notebook to find Deandre Knowles looking down at me.

"Hey, man, what's up?"

"Nothing. I was here doing some research on a paper, and I saw you sitting over here. So what are you doing writing in your diary?" I laughed.

"I'm trying to get it in for my Western Civ. class," I lied.

I didn't know Deandre that well other than he was this weird cat I had Shariece's class with. He wasn't the kind of brother I would hang with, plus there was something about him that creeped me out. I made sure to never call Shariece by her first name in or outside of class to fellow students and the faculty in the English building. We were careful about not bringing any unwanted attention to ourselves. I almost slipped one time in class and called her Shariece, but caught myself before I said anything.

"So you mind if I sit down?" Deandre asked. He had already pulled out a chair before I could answer. Honestly, I was in the moment with the poem and didn't want to be bothered. "So what's up with Ms. Mills?"

"What do you mean?"

"Did you see what she was wearing in class on Wednesday? I thought for sure her titties were going to slip out of that blouse she had on."

I was getting madder and madder each time Deandre mentioned Shariece's name. I wanted to jump across the table and rip his fucking throat out.

"No, I didn't notice."

"You would have to be blind not to see. Those sweet-ass nipples of hers pressing through that fabric. I bet she stays in heat."

I didn't know what happened, but it was like something in me clicked, like someone had pulled a pin from a hand grenade. I jumped up knocking over the table that separated us, sending Langston and Alice crashing to the floor. I grabbed Deandre up by his T-shirt as people that sat nearby scattered, parents pulling their children to them in hugs. I tried to kill Deandre.

"What the fuck did you fuckin' say about Shariece?"

It took one of the bookstore staff and security guards to pull me off of Deandre.

"I knew it. I knew ya'll was fucking. So tell me, Jay, how good is that cougar pussy?"

I tried to break loose from the bookseller's grip, but he was stronger and bigger than me.

"If you two don't calm down, I'm calling the cops."

"Get off me," Deandre said.

Malcolm, one of the managers of the store, arrived on the scene.

"Escort him out of the store," he told the security guard. He held Deandre by the arm and walked him toward the entrance that led into the mall.

"Yo, Jay. You ain't the only one who's hit that."

"Emjay, do you know that guy?" Malcolm asked.

"He's nobody, just some loser." Malcolm helped me stand the table back up off the floor. Luckily, the books were not damaged. "Man, I'm sorry about all this. He pissed me off and I lost it."

"I can't have this kind of thing going on in the store."

"I understand, and I'm sorry. It won't happen again."

"I usually bar customers away from here for fighting, but since you're a faithful customer, I'll let it go."

"Thanks, man, for not calling the cops, and again, I apologize."

I placed the books back on the shelf in the poetry section. I was reeling from the fight still, and I would have broken every bone in that fucker's body if they hadn't pulled me off his ass.

"What the fuck did he mean, talking about he's not the only one who's hit that?" Deandre's words stuck under my skin like splinters. I began to wonder if there were other students Shariece had fucked. Who else had she been with? Did she fuck Deandre? She does wear tight shit in class. Who else has she spread her legs for?

I was so pissed; I skipped the rest of my classes. I couldn't shake the thought of Shariece and Deandre fucking. "So what, she does me on Mondays, Wednesdays and Fridays and lets him eat her pussy on Tuesdays and Thursdays? I pulled a bottle of Jack Daniel's out of the refrigerator. I thought if I was drunk enough, it would wash out the nasty thoughts I had of him fucking Shariece, but after polishing off the rest of what was left in the bottle, it wasn't enough to make me forget, to numb the images of the two of them together. I noticed Shariece's iPad on the dining room table. My laptop was back at my place, and I needed to let my teachers know that I was sick and would come by their offices later in the week to get lecture notes and any homework assignments. There was a Christmas list of emails—some from students, others from teachers. There was one I didn't recognize labeled *Hot for Teacher.* I wasn't sure it was a good idea to invade her privacy, but hell, it wasn't my fault she'd left her iPad on. "Fuck it," I said and opened the email. The message in the inbox simply read *see me,* and above it was an attachment. As soon as I opened it, I wished I hadn't. "What the fuck?"

THIRTY-THREE
SHARIECE

I love you. Those three words had been dancing in my head all day. Worrying about this damn video Deandre has of me, has given me a migraine to kick the ass of all migraines, but I guess playing the conversation back in my head doesn't help to relieve the pain. I can either sleep with him, or lose my job and Emjay. I think about how it happened, about the first time Emjay and I hooked up. It was four years ago, Memorial Day at Leandra's cookout. It was small with Delora and me, and Nishelle, Sabrina and her boyfriend, Krista, and Javonte from Radiance. Emjay pranced around the house and yard half the day shirtless. Next to Nishelle and Javonte, I couldn't keep my eyes off him. I don't think that Leandra ever noticed, but maybe she did and never said anything. Emjay was sixteen, but could pass for twenty, twenty-one with his six-three physique. I blinked and before I knew it, he had become a full-grown, handsome young man. It was uncanny that he looked so much like his daddy. You would think it was Rick standing there talking to you. I pretended I didn't notice him staring at me during dinners at Leandra's whenever I came over. It wasn't how a godson looks at his godmama.

The day of the cookout, I was in the kitchen helping Leandra and Nishelle prepare cole slaw and carrot salad while Emjay was outside playing basketball with one of the neighborhood kids. The way sweat glistened off his chest, the way his dick pressed against the nylon fabric of the shorts was enough to make my pussy wet. I was slightly buzzed from all the boozing. Leandra had just about every beer you could name, and enough liquor to put an elephant down, from red wine to Jack Daniel's. When it was time to eat, Emjay and Edmond Payne from next door had walked inside, drenched from head to toenail in sweat.

"Jay, you need to go shower before you eat," Leandra had said. "Why? We're going to be eating outside anyway, right?"

"It ain't sanitary for you to be sweating around all this food. Boy, now go shower and then join us outside to eat."

Jay had given me this seducing glare, cutting a wink at me as he ran upstairs to shower. There wasn't a place on the table that didn't have a bowl of something: potato salad, carrot salad, deviled eggs, baked beans, chicken, ribs, hot dogs, hamburgers. You would have thought it was a family reunion with all the food Leandra had made including dishes Nishelle and others had brought.

"Hey, I'm not feeling so good. I'm going to go and splash some water on my face," I had told Leandra.

"That's because of all that beer you've been drinking. I told you not to be drinking that shit on an empty stomach."

"Thank you, Ma, for that advice."

"All right, keep on," Leandra had said.

I could barely make it upstairs the way my head was spinning. That Jack Daniel's Honey and Coke was kicking my ass. I went to Leandra's room to freshen up. Emjay's room was directly across the hall. The door was slightly ajar. He was standing ass-naked in the middle of his pigsty of a room, drying off. He was just as hot in the buff as he was with clothes on with a big hateful horse-hung dick between those muscled legs of his. I walked off before he caught me standing there. Leandra's room was so pretty with a white and egg yolk-yellow color scheme. I went to the bathroom to splash water on my face in hopes it would ward off the buzz that had come over me. I was about to make my way back downstairs when Emjay stood in the doorway wearing a pair of cargo shorts and nothing else. A treasure trail of chest hair ran down his torso into his shorts.

"Damn, you scared me," I said, holding my hand up to my chest.

"Sorry."

"Are you ready? Everybody's about to eat."

"Why don't we chill up here for a minute," Emjay said. He walked in and closed and locked Leandra's bedroom door. I remember standing there like my feet were encased in cement blocks. I swooned when Emjay caressed the side of my cheek. I had never been touched like that by any man. He kissed me, shoving his tongue in my mouth. I nudged him away knowing good and damn well I wanted him.

"Emjay, we can't do this."

"What, I locked the door."

"No, I mean this, we can't."

"Why not?"

"What do you mean why not? I'm old enough to be your mama."

"I see how you look at me, and you know what; I look at you the same way."

"Do you know what would hap—" Emjay sealed my words with another kiss before I could push the rest of what I had to say out of my mouth. This time, I didn't stop him.

He grabbed my ass hard into his hands, pressing me into him

until I felt his dick rise and thicken against my thigh. I knew it was wrong, that Leandra would hurl me out of her bedroom window if she walked in on us, but the selfish Shariece in me took over, the I-don't-give-a-fuck Shariece that had no problem acting on what were mere fantasies when she found herself alone in bed, running her fingers between her legs when Emjay wasn't around to quench her lust for dick. He smeared me on the bed like a dirty secret. Pings of electrical sexual shockwaves ran along my body when he squeezed my breasts, ran his fingers around my nipples.

"If Leandra ever finds out—"

"She's not going to find out."

Emjay slid his shorts down off his ass, around his legs. He hunched my faded, denim skirt up over my booty. The only thing that was separating us was my thin layer of cotton, lavender panties he gently eased down my thighs. I gasped the minute his dick slipped between the lips of my pussy. Some would say that I robbed the cradle, but the pussy wants what the pussy wants. The deep-dicking Emjay was giving me was truly one for the record books. I slid my legs around his, pulling him into me, allowing that big, juicy dick of his to tame a woman's pussy proper. I kneaded his back, groped his firm, dark-chocolate ass as he ran me through. We didn't have much time before Leandra began to wonder what was keeping us. Emjay muffled my mouth with his hand as he fucked me. Good thing, too, 'cause I'm a screaming, talk-dirty-to me kind of bitch, something Emjay is now fully aware. The dirtier he talked, the hotter it made me. Emjay grunted until he came, shooting what felt like torrents of cum. We were quick to get dressed and back downstairs before Leandra and the others would start to wonder where we were.

"You walk out first, and I'll come out twenty minutes after you," I told Emjay.

"When can I see you again?" he asked as he fastened his shorts.

"Are you serious? There is no doing *this* again. It's a one-time thing, that's all."

"It doesn't have to be."

"Emjay, listen to me. We can't do this."

"Why not?"

"Because one, Leandra could find out, and two, I like breathing."

Emjay grabbed, and kissed me one last time before he exited Leandra's bedroom. It was then that I knew that none of what I said to him had sunk in.

I didn't look at Emjay all that afternoon. Every time I looked at Leandra, a feeling of guilt would come over me like a fever, but I couldn't stop thinking about Emjay and what had happened in Leandra's bedroom. Emjay would call wanting to get together, but I would ignore his calls and erase the numerous X-rated voicemail messages he would leave on my cell, but I finally gave in when my vibrator simply wasn't as good as the real thing.

The second I dialed the last digit of his number, I thought to hang up.

"Hello."

I didn't say anything at first.

"Shariece, is that you?"

"If we are going to do this, we have to be careful."

"Yeah, sure," Emjay said nonchalantly.

"Emjay, I mean it. This isn't a game. If Leandra finds out about us, there's no telling what she'll do."

"I understand. It will only be between you and me."

We would meet up once a week at Motel 6 out near Lake Jackson. I wasn't taking any chances, and wasn't going to run the risk of Leandra or anyone else seeing me, or Emjay's car in the parking lot. The second time we got up, he went all-out, came to the motel with wine I'm sure he had stolen from Leandra's liquor cabinet. Emjay treated me with love, class and respect, a big difference from the scrubs I often dealt with at clubs and bars.

I struggled with the love I developed for Emjay and my friendship to Leandra. For two years, we secretly met, never at the same motel until I told Emjay that I wanted to tell Leandra about us. We both knew that it wasn't going to be easy. You don't take the news of your best friend sleeping with your son, with a smiling face and a congratulatory pat on the back. We were going to tell her at dinner the day before she found out about us, but I'd learned the hard way that things don't often go as planned, which is why I was going to tell Emjay about this mess I was in with Deandre.

THIRTY-FOUR
SHARIECE

could barely make it up the stairs of my apartment complex; I was so tired. I saw Emjay's SUV parked in front, so I was glad he was home 'cause I was in desperate need of one of his state-of-the-art back rubs. Just as I was about to push the key in the lock to open the door, it flew open.

"Damn, baby, you scared the hell out of me."

Instead of helping me with the groceries, and when Emjay walked off with a grimace without the usual greeting of a kiss and "hey baby," I knew something wasn't right, that he was angry about something, that maybe he didn't get the movie theater job he wanted.

"Baby, is everything okay?" I asked as I set the bags of food and my attaché case on the kitchen table.

"I'm good," he said sternly. I always knew he was mad or didn't want to talk about something based on these one- to two-word answers he would give. *Hate when he does this passive-aggressive shit*, I thought. I wasn't sure I wanted to know what was bothering him.

"How did the job interview go?" When I attempted to cuddle with him, he jerked away. "What's wrong with you?"

"It might be better to show you what's wrong."

As soon as he grabbed my iPad off the coffee table, I knew he had seen the video. I remembered when I got to campus this morning that I'd left it on the dining room table. As soon as he opened the attachment, I wanted to jump out of my skin.

"I can explain."

"What is this, Shariece? Who took this?"

"I got the email on Monday while I was in my office grading papers."

Emjay got up and began pacing the living room floor. I could sense the anger that was coming off of him.

"What the fuck. Somebody videotaped us." I knew that if I told him it was Deandre, not even God could keep him away from beating his ass. "You know who it is, don't you?"

"Jay, I don't know who sent the video. The email doesn't look familiar. When I responded to it, my message was kicked back to me."

"Well, whoever the fuck he is, he wants you to meet him."

"I have no plans to meet up with whoever this is," I lied.

"You don't have to, 'cuz I'm going to get up with this sick fuck myself."

"And then what?"

"What the hell do you mean and then what? I'm going to break their fuckin' neck."

"And *that* is exactly why you're not going anywhere near this man."

"Hold up, how do you know he's a dude?"

"What?"

"You just said you don't know who it is, Shariece, so how do you know it's a guy?" I had never seen Emjay so pissed. "You know this nigga, don't you?" I scrambled for the right words. "Did you meet up with this motherfucker already?"

"Jay, I got us into this. This is my—"

Before I could push out the rest of what I had to say, Emjay turned over the coffee table in an angry rage. "Fuuuck!"

"Baby, calm down."

"Shariece, have you seen that fucking video? I'm on that shit too."

"But I stand a lot more to lose. If this gets out, it could ruin me. I'll never walk into another classroom again."

"I can't believe you said that. You think that I don't have nothing to lose? Do you think that I can just go on with shit as usual with something like that floating around?"

"I didn't mean it like that."

"I could get kicked out of school. Shit like this could follow me, us around for the rest of our lives, but that's cool; maybe I'll have a great career in the porn industry."

"I told you I'll handle it."

"So what does he want? I know ya'll didn't meet to talk about the fucking weather over chocolate frosties."

"You need to calm down."

"Don't tell me to calm down, and stop talking to me like I'm a fucking teenager and tell me what happened."

"Nothing happened, Jay!"

"What does he want, money?"

"He doesn't want money."

"I find that hard to believe. This dude's blackmailing you and he doesn't want money?"

"He wants me to write him a letter of recommendation?"

"Hold up. This motherfucker's a student?"

"I told you I'll take care of it, goddamn."

"What else does he want?"

"That's it," I lied.

"Bullshit. What else does he want?" All of Emjay's yelling had given me a headache.

"He said he would give me the copy of the video if I had sex with him."

"So that's what his ass meant at the bookstore?"

"Who?"

"Deandre Knowles showed up at the bookstore today asking me questions about you."

I noticed scarring on Emjay's knuckles. "Jay, what happened to your hand?" He covered his bruised left hand with the right one. "Did you and Deandre get into a fight?"

"I wasn't going to let him disrespect you."

"That's your answer for everything. If somebody says something you don't like, you get in their face?"

"If they disrespect me and you, you're damn right."

"You can't go punching people every time they do, or say something you don't like. It's no wonder you didn't get carried off to jail."

"I can take care of myself, just like I'm going to take care of Deandre. I'm going to get the video, all the copies, then I'm going to finish beatin' that ass."

"You are not going anywhere near him." Emjay looked around the living room. "What are you looking for?"

"My car keys. I'm going over to Deandre's."

"The hell you are. You're drunk. There's no damn way I'm going to let you drive in your condition." I wrestled the keys out of his hand.

"Shariece, stop playing and give me my keys."

Emjay could barely stay upright.

"I told you; I got this."

"You're gonna fuck him, aren't you?"

"You need to lie down somewhere and sleep it off."

"Mama was right about you. You're nothing but a ho."

I knew he didn't mean what he said, that it was the vodka talking. Emjay stumbled back onto the sofa where he passed out. I rummaged through my purse for the napkin Deandre wrote his number and address on. I retrieved it from the bottom of my bag smudged with makeup. I dialed his number as I watched Emjay snore on the sofa.

"What up, this is Dre."

"It's me. We need to talk."

"Hey, baby girl. I was just thinking about you. Have you given any thought to what we discussed?"

The mere sound of his voice made me want to throw up in my mouth. "I'm coming over."

"I'll be here, hard, willing and able."

I hung up before he could say another word. It was time to put an end to all of this. First, Myrick's psycho crazy-ass, now Deandre.

"This ends now."

THIRTY-FIVE
DEANDRE

"I'm gonna beat the breaks off that pussy." I popped an Altoid into my mouth and sprayed on some Tommy. Breath: check. Armpits: check. I pulled two wineglasses I'd bought from Picr 1 Imports, from the cabinet and a bottle of Merlot out of the refrigerator. My dick was already harder than granite to the thought of deep-dicking Shariece. She'd be speaking in tongues by the time I was done with her, won't be able to walk for a week. "Drink enough of this liquid candy, and I'll forget that pretty boy sucker-punched me today. One lick in was all his ass was going to get. He better be glad that toy cop pulled us apart today 'cuz I would have killed his high-yellow ass. Where I come from, niggas play for keeps. I should have went strapped. Shit never would have gone down like that had I had my piece on me. But fuck that nigga. He ain't worth it.

When the glare from Shariece's ride seeped between the blinds on my window, I checked my shit one last time. Breath, armpits, balls, check, check and check. I looked at myself in the mirror admiring how good I looked. "I would fuck me." I was about to answer the door when I remembered something. "Fuck, I almost forgot the camera." I had it set up between some photography books on the entertainment center where I had it pointed directly at the sofa. "Press play, press record, done." Shariece rang the doorbell twice before I answered. "Damn, you want this dick bad, don't you, baby girl?" I walked over smelling and feeling good.

"We need to talk," she said, busting up in my crib looking like a bitch on a mission.

"Well, hey to you too, baby." Shariece had this serious look on her face.

"What did you do to Emjay?"

"What did *I* do to him?"

"He saw the video."

"Okay, and?"

"He said he saw you in the bookstore. What did you tell him?"

"That nigga is something else. He walks around like he wipes his ass with diamonds, the way he kisses your ass, such a fucking teacher's pet. I see how he looks at you in class; you try to play it off like you ain't feeling him. I suspected something was going on with the two of ya'll, but I couldn't put my finger on it."

"He knows now that you videotaped us."

"So you came clean, huh? I didn't think you had it in you."

"He found out when I left my laptop on."

I walked over to the table where I had the bottle of wine and two glasses. "That's fucked up. Sorry to hear that."

"If you were really sorry, you wouldn't be blackmailing me."

I popped the cork off the bottle and poured. "Let's not talk about that right now. Let's have a drink."

"I didn't come here for all that. Here's the recommendation letter; now where's the flash drive with the video on it?"

THIRTY-SIX
SHARIECE

I wanted to jump clean out of my skin if not the nearest window when I caught a whiff of Deandre's cheap-ass, bargain-bin cologne. "I will erase the video if you kiss me first."

I would have preferred to kiss a skunk's ass than Deandre.

"If I kiss you, will you give me the flash drive?"

"Sure, baby, anything you want," he said as he drew in close to me, putting his grimy-ass hands on me. I trusted Deandre about as far as I could throw him.

"One kiss," I told him.

I braced myself as he came closer. I balled both of my hands into a fist as he kissed me. I made my lips tight, so he wouldn't try to stick his nasty tongue in my mouth. I wouldn't touch someone like Deandre to scratch him, but I didn't have a choice if I wanted what I came for. I shut my eyes tight wishing I was anywhere other than his apartment. The smell of onions on his breath that he attempted to mask with an Altoid was enough to make me dry-heave. I didn't object when I felt him grab my booty, but a small price to pay to save Emjay and me.

"Okay, you got your damn kiss; now where's the flash drive?" When Deandre tugged me hard against him, I could feel his hard-on against my thigh. His hands tightened like a vise grip on my ass. I could feel his dick pressing against my thigh. "Get the fuck off me."

"Girl, stop tripping, damn. We had a deal." His hands felt like iron braces on my arm. This bastard was losing his mind. "You give me what I want, you get what you want."

My heart was pumping crazy in my chest. I had wandered into a snake's den, and it was up to me on whether or not I was going to get bitten. Deandre kept kissing me, licking my neck and chest. Like I said, jump out of my skin. I thought back to when all this had started, wishing I could go back into a time machine to that day we were in my office. It was because of me we were in this situation.

When Deandre tore at my blouse, I pushed him off me. "What the hell is wrong with you?" I asked as I wiped my mouth with the back of my hand.

"I like it a little rough," Deandre said, as he cut me a devil-slick grin.

"I'm not doing this." Deandre looked at me with a menacing glare.

"I love a bitch that plays hard to get." He started to rip at my blouse again.

"Get off me!" I screamed. We struggled. Deandre threw me down on the sofa, got on top of me and pushed his hand up under my skirt, trying to get at my panties.

"Whatcho got for me, Mrs. Santa."

I tried to push him off me, but his hold was too strong.

"Get off!" I scratched him across his face as hard as I could.

"Fucking bitch." Deandre backhanded me across the face. The sting was instant. I could taste blood forming in my mouth as he manhandled me with brute force. The fear I felt turned to rage, so with all my strength, I kicked him in the balls with my knee. When he braced his balls in pain, I threw him off me onto the floor, causing the bottle and wineglasses to tumble to the floor.

"You goddamn bitch." When he tried to make his way up on his feet, I took the stem of one of the broken wineglasses and slashed him across the chest. Deandre felt at his chest where I drew blood. "Bitch, I'm gonna fucking kill you."

"You move and I'll slice your fuckin' throat." Deandre looked at me and knew I meant every word I said. "Now where the fuck is the flash drive?"

"I'm fucking bleeding," he said.

"I don't give a fuck," I huffed. "I'm not going to ask your ass again."

"It's in my book bag over there in the recliner."

"If you move, I'll shove this in your stomach." I rushed over to the desk where a blue backpack sat in a Lay-Z-Boy. I rummaged through it until I found the flash drive.

"You ain't nothing but a fucking tease."

I noticed his laptop that was sitting on the kitchen counter.

"Is this the only copy?"

"Fuck you."

I took the broken-off stem from the wineglass and ran it along the other right side of his face that was scratched. "I asked you a question. Is this the only copy?"

"Yeah, damn, that's the only copy," Deandre said, holding his hand up to his face. I didn't cut him deep, but enough to draw blood. I took his laptop and slammed it on the kitchen floor. I made my way to the door. I couldn't wait to get out of there. "Take your underwear off."

"What?"

"You heard me; take off your underwear. I don't want you chasing after me after I leave, so take them off."

Deandre was hesitant, but he did what I told him.

I laughed when I caught a glimpse of his circus peanut-size dick. "Are you serious? Is that what you were going to fuck me with?"

"Fuck you, bitch."

"Oh, you wish, motherfucker." I couldn't get out of there fast enough as I jumped in my car and hauled ass.

THIRTY-SEVEN
MYRICK

When I saw Shariece walk out of her apartment, I almost couldn't believe how beautiful she looked, even with the few pounds she had put on since I had last seen her, which was in a Leon County courtroom, days before I was sentenced. I followed her to an apartment off of Jackson Bluff. "Must be the boyfriend's crib." Shariece was at his place for a good long time. "Up in there fucking, I bet." Rage came over me at the thought of her fucking another man. I clenched the knife in my hand I had pulled from the glove box. My initial thought was to kill them both, but the thought of laying a hand on my Shariece made me sick to my guts. The only way she and I would ever have a chance to reconcile was to get rid of him. I waited for two hours in the parking lot until it got dark when Shariece finally came out, storming down the stairs of the second-level apartment complex. She looked scared. "What the fuck did he do to her?" I watched her drive off before I went up, gripping the knife tightly as I held it out of sight in one of the pockets of my hoodie. I was dressed in black, wearing a cap and dark shades. I made my way up to apartment 2B, the same crib I saw Shariece run out of, and rang the doorbell. He didn't answer, so I banged on the door.

"Hold the fuck up, damn," I heard him say. Yeah, he sounded like a pussy. *When did she start dating punks?* I could hear this motherfucker stomping toward the door from inside his crib. He flung the door open wearing only a pair of ugly-ass purple satin boxers, holding a wet dishcloth up to his face.

"Who the fuck are you?"

I grabbed him by the throat and pushed him back inside and slammed the door behind me with the butt of my left foot.

"So you're the boyfriend."

"Man, who the fuck are you?" he asked, attempting to break free from my grip, but the more he struggled, the tighter I made my hold. I could have busted his windpipe if I wanted to, but that would have been too easy, and I like to have a little fun first, and I was going to play with this one like a new action figure. There was a long gash across his chest that ran from the left armpit to the right, so Shariece had already worked his ass over. There was glass and a busted computer on the floor, so I knew whatever had gone down, it was nothing nice.

I pushed him back over one of the end tables, causing a lamp to crash and break to the floor.

"Did you hurt her?"

"Hurt who, man? Who the fuck are you?"

I kneeled down at him as he felt pain in the lower part of his back. The minute I brandished my knife, I could feel his fear seep in.

"I'm not going to ask you again. What did you do to her?"

"To who?"

"Shariece!" I yelled, as I planted the sharp top of the blade into his leg. He hollered out as blood seeped from the deep gash I had made. I took the knife stained with his blood and held it up to his throat. "Did you hurt her?"

"Man, I didn't do shit. Look at me. I'm the one bleeding." *I get out of prison only to find that this is who she's been shacking up with? She replaced me with a twelve-year-old?* "You tell that bitch that I'm going to put her ass on blast to anyone who will listen. She's fucked with the wrong—." I slashed him across the throat before he finished his threat. He grabbed at his throat, throttling about as he attempted to stop the blood gushing from his neck.

I watched as the last seconds of life drained out of his eyes as blood pooled into the carpet. "You can't do anything if you're dead."

THIRTY-EIGHT
LEANDRA

My back was killing me. "I can't sleep on that sofa." Taj was dead to the world, sounding like a freight train in my ear with all that damn snoring. It reminded me I needed to stop by Walgreens and get him some of those nasal strips Nishelle had told me about. I was willing to try anything to keep him from doing all that snoring. Ask Taj, and he'd swear up and down that he didn't snore.

I woke up to him spooning me with his arm snaked around my waist. He felt hard and warm against me. That's what I love about Taj, his ability to make me feel safe, like nothing can hurt me, which was something I never felt when Rick was alive. Can't believe he's been dead for twenty-two years. After I buried Rick, there was barely time to mourn the man. I was a single mother who had a son to raise into a man. I wanted Emjay as far away from the street life as I could get him. I would rather see him dead than to end up like his daddy selling dope or running with one of these gangs out here. I've seen too many kids die from all this craziness out here. Saw on the news last night that a six-year-old boy was shot and killed by his eight-year-old brother after finding his daddy's gun in the house. I don't know what I would do if something ever happened to Emjay. I don't have nobody but the good Lord Jesus to thank for leading my boy in the right direction. And to think that I raised him all by myself. Lord knows, it was hard, but I did it.

I walked to the bathroom to see if there was something in the medicine cabinet to numb the pain in my back I had endured from that lumpy sofa. "Please let me have some Aleve in here." I jinxed it as soon as I opened the medicine cabinet to find that I was out. There was only Tylenol and Ibuprofen, which was nowhere near as good. "Add Aleve to the list along with nasal strips." I had some Icy Hot, but I wanted something to work on contact. I popped two Tylenol and hoped the pain would quickly go away.

The digital clock that sat on one of my bedside tables read four minutes past eleven. "Feels later than that." Taj was dead to the world snoring and drooling on my sofa. With the crazy hours he'd been putting in at that magazine, I let him sleep and went to the kitchen for a little late-night snack. I raided the cabinets to find a box of Cheez-Its sandwiched between a box of Sugar Smacks and Honey Nut Cheerios. I grabbed the box of snack food from the cabinet and sat down at the kitchen table where something that looked like a book manuscript sat opposite me. My interests had piqued. I glanced down at the bottom of the title page that read *Directed* by Jimi Bryan Productions. I flipped through a few of the pages to the casting list where I recognized Taj's name with *Dillon Durke* typed next to it. I began to read the words typed in courier. There was dialogue like "feed me that big black dick" and "break that dick off in me" running through my mind like ticker tape. It was then that I knew what it was. "Is this what he's been working on?" I noticed that this Dillon Durke role he was playing included him fucking a man named Vance. I read until I felt myself get sick to my stomach. I sat and thought all the phone calls he made to me saying that he would be home late, that I shouldn't wait up. "Fashion shoot, my ass." I grew angry and pissed as I thought of all the lies Taj had told me night after night. I hauled off to the living room with the script rolled tightly in my grip to where Taj was sleeping.

I stood over him. "Taj, wake up." He didn't hear me, but just kept on snoring and drooling like an overgrown-ass baby. "Taj, get up!" I yelled. He rolled over on his left side, turning his back to me. I was so hot, I could have spat lava. "Taj, wake yo' ass up!" I yelled, whacking him across his head with the thick, rolled-up script. He was lucky it wasn't something harder than that.

"What the hell," he said, with his eyes squinching to the lights of the ceiling fan that hung in the center of the room.

"What the fuck is this?"

"What is what?"

"This shit right here," I said, hitting him in the head again. Taj shielded his head with his arms in protection from my assault. "Is this the kind of shit you do when you're working these damn sixteen-hour days with the magazine?"

"Baby, what are you talking about?"

"Taj, don't play games with me. I'm not in the mood. I saw this sitting on the kitchen table. What the fuck have you been out here doing all time of the night?"

Taj's eyes adjusted to the ceiling fan light. "It's just a script."

"I know it's a script. I'm not stupid. I can also see in here that your name is on here where you play some dude named Dillon Durke."

Taj sat up, rubbing sleep out of his eyes. "Lee, I can explain."

"You're not working on a fashion shoot, are you?" He looked at me like he was reaching for the next lie to tell. "Are you really a photographer?"

"Okay, look, a few months before I met you, I fell on hard times."

"Oh, I bet. Fell on a hard dick, you mean."

"It's nothing like that. I was going to school like I told you, but I lost my financial aid after failing a few classes. I came close to being evicted out of my crib and losing my SUV."

"So, you what, went out and started fucking other men for money on camera?"

"Lee, you know how hard it is out here to find a job. I busted my ass applying for anything I was qualified to work, and putting in applications for every 'now hiring' sign I saw. The only thing I could get was flipping burgers at Mickey D's or working at Walmart like every other black man in Tallahassee."

"Flipping burgers is better than doing this shit."

"I was going to tell you."

"When exactly were you going to tell me that you suck dick for money?"

"Shut up. I don't suck nobody's dick."

"Then what then?"

"I…"

"You let faggots suck on your dick, is that it; or do you let them fuck you?"

"I don't do nothing I don't want to do; let's get that shit straight."

"So are you gay, Taj?"

"Fuck no. I ain't no faggot."

"Then why are you doing this shit here for?"

"I do it for money, that's it. I don't get fucked and I don't suck no nigga's dick. Jimi gave me the script to look it over, to offer up some suggestions."

I sat there with my hand against my forehead.

"You come home to me, and stick your dick in me after you've fucked men up the ass. You're disgusting."

"It's not even like that." When Taj tried to console me, I pulled away. "Don't touch me."

"Jimi runs a clean production company. Everybody gets tested."

"Oh, so that shit is supposed to make me feel better about you letting guys suck on your black-ass dick?"

"I was trying to figure out the right time to tell you."

"Nigga, there's no right time to tell somebody some fucked-up shit like that. You got gay niggas slobbering all over your dick."

"Baby, it's just a job, that's all."

To hear him call me *baby* was enough to turn my stomach. "I can't believe I'm hearing this shit right now."

"I'm clean, Lee, and I don't bring nothing home to you."

I could no longer stand to even look at Taj. "I think I'm going to throw up."

"Lee, I'm sorry that I wasn't upfront with you. You gotta know that I didn't mean to hurt you."

"But yet and still, you have. You know the fucked-up part isn't that you work in gay porn; it's that you lied, Taj, about what you do for a living."

"I guess I was afraid of how you would react."

"Oh, fuck you. You're not a fuckin' child. Why do men feel like they always gotta lie about every little-ass thing? How can ya'll sit here, fix your mouth and say you love somebody, but then go behind a bitch's back and lie?"

"Other than I'm sorry, I don't know what else to say to you."

"Who are you? Who the fuck is the man that I've been sharing my bed with for the past six months?"

"I'm still the same Taj Bowman that you met at the Blue Moon. I haven't changed, baby girl. I'm still me."

"Shit, I doubt that."

"Let me ask you this: would you have gone out with me had I told you what I do for a living?"

"Whether I would have gone out with you or not, is not the damn point, Taj, and you know it. You lied, Taj. You looked me dead in my face for months on end and lied to me. It doesn't matter how I would have reacted. We're supposed to tell each other everything. What else are you keeping from me?"

"I'm not hiding anything else."

"What, you got like a litter of kids out here that I don't know about, maybe you on the down low with some nigga, or maybe he's the one you playing house with and I'm the down-low bitch. Is that it?"

"I told you. It's only a paycheck, that's it. I don't have any kids unaccounted for and I'm not on the down low with nobody."

"How am I supposed to believe anything that comes out of your mouth? First, my son and my best friend have been fucking around behind my back, and now I find out my man is on some gay-for-pay bullshit?"

"Look, the bottom line is, I was afraid of losing you if I told you the truth."

"Yet, you have lost me with a lie."

"What?"

"You know what; you're a grown-ass man. I can't stop you from doing nothing you don't want to do. If you want to fuck men, fine, but I'll be damned if you're going to make a fool out of Leandra Fox." I hurled the script at Taj. "I want you to get your shit, and get the fuck out of my house."

"Baby, come on, let's talk about this."

"Fuck you. I'm done talking. I want you and all your shit out of my house, and I want you out of my life; we're through."

THIRTY-NINE
TAJ

Everything I carried over from Lee's was enough to fit into a small suitcase. She had locked me out of the bedroom, which was a first. "I know you don't want to talk or see me right now, Lee, but I'm not giving up on you; I'm not going to give up on us. I know there's nothing I can say to make this better, but I'm damn sure going to try. I'm going to talk to Jimi and tell him that I quit, that I can't do it anymore. I don't give a damn if I wind up working at Burger King. At least I will have you. If you need to reach me, you know where to find me. I will understand if you don't want anything to do with me again, but know that I love you and I will always care about you." In a perfect world, I wanted her to fling the door open, throw herself into my arms and confess her undying love to me, but I knew with how she had gone off on me, the chance of that happening was zero. I threw my suitcase filled with whatever I had brought over, and set it on the floor in the backseat of my car. I took the script that Jimi had given me, that had literally fucked up what I had with Lee, and flung it out of the window. It was time that I leave that world. I was getting sick of the drug use, the late-night hours, and it was past time for me to clean my life up, go back to school, finish my degree.

I honestly didn't feel like going back to my place. Sitting at home and feeling sorry for myself, would have only made things worse. I called up my boy, Deandre to see what was up, but his phone kept ringing until it clicked over to voicemail. "This is Dre, you know what to do." I hate that voicemail shit, so I didn't bother to leave a message, but instead decided to drive over to his apartment. Dre would always give me good advice, especially when it came down to women. Yeah, he could do some fucked-up shit sometimes, but he was my boy, and really was the only brother I trusted. I was relieved to see that he was home after seeing his silver Charger parked in the lot of his apartment complex. I rushed up to the second floor and knocked on the door, but there was no answer. When I knocked again, the door eased open. Deandre was lying on the floor in a pool of blood.

I rushed over to him thinking that maybe he was still alive, but I could tell by the deep slash across his throat and death in his eyes, that Dre was dead. There was glass everywhere; the place looked like it had been ransacked. My hand was shaking when I took out my phone to dial 9-1-1. The stench of blood was enough to make me dry-heave, so I ran outside where I threw up outside of Dre's apartment. It didn't take the cops long to get to his place when I told them that somebody was dead. They take their sweet-ass time if it's anything short of someone being murdered. Two cop cars arrived at the complex with blaring sirens that lit up the lot. Before long, the place was teeming with po-po, paramedics and firemen. This bald cop in plain-dress clothes, Italian-looking, who looked like he was made for breaking balls, arrived on the scene.

"Can ya'll cover him up, damn." The cop glanced over at me when one of the uniform pigs pointed me out to him. I've watched enough episodes of *The First 48* to know that he was one of those homicide detectives.

"Hi, I'm Detective Stambler." He fished a small memo pad out of one of the breast pockets of his shirt. "What's your name, son?"

"Taj Bowman."

Cops and coroners filled Deandre's apartment, stomping thoughtlessly all over the place, touching shit with their latex gloves, treating it like it was some kind of damn biohazard.

"How do you know the deceased?"

"His name is Deandre Hartman. He was a friend of mine."

"What time did you arrive on the scene?"

"I don't know. Around one-thirty, two o'clock."

"So what did you see when you arrived on the scene?"

"I knocked on the door, but there was no answer. When I pushed the door open, that's when I saw Deandre lying dead on the floor."

"Do you know anyone who would want to hurt Mr. Hartman?"

"No, no one I can think of."

"Are you sure?"

"I told you, no, there's nobody. Man, do all these cops have to be in there like that, walking all around his body and shit. They need to have some fucking respect."

The cop directed one of the coroners to put a sheet over him.

He waved at one of the uniform cops and told him to cover Deandre up.

"Well, Mr. Bowman, I don't think we have any more questions for you. You're free to go, but stick around. We may need to ask you some more questions."

"What? That's it?"

"If we have more questions, we will give you a call."

"So, I'm supposed to what, sit around with my thumbs up my ass to find out what happened to my friend?"

"Mr. Bowman, there's nothing you can do here."

"It's obvious someone killed him."

"You don't know that."

"Well, he didn't slash his own damn throat."

"Marc, we found something," one of the CSIs yelled. He pulled a camera off the entertainment center.

"What is that?" I asked.

"Mr. Bowman, you need to leave. We will call you if we have any more questions or details of the case."

"Whoever killed Deandre is on that camera."

"Officer Whalen, could you please escort Mr. Bowman off the premises?"

I took one last look at Deandre's body knowing that the next time I would see him again would be at his funeral.

"Fuck off, I'm leaving," I said as I tugged my arm away out of that pig's grip when he attempted to take me by the arm and escort me out of Dre's apartment. My life was unraveling at the seams. I had lost my girlfriend and my best friend all in the same day. What the fuck was going on?

FORTY
EMJAY

When I managed to pry my eyes open, beams of sunlight speared in from between the slits of the Venetian blinds. My head felt like a wrecking ball had hit it. I was slightly disoriented, not sure what day of the week it was until I looked at the time and the day on my cell phone. It was seven minutes after nine, Thursday morning, the day of the poetry reading. The aroma of chocolate chip pancakes permeated throughout the room. The half a bottle of whiskey I had downed last night felt like it was coming out of every pore in my body. I usually would beat anyone to the kitchen table for chocolate chip pancakes, but the way my head was throbbing and the iron butterflies that were fluttering around in my stomach, chocolate chip pancakes had might as well smelled like chitterlings. I sat on the edge of the bed allowing my brain to shake itself loose from the liquid haze. I remembered bits and pieces of the fight Shariece and I'd had. It was about the video, that perverted shit Deandre had taken of us.

"Good morning," Shariece said, as she walked in holding a tray that held a plate of chocolate chip pancakes, bacon and a glass of milk.

"How are you feeling, or do I need to ask?"

"Other than my head feeling like someone had taken a sledge-hammer to it, I'm breathing."

Shariece set the tray of food on one of the bedside tables. "This will help with the hangover." She handed me a glass of water and two small, light-blue pills. "What are these?"

"It's two Aleve. I swear on the Bible by them."

I took the pills, popped them into my mouth, and chased them down with a swig of water. "Hangovers were the only thing I hated about drinking. I didn't throw up nowhere on the floor, did I?"

"Thankfully, no."

"Good to know I can still hold my liquor."

"You need to put something on your stomach."

"I'm surprised you're here."

"Why is that?"

"After the things I said to you last night, surprised you still want anything to do with me."

"I know that was just the whiskey talking. I know you didn't mean none of it."

"I need to talk to Deandre about that video."

"Speaking of which." Shariece opened the bedside table and pulled out a flash drive.

"What is that?"

"It's a flash drive with the video of us on it."

"How did you get a hold of that?"

"Jay, I told you that I would take of it and I did."

"What do you mean you took care of it?"

Shariece took a deep breath. "I went to go talk to Deandre last night about getting the video."

"Goddamn, Shariece, I told you not to go to his apartment without me."

"Baby, stop, okay. Look, all that matters is that I got the flash drive."

"Are you sure that's it?"

"Yes. I looked at it and it's the video."

"How do you know that he doesn't have copies laying around somewhere?"

"He doesn't."

"You know that for sure?"

"It took some convincing. He doesn't have any copies."

"What do you mean, convincing?"

"I know what you're thinking and I didn't fuck him to get this."

"So when you went over there, what happened?"

"I didn't get in the apartment good before he started pawing all over me. Jay, it was nothing I couldn't handle."

"So how did you get that from him without sticking your pussy in his face?"

Shariece sucked her teeth. "How many times do I have to tell you that I didn't fuck him? I didn't fuck him, I didn't suck his dick, I didn't even tickle the man."

"I believe you."

"It doesn't sound like you believe me."

Honestly, I wasn't sure what to believe.

"It wasn't easy to get the flash drive. He got a little rough with me."

"What do you mean? Did he put his hands on you?"

"He slapped me."

"Take your shades off."

"It's really not that bad."

"Baby, let me see." Shariece hesitantly pulled the shades from her face, exposing a dark bruise that was two inches below her eye.

"Did he do that to you?"

"Forget about it. It's nothing."

"Tell me what happened?" Shariece began pacing the bedroom floor.

"I know I shouldn't have gone over there without you. I admit that was stupid."

"True."

"But I knew that had I taken you with me, things would have been a lot worse."

"I would have broken his damn neck."

"Which is exactly why I didn't take you with me, plus, you were drunk anyway."

"So what the hell happened when you went over there?"

"I went to exchange the tape for the letter. It's obvious he had something else in mind because he came to the door wearing next to nothing. I wanted to tell him to go fuck himself and walk back out of the door, but I had to get that tape not just for myself, but for the both of us. I got us jammed up, so I needed to get us out of it."

"Shariece, I admit that we should have been more careful, but Deandre was the perverted fuck who videotaped us, and tried to blackmail you. He's sick. I don't blame you for doing what you had to do."

"I gave him the recommendation letter, but when I asked for the flash drive with the video on it, he wouldn't give it up until I kissed him."

"What the fuck?"

"I didn't kiss him. Deandre kissed me. When I pulled away, that's when he started to get rough, pulling at my blouse, grabbing me by the arm and threw me down on the sofa."

"Did he rape you?"

"He tried to when he figured out that I wasn't going to fuck him."

"Fuck, I should have been there."

"He threw himself on top of me, pulling at my clothes. I scratched him and threw him off me. When he tried to get up, I cut him with a broken wineglass."

"Shit. Was that enough to keep him off you?"

"I told him that if he didn't tell me where the flash drive was, I would slit his throat."

"So he told you where it was?"

"Deandre didn't really have a choice at that point."

"Did anyone see you?"

"What do you mean?"

"Did anyone see you come out or go into his place?"

"I don't know."

"Nothing, it's cool, baby. I'm just glad you're okay."

"I got out of there as quick as I could."

"So you're sure this is the only copy?"

"He claimed it was, but I smashed his laptop just to make sure, and I took every single flash drive I could find. I wasn't taking any chances."

We checked each flash drive to make sure there weren't copies of the video lingering around. Shariece deleted the attachment that had Deandre sent. We took all the drives to the stove, turned on one of the caps, and burned them. We watched them melt into a black liquid sludge.

"I'm sorry," Shariece said.

"For what?"

"For not listening to you."

"The most important thing is that you're okay." I slid my arm around Shariece and pulled her close to me.

"I'm just glad it's over and we can get on with our lives."

"You and me both," I said.

FORTY-ONE
MYRICK

July, 1991

The cops had ruled Mama's death an accident. Rashawn and I had to go live with our Aunt Inez in Carrabelle. I hated it there. It was ten times smaller than Tallahassee and everyone's idea of fun was sitting in the parking lot of Walmart, riding in shopping carts. Auntie Inez was nothing like Mama. She was Glinda the Good Witch compared to Mama's wicked ass. I wondered how in the hell they were even cut from the same cloth. Rashawn was at a loss without Mama constantly reminding him how handsome he is, and how his pretty ass could do no wrong. Rashawn went from being a straight-A geek to putting needles in his arm, and I was loving every tragic minute of it. She didn't pull any of that special treatment shit with him like Mama did. Auntie Inez fed us and made sure we had a warm bed to sleep in, but I think all she cared about was how much money she would get back on her income tax every year when she claimed two more mouths to feed including our cousin, Kirk.

I remember making trips on Thanksgiving and Christmas to

visit Auntie Inez back when we were kids. Kirk was always trying to fuck with me and Rashawn, try to boss us around, tell us where to sleep and what toys we could and couldn't play with. We found out when we moved in with Auntie Inez that old habits die hard. One day after being tired of being bullied, I decided to put Kirk' ass in his place. Auntie Inez was out on another one of her dates. *Apple doesn't ever fall too far from the tree,* I thought. Kirk was in charge to babysit even though the three of us were grown teenagers who could take care of ourselves. Kirk would get worse when Auntie Inez wasn't around; telling us we had to follow his rules and do what he wanted. "Where the fuck is that written?" I asked. Kirk didn't say anything, but walked up on me and punched me as hard as he could in the gut. Putting his hands on me was his first mistake, and his last. Rashawn always went along with Kirk knowing that he would get a dose of what I got if his ass didn't fall in line. What Auntie Inez didn't know is that Kirk had a thing for messing with boys. Now I don't know if he was a fag or not. He was always weird even back when we were kids. He used to make me, him and this retarded boy named Grady take our dicks out, and rub them together. I thought he had outgrown his perverted phase until he started coming in my room. I would catch him trying to touch my dick under the covers while I was trying to sleep. I would push him off me, but he would punch me in the stomach and say, "Lay your ass down." I used to shut my eyes tight when he would put my dick in his mouth. I was about nine or ten the first time it happened. When we moved in with Auntie Inez, I found out that Kirk was still a nasty perverted fuck. Who knows how many boys he had messed with over the years? It was a little after midnight when he crept into my and Rashawn's room. I would act like I was asleep, but wasn't. I remember how the hinges on the door creaked when Kirk walked in. I could sense him standing over me from all the body heat he was giving off.

"Wake up," he whispered loudly in a demanding tone. I ignored him at first as I gripped a straight-edged razor in my hand under my pillow.

"Nigga, I know you ain't sleep." I pried my eyes open to find him standing over me with his dick protruding from the gape of his pajama pants.

"Suck my dick." I glanced over at Rashawn whose back was turned to us. I knew his pussy-ass was faking, that he heard every word that was said, but as usual, he was too chicken shit to say or do anything. Why Kirk always went after me, I had no clue. Maybe it was because he liked boys tough and hard to fuck with.

"Do it, faggot, suck my dick."

"Fuck you," I told him, as I tightened my grip around the handle of the razor.

"Fuck did you say?" When he punched me in the kidneys, that's when I raised up and slashed off the tip of his dick. That shit was so fast, I don't even think he knew what had happened, what I had done until he saw all the blood gushing from the cut. I sat in bed and watched as Kurt grabbed his privates, screaming in pain. There was blood everywhere: my bed, the floor. Kurt looked like he had been dipped in blood. His screams were enough to wake up the whole neighborhood. Rashawn didn't move until he heard Kirk screaming. I had never heard anyone yell and holler as loud as he did. It was like he was dying, and maybe he was, but I knew he would never put his hands on me again. Blood was running down his leg, pooling on the floor.

"Myrick, what the hell did you do?" Rashawn yelled, standing there, watching Kirk bleed to death. I ran over to him armed with the razor and held it at his molesting-ass throat.

"Open your mouth."

"You cut my dick," he yelled, as he cupped the area that was gushing blood.

"And I'll hack off the rest if you don't open your fucking mouth."

"Man, what the fuck?" Rashawn yelled.

"Rashawn, shut the fuck up!"

"I'm not going to tell you again, open your fucking mouth." When Kirk hesitantly did what he was told, I took the severed tip of my cousin's dick and stuffed it into his mouth. "Now you know what your own dick tastes like, bitch." Kirk puked and began to shake.

"We need to call nine-one-one," Rashawn yelled.

"Fuck him. Let his ass bleed to death."

I sat on the edge of my bed with the razor as Rashawn called for help. Unfortunately, the doctor was able to piece his dick back on, but he would be pissing in a Ziploc bag for the rest of his life. The cops removed me after Rashawn snitched and told them everything about what happened. I was put back into Child Protective Services until I aged out at eighteen. I didn't give a fuck. I was glad to be out on my own finally. I was my own man and didn't have to answer to nobody. I went back to Tallahassee the minute I got enough money saved up from working as a dishwasher at the Waffle House. Killing Mama awoke a craving in me to kill. It was like it was in my blood or something, like I had been possessed. To look into the eyes of my victims, and see the last signs of life leave them, made me feel powerful, like there was nothing I couldn't do. From that point on, if anyone got in my way, kept me from getting what I wanted, I would come down on them like a hammer. Nobody would ever hurt me again. If anyone was going to do any hurting, it was going to be me from now on.

FORTY-TWO
LEANDRA

After my fight with Taj, I wasn't in the best of moods. I didn't want to stay home and be pissed off all day, nor did I want to go to the salon and sit around in my office sulking, thinking about how Taj had lied to me, thinking about him sticking his dick up another man's ass for money. I had hoped by burying myself in work, it would take my mind off his confession, but it was all I could think about, visions in my head of men sucking his dick. I mean, out of all the jobs he could have gotten: busboy, server, flipping burgers, digging ditches, he takes a job doing gay porn. "Why do men feel like they have to lie about everything?"

"Because they know we will beat the black off their asses if we find out." Nishelle startled me when I turned around to find her standing in the doorway of my office. "My bad, girl. I didn't mean to eavesdrop."

"No, it's fine. I was just thinking out loud."

"Is everything okay? You've been a bit distant today."

"Everything's fine," I lied. I wasn't sure if anything would ever be fine again. "I've just had a lot on my mind."

"You want to talk about it?"

I leaned back from the mounds of paperwork that littered my desk. "Nishelle, if I tell you something, will you promise to take it to your grave?"

"Of course, absolutely," Nishelle said as she closed the door and sat down across from me at my desk.

"I'm serious. If you tell anyone at all about what I'm about to tell you, there will be nowhere for you to hide," I said in a kind of half-joking tone.

"I swear on my mama, on God's good Bible, I won't utter a word." Even after Nishelle swore on her mama and God, I was still hesitant to tell her my business.

"It's about Taj."

"What about him?"

"Me and him had a huge fight last night."

"About what, what happened?"

"He lied to me, Nishelle. He lied about everything."

"What did he lie about?"

"Well, you know how I've come in here and bragged about him being this big fashion photographer and whatnot, and how he works for all these big-city magazines and has done photo shoots with models."

"Yeah."

"Girl, I found out all that was a lie. He doesn't work for any magazine, and he's not a fashion photographer."

"What do you mean? Where does he work?"

"I found out that he does porn."

"PORN!" Nishelle shouted out.

"Keep your voice down, damn."

"He told you this?"

"Only after I came across this script that he left on the kitchen table."

"What did you do?"

"I confronted his ass about it. He couldn't deny it being that his name was typed next to the character he goes by in the porn movie."

"Leandra, you must have lost your shit."

"I lost it all right. I kicked his ass out and told him that I never wanted to look in his lying-ass face again."

"Good for you. Anybody would have done the same thing finding some shit like that out about their man."

"Even if you um…found out that he does gay porn?"

"Oh, hell no. Taj is on some down-low shit?"

"I don't really know. If you found out that your man was doing gay porn, what would you do?"

"What do you think I would do? I would probably shoot his ass."

"Come on, Nishelle, not kill the brother."

"I would put the gun to his damn head and pull the trigger." It was shocking to hear this from Nishelle, someone who seemed like she wouldn't hurt a fly. "Look, I don't have nothing against gay people, but if I found out my man was dipping his pickle in that jar, murder is the case they would be giving my ass. A lot of those dudes that do porn don't wear protection. Javonte told me all about this barebacking shit they do. Leandra, if you haven't gotten tested yet, you better run to the clinic."

"Taj told me they get tested every six months, and that he doesn't do anything without a rubber."

Nishelle sucked her teeth and folded her arms in front of her. "And you believe him? If he lied about what he does for a living, what makes you think he's not lying about being clean? No, girl, I wouldn't trust it. Who knows what he could be bringing home to you?" Nishelle had a good point. *Yeah, he told me they use protection and get tested, but how do I know that for sure? It ain't like I'm on the set with Taj 24/7 to see who he's sticking his dick in.*

"You did the right thing, Leandra, by kicking his ass out. No way would he be running up in my Queen Victoria after he's had his dick in a man's booty."

I laughed at Nishelle's crazy ass. "Your Queen Victoria?"

"Yeah, girl. That's what I call it. My Queen Victoria, my fine China."

"Oh Lord, not your fine China, girl."

"My fine China, my purse."

"Your pocketbook."

"Yeah, see there you go."

We both laughed to the slang vagina terms. "So you don't play that 'stand by your man' bullshit, huh?"

"Leandra, I'm sorry. I *might* be able to take him cheating on me with another woman, but another man? I have to draw the line somewhere."

Nishelle was giving me a whole lot to think about with the situation. I didn't think I would go as far as killing somebody though. "Seems like as soon as I open my heart up to someone, they take it and rip it out of my chest and kick it in the dirt. And what's the first thing they say when they've gotten caught in the act? 'I didn't want you to get hurt.'"

"But the more they keep from us, the more that shit hurts," Nishelle said.

"Exactly, and honestly, I love Taj, but I don't know if I could deal with this porn stuff."

"Your story reminds me of this movie, or documentary or something I was watching on TV about straight men that do gay porn for pay. 'Gay for pay' is what they call it, and there was this one white guy who actually had his wife on the set with him."

"To do what?" I asked.

"He said he couldn't get hard, so she would be there on the set to help him get it up."

"Like a fluffer?"

"Is that what it is?"

"They basically help the guys in porn movies get hard."

"Well, I wouldn't know. Look, Leandra, it's your life. I'm just saying that if it was me, I wouldn't put up with that kind of foolishness." Nishelle sat in front of me with her arms folded at her chest, her lips twisted in a sneer almost.

"Every woman's different, I guess," I said.

"Anyway, I better get back out here before Sabrina puts a missing person's report out on a sister. You know how she gets."

"How do you like your new position?"

"Leandra, you should have seen the look on Sabrina's face when you told me that you gave me Krista's chair. Shit was priceless. By the way, did you get a chance to go by her apartment to check on her?"

"Girl, with all this mess that's been going on with Taj—. Oh, of course. I'll probably go by her place after work to see what's up because she hasn't been answering her phone. Every time I call, it goes straight to voicemail, and it's not like her to call or not show up for work."

I admit that I was a little worried about Krista myself. For her to take off for weeks on end and not let somebody know if she's all right isn't like her.

"She probably took off to Vegas somewhere with one of her flavors of the month, who knows?" I tapped my pen on my desk strewn with invoices, receipts and folders.

"Yeah, you might be right. I'm sure it's nothing. She'll pop up when you least expect it," I said.

"True. Well, let me get back out here."

"Hey, remember what I said now. Not a word of this to anybody."

"I have no idea what you're talking about," Nishelle said, smiling.

"Thank you, girl."

"What are friends for."

I couldn't worry too much on Krista right now. Taj and I needed to have a serious talk, but that would have to wait considering I was about to throw up the sausage, egg and cheese biscuit I'd had for breakfast in the trash can at my feet.

FORTY-THREE
TAJ

I sat in pitch-black dark over the news of Deandre's death. I couldn't shake the scene out of my head of seeing him lying there in a pool of his own blood. I mean, who would kill him and leave him lying there like that? Damn, his head was barely attached, some real, brutal, fucked-up shit. When I flipped on the TV to see if there was anything on the news about Deandre, my phone rang. It was Jimi. He was the last man I wanted to talk to, but if I didn't answer, he would only blow up my phone fifty-eleven times until I picked up. "What's up, Jimi?" I asked.

"Taj, hey, what's up?"

Other than finding my friend dead on the floor at his crib, I'm good was what I wanted to say, but didn't. "Sitting here watching the news, man, what do you want?"

"I wanted to know if you got a chance to look at the script I gave you."

"Yeah, I read it and made some notes."

"Great. When you come in, we can talk about your ideas."

"Well, the thing is, I seemed to have misplaced the script with my notes on it, and can't find it anywhere."

"Don't worry about it. I have plenty of copies here at my office. I also have Vance and the new guy, Montez coming in later. I was hoping the four of us could get together and run lines for the new film." The way I was feeling, I could give two shits about dick and ass, number one, and number two, people who buy these DVDs, don't care about dialogue. They put their shit on mute half the time and beat off to the fuck and suck scenes, but money was money, and now that I had lost not only my best friend, but my lady too, so I didn't give a fuck. I needed something to take my mind off Leandra and Deandre. "T, did you hear what I said?"

"What? Yeah. Let me take a shower and I can be there in ten minutes."

"True. I'll see you in ten."

All I did was stand under the hot water, caught in a daze of the events that had occurred in the last twenty-four hours. When I got to Jimi's, there were three cars parked in the driveway. Jimi's Beamer, Vance's Spyder, and a 1996 Camry that had to belong to the new swinging dick Jimi had hired. When I walked up to the door, I rang the bell. "Come on in, T." It was Jimi's voice. The second I turned the gold-plated knob, I heard a series of moans reverberating from the living room. When I walked inside, there was Vance on all fours sucking Jimi's little-ass dick and taking it up the ass by the new kid. There they were in the center of the living room that reeked of poppers and ass, going at it like a bunch of wild zoo animals, Vance licking across the shaft of Jimi's dick as if it were dipped in chocolate while Montez was pounding Vance's ass hard and rough. Of course he was taking it like the porn pro he is. "Hey, you made it," Jimi said.

"Jimi, I thought we were going to talk about the notes I made on the script."

"We are. This is only a rehearsal. This is the new guy Montez I was telling you about the other day."

"What's up," the new guy said, as he cut me a sinister glare before he turned his attention back to deep-dicking Vance who was too busy sucking Jimi's circus peanut of a dick to say anything. Jimi was armed with a handy-cam filming the nasty scene. "Why don't you strip and join us? Montez here is versatile and says he's a huge fan of yours and would love to get fucked by the famous Dillon Durke."

I looked at the three of them going at it and realized that I didn't want to do this shit anymore, that even though I was making bank, some things are not worth selling your soul for. I didn't want to be in my thirties and forties and still fucking for money. I knew that if I stuck around, I wouldn't last and would end up being some messed-up, coked-out drug addict like Vance, and from the looks of Montez who looked all of eighteen, Jimi would use him up until he was no good to him anymore. "I'm out of here, man; I gotta go." I couldn't get out of there fast enough. "Where are you going?" Jimi asked. I didn't answer, but kept on walking. "Taj, where the fuck are you going? Get back here."

"I quit, Jimi."

"What the fuck do you mean, you quit. You're locked in a contract. I still own your pretty ass for two more films."

"So sue me. I really don't give a fuck. I'm done with this shit."

Jimi stood ass-naked in the door all red-chested with Vance's spit dripping from the head of that circus peanut he called a dick, not caring who saw him. Neighbors, kids, dog catcher, the damn ice cream man, nobody.

"Come on, man. We were just having a little fun. Come back inside; let's talk about your future."

"I'm done, Jimi. How many times do I need to say that shit? I'm done; I'm out of the porn business."

"So you're going to turn your back on all that good money just like that? Taj, you're my top-selling star. I have big plans for you, baby: convention appearances, red carpet events. Did I tell you that I've been approached about you doing a sex toy line? I'm talking dildos, vibrators, you name it. Come back inside. We'll talk about it over drinks."

I got in my car and cranked it up until it roared to life. "Good luck with everything, Jimi."

"You think it's that easy? I own your ass, Taj, you hear me? I own you, you black son of a bitch!"

I hauled ass, burning traction knowing I would never have to lay these pretty brown eyes on Jimi's sleazy ass again. I was smiling ear to ear without a pinch of regret.

"I'm coming for you, Leandra."

FORTY-FOUR
SHARIECE

After Emjay and I burned the flash drives, it felt like an anvil had been lifted off my shoulders. It was finally over and now things could get back to some sense of normalcy. I thought for a second to just give in, to give Deandre what he had wanted: sex, but who's to say that fucking me would have been enough for someone like him? First sex and then money. It would have been a continuous cycle of blackmail, secrets, lies and destruction, and I wasn't about to lose Emjay over it all. I'm surprised I've been able to keep it together this long. I only wanted to move forward and put this whole nightmare behind me. If God was trying to teach me a lesson, consider it learned.

It was the week before Thanksgiving and I needed to catch up on grading papers and simply getting my head back in the game of teaching. All I wanted to do was relax, spend the holiday with my man, and sit down to a nice Thanksgiving dinner with all the trimmings. I usually went to Leandra's for the holidays, but since our friendship was on the rocks, spending Thanksgiving with her was out of the question. It's too bad too, because she puts her foot in some greens and chitterlings. Why spend the whole day over a stove like some kitchen witch, anyway, when I can have my friendly neighborhood Boston Market cook the meal? I'd just throw everything in plates, bowls and a cooking sheet and Emjay wouldn't know the difference. This would be our first Thanksgiving together. A day of cuddling up under him on the sofa with some store-bought sweet potato pie while watching *The Twilight Zone* marathon on TV.

As I recorded grades into a document on my laptop, I glanced at the time at the bottom right-hand corner. *7:40*, it read. Emjay was set to read at the Epitome Coffee House at 8:30. I was so proud of him. I only wished Leandra could be there to hear him read. If Emjay kept his writing up, not even the sky would be the limit. I missed my best friend. I was on my way out the door when I bumped into Bonita in the hallway. She was looking sharp in a red, sleeveless dress that was tight in all the right places.

"Uh-oh, go 'head, girl."

"You like it?" Rochelle asked as she pressed the dress down with her hands along her thighs and booty. "Girl, it ain't wearing you; you're wearing it."

"It's been sitting in my closet under plastic for weeks. I got it on sale at Macy's. I was going to wear it to church, but I don't think it's really what you would call a church dress."

"If you walked into church wearing that, you would give the pastor a heart attack."

Rochelle laughed. "You're probably right."

"So who's the lucky guy?"

"This guy I met at the Top Flight Club. He's a dispatcher at the Tallahassee Police Department."

"Nice. Is he fine?"

"Very. He's originally from Carrabelle, and moved here at eighteen."

"He sounds nice."

"He seems sweet, yeah. I think he's taking me to this new place called Liberty that just opened up in Midtown."

"So do you have any plans for Thanksgiving?"

"It's only me and my boyfriend this year. I'm making him dinner," I said, as I spat my half-truth like a cherry pit in Rochelle's face.

"That sounds romantic." I thought of how close I came to Rochelle finding out about me sleeping with one of my students and how totally fired I would have been. "Girl, I can't wait until the break. I want to sleep for a month."

"I hear that. It'll be nice to not have to get up at six a.m."

"How about you, any turkey day plans?" I asked.

"I will probably go visit my mama, brother and his family in West Virginia. My brother called and said that she hasn't been doing so well."

"Sorry to hear that. Is she sick?"

"She's in stage three of Alzheimer's disease."

"My goodness, that's terrible."

"Yeah, my brother says that she's been asking about me and I miss her. I'm thinking about moving up there to be closer to them and my nieces and nephews. He's got his own wife and kids to take care of and he can't always be there."

"Does she have a nurse who comes by to check on her?"

"Yeah, but she's only part time and my mother's insurance can't afford a full-time nurse to be there with her."

"Rochelle, I'm so sorry."

"Thank you. I told my brother that I would decide something before the end of the year. He could really use the help with her. My daddy died eight years ago and we're all she has."

"Well, do what you have to do. Family is everything."

"Listen to me all doom and gloom before my date," Rochelle said.

"I'm actually running late to an engagement of my own."

"Well, come on, walk to the parking lot with me. Jarrell is picking me up."

"Damn, with a name like that, he must be fine. When he sees you in that dress, his mouth is going to drop to his feet."

"Let's hope so. It was a miracle that I was able to fit in this dress."

The night air slapped us in our faces as Rochelle and I made our way outside.

"Damn, it's getting cool out here," I said.

"Old Man Winter will be here before you know it, honey. There's Jarrell's car right there."

A black Escalade that shined under the white parking lot lights sat idle with tinted black windows. The whole thing looked odd. I was having one of my bad feelings about this guy.

"Well, be careful, have fun and I want to know all the details of your date tomorrow, and I'll pray for your mama."

"Thank you, girl. She's going to need them." Rochelle embraced me with a hug. "I'll call you," she said.

When Rochelle got in the gas-guzzling SUV, the light flashed on, but her date had his face turned away from me. I rubbed my arms as that creepy feeling tickled my skin.

My heart was bumping beats triple time when I pulled into the lot of Black Dog Cafe. I was nervous about meeting Emjay's friends, hoping they would like me and that I didn't look like some old maid sitting up in there with all those young'uns. I checked my face in the visor one last time, primping my hair, dabbing away excess lipstick from my mouth with a Kleenex, making sure there wasn't any on my teeth. Yeah, I knew I looked good. I laughed to the thought of Deandre back at his place nursing the wounds I had inflicted. All the bandages and witch hazel alcohol in the world wouldn't heal his ego. He thought I was one of these candy necklace bitches he thought he could get over on. I was a grown-ass woman, not a Girl Scout, and he knew that now. If he knew what was good for him, he wouldn't show up in my classroom. If I never saw that perverted bastard again, it would be too soon. He'd better stay as far away from me as he could possibly get by human, dirt bucket standards. If Emjay saw him, he'd put him in traction.

I dropped my compact in my clutch, stepped out of the car, locked it, took a deep breath and walked toward the coffee house. I looked past the sea of young folks, some of the boys checking out a sister. *Feast your eyes on a real woman*, I thought to myself. I let these thirsty pups take in every inch of my body. Hell, I even caught the eyes of a few white boys. There's nothing wrong with looking at my booty, don't touch. This brown sugar is bought, paid for and is the property of one Shariece Mills. I didn't see Emjay in the crowd until I felt hands slip around my waist. I looked over my shoulder to find my man standing behind me. I could smell his Polo Red cologne permeating off his body.

"Hey, baby," I said.

"You made it."

"Am I late?" I asked.

Emjay slid around in front of me. "You are on time always. You look amazing."

"Thank you. I just left the office. I got a good chunk of my grading done, so that's a relief. How are you feeling? Are you nervous?"

"A have a few baby butterflies in my stomach, but I'm more psyched to get on stage and perform more than anything. I feel like I never stopped, you know? The energy in this place is bananas."

"I see. I haven't been here in a while. I see they've remodeled the place. It's beautiful. I'm so excited for you."

"Are you feeling okay?"

"Now that all that drama with Deandre is over, I'm feeling much better."

"We can finally move past it. I just want you to be honest with me and not feel like you have to hide anything from me," Emjay said.

"I know, and from here on out, no more secrets."

"Do you know how bad I want to kiss you right now?" Emjay asked.

"I know, but we have to be careful—at least until the end of the semester."

"I'll try."

"What up, breeder, you made it," Dash said.

This brother with thick dreads that draped over his shoulders and down his back came out of nowhere. "What up, dick licker." The two of them went at it like two high school footballers, cracking on each other like their tongues were wet locker room towels.

"Shariece, this is my oldest and *gayest* friend in the world, Dash Howard. Dash, this is my girlfriend, Shariece."

Did I hear him right? Did Emjay just introduce me as his girlfriend? Hearing it seemed like it was official.

"So you're the Shariece my man can't stop talking about?" Dash whispered as he softly shook my hand.

"I better be the *only* Shariece he's been talking about," I said, smiling.

"You were right, bro, she's beautiful."

"Aww, thank you, you're sweet, Dash."

"I didn't pay him to say that," Emjay joked. The three of us burst out laughing. The café was filling up, schools of people sipping on specialty coffee, immersed in conversation. The clank and clatter of cups and plates reverberated throughout the coffee bean-smelling café. I wondered with all the noise how anyone got any work done.

"Hey, the gang's all here. Everybody except Chadae. She says she's going to be a little late."

"What time do I go on?"

"I put you down for like an eight-forty to nine o' clock slot in case you were running late. Is that okay?"

"That's cool. I'm down for whatever."

"Plus, I figured it would give you a chance to get something to drink and chillax with the guys." He turned to me. "Shariece, you want something to drink? Everything is on me tonight," Dash said.

"I'll have a pumpkin spice Frappuccino."

"What about you, Mr. Poet? The usual?"

"Iced coffee, heavy cream," Emjay said.

"The guys are sitting over there at the big round table in the corner by the stage," Dash pointed out. "Go say hello."

"Is that Brant? Damn, he done got big. Come on, baby, I'll introduce you."

Emjay pulled me by the hand through the crowd. It made me happy to see him in his element.

FORTY-FIVE
EMJAY

Damn, Shariece looked like liquid sex. I'd be lucky if I could get through the night without getting wood. I rolled my tongue back in my mouth knowing that I would need it later to lick her from her red, pedicured toenails to her full, glossed lips.

I sneaked up behind Brant and slapped him hard on the back of the neck. He turned around. "Jay, what's up, boy," he said as he picked me up in a big bear hug.

I could already feel the blood flow being cut off from my feet. "Damn, bruh, put me down, dang."

"I see you've put on some pounds. What, you eat a small child before you came?"

"More like a busload of kids," Elsias chimed in, who was another good friend of mine from Rickards High School.

"What's up, El-B?" We came together in a hug that wasn't as rib-cracking as the one Bigfoot Brant had given.

"Man, whatever, Ya'll brothers know I got a glandular problem," Brett said, rubbing his belly.

"More like pulling your big butt from the all-you-can-eat buffet," Chadae said.

"Cha, is that you?" I asked.

"The one and only."

Shariece looked at Chadae oddly as I roped my arms around her. While Brant had put on weight, Chadae had lost all of her baby fat. Home girl was fine, but she didn't hold a candle to Shariece.

"I would like you all to meet Shariece."

"Hey, Shariece, how you doing?" Brant said, shaking her hand.

"Try not to break the lady's hand," Chadae said. "I love your blouse. Where did you get it, Lane Bryant?" Chadae's outer shell might have changed, but she was still a bitch. Shariece wasn't too happy with Chadae's dig, but she would check her before the night was over with if Chadae kept on.

"No, actually, I bought this from Macy's," Shariece said. I knew that I didn't have a thing to worry about, that Shariece could hold her own with this bunch, and didn't need me to ride to her rescue.

"Well, ya'll pull up some chairs. We have a lot to catch up on," Elsias said. "Since our boy Emjay here don't come around anymore." Chadae sat next to Elsias, me next to Brant, while Shariece sat next to me.

"Yeah, I know. I've just been so busy with the school thing that I really haven't had time to hang out much."

"I know that feeling, Jay," Chadae said. "These nursing classes are kicking my butt up and down campus. I'm in class all day and studying at night. I barely have time to eat, much less get some sleep."

"So how's your mama doing, Jay?" Elsias asked.

"She's good," was really all I could say about Mama, considering we hadn't spoken in three months.

"Is she still running that salon over there on South Adams?" Brant asked.

"Yeah, it's still going strong. I helped her do some remodeling to it last year, so business is good."

"Does she still make those cherry cheesecakes with whipped cream and walnuts sprinkled on top?" Brant asked.

"Yeah, she'll probably be making one for Thanksgiving."

"Your moms make the best cherry cheesecake."

"Man, is that all you think about? Food?" Dash asked as he set our drinks on the table.

"What else is there?" Brant asked as he patted his belly.

"Brant is like a bottomless pit when it comes to food. Will eat anything if it ain't tied down," Dash said.

"Do you think your moms can make me a cheesecake for Thanksgiving?"

"Only one?" I asked, laughing.

"I'll pay her for two."

"Dang, you greedy," Chadae said. "You don't need cheesecake. Weight Watchers is what you need." Everyone laughed while Shariece smiled politely with her hands folded neatly in her lap.

"I'll talk to her about making you a cheesecake. She won't mind making you one. One thing she likes about you, Brant, is that you bring your appetite. This brother never turned down an invite for dinner. He ate at our house more than at his own," I said.

"I think he ate at all our houses like that," Elsias added.

Brant took one of the sugar cookies that were sitting on a plate in the middle of the table.

"So Shariece, what do you do?" Chadae asked. Everyone got quiet as if Shariece was about to say something astounding and eye-opening.

"I'm a teacher at Tallahassee Community College. I teach English."

"Cool. How long have you been teaching?" Chadae asked.

"For about four months now."

"Do you enjoy teaching?" Chadae asked.

"I love it. To be able to influence people, teach them that there's more than one way to think about an issue, it's great."

"So are you and Emjay just friends?"

"Chadae, seriously?" Dash said.

"I'm just asking her a question; what's wrong with that?"

"Stop interrogating the woman, damn," Brant said.

"Shut up. Have another cookie, B," Chadae said.

"We're friends. This is actually my first time hearing Emjay read, so I'm here for support," Shariece said.

"I think we all are. It's about time they got some real talent up in here instead of all these white folks getting up on stage reading poems about flowers and country cabins and shit," Chadae went on. "Emjay is going to show them how to do a damn thing."

"That's what's up," Brett said, as he rubbed my shoulder.

"True. What are you going to spit tonight?" Elsias asked.

"I got something new I'm going to reveal on stage for the first time. Trust though, ya'll won't be disappointed," I said.

"Oh, we already know," said Dash.

I was nervous, anxious and excited all at once. "I hoped I wouldn't get up there and fuck up."

"Never that, son," Elsias said.

"You still got it, trust," said Dash.

"Jay, do you remember when we took your moms' car and went joy riding?" Brant asked.

"Oh damn, I almost forgot about that."

"We got into your mom's Crown and got drunk off our asses."

"Yeah, and I remember you throwing up on the floor too. Had the whole car smelling like red beans and rice and Crown Royal."

"Eww, how long ago was this?" Chadae asked.

"We were like fifteen. All Jay had was his learner's permit."

"Man, do you know how long it took me to get the smell out of my mom's car? I remember grabbing every cleaning supply she had trying to scrub puke out of the carpet." Everyone roared with laughter.

"'Why does my car smell like vomit?' Mama kept asking me."

"What did you say?" Brant asked.

"I acted like I didn't know what she was talking about. It wasn't like I was going to tell her that we took her car to go joyriding up and down Tallahassee."

Brant laughed so hard he cried.

"Oh, we can all laugh about it now," I said. "Crazy thing was, we didn't get stopped once by the cops."

"Seriously?" Chadae asked.

"We drove to Panama City, and didn't get pulled over."

"Ya'll were lucky. Cops probably would have put ya'll under the jail had you gotten stopped," Chadae said.

"How were you able to get your mama's car without her knowing?" Elsias asked.

"His moms had gone out of town, and she left him the keys," Chadae said.

"It was to some hair convention in Tennessee, that year, I think. 'You drive to school and straight back home. Don't drive my car at night,' she said," Leandra said.

"We were bored and this crazy-ass boy got it in his head to go out and try to pick up girls," Chadae said.

"Figures," Chadae said.

"Hey, I recall that you were one of those girls we picked up at Popeyes," Brant said.

"Ya'll thought ya'll had real swag," Chadae said.

"We had swag coming out of our asses and you know it," Brant said.

"Whatever... whatever." Chadae laughed.

"This fool wanted to drive all the way to Miami, talking about going to damn South Beach and he was dead serious too," I said.

"So what did ya'll do?" Shariece asked.

"We spent the weekend chilling in Panama City and came back like that Sunday morning. Mama didn't get back from the hair show until like six that night, but that next day, she was on my ass about why the car reeked like throw-up."

"That's so nasty," Chadae said. "How long did it take you to get the smell out, Jay?"

"Like three weeks. Mama made me spend my allowance money on getting the seats shampooed."

"So she never found out about you and Brant driving to Panama City?"

"No one ever did."

Shariece placed her hand on my knee, looked at me like she was saying my secret was safe with her. Her touch was enough to make my dick bang against the wall of my underwear. All I wanted to do was pick Shariece up, lay her on the table and ravish her fine ass right there in front of Brant, Dash, Elsias and Chadae as they watched in total shock and awe, café patrons capturing every thrust on their cell phones, but that was the kind of shit that got us into hot water in the first place. I had to take care of my hard-on because the last thing I wanted to do was go on stage popping wood. I sent Shariece a text message. *Meet me in the men's room, ten minutes.* I watched her pull her phone out of her purse and read my message.

"Ya'll, I'll be back."

"Where are you going?" Chadae asked.

"I have to take a leak before I go on stage to read," I lied.

I sauntered off to the bathroom where my dick was so hard it hurt. Two of the stalls closest to the door were occupied with guys taking a piss. I took the last stall at the end of the shitter—the bigger, roomier one. I undid my jeans and tugged my hard-on gently out of white, cotton underwear. Gently, I started to massage it, running my thumb over the thick head of my dick. The two men pissed, flushed, washed their hands and exited out of the bathroom. A minute after they left, I heard the door being pushed open as hinges let loose a squeal.

"Emjay, where are you?" It was Shariece. I cracked the stall door slightly to let her know where I was. She slid in between me and the door.

"What are you doing?" She smiled, glancing down at my thick, nine-inch erection.

"Baby, I need you to take care of this before I have to go on."

"Jay, right now, are you serious?"

"I can't go on stage with a hard-on. Come on, baby, please."

"Damn, you picked a fine time for this shit now." Shariece sat on the commode and placed her purse on top of the tissue dispenser. "We gotta hurry before Dash and them suspect something," she said. She held my dick at the base as she started to lick the head of my dick.

"Damn, fuck, that's what's up." Her tongue was warm and wet, feeling on point to the touch. She threw her lips around the full plumpness of my dick head, making them tight as she began to suck my dick hard and fast, licking along the shaft of my meat like a chocolate pudding popsicle. With all the crazy shit that had been going on with Deandre, neither one of us was in the mood for sex, so this was the first time since finding out that he had videotaped us, that we had been able to be intimate. I only wished we were at home in my bed instead of in a bathroom that reeked of stale piss and liquid soap. A blow job was exactly what I needed to relieve all the stress and pressure that I was feeling from the last couple of weeks. Shariece took inch after inch in her mouth as she swallowed me, her nose grazing in my thatch of soft, black crotch hair on my groin. She held onto both railings as she sucked, both sides of her jaws caved in as she hugged my dick with her mouth. Damn, my baby had that good head game. Shariece was going in hard when someone walked in. "Shit." I thought she would stop, but she kept at me with her eyes shut like we were the only two in the bathroom. Shariece kept quiet so as to not draw attention. Pearls of spit trickled down my shaft, dripping off the end of my balls. The brother who had walked in pissed, washed his hands and left, oblivious to what we were doing. This was only the second time I had gotten my dick sucked in a bathroom. The first was when I got head in the shitter in the ninth grade by Chadae, another secret I would take to my grave. She can suck a dick, but has nothing on Shariece. I don't know what was turning me on more: Shariece blowing me in the bathroom or the thought of getting caught. She began moving her hand up and down the long, thick shaft as she enveloped my appendage with her mouth, taking nine inches to her throat. "Baby, I'm about to come," I warned her, but she didn't slow up, but sped up her blow job work until I came, shooting torrents of cum. Shariece throated my load effortlessly, taking every drop I had to give. She gently pulled away, my dick drenched with her spit.

"I wish I could fuck you," I said.

"I plan on it when we get home," she said, smiling. Shariece adjusted her dress, pulling it down her ass and thighs as I tucked my drained dick back into tight-whites and denim. "That Chadae is a real piece of work."

"I'm surprised you haven't clawed her eyes out yet."

"The night is still young."

"She's cool when you get to know her."

"You mean when she's not being a prissy bitch."

"Stop," I said, laughing.

"I saw how she was drooling over the table at you. Do you two have history?"

"We went on a couple of dates, but it never led to anything."

"Let's go before someone catches us."

"You go first, and then I'll follow you out," I said, as I tucked in my shirt.

Shariece wrapped her arms around me and gave me a wet-hot kiss. "That's for luck," she said. "With you by my side, I don't need luck." She exited the bathroom and I followed behind her ten minutes later. Shariece was back at the table sipping her pumpkin spice Frappuccino like she was never in the men's room sucking my dick.

"What did I miss?"

"Nothing yet," Chadae said, smiling. "Dash is about to kick off the reading. Are you ready for your comeback?"

"This brother never left," Brant said, as he gave me a pat on the back.

Dash got the crowded café that was standing room only, revved up. He was a natural on the mic. I listened as he read off my bio I had typed up on an index card. As soon as Dash said my name, the crowd let loose a roar of claps and whistles. The love people were giving off sent a jolt of energy through me. I remember how nervous I was before my first reading. I was a senior in high school and Dash was the only friend I'd told about reading at The Warehouse on Gaines Street after finally getting up the nerve to recite my poetry in front of a live audience. Dash swore he wouldn't tell anyone. "You gotta let me tell Brant and Chadae at least," he'd said. I had said no at first, but Dash not being able to take hell no for an answer, twisted my arm. A few days before the reading, I went to a T-shirt shop and had my buddy Hank paste "Got Poetry" on the top left-hand corner of a blue T-shirt. I thought I was Eldridge Cleaver or somebody with my militant blue and black camo pants and black Army boots. The idea was some corny, cheeseball shit thinking back on it now. I still have that T-shirt with holes in it and blotches of bleach stains. I almost lost it when I saw Ma using it as a dust rag and snatched it out of her hands.

"Emjay, what do you want with that old shirt?"

"It has sentimental value," I told her. "It'll be something I can look back on when I become a famous writer someday."

"I don't care what you become as long as you stay in school, off the street and don't come up in here with a baby. I am too drop-dead gorgeous to be somebody's grandmama."

First time I read other than in front of my dresser mirror, my throat was dry and my palms were sweating. *Don't fuck up, don't fuck up*, I thought to myself as I fished three poems I had folded up in the back pocket of my cool camo pants. I was channeling all of my favorite poets: Amiri Baraka, Nikki Giovanni, Alice Walker and my all-time favorite, the man himself, Langston Hughes. I spat three poems and got off stage, happy to get it over with and even happier that I had the balls to do it. I guess I was good, because the host invited me back to read again and before long, I had a following. I did poetry slams all through my senior year in high school and then stopped a few months before starting college. Now, there I was after almost a year of not doing poetry slams, about to get back behind the mic.

Don't fuck up, don't fuck up, I chanted in my head.

Armed with five new poems, I started with a piece I wrote for Shariece. All eyes were on me, waiting with baited breath to hear me wax poetic. When I looked out and saw Shariece, I knew everything was everything and began to read the first line of the love poem.

FORTY-SIX
EMJAY

I was fifteen when I began to develop feelings for Shariece that went deeper than any relationship between a godmama and godson. I didn't have a problem getting girls. Hell, they were practically throwing themselves at me the way they were on my jock, leaving their numbers in my locker written on torn pieces of notebook paper with little black and blue hearts doodled next to their names. Alexis, Shanel, Raven, Porsha, Latoya, and even Chadae were on my dick, but I wasn't love jonesing for none of them chicks. They would be blowing me under the football bleachers and in janitor closets, and I would nut all over their blouses as my mind ran dirty thinking about Shariece. I didn't tell anyone how I felt about her. Not even Dash. I was scared that if I told Mama, she would think I was nasty, that something was wrong with me for having feelings for Shariece, but damn, it wasn't like we were blood related. So not being able to tell anyone, I wrote a poem about how I felt in this purple notebook I kept between my mattress. Most of them were sex poems about girls I finger-fucked and poems about not having a daddy around growing up. Paranoid that Mama might find my notebooks along with my stash of stroke mags, I moved everything from my bed to a secret compartment I cut in the floor in the closet. I still have that notebook, reading some of the corny poems I wrote back when I was in junior high.

I didn't act on my desires until four years later. I would catch Shariece checking me out at pool parties and cookouts Mama would have at the house. It wasn't in a godmama kind of way, but more like I was something succulent she wanted to sink her pretty white teeth into. Dash, Big Brant, Elsias and this girl, Anissa I was dating—well, more like fucking at the time—were at a Memorial Day pool party. Anissa was fine, but she was clingy as hell, blowing up my cell 24/7 wanting to know where I was and what I was doing every second of the day. Two in the morning, she would call me sometimes. "What are you doing?"

"I'm sleeping, girl, damn."

"Sleeping with who?" she would ask. If I wasn't with her, I was fucking someone else, as far as she was concerned.

"Bye, Anissa." I broke up with her the next day when I got tired of that fatal attraction bullshit she was pulling. A few days later, after I broke up with her, she would call and then hang up like I didn't know it was her crazy-ass calling me, so I had my number changed and warned all my boys about her. I was officially done with high school girls after Anissa. I was over that cheerleader, prom queen pussy. It was time I graduated from Sloppy Joes and applesauce to steak and lobster.

I spent all day putting on a show for Shariece, flexing my muscles, showing her what she had been missing. I eventually wandered off from the fray back to the house where I took a shower. I could feel Shariece on my heels as I made my way to the house. I left the bathroom door open and let loose moans when I heard her easing up the stairs. Shariece sauntered into the bathroom and looked over at me in the tub beating my meat, soapy water splashing as I furiously jacked off. She sat on the edge of the bathtub, eased her hand in, taking the place of my own, grabbed my dick, and started stroking me off. I gripped the lip of the tub as Shariece slid her hand up and down my hard shaft. Within five minutes, I came, cum mixing into warm, cloudy bathwater. She dried her hand with a towel and slipped out as easily as she slipped in, closing the bathroom door behind her. Shariece didn't pay me much attention after the bathtub beat-off incident. Guilt-ridden for what had happened, I guess, but I didn't regret a single second. Hell, I wanted more. Every time I rubbed one out, I thought of Shariece's hand gripping my dick as if it were a stripper pole. I figured she didn't want anything to do with me after that, but I later found out that Shariece wanted me about as much as I wanted her. I was hitting that once, sometimes twice a week, meeting at various motels for full-on fuck sessions. We were about as careful as two people in love could be, yet we both discovered after getting caught by Mama that you can never be too careful.

FORTY-SEVEN
MYRICK

nstead of some overpriced restaurant, Rochelle and I decided to go back to my place for dinner. "I cook a mean T-bone steak," I said.

"I bet you do."

When Rochelle began to caress my thigh, sliding her hand up to my crotch, I knew she was like all the rest of them: a filthy whore and ridding the world of filthy whores was the only job I was put on God's green earth to do. I simply looked at her and mustered up a smile. When we got to the house, I lit some candles and put on Teddy Pendergrass' "Come On Over to My Place."

"Oh, that's my man, Teddy," Rochelle said as she started dancing slow in the middle of the living room. I hoped that with enough air freshener and potpourri, it was enough to mask the smell of blood and death. Rochelle didn't say anything, so I guess I was in the clear.

I took two steaks and two baked potatoes out of the refrigerator before I fired up the grill that was on the deck out back. "Would you like a glass of wine to take the chill off?" I asked.

"Do you have red wine? White upsets my stomach."

"Red wine it is." I plucked a bottle of Merlot out and two wine-glasses out of the cabinet above the kitchen counter. I twisted off the corkscrew and poured. Rochelle was singing along with Teddy with her back turned to me when I pulled a small vile of Rohypnol out of the inside pocket of my jacket. "A little something to take the chill off all right," I said to myself as I sprinkled a smidgen of the drug into Rochelle's glass. I stirred it in with my finger so Rochelle wouldn't taste anything unusual. I joined her in the living room where I handed her the glass of wine. Her fingers grazed against mine as she took her libation. I would have preferred Shariece be here instead of Rochelle. Damn, she still looked good. She's put on a few pounds, but she's thick in all the right places unlike this bitch in heat who was twirling around in my living room. I watched eagerly as Rochelle took her first and last sip of wine of her life. I set my glass on the coffee table and took Rochelle into my arms. She rested her head against my chest as we danced. "So who was that you were talking to back at the college?"

"Who?"

"That woman you were laughing with. Is she one of your students?" I asked, playing like I didn't know who Shariece was.

"Oh, you're talking about Shariece. No, she's an instructor in the English Department. Do you know her?"

We danced as one Teddy Pendergrass song rolled into another and another. "She looks familiar to me."

"Shariece is amazing. One of my best instructors and the students seem to like her. She works harder than any of the faculty members, she's always in the office burning the midnight oil, she comes to every staff/faculty meeting, and she's only been with me for a few months. I don't know what I would do with—" Rochelle stopped in midsentence, her body slumped heavy into my arms. I pulled her gently by her hair and sure enough, she was out like a light. I dragged her over to the sofa and laid her down while I went to the basement to gather my tools. I met Rochelle at the Mockingbird Cafe. I'm a sucker for a woman drinking alone. Easy pickings are what I call women like her. I was pleased with the job Krista had done in discovering the whereabouts of Shariece. Girl would have made a damn good private investigator. I kind of regret killing her, but she was a liability and I couldn't risk her getting pinched and leading the cops to me. Rochelle was nowhere near my type. Too much on the boney side. I hadn't been on a college campus since I had killed that freshman in her dorm room last year. She was a fighter, that one. I cut out her heart and hazel eyes to remember her. Karissa had pretty, butterscotch skin. Poor thing was sitting alone in the food court eating French fries. Easy pickings. She went on about how her friends all went out of town for spring break and she was stranded for a week on campus. "I'm too fat to be seen in a bathing suit anyway," she went on.

"Come on now, don't put yourself down like that. You're a pretty girl." The ones with low self-esteem are like melted milk chocolate in my hands after I've stroked their fragile egos.

After returning from the basement, I cleared off the dining room table and spread out a blue, plastic tarp. Rochelle was knocked out still. I didn't have a lot of time before she came to from the roofie I had slipped her. I laid the assorted row of knives on the counter facing the dining room table. I always make sure my instruments are sharp and quite clean. I can't stand filth. Karissa invited me up to her dorm room which was on the other side of campus. "Is everyone gone?" I asked her, making sure that there wouldn't be any witnesses when she screamed. "I have a roommate, but she's at work."

"Good, so we won't be disturbed," I said, as I copped a feel of her juicy ass in tight low-riders. Karissa laughed as she slid her key card to open the door. The minute she got the door open, I pushed her in. "Dang, Big Daddy, what's the rush?" Karissa rubbed my chest, pressing her hot-blooded body against mine. Her lips shimmered with gloss as she kissed me. She smelled sweet like cherries. I returned her advances, shoving my tongue in her mouth, taking her apple bottom booty in the vise grips of my hand. My dick got bone-hard through it all. Karissa wasn't worth it. She was too easy like all the ones before her. "Fuck me," she said, as she ripped at my shirt. "Fuck me, daddy."

I kept kissing her hard, rolling my tongue around hers. "You have a nasty mouth, you know that?"

"Yeah, you want to stick that big black dick in my nasty mouth, don't you, huh, daddy?"

I couldn't stand it anymore. I slid my hands around her throat and applied pressure. "Shut your filthy mouth."

Karissa clawed at my hands as she struggled for breath, yet the more she struggled, the more pressure I exercised until those pretty hazel eyes of her rolled back into her pretty head. I choked her out until I heard her neck snap like a twig. I laid her lifeless body on the bed I assumed was hers. She looked like she was asleep. Because she kept scratching at my hands, I took some tissue from the bathroom and carefully wiped her fingernails free of any traces of skin. I took my knife out of the inside of my jacket pocket and performed a quick surgery, cutting out not only her heart, but her eyes. They were much too pretty to waste. I took two individual plastic sandwich bags and placed Karissa's heart in one and her eyes in another. I covered her over with the sheet from the other bed. "Thank you," I whispered, kissing her on the forehead.

When I got back to my car, I parked under a tree in a vacant lot. I unzipped my jeans, took my dick out and jacked off as I watched Karissa's beautiful hazel eyes staring back at me through the sheath of plastic. "You like that, baby? You want this dick?" Within two minutes, I came all over my hands and jeans.

I picked Rochelle up in my arms and laid her on the dining room table. I unbuttoned her dress, exposing her breasts cocooned in a black lace bra. I used my knife of choice to cut the bra off. Her breasts were voluptuous with deep, milk chocolate-brown nips. I traipsed over the left one with my thumb, squeezing it gently between my thumb and index fingers. "Dirty whore titties," I said. I took some phone cord and tied her wrists to the legs of the table. To muffle her screams, I placed duct tape over her mouth even though no one way out here in the sticks would hear her. As I ran the knife slowly down Rochelle's chest and stomach, I realized that I hadn't thought about what I was in the mood for. "Heart? Spleen? Liver? Kidney?" Rochelle was coming out of unconsciousness. I looked into her eyes and said, "You're up in time for dinner." Rochelle started to scream through the tape, but her shrills came out muffled. "Grilled liver and onions sounds delicious." When I took the knife and made the incision, Rochelle shrieked out in pain as I cut. I cut until there was a wide enough gape to remove her liver. She died as I began to remove her organ. There was blood everywhere. "I'll clean up after dinner." I placed the liver on a plate, rinsed over water, seasoned it with salt and black pepper and tossed it on the grill with chopped onions. I placed Rochelle's liver with onions on a plate before I refilled my glass of wine. I sat at the head of the table and cut, savoring the first bite. "Just as I thought, everything tastes better on a grill."

FORTY-EIGHT
SHARIECE

It was a little after ten when Emjay and I got home from the poetry reading armed with Chinese takeout from the Red Dragon. I had never seen him look so happy. "Did you see me up there? That crowd was fire," he said as he set the food on top of the dining room table.

"Of course I did. I was right there cheering my baby on," I said before I kissed Emjay.

"I didn't realize just how much I missed being up there until tonight."

"That first poem you read, was that about me?"

"Did you like it?"

"Like it? Baby, it's one of the most beautiful, heartfelt things anyone has ever done for me. It took everything in me to keep from crying."

"I hoped you would love it."

"I want to frame it," I said as I took brown rice and pork dumplings out of the bag.

"Dash thinks I should put some poems together for a collection, but I don't know if I have work that's good enough for a book."

"Of course you do."

"Will you help me put them together? Sort the good ones from the not so good?"

"Of course. We can sit down and read them and put them together in some kind of order."

Emjay pulled me into his arms, cupping my booty with both hands. "I would have been a mess of nerves if you hadn't have been there tonight."

"I wouldn't have missed it for the world."

"I'm just—"

"What?"

"I just wish my mama could have been there. She's never seen me read."

"Did you call her?"

"Yeah, but she didn't pick up, so I left a message. She never got up, so it's whatever."

I knew that it hurt Emjay that Leandra didn't return his messages and wasn't there to see him read. I also knew what a stubborn heifer she could be, that she was only punishing Emjay to spite me. "Ever since the whole incident at the house, I haven't felt right about the two of you not communicating. There's no reason why she shouldn't have been at your reading tonight. Yes, Leandra and I have our issues, but that's between me and her. She shouldn't punish her son for that."

"I don't know, baby. I really thought she would have gotten over all of this by now, that she would have met me halfway at least."

The aroma of sweet and sour chicken instantly began to waif through my apartment. "Leandra is stubborn like you are. I know her. She will take a grudge to her grave and isn't going to meet nobody halfway nowhere, so you suck it up and go to her and talk to her."

"Mama doesn't want anything to do with me. She proved that by not coming to my reading tonight."

"Then make her talk to you. Go to the house. If she's not there, go by the salon."

"I doubt she'll want to see me."

"Maybe. Maybe not, either way she has to talk to you."

"I do miss her."

"I know you do."

"But what about you and her?" Emjay asked.

"Don't worry about that. Leandra and I will have our day."

"Sounds like ya'll are going to have a gun fight," Emjay said as he plucked two plates out of the cabinet above the counter top.

"That's your mama and not me, not anybody should stand in the way of that."

"Babe, you're not standing in the way of anything."

"I know, but you know what I mean. She's your mama, Jay, the only one you have."

Emjay sighed as he spooned brown rice and sweet and sour chicken onto our plates. "Okay, I'll go by the house tomorrow." We were about to sit down and eat when the bell rang.

"Are you expecting someone?" I asked.

"Not that I know of," Emjay said, walking to answer the ring. "Maybe it's a publisher wanting to talk to me about a book," Emjay joked. When he opened the door, my heart sank when I saw a police officer and a tall black man dressed in business attire. I noticed a badge and gun hooked in the waistband of his slacks. "Hi, can I help ya'll?"

"Is this the residence of Shariece Mills?" I was a fan of enough cop shows to know that this brother was a detective.

"I'm Shariece Mills. What's going on?"

The white uniformed cop who looked a little like a young Mark Wahlberg and the detective walked in. Emjay closed the door looking just as surprised as me. "My name is Detective Newburn, and I would like to ask you a few questions."

"About what?" Emjay asked.

"Is this your son, Ms. Mills?"

"No, I'm her—."

"He's my godson," I said, cutting Emjay off. "What kinds of questions?"

"It's in regards to one of your students, Deandre Jackson." I figured that pervert had filed assault charges against me.

"Deandre Jackson? What about him?" I asked, trying my damndest to look calm and cool. "You're an instructor at Tallahassee Community College, correct?"

If this fool had done his homework, he already knew that I taught at TCC. "Yes," I answered.

"Mr. Jackson is a student of yours?"

"He's in my ten-fifty Freshman Composition class, yes, why?"

"When was the last time you saw Mr. Jackson?"

Visions of Deandre pulling at my clothes and forcing himself on me flashed in my head. "I saw him in class two weeks ago."

"And how did Mr. Jackson seem to you when you saw him in class?"

"How did he seem to me?"

"Did he seem distant, or like he was upset about something?"

"No, not to my knowledge."

"Not to your knowledge," Detective Newburn said, cutting me a sinister glance. "Ms. Mills, would you mind coming down to the station with us?"

I knew that when a detective asked you to come with them

to the police station, you were in deep shit. "Okay, stop. What's going on?"

The two cops looked at one another like they weren't sure how to answer my damn question.

"We just want to ask you a few more questions," the detective said.

"Am I under arrest?"

"No, but we would like to continue this downtown, and your cooperation would be greatly appreciated."

"She's not going anywhere with ya'll," Emjay said, like he could actually do something about them dragging me to the police station.

"Emjay, it's all right. I don't have anything to hide."

"Then I'm going with you."

"You can't go with her, Sir, but you can meet us down there," Detective Newburn said.

As much as I was trying to stay calm, I was honestly scared to death, yet I was curious to know what they had found out.

FORTY-NINE
SHARIECE

When I stepped past the double-glass tinted doors of the Tallahassee Police Station, I felt like the last woman walking toward death row with the uniformed cop holding my left arm and Detective Newburn holding my right. I knew I would be able to hold it together as long as Emjay was by my side. He beat us to the station, but they wouldn't let him follow to wherever they were taking me.

"What are you doing? I'm going in with her."

"I'm sorry, I'm Mr. Fox, but you're going to have to wait out here while we speak with Ms. Mills."

"No, fuck that, I'm going in with her." I could tell that he was getting irate and trying the detective's patience.

"Emjay, stop, it's fine."

"No, it's not fine. You've come down here voluntarily and we want to know what's going on."

"We only want to ask Ms. Mills some follow-up questions, son, that's all."

"Emjay, please let these officers do their job." He looked puzzled like he wasn't sure what to do. "If you would like, you can watch us in the room opposite this one to see what's happening." Emjay looked at me, searching my eyes for answers.

"Go ahead," I told him.

We walked down a hallway of shiny purple-and-white checkered linoleum where both sides of the walls were decorated with pictures of police officers who were awarded for either their heroism or their time protecting and serving. We stopped at a black door where Detective Newburn used a key card to gain access. The room was cold with a table, two chairs and a flat-screen TV that hung in one of the top-right corners. My heart was beating so crazy I thought it was going to explode. If I could snap my fingers to disappear, I damn sho' would have. "Have a seat, Ms. Mills. I need to get something from my office."

I had no idea why I had been dragged down to the station. Detective Newburn had finally returned thirty minutes later armed with a folder and a legal pad, the kind that guilty people scribble confessions on. The chill in the room was enough to make my nipples hard. I folded my arms across my chest to keep warm. "Okay, let's get started. Where were you between the hours of nine and ten p.m. on Tuesday, November 18th?"

"I was home grading papers."

"Can anyone verify that?"

"Emjay was at my place that night watching TV."

"What was he watching?"

"What was he watching? I don't know. It was some cop show."

Detective Newburn gave me this look like he disapproved of my answer. "Okay, Ms. Mills, I'm going to be frank with you here. We found Mr. Jackson dead in his apartment last night."

"Wait, what?"

"It appears that his throat was cut."

"And you all think that I had something to do with his murder?"

Detective Newburn took the remote that was sitting on the table and aimed it at the TV that hung in the top right-hand corner of the meat locker-cold room. "While we were collecting evidence, we found a video camera tucked away between some books on a shelf in Mr. Jackson's apartment. This is what we found." My heart skipped triple beats when I saw myself fighting with Deandre. The scene of me slashing him across his chest with the stem of the wineglass startled me. Minutes later, the video faded to static. "This was taken between nine o'clock and ten the night of the murder, so would you like to start over or do you want to play this the hard way?"

I stared long at Detective Newburn deciding that it was in my best interest to come clean about everything. "Okay, I was there, but I swear to you Deandre was alive when I left."

"Tell me what happened that night."

I tucked my hands under my arms and began to tell my side of the story as to what had happened that night. "Deandre was black-mailing me. He had taken a video of me in a compromising position with one of my students. He sent me an email with the video attached and told me that he wouldn't send a copy of it to my boss if I did what he wanted."

"What did he want?"

"Deandre said if I wrote him a recommendation letter for film school and had sex with him, he would give me all the copies of the video, and I would never have to see him again."

"Who is the student you were sleeping with?"

I paused for a bit, hesitant to answer. "What difference does that make?"

"Was it with Mr. Fox?" I didn't admit that it was Emjay but didn't deny it either. "So you met Mr. Jackson at his apartment?"

"I was only going over there to talk to him about giving me the flash drive with the video on it. I gave him the letter, but when I told Deandre that I had no intention of having sex with him, he got mad and forced himself on me. There was a struggle, he fell on the floor, and I guess he knocked the glasses over. I was too busy trying to stop him from raping me. He wouldn't get off me so I grabbed a piece of the broken glass, and cut him."

"Did he ever give you the flash drive that the video was on?"

"No, but I found about four or five of them in his bookbag. I didn't know which one had the video on it, so I took all of them."

"And then what happened?"

"I got the hell out of there. I swear Deandre was alive when I left. He was cursing and yelling at me as I made my way down the stairs of his apartment complex."

"We did, and everyone is claiming that they didn't see anything, which isn't surprising. In a neighborhood like that, no one sees, says or hears anything."

"Detective Newburn, you have to believe me. Deandre was alive when I left there."

"Where are the flash drives that you took from his apartment?"

"I burned them."

"You're not lying to me, are you, Ms. Mills?"

"No, I'm not lying. I found the one that had the video on it and burned it."

"We collected evidence from Mr. Jackson's bedroom and discovered several shoeboxes filled with videos dating all the way back to 2009. Apparently, you were not the only woman he had done this to."

"Oh my God, what?"

"Okay, just hang tight for me for a minute here," Detective Newburn said as he tucked the legal pad inside the folder and exited what was obviously an interrogation room. I couldn't say that I wasn't surprised by the news that there were other tapes of women, victims of Deandre's nasty perversion. I may not have killed him, but he damn sure had it coming. After hearing the news about the other tapes, anyone could have killed him. Detective Newburn returned five minutes later, this time with the tall, Larry Bird look-a-like behind him. I called Emjay to let him know what was happening. "Ms. Mills, please stand up," Detective Newburn said in a demanding tone.

I was so shaken, I wasn't sure I could stand. "What's going on?"

"Shariece Mills, you have the right to remain silent..."

"What? You're arresting me?" The detective didn't utter a word as he stood there with his hands in his pockets as the uniformed officer slapped handcuffs on me and escorted me to booking.

"Emjay, what are they—" I couldn't speak. The rest of my words caught like fish bones in my throat before I began to cry.

"Baby, I'm going to get you a lawyer. Don't tell them nothing, baby. I'm going to get you out of here."

The cuffs ate into the skin of my wrists as I was carried away; the words of *you're under arrest for the murder of Deandre Jackson* beat against my brain.

"I promise, Shariece, I'm going to get you out," were the last words I heard from Emjay as I disappeared behind another black door.

FIFTY
LEANDRA

Today was one of those days where I didn't feel like doing nothing but lying on my ass. I had this gut feeling that if I stepped outside my house, everything would go to opossum shit. The anger I was feeling after finding out what Taj's lying ass did for a living was through the roof. I was trying to find the right time to tell you, Taj had said. News flash, motherfucker, there is no right time to tell your woman that you fuck men in the booty for money. I don't know what burns my titty the most: the fact that he's on some gay-for-pay shit, or that he lied to me about it. I blame myself for even getting involved with Taj. A man sweet-talks me, tells me how pretty I am, and before I know it, my Victoria's Secret panties are down around my ankles like a hula-hoop. After Emjay moved out, I had a bad case of the empty nest, doing nothing but sitting at home eating Lean Cuisine TV dinners and staring at four white walls. I never thought I would miss that loud, terrible rap music bumping from Emjay's room or years of cleaning up after him after it looked like a tornado had hit his room. With the mess that had happened with Taj, I missed Emjay more than ever and wished he was still living at home. I didn't realize just how good he was at his writing until I saw him read last night. I sat at the back of the café so he and Shariece couldn't see me. Shariece looked like she had put on a few pounds, but who was I to talk the way I've been eating. Since our fight, my diet has gone off the rails. I didn't know just how much I missed them until I saw them at the poetry reading. Emjay looked thin like he hadn't been eating well. Figures. Shariece can barely boil bologna.

When Emjay moved out, I was excited at first to finally have the house to myself. I could finally have some male company over. My number one rule was to never bring a man home around Emjay. A week after he'd moved out, I started going out again. It was better than sitting at home stuffing my face with ice cream and greasy potato chips. I felt like dressing up and dancing, shake off some of this ass I had gained. The night I met Taj at the Top Flite Club, I had on a leopard print skirt and a black Dsquared2 blouse with some black Jimmy Choos to match. When I walked into the club, mouths dropped and all eyes were on me 'cept the ladies who were obviously drunk off *hater aid*, as Emjay once put it. The club was packed and hot from all the body heat being given off. I saddled up to the bar where Taj was working as one of the bartenders, a job he wasn't the best at, considering I had to wave my titties in his face to order a drink.

"What can I get for you?" he asked, as he glanced at my breasts tight in the designer blouse. "Vodka cranberry."

"Single or double?"

"A double." My day was crazy at the salon, and a double was what I needed to help me forget that a church group of ten women all came into the salon at once to get their hair done. Taj returned with my drink, and when I tasted it, there was more cranberry juice in the glass than vodka. *Where the hell did he learn how to make drinks*, Bartending for Dummies? Being that he was busy and was the embodiment of fine, I didn't break his balls about the worst vodka cranberry I'd ever had. From where I was sitting, I had a stellar view of his bubble-luscious football player's ass and broad shoulders that were perfect for resting my legs on while he ate my pussy. His dark-chocolate muscles glistening under the club lights made my pussy throb. I knew the minute I saw him, I would have him. Even if I did have shoes older than the brother. I hung around until final call sipping on one bad vodka cranberry after the next watching women that were less than practically throwing their pussy up in his face. That's the problem with today's twenty-first-century chick. Lots of ass, but no class. No need to throw yourself at a man. It's only dick.

I took the slice of lime that was left and sucked the juice out of the pulp.

"You want another one, baby?"

"No, I think two is my limit," I said, handing him my debit card.

"Forget about it; it's on the house."

"Thank you."

"You okay to drive home tonight?" Taj asked.

Due to the lack of vodka in all the two drinks I'd had, I wasn't even buzzed. "I think I'll make it. It looks like you had a busy night."

"Everyone is trying to get their party on before school starts back," he said, as he wiped off the bar. I watched Taj's lips move, thinking how they would feel against my own.

"Do you have any plans after you get off?" I asked.

"Most likely go home and go to bed."

"Sounds like a plan to me, let's go," I said boldly. Taj looked at me with amused disbelief. "You can follow me back to my place," I told him.

"Yeah, okay, that's cool. Give me a few minutes. I need to clock out."

As I drove home I started to think: *I hope he's not crazy. He's too damn fine to be psycho.* I was horny and couldn't wait to wrap my lips around what I was sure was an endowment of gigantic proportions. A woman can only finger-fuck herself for so long before she wants to be run through with some good dick. The minute we got in the house, Taj took me by the waist, pulled me to him and planted a kiss on me, squeezing my ass with those big Shaquille O'Neal hands of his. Our tongues intertwined as Taj squeezed my ass harder. I slid my hand along the thick bulge that tinted his black jeans, a dick aching to be released.

"Let's go upstairs," I said. I took him by the hand and led him upstairs to the bedroom. If Taj did turn out to be a black Jeffrey Dahmer, I had something for his ass in my bedside table that was cocked and loaded. We both got undressed. When Taj peeled off his shirt, exposing firm abs and pecs, my mouth damn near dropped to the floor. I kicked off the Jimmy Choos that had been putting a killing on my feet all night, but it's like I always say, beauty is pain. My breasts popped from their black, laced prison when I released the hook in the back. Taj began licking my nipples, running circles around them with the tip of his tongue. I couldn't remember the last time a man had touched me so sensuously. Taj smeared me onto the bed, kissing me deep as he slid the white boxer briefs off his bubble-butt like it was a second skin. His dick was fat and hot pressing against my pussy. He looked deep into my pretty brown eyes as he slipped his dick inside me like a sweet secret. I hooked my legs around his mid region as he deep-dicked me with long thrusts. Taj was hitting every spot, swerving, stretching my sugar walls like a pussy-fucking pro. He grabbed my ankles as if they were handle bars, fucking me crazy as I clawed at his firm, molasses-brown ass. After almost an hour of lovemaking, we had come to climax; the two of us collapsed into a heap of sweat and exhaustion. The last time I had gotten fucked that deep was when Rick was alive.

"Are you okay?" Taj asked.

"Oh, I couldn't be better." Taj ended up sleeping over that night. I got up the next morning and made him blueberry pancakes, grits and ham steak. I wasn't about to let dick that good get away.

"So can I see you again?" Taj asked.

"I'm sure something can be arranged," I said as I was making the pancakes.

"That's good, because I want to take you on a proper date." I should have known then that if everything was going right, it was just too damn good to be true. Nobody is that perfect. Thinking on it now, I wonder if he was fucking men on the down low all those times he was with me. How many asses has he stuck his dirty dick in? It doesn't matter. We've done as far as I'm concerned.

FIFTY-ONE
EMJAY

I kept thinking that I was going to wake up in a cold sweat and discover that the last twenty-four hours was a bad dream. But I would actually have to sleep in order to have any kind of dream, good or bad. I tossed and turned all night thinking about Shariece being arrested for murdering Deandre. If I could, I would dig that sick fucker up and kill him again for what he'd put me and Shariece through. This might have been fucked up to say, but I was glad he's dead. That's what happens when you fuck with somebody's life. Unless I hear it from Shariece's mouth, I don't think she killed him. And if she did, it was obvious judging from the video that it was self-defense. I'm not the least bit surprised that sick piece of shit tried to videotape himself having sex with Shariece. That tells you right there he had no intention of turning over any copy of the video. I wish to God I had gone over there instead of Shariece. He would have been glad to hand copies of the video over to me after I beat him within an inch of his sorry-ass life. I felt helpless thinking about her sitting in that jail. I would have taken her place in a heartbeat if I could. What the fuck was Shariece supposed to do, just lie there and let that bastard rape her while he videotaped it? I could tell from the look on her face when that detective showed her the video that she had no idea what was going on. Shariece could easily be lying in the morgue instead of Deandre. I couldn't help but be pissed off with her. I mean I get that she didn't want me involved, but I'm your boyfriend for fuck sake, and as such, it's my responsibility to protect my lady, especially when some psycho perverted fuck is playing Russian roulette with her life. It killed me that I had to sit back and watch that detective interrogate Shariece like that, to watch Deandre force himself on her. With everything that had happened, I'd decided that I didn't want to hide anymore. I love Shariece and I'm sick and tired of treating our relationship like it's some sort of dirty secret. I mean, who gives a fuck if she's ten years older than me? We were both grown-ass adults who were perfectly capable of making our own decisions. I understood the hiding at first because I was one of her students and that her job could be affected if anyone found out, but hiding was what got us in this shit in the first place. I didn't give a fuck who knew anymore. I'd stand on any rooftop at this point and shout it to the world if I had to.

FIFTY-TWO
LEANDRA

I was waiting on my Pumpkin Spice Latte I had ordered at Starbucks when I heard my phone ring. When I pulled it out of my purse and saw that it was Taj calling me for the umpteenth time, I pressed ignore and dropped it back into the abyss of makeup, change, chewing gum wrappers, old receipts and crumpled wads of tissue. "Ain't nobody got time for you," I said to myself, letting the call go straight to voicemail. I wanted Taj to know just how livid I was for keeping me in the dark about his down-low lifestyle, and that I wasn't trying to hear a damn thing he was trying to say. I'm too smart and too strong to continue to fall for a man's bullshit. First it was Rick, then my own son, and now Taj. My days of being a fool were officially over. With the way I'd been feeling today, I was in no mood to hear more lies and apologies. The minute I finished my lunch at Popeyes, I ended up over the toilet throwing up red beans and rice.

"I knew it was something about that chicken that didn't taste right. I should sue their asses," Delora warned me not to go to the one on Tennessee Street. I figured my stomach was trying to get used to greasy food again after being off this rice cake and Naked juice diet I was on with Shariece. I couldn't stand the taste of vomit in my mouth after throwing up. I only hoped I could keep this latte down long enough to get me through the rest of the day. Between being lied to and puking my guts out, drowning my sorrows in work was exactly what I needed.

I had a bone to pick with Sabrina about the less than impressive job she'd been doing running Radiance while I was gone. Nishelle was busy giving Mrs. Dorsey, one of our regulars, a wash while Javonte was giving Mrs. Maddox, the mayor's wife, an eyebrow arch. I had Sabrina working the receptionist desk when she didn't have any clients on the books, which she hated, but Nishelle loved every minute of watching Sabrina squirm. Nishelle was the only one in the salon who knew what was about to go down. When I returned from lunch, I could see through the window Sabrina sitting with her feet cocked up on the desk, filing her nails like she owned the place. You would think she would have taken her feet off the desk I'd bought and paid for when I walked in, but this bitch didn't budge, and I was starting to see exactly what Nishelle was talking about. Sabrina had gotten complacent and it was time to put her nail filing-ass in check Leandra Fox style. "Sabrina, come on, I need to see you in my office for a minute."

She placed the nail file on top of the appointment book and followed through the salon to my office. "Did I do something wrong?"

"I just want to talk to you, that's all," I said. I wanted to get her behind closed doors and out of sight of customers and my employees in case she made a scene. "Have a seat," I said, as I closed the door behind her. I hooked the strap of my purse on the back of my desk chair and set my Pumpkin Spice Latte next to the phone on my desk. "It has come to my attention that while I was in the hospital, you were bringing friends of yours in the salon, who were not paying customers, but sitting in the shop being loud and harassing clients."

"Who said that?"

"It doesn't matter who told me."

"'Cuz somebody's lying on me then. My friends have never been in here sitting around."

"You know that I have a zero tolerance for that kind of behavior in my salon. If they are not in here to get their hair done, to get a manicure or pedicure or a massage, I don't want nobody hanging around in my shop wasting time. It makes not only me look bad, but it looks bad for the salon."

"Leandra, I swear, I didn't have nobody in here sitting around." Here it was again, someone else lying to me.

"Okay, fine, whatever. I'm only letting you and everyone else know, which brings me to another matter. I was doing inventory on Tuesday and I noticed that some of the product has gone missing without properly being logged in."

"I know you're not accusing me of taking nothing out of the salon," Sabrina said, as the bass in her voice rose.

"I'm not accusing you, but—"

"You must be accusing me of something since I'm the only one sitting in your office in front of you right now. I don't see Javonte and Nishelle up in here." I wondered who she was yelling at because I was the wrong bitch to get loud with.

"When I made you assistant manager of Radiance, it was understood that if I was on vacation, at a meeting or sick for any reason, that you were in charge of everything, that you were responsible for the day to day that goes on in the shop."

"And that's exactly what I've been doing."

"Then explain to me why there are thirty bottles of Pantene unaccounted for?"

"Leandra, I don't know. Maybe they forgot to include the thirty bottles of shampoo in last week's shipment. Look, I don't know what happened to any shampoo. I don't own this salon and I don't write the checks. I don't know anything about any inventory going missing. You might want to ask Javonte and Nishelle since they work here too. Hell, maybe Krista took the shampoo. Maybe that's why she hasn't shown up for work."

"You are the only one with the keys to the inventory closet."

"Man, if I was going to steal something, why would I take shampoo?" Sabrina sat in front of me mad with her arms crossed tightly at her chest. "So am I fired?"

"I'm going to have to let you go, yes."

"What? Are you serious?" Sabrina asked, jumping up out of her seat." I stood up in case she got the bad idea in her head to throw punches. "This is fucked up, Leandra. I told you I didn't take no shampoo."

"I'm going to need the keys to the store and the inventory closet."

"They're in my purse in the drawer of the desk out front."

"I'll follow you out to get them." Nishelle and Javonte stared at us as we walked to the front of the salon.

Sabrina opened the bottom drawer, took out her purse and threw the keys on the table. I noticed as she cut a nasty glare at Nishelle. "It was that bitch, Nishelle, wasn't it?"

"It doesn't matter who told me."

"She's always bopping her boney ass around here like her shit don't stink, kissing your ass at every turn."

"You better watch your mouth."

"No, that dizzy bitch lied on me and I'm about to settle this shit." Sabrina stormed back into the salon area filled with customers.

Nishelle was busy hot-curling Mrs. Dorsey's hair when Sabrina made a beeline toward her. Javonte sandwiched himself between them knowing something was about to pop off.

"Sabrina, you need to leave," I said, but she ignored me.

"What the fuck did you tell Leandra, Nishelle?"

"I don't know what you're talking about," she said, looking cool and collected.

"Bitch, don't play dumb. I know it was your ass that told her I was stealing when you know good and goddamn well I didn't steal shit." All eyes in the shop were on Sabrina and Nishelle, gawking at them like they were prize chickens in a cockfight.

"I didn't tell Leandra nothing, first of all, bitch; and second of all, you better be glad Javonte holding your stank breath-ass back, 'cause you 'bout to get a beat down." Nishelle wasn't playing, armed with the set of hot curlers.

"What's up then? High-yellow, cornbread-ass bitch. Whatchu gon' do?"

"Ya'll need to chill with this shit. Ya'll our friends," Javonte said.

"Fuck that ho," Sabrina yelled. "I've never liked your prissy ass no way."

"Leandra, you better get her out of here or somebody's going to jail today," Nishelle said.

"Fuck you, ho', you ain't saying shit," Sabrina said.

"Sabrina, I'm not going to tell you again," I said.

"I ain't leaving until I get my last check from this sorry-ass salon." As much as I wanted to take Sabrina and drag her by her two-tone weave, I knew if I put my hands on her, she would call the cops and have me arrested for assault. "By Florida law, you have to write me my last check if you terminate me from employment."

I didn't know dick about any Florida law that stated that. All I wanted was Sabrina out of the salon and away from my clients. I wrote her a check for $400. "I will mail the rest of your money to you next week."

"If anybody's stealing, it's that bitch," Sabrina said, jabbing her finger in the air in Nishelle's direction.

"Whatever, bitch. Bye, so long, see ya."

"Nishelle, don't let me see your ass on the street. I'mma fuck you up."

"Get the fuck outta my salon, Sabrina," I said.

"Fuck you, Leandra. This place has gone to shit anyway. I'm going over to Super Cuts to help put you out of business. I hope you don't make a penny in this motherfucker." Sabrina grabbed her purse and stormed out, pushing the door open like she wanted to break it off the hinges. "Fuck all ya'll bitches!"

Clients were gossiping like a bunch of hens as they sat under blow-dryers.

"Nishelle, are you okay?" I asked. She went back to curling Mrs. Dorsey's hair like nothing happened.

"Oh, I'm Gucchi. Ain't nobody scared of Sabrina. Big ain't bad."

"Girl, I saw you with those hot curlers in your hand and knew I had to get between ya'll before it got real messy," Javonte said.

"I was going to burn her ass too." Javonte and Mrs. Dorsey chuckled.

"Thank you, Javonte, for stepping in," I said. "I was about to call the cops."

"You would have had to call them on Sabrina. Them, or the ambulance, because I don't fight bitches; I kill bitches," Nishelle said.

"Nishelle, watch your language and ya'll get back to what you were doing. I will talk to ya'll after business hours."

I felt that I needed to apologize to my clients for the scene that they had just witnessed.

"I want to say that I'm sorry, ladies, for what ya'll just witnessed.

It wasn't classy nor professional, so my deepest apologies. I will take five dollars off your cuts today for having to witness that."

It was a little after seven when we closed. Javonte was sweeping up loose pieces of hair while Nishelle and I counted out for the evening. My feet were killing me and all I wanted to do was go home and veg out in front of my fifty-inch flat-screen TV. "Ms. Leandra, I didn't want to say anything with all that mess that was going on earlier, but I saw Sabrina on a couple of occasions take hair grease and shampoo from inventory and not pay for them," Javonte said.

"And why in the hell are you just telling me this now?"

"I don't know. I wanted to stay out of it and figured you would find out about it sooner or later."

"Now see, I should fire *your* ass for that, Javonte, because you should have opened your mouth and said something."

"I will for now on. If I see anything strange going on or any inventory missing, I will let you know."

"Oh, I've decided that it's not going to be up to you or nobody else because I'm going to have some cameras installed in here."

"Damn, for real?" Nishelle asked.

"I should have done it when I opened the salon. Stealing from me is unacceptable. Ya'll should understand that when stuff like product goes missing and unaccounted for, that's money out of your pocket."

"So am I fired?" Javonte said.

"I've already fired one person today, so no, but if you see something, say something. It hurts me that someone ran my place and was stealing from me all the while. And I'm going to tell ya'll what I told Sabrina. I'm fine with you having friends to stop by, but don't let it interfere with your work and don't have them hanging around in the shop if they're not going to get a manicure, an eyebrow arch, something. This is my business, not a nightclub. If I don't have loyal and honest stylists working for me, there's no point in having you two here."

"Well, you already know how much I love working here," Javonte said, "so I am letting you know that I'm loyal to you from here on out."

"Me too," Nishelle said, "and I want to apologize for cursing and stuff in the salon. You know that ain't me."

"I know, and thank you for your apology."

After all the earnings for that day had been counted and the salon cleaned to my satisfaction, I switched off the lights in my office, the break room and the main part of the salon.

"All right, I will see ya'll tomorrow morning."

"Bye, Leandra," Nishelle said.

"Bye, Ms. Leandra," Javonte said.

Just as I was locking up, Taj walked up on me. "Damn, you scared the hell out of me," I said, holding my hand up to my heart that had skipped a couple of beats.

FIFTY-THREE
TAJ

orry, baby," I said.

"Can we talk?"

"Taj, it's been a long day. I had to fire my assistant manager today and I just want to go home and soak my feet."

"A friend of mine is dead."

"Who?" she asked, with a puzzled look on her face.

"Deandre. After our argument the other night, I went over to his apartment and found him dead."

"Come on inside." Leandra and I walked back inside the salon and sat down on the brown leather sofa in the waiting area. "Are you okay?"

"As well as could be expected, I guess, just a little freaked out from seeing him lying there like that."

"What happened?"

"I went over to talk to him. I saw that his door was open. I went in and there was Deandre lying on the floor in a pool of blood."

"My God, Taj. Did you call the police?"

"Yeah, they asked me a few questions and then let me go."

"Deandre's throat was slashed."

"Jesus."

"Knowing Deandre, it could have been anybody. He wasn't exactly liked by a lot of people and he pissed off a lot of people."

Leandra shook her head. "What is this world coming to?"

"They found a video camera stashed on the entertainment center."

"What was he doing?"

"Ain't no telling. I didn't say nothing to the cops, but he was into some pretty heavy shit."

"Is he the guy you worked with on the movies?"

"No, no, not at all. Deandre would do shit like install cameras in the toilets of public women's bathrooms. I told him that if he kept on, it would catch up with him; now he's dead."

"Yeah, but Taj, that doesn't give anyone the right to take his life. Doesn't matter what someone did." Lee was right. I didn't agree with most of the sadistic shit he did, but he didn't deserve to be killed like that—even if Deandre was a weirdo. "I hope they catch whoever did it and fillet his ass."

"Don't think like that." Leandra caressed my forearm. She had no idea how much I needed that, to feel her touch.

"I miss you and I want you back."

"Taj, it's not that easy."

"I love you and I want you back in my life."

"I can't be with someone who lies to me, who keeps secrets. You know how messed up I was when I found out about Emjay and Shariece."

"I quit doing porn."

"What?"

"I went to Jimi and quit." Leandra sighed, folding her arms at her chest. "I thought you would be cool about me quitting."

"I don't think it even matters at this point. The fact remains is that you lied to me; you told me you were a fashion photographer when what you really do is fuck guys for money? I mean, if I hadn't have found that script on the table, were you ever going to tell me?"

"Of course I was, but how do you tell your girlfriend that you do porn for a living? I was afraid of losing you."

"Look, I'm sorry about Deandre; my condolences go out to you, Taj, but I can't do this right now. I need some time to clear my head. Can you understand that?"

"I'm sorry for lying to you, for hurting you." I felt disappointment weighing down on my shoulders like a ten-ton elephant. As I struggled to get back into Leandra's good graces, I got a call from Detective Newburn. "Detective, hello."

"Mr. Bowman, I'm calling to let you know that we have a suspect in the murder case of Deandre Jackson."

"You do? Who is it?"

"We have a Ms. Shariece Mills in custody."

"Wait, hold up, did you say Shariece Mills?"

Leandra cut me a startled look when she heard me say Shariece's name. "What's going on?"

"Yes, do you know Ms. Mills?" the detective asked.

"She's my girlfriend's best friend."

"Can the two of you come down to the station?" Detective Newburn asked.

"Yeah, give us twenty minutes." With a feeling of disbelief, I ended the call.

"What is it? What about Shariece?"

"They just arrested her for Deandre's murder."

"What?" Leandra said.

"Detective Newburn wants to talk to us down at the station." My head was spinning as it tried to process the news I had gotten from the detective.

"There's no way. There's no way Shariece could have done this.

She's capable of a lot of things, but murder sure as hell ain't one of them."

"How do you know what she's capable of?" I asked.

"Excuse me?"

"You think just because ya'll go shopping and get manicures, you know her?"

"She didn't do this, Taj. There has to be an explanation."

I drove like hell, hoping that I wouldn't get stopped for speeding. I wasn't what you would call a fan of the police or police stations being that I'd spent my fair share in jail.

"You think she killed Deandre, don't you?"

I didn't want to fight. I was curious to know what the detective had found out. "Let's just see what Detective Newburn has to say."

Leandra and I walked through the tinted, double-glass doors. This Mexican cop was sitting at the desk behind plated glass. *Torres*, his name tag read.

"Can I help you?" he asked.

"We're here to see Detective Newburn. My name is Taj Bowman." Speedy Gonzalez looked at us suspiciously. He probably thought we were in a gang. Some of us work for a damn living; we don't all hang out on liquor store corners. If it was up to cops, there would be no lawyers, no courts or judges. They would take us out to the woods and blow our brains out, no questions asked. Just because Dude is Mexican don't mean shit.

"I'll let him know you're here; have a seat," Speedy said. He kept his eyes glued on me and Leandra as he yapped on the phone.

Five minutes hadn't even passed before Detective Newburn reared his shiny, bald head. "Mr. Bowman, thank you for coming down."

"What happened to Shariece? Where is she?" Leandra asked in a panicked tone.

"Detective, this is Shariece's best friend, Leandra Fox."

"Mrs. Fox."

"It's Ms. I'm not married. What is going on with Shariece?"

"Come to my office. We can talk there." The anticipation was killing me. When we got to Detective Newburn's office, he shut the door behind us like he had a deep-seeded secret he was itching to let me and Leandra in on. "We brought Ms. Mills here last night to ask her a few questions about her whereabouts on the night Mr. Jackson was killed and what her connection was with him. She didn't want to come clean at first, but she did tell me that she did go to Mr. Jackson's apartment the same night he was killed."

"What? Did she tell you why she was there?" Leandra asked.

"She claims that Mr. Jackson was blackmailing her, that apparently he had a video of her and another student having sex."

"My God, are you serious?"

Detective Newburn sat on the edge of his desk in front of us with his arms folded at his chest. "She says that Mr. Jackson would give her the video if he had sex with her."

"Of course he did," Leandra said.

"She went to his apartment to talk to him about giving her the copy of the video, but claims that she had no intention of having sex with Deandre."

"Do you believe her?" I asked.

"Well, there was a video on the handy-cam we found at Mr. Jackson's apartment that shows that they argued, and there was a scuffle between Shariece and Deandre. We see her cutting Deandre and then the video goes to static. I guess there was no more memory left on the camera."

"Damn," I said.

"I don't believe it," Leandra said. "I don't believe she did this."

"Leandra, baby, they have her on video."

"I don't give a damn what they have. I know Shariece. She wouldn't hurt a gnat. Hell, one time when I tried to kill a fly that had gotten in the kitchen, she kept hollering at me not to kill it. She let the window up to let the fly out. No, Shariece didn't do this."

"Well, Ms. Fox, she's the only prime suspect we have right now." Leandra had grown teary-eyed to the news of Shariece being accused of killing Deandre.

"There's something else," said Detective Newburn. "We were going through Mr. Jackson's belongings and found two thousand VHS tapes and hundreds of flash drives in a locked desk drawer. Many of them were of women in public restrooms. Apparently, he had lipstick cameras in the toilets of the stalls."

Leandra looked at me and I at her. "Anyone could have killed him. Maybe somebody's husband or boyfriend found out about the tapes and killed him. You said it yourself, Taj. Anybody could have killed him. Something like that, I would want him dead too."

"Ms. Fox, I don't think you understand. We have Ms. Mills' prints on the murder weapon."

"I want to see her," Leandra demanded.

"What?"

"I want her to tell me to my face that she did this."

"Baby, are you sure. I mean, you're upset."

"I have to see Shariece."

"She's in D-Unit. I will show you the way," Detective Newburn said. Just as I was about to talk Leandra out of seeing Shariece, Speedy burst into the office and whispered something to the detective under his breath. He was short for a cop. "Okay, thanks for letting me know." Speedy exited the office, paying me and Leandra no mind. "Her boyfriend is here."

"Emjay? Emjay is here?" Leandra asked.

"You know Ms. Mills' boyfriend as well?"

"He's my son."

FIFTY-FOUR
EMJAY

I waited an hour to be called up to see Shariece. I sat in the lobby that reeked sickly of bleach and feet. My palms were sweaty and I couldn't stop from tapping my Chuck Taylors against the glossy white-and-purple checkered linoleum. I couldn't imagine what Shariece must have been going through. If I could have busted her out of this hellhole, I would have. I flipped anxiously threw a tattered old issue of *People* magazine until I couldn't take it anymore and hauled back up to the front desk where the Mexican cop sat. "Man, what is taking ya'll so long? I've been waiting a damn hour." Before I could get an answer, Detective Newburn, Taj and Mama exited from a white door. "Ma, what are you doing here?"

"We heard what happened to Shariece. Are you okay, baby?" she asked, wrapping her arms around me.

"No, I'm not okay. They got Shariece in here on some murder charge, and she didn't do it. Mama, it's Shariece. She didn't kill anybody."

"Of course she didn't. Detective Newburn, we want to see her."

"Usually we only allow one visitor to see an inmate, but I'll make an exception this time."

"Thank you, Detective," Leandra said.

"Are you coming?" Mama asked Taj.

"I'll wait in the lobby. The two of you should go up."

I hadn't seen Taj since the dinner at Mama's. They patted me and Mama down, told us to empty our pockets. I guess they thought we had a paper clip to pick the lock, or some shit. Ma looked annoyed as they rummaged through her purse. We had to put our car keys in a bowl and then walk through the security alarm. It didn't sound, so I guess we were in the clear. They gave the three of us tags that read *D-Unit* and told us to clasp them on our shirts.

"Walk down the hall, take the elevator to the fourth floor. She's on her way down," Detective Newburn said.

"How are you holding up?" Mama asked.

"I'll be better once I get Shariece out of this place."

"Detective Newburn told us what happened, about that Deandre person blackmailing Shariece."

"She didn't kill him. I saw the tape, but she didn't do it. Somebody must have gone to Deandre's apartment after she left."

"Who?"

"I don't know, but I'm going to find out." Mama and I were the only ones in the unit waiting for Shariece to come down.

"Where is she?" Mama asked.

"They said she was on her way down," I said, as I looked from behind the plate glass smudged with fingerprints. Schools of women swarmed the jail wearing navy-blue jumpsuits that read *Leon County Jail* in large white letters on the back of their shirts and on the side of their pants. I didn't want to think about what Shariece must have been going through. "I wished I had never heard the name Deandre," I said, as I waited patiently. "Detective Newburn said there was a video he took of her having sex with another student. Was that student you?"

I was embarrassed by the thought of telling Ma that I was the one, that I was that student in the video. "We made one mistake and look where it got us."

"Oh Lord, Emjay."

"It was stupid, I know."

"Does her boss know about the two of you?"

"I'm not sure. I really can't think about that right now, Ma. The most important thing right now is finding out who killed Deandre and getting Shariece out of here."

"I know you're not thinking about going out there to find his murderer," Ma said.

Before I could push an answer out of my mouth, I spotted Shariece making her way toward me and Mama. She was both happy and shocked to see us sitting on the other side of the glass waiting for her. She looked good considering. We picked up our phones simultaneously. "Hey, baby. How are you holding up?" I asked.

"Scared, but I'm trying to stay strong."

"We're going to get you out of here," Mama said, "we know you didn't kill that boy."

"I went to court this morning. My bail is set at one-hundred thousand dollars."

My jaw dropped when I heard how much it would be to get Shariece out of that hellhole. "Don't worry. I'm going to go talk to a lawyer," I said.

"I'm a black woman accused of murder. No one gives two shits about me."

What she said was messed up, but true. No one cares if we kill each other off. If Shariece were blonde, blue-eyed and pure as the driven snow, she would be deemed a hero.

"Stop talking like that, Shariece," Mama said. "We care about you and we love you."

"Leandra, I'm surprised you're here after what I've put Emjay through. I'm so sorry."

"Forget about all that, baby girl. It's water under the bridge. The only thing you need to be focused on right now is walking out of these doors a free woman." Shariece laughed through the tears that welled up in her big, brown eyes.

"Please forgive me," she said, pressing her hand against the glass.

Mama returned the gesture. "There's nothing to forgive you for, best friend. If anyone is asking for forgiveness, it's me. I've been acting like a total bitch, and these past few months have been hell without the two of you in my life. I admit that I wasn't ready for you to grow up, Jay. You're my son turning into a man before my eyes and I didn't want to turn you loose. When you moved out, I was terrified of losing you."

I gave Mama a hug. "You could never lose me, Ma. It doesn't matter how old I get; I will always be your baby boy and I will always be here for you."

"I love you, baby."

"I love you more, Mama."

Ma turned her attention toward Shariece. "And you and I are going to rebuild our relationship again when you get out of here."

"If I get out," Shariece said.

"What Emjay and I need you to do is stay positive. You gotta keep your head up and trust that we are going to do everything we can for you. Can you do that, Shariece?"

"I'll try."

"No, you can do better than try," Mama said. "Promise us that you will stay positive. This will not beat you as long as you keep me, Emjay and God in your heart."

Before I could throw in some words of encouragement of my own, a female voice chimed in. "You have three minutes remaining."

"They're about to cut us off," I warned Mama.

"I don't want to leave you," I said.

"I don't want you to leave," Shariece said, crying.

Thick tears streaked Shariece's face knowing that I had to leave without her.

"I will get you out," was the last thing I said before our conversation was cut short.

Mama and I left, walking toward the elevator. "Fuuuuuuccck!" I yelled as I repeatedly punched the painted, cinderblock wall.

"Jay, calm down."

"What are we going to do? I don't have a hundred thousand dollars."

"We'll find a way."

"I told her not to go see Deandre by herself. I told her that she could get hurt, but she went anyway."

"You know she's always been headstrong. There's no convincing her otherwise."

"Ma, I think someone went to Deandre's place the same night Shariece was there. She swears to me that he was alive after she left."

"Detective Newburn said they found hundreds of flash drives and videotapes in his bedroom of women in public restrooms, some of them underage, so anyone could have killed him."

"And I need to find out who that anyone is."

"I know that look. Don't do nothing crazy, baby."

"Shariece could be facing life in prison, Ma. Or worse, the death penalty, so I'm willing to do a little crazy if it means clearing her name."

My mind was made up and I was going to do whatever it took to save the woman I loved.

FIFTY-FIVE
TAJ

My phone buzzed for the fourth time in the pocket of my khakis. I decided against ignoring it this time. "Damn, do I have to tell you in twelve different languages that I quit?" I hesitantly answered. "Jimi, I really can't—"

"Man, I have been trying to reach you all afternoon," he said before I could finish my sentence. "What's going on?" I asked.

"It's Vance. He's not waking up."

"What do you mean he's not waking up?"

"I think he took too much shit." Jimi sounded hysterical on the phone, hollering and sounding crazy.

"Then call nine-one-one."

"I can't call the cops, man, you gotta help me." I didn't have to do shit but stay black and die. Since when was Vance's business mine? Leandra and Emjay stepped off the elevator. "Okay, just hang tight. I'm on my way."

"Hurry up, man. I don't know what to do," Jimi said.

"What's going on?" Leandra asked.

"I have to go. It's an emergency."

"Seems to be a lot of that going on around here."

"I'm sorry, baby."

"It's fine, go. I'll get a ride from Emjay back to the shop."

I kissed Leandra on the forehead and said, "I'll call you tonight."

When I got to Jimi's, the place was a mess—needles and traces of cocaine strewn on the coffee table like Monopoly pieces. "Jimi!" I yelled.

"We're in here." I walked toward the bathroom to find Jimi sitting on the edge of his bathtub cradling Vance's head in his arms. Vance was deathly white.

"What the fuck happened?"

"We were smoking up and he started seizing. His eyes rolled back into head. I've been trying to wake him up."

"Where's Montez?"

"That twink bolted when Vance started seizing."

I felt his neck for a pulse. There wasn't one. "We need to get him to the hospital."

"No hospitals," Jimi said, snapping at me. "Look at this place. If we take him to the hospital, they will start asking questions, and then call the cops. I'm not going to prison because of this junkie."

"Help me lay him flat on the floor," I said. Jimi grabbed Vance by the legs while I took him by the shoulders. We gently laid him on the cold bathroom tile. I started to give him mouth-to-mouth. I put my ear to his chest in an attempt to hear a heartbeat. "Fuck," I said. I began to press down on his chest in an effort to get his heart beating again. I didn't know shit about CPR. "Please, God, wake up," Jimi said. "I can't go to prison." Jimi was whining like a punk. He was always trying to come off hard, but really, he was soft as butter.

"Come on, Vance, wake up!" I yelled, as I began to beat on his chest with a closed fist.

After the third try, Vance came to, coughing and heaving. I rolled him over on his side, scared he would choke on his tongue.

"Thank you, God," Jimi said. "You crazy junkie fuck, you scared the crap out of me."

"We still need to get him to the hospital," I said.

"He's fine now, right?"

"Yeah, but we don't know what could be wrong with him."

"He had too much drugs, that's all. Look at him, he's good. You're all right, ain'tcha, Big Vance?" Vance shook his head. "Jesus, I thought the bastard was going to die, but he's okay thanks to you." I wanted to put my fist through Jimi's sleazy mug, but he wasn't worth it. "He needs to walk it off, that's all, get some food in him other than a crackhead lunch." I knew there was no getting through Jimi's thick skull. "I think I can handle it from here, Taj. Thanks for coming over."

"I am so done with this shit. I'm done with you, him, the whole fucking shit show. If he dies, it's on you." I took one last look at Vance and walked out of the bathroom, past the living room toward the door. "Don't ever call me again. You two are on your fuckin' own."

"Oh, yeah? Do you really think it's that easy to just walk away? You signed a contract, Taj."

"Do you think I'm going to step foot back on your set after this? Vance almost died, Jimi."

"I'll get him some help. Truth is, he's used up anyway. He shows up for work late, he can't stay off the candy long enough to fuck; I've had it. I need fresh meat, some new blood and you're it, Taj, baby. You're going to make me a shitload of money."

"Fuck you and your contract. I'm done. I'm out."

"You're done when I say you're done. I have plans for you and that Mandingo dick of yours. Tours, special appearances, calendars, sex toys, you name it. We are going to be so—"

I grabbed Jimi by his throat. "You might want to get your hearing checked. I quit. You can take your contract and shove it up your pasty-white ass."

"Take your hands off me," Jimi warned like he was going to do something. I shoved him back against the coffee table and hauled my ass out of that pig pit he called a house. "This isn't over. I own you, you fuck. You signed a contract and that makes you my property." As loudly as Jimi yelled, I wasn't trying to hear him.

"Fuck you," I said as I happily hauled my ass out of there.

FIFTY-SIX
MYRICK

After spending ten hours hacking up Rochelle's body, I grabbed four black plastic construction bags from the basement, tossing in legs, arms, head, hands and torso. All except the feet and fingers, which I bagged separately to burn later. I doubled the bags so they wouldn't leak in the back of the Suburban, and bound them with duct tape. I laid some tarp down still, just in case. You never know where blood is going to end up. Rochelle's heart was the only thing I kept. I thought to dispose of her in the Dumpster behind a movie theater that was a few miles from where I lived, but I didn't want to take the chance of being seen by anyone. So I went with the twenty-four-hour city dump instead where there were no cameras and there wouldn't be any people at 3 a.m. I was too tired to drive all night trying to find a space to get rid of the body. The dump was about thirty minutes across town, but it was worth the drive. I drove until asphalt turned to gravel and dirt. I pushed my SUV around corners and bends. I dimmed my lights as I approached the fenced entrance. "Good. I'm the only one here." I had to make it quick. I pulled up alongside one of the large containers. The minute I stepped out of my car, the putrid stench of garbage slapped me in the face. I let the back door up and dragged the two heavy construction bags out. I threw one over my right shoulder and hurled it into the Dumpster. I did the same with the other and hauled ass out of there.

When I got home, I could still smell Rochelle's blood on me. I switched on the TV in the bedroom. Sound coming from something other than the cicadas outside made me feel at ease. I emptied the wineglasses in the sink to wash later before I went to the bathroom and filled the tub with hot water and bleach. I threw my clothes in a ball on the floor. I sat in the tub, took a Brillo pad and scrubbed my legs, arms and hands raw. I kept my fingernails trimmed so they wouldn't act as trappings for blood and skin. I scrubbed until my skin burned, until the only traces of blood left were mine from the bleach bath. I stepped out of the tub of bleach and bloody bathwater and grabbed a towel. As I dried off, that's when I heard the news report on the TV in Mama's room about Shariece being arrested for murder. "No, that's not right. It can't be." I watched and sure enough, it was my baby's face plastered all over the news. She had been taken into custody for the murder of some loser by the name of Deandre Jackson. "That's not him. That's not the boyfriend. Fuck, that's not the fucking boyfriend! Who the fuck is Deandre Jackson?" *Bail is set at 100 hundred thousand dollars*, the anchor said. "No, that's not him? That's not the guy." The thought of Shariece being pinched for something I had done made me sick to my stomach. "I can fix this." I pulled open the doors of the closet and reached behind boxes and clothes for a small shoebox. Inside was some money I had stashed away. It was two- hundred thousand damn near, more than enough to bail Shariece out of the shithole they had thrown my baby in. This was money Mama had given me for school.

After everything that had happened with the trial and her testifying against me, I had forgiven her. Being locked up made me do a lot of thinking about what had gone down that night, and hell, I would have called the cops on my ass, too. I couldn't stand the thought of losing Shariece. I would write her every day, apologizing in each letter. I had told her that I'd bared no ill will against her. I had told her that I'd forgiven her and that I understood. Every one of my letters was returned to sender.

I didn't sleep all night for thinking about Shariece. "Can't imagine what she must be going through." I got dressed and grabbed the shoebox of money. "It all ends today. I have plans for you, Shariece, baby."

It didn't take me long to get to the police station. My palms were sweating and my heart was thumping crazy in my chest as I sat in an attempt to pull my shit together. I hadn't seen anything on the news about the trail of bodies I had left behind, so I figured they weren't on to me yet. Most of these Barney Fife pigs don't know which way is up half the time. Tallahassee's finest, my dick. I knew the chance I was taking, that the cops would pounce on me the minute I walked through those doors, but for the sake of Shariece, it was a chance I was willing to take.

With the shoebox of cash tucked under my armpit, I walked into the police station where a uniformed cop was sitting behind a plate of glass. He had coffee bean-brown skin, speckles of white in his hair and wore glasses, looking like somebody's granddaddy. I was surprised that the force still kept old-timers like him on the job. He zeroed in on me like a heat-seeking missile the minute I walked through the door. He probably thought I was carrying a bomb. It's not every day someone walks into a police station with a shoebox of money. "How you doing?" he asked. "What's up? Do you all have an inmate here by the name of Shariece Mills?"

"Let me check." *Slade*, his chrome-plated name tag read. He ran his fat fingers across the keyboard in search of Shariece's name. I took the lid off the shoebox, unveiling the contents inside, putting this desk jockey pig at ease. "We have a Shariece Mills here who was brought in two weeks ago."

"Great. I'm here to post bail for her if that's possible."

He gawked at me curiously. "Are you a family member?"

"No, I'm a good friend." What difference did it make if I was family, a friend or Bobo the damn clown? "So is a cash bond okay?"

"We don't normally take cash at this hour, but that's fine." Officer Slade took the lid off the box of cash, and began counting. He pushed a form under the glass for me to fill out.

"Would you like a receipt for this?"

Was this brother serious? "No, just make sure that it gets posted." I realized that it was time to stop hiding. It was time for me to get my woman back.

FIFTY-SEVEN
SHARIECE

I had given up on sleep in this place. My head was throbbing from another one of my migraines, and my back was kicking my ass. The cheap, generic aspirin I had to wait two hours for clearly wasn't working. When I had told the guard that I couldn't sleep, she didn't give two shits. "What do you think this is, a five-star hotel?" she had said. "You eat what we tell you to eat; you sleep when we tell you to sleep. Where you're going, princess, you can expect to have plenty of restless nights." Bitch. I would have been wasting the breath God gave me trying to explain to that ice queen that I was innocent, that I didn't kill anybody. Damn cops are going to believe what they want. If it was up to them, they would shoot first and ask questions never. No judge, no lawyer, no jury of your peers, just a bullet to the head. I wish to God I had never gone to Deandre's apartment that night. A day, an hour, a minute doesn't go by that I wish I had stayed away. Why would I throw my life away on a kid? God knows that I didn't kill him and I had faith that He will see me through this. I would give my right titty to be in my own bed right now, cuddling up under Emjay, laughing to old episodes of *Martin* on TV One. I would give my left tit for a steak and baked potato right now. All they gave you in this rotten place was bologna between two stale-ass pieces of bread, half an orange and water. I couldn't stand bologna when I was a little girl and couldn't stand that nasty meat now. My hair was a mess, I was losing weight, which might not be a bad thing, and I was horny. There is no way in hell I could do prison. A woman like me would not survive a place like that. I could barely endure jail. A single minute in this hellhole was enough for any God-fearing, law-abiding female. If I did end up doing a bid, at least I wouldn't have to hear Denise screaming her crazy head off. Every night this time, she wakes up hollering from nightmares. The ice queen guard says she's in for killing her baby. Says the girl was so high on PCP, she had no idea that she put her baby in the microwave. A chick like that, they should skip the trial and put her baby-killing ass under the prison. I mean damn, how in the hell do you not realize that you're putting your baby in a damn microwave? I have always believed that people who harm children, their life should be forfeit, just automatically put to death. Why are they even wasting their time with her? Need to do something with her, take her to Chatta-hoochee somewhere. People think that just because Tallahassee is a small town that nothing ever happens here. You are just as likely to get killed as you would somewhere like Miami or New York, and the more you try to cover shit up, the louder it's going to smell. I hope Emjay and Leandra could get me the hell out of here. Even if I did get out of here, I wouldn't have anything left. Sure by now my face was plastered on the cover of every rag in Florida and on every news channel. Rochelle ha probably had my office cleared out. I would have no money coming in and worse yet, I'd be looked at as a pariah. Had I told Deandre to go fuck himself, maybe none of this would have been happening. No matter what happened, everything was going to change.

"Mills, you're out." It was the ice queen with the heart of junkyard aluminum. I looked at her like she was cray-cray.

"What?"

"Someone put up your bail. You're free to go."

"Is this some kind of joke, because if it is—."

"Do I look like the kind that jokes around? Now come on, get the hell out of my jail."

She didn't have to tell me twice. "Was it my boyfriend who put up bail?"

"No clue. I just do what they tell me. They told me to let you out, so that's what I'm doing, but you're welcome to stay if you want." I didn't find her dry humor nowhere in the vicinity of funny. I gladly put one size nine in front of the other and followed her out of the eight-by-ten shithole. Emjay and Leandra had come through. I didn't have a doubt in my mind that they wouldn't. Leandra probably took a second mortgage out on the house. I don't know what I would ever do without her. I was going to pay her back every red cent when I got back on my feet. I thought I would see them waiting when they took me down to be processed out, but there was no sign of Leandra or Emjay. *That's strange*, I thought. All of my belongings were returned to me and I was free to go. Hard to believe that I would ever say the word *free* again the way things were looking. What just happened? I wanted to pinch myself, but was afraid that if I did, I would wake up back in my cell in a cold sweat, realizing that it was all a terrible dream. Two things I wanted to do were feel Emjay's arms around me again and take a long, hot bath to soak the stink of the Leon County jail off of me. I called Emjay. The phone rang once before he answered. "Hey baby," I said.

"Hey, I'm on my way to see you now." It was good to hear Emjay's voice.

"I'm going to need a ride home."

"What do you mean?"

"I've been released. Didn't you and Leandra post my bail?"

"No. Ma and I have been talking about getting you a lawyer."

"Well, somebody did, because they've just released me."

"Are you serious?"

"They told me that someone posted my bail, and that I was free to go. I thought it was you and Leandra."

"No, I've been fishing through the phone book trying to find a good criminal lawyer. That's weird. Maybe it was the director from the school."

"Rochelle? I don't know; I doubt that. She probably never wants to see my face again."

"Well, baby, it's fantastic news either way. If I knew who it was that did this, I would kiss them."

"You and me both."

"I just left my place. I'm about ten minutes away from the jail now," Emjay said. I looked out of my car window at a sky full of stars.

"Hurry. I'll be outside waiting."

I sat on a bench in front of the entrance of the jail as the realization of my freedom was slowly seeping into my mind. I racked my brain trying to figure out who could have posted my bail.

FIFTY-EIGHT
MYRICK

When I saw Shariece sitting in front of the jail, all I wanted to do was run up to her and throw my arms around her. I saw how good she looked and knew that my journey to get to this point was all worth it. But my eagerness turned to anger when I saw this silver SUV pull up in front of the jail alongside Shariece. This boy, who was probably still suckling from his mama's titty, got out to greet my woman. And when they kissed, it took everything in me to keep from putting my fist through the windshield. "Who the fuck is that?" I tailed behind them careful to keep my distance. They led me to a house in the country that was a good twenty minutes out of town. The image of them kissing was like repeated stabs through my heart. I parked at the end of the studio apartments as he pulled in front. I waited a few minutes until I thought they were inside the house to make my move. "I'm too close to let anyone get in my way." I pulled the .38 automatic out of the glove box and eased up toward the house. I peered through one of the front windows to find them kissing and necking. The angrier I grew, the tighter I gripped the gun in my hand. "Fucking whore." Shariece disappeared out of my sights, leaving this loser to scrounge around in the kitchen. My heart felt like it had been ripped out of my chest and thrown in the dirt. How could she let this broke-ass, high-yellow wannabe motherfucker put his hands on her? I quietly turned the knob of the front door and tipped in. I could hear the shower going from the bedroom. This nigga was rummaging around in the refrigerator with his back facing me. Dumb fuck didn't even hear me walking up behind him. Just as he turned around, I hit him over the head with the butt of my burner. He dropped to the kitchen floor like I sad-ass sack of potatoes. I aimed the gun at him about to shoot him when I heard the shower water stop.

"Honey, I'm home," I whispered as I crept down the hall toward the bedroom.

FIFTY-NINE
SHARIECE

almost forgot how good a bath felt. We had showers twice a week in the jail, but there's nothing like soaking in a hot bubble bath. I was already starting to feel like a human being again. All I wanted to do was put the last couple of weeks behind me, pretend for just a short while that it never happened. I didn't want to turn on the TV to find that I was being talked about. My cousin Sedrick's cabin was the perfect getaway from the crazy city. "Baby, those hamburgers smell too good." I walked out of the bathroom in my robe, toweling my hair dry.

"Hey, baby, did you miss me?" The sound of *his* voice curdled my blood. It was Myrick.

"What the fuck?"

"I've missed you so much."

"How did you…where did you?"

"Speechless. That's a good sign."

I stumbled back until my hips hit the dresser that was on the right side of the bed. My heart rate quickened when I saw Myrick standing in front of me. "You're supposed to be in prison."

"They let me out on good behavior."

"Get the hell out of my house."

"Or what? You're going to call your little boyfriend? Come on, Shariece, what are you doing, babysitting?"

"What did you do to Emjay?"

"Don't worry about him. I took care of him." I screamed as loud as I could, but stopped when I noticed the gun he was holding in his hand. "I took care of your little teenager."

"What did you do to him, you crazy motherfucker?"

"Is that any way to talk to your soul mate?"

Myrick was the only thing that stood between me and the bedroom door. I felt along the dresser, grabbed up the ashtray, and hurled it at Myrick. I ran, but Myrick grabbed me and slung me onto the bed. He straddled me, pressing down on me with his weight. I punched and kicked, screaming for help. When I scratched him across the face, he gawked at me with wide-eyed anger and backhanded me across the face, and held the gun at my right temple. "Woman, what the hell is wrong with you? Why are you acting like this, Shariece? If anything, I should be the one pissed off, catching you kissing all over that fool in there. I could slit your throat and blame it on your little fuck buddy in there." Myrick gently swept hair out of my face with the nose of the gun. "But you see I'm not going to do that. Your throat is much too pretty," he said, as he ran the black steel along my chest, pushing open my robe. Myrick licked his lips when he stared at my wet breasts. All I could do was cry out as he circled the right nipple of my breast with the gun. "Damn, you're beautiful." I knew my only way out of this was to play by whatever sick game Myrick had in store. I caressed his arm to calm him down. His eyes began to soften, the irate expression on his face, relaxed. "If I take my hand away from your mouth, you promise not to scream?" I nodded yes. "The last thing I want to do, baby, is hurt you, but I will if you make me." I nodded my head again. Myrick eased his hand away. Beads of sweat plummeted from his face. Myrick got off of me. I was careful not to make any sudden moves. I was frantic thinking about Emjay. "You have no idea the things I have done to get to you."

"What do you want, Myrick?"

"I just want us to be together. I want it to be like it used to be."

"It can't be like it used to be."

Myrick wiped his mouth with the back of his wrist. "Come on now. You wouldn't say that if you knew how many people I had to kill to be with you."

"Oh my God, what did you do?"

"Did you get any of my letters? I wrote to you every day."

"I got your letters, but I threw them away. It made me sick to my stomach to so much as touch them after what you did to me."

"It's all good, boo. I'm better at confessing my undying love to you face to face anyway." Myrick was scaring me the way he waved his gun about. "I had to pull some Veronica Mars shit to find you, but thanks to a loyal prison pen pal of mine, she was able to track you down. I told Krista about all the pain you caused me; how you were the reason I was locked up."

"They should have given you life in prison."

"She found out where you lived, where you worked, even where you did your banking. She should have been a private detective. She was much smarter than what she gave herself credit for. Too bad I had to kill her. She was a liability and would have ratted me out to the cops eventually."

"You're nothing but a cold-blooded murderer."

"You want to watch your mouth with me. Don't make me

regret bailing you out of jail." I looked at Myrick surprised by his revelation. "It was nothing, really. Anything for my girl."

As Myrick continued running off at the mouth, it had come to me. "Oh my God, it was you, wasn't it? You killed Deandre?"

"Who? Oh, you mean that perverted fuck that tried to rape you?"

"You were there?"

"Hell yeah, I was there. I followed you to his crib that night. I thought he was your little teenage boyfriend, but I found out he wasn't when I saw that...*boy* kissing on you at the jail. It's just as well though. I took care of them both." Tears welled in my eyes, streaking my face. "Ah, come on, girl. Why the waterworks? This is a celebration. You and I are finally reunited. Reunited and it feels so good." Myrick laughed. "I love that song." I pulled away when he caressed my face with the hands that had killed Emjay. "The night I saw you talking to Rochelle, you looked so good."

"What did you do to Rochelle?"

"Don't be mad at me, baby. We just went on a couple of dates, that's it. She don't hold a candle to you. It's all good though. You don't have to worry about her anymore. I cut her heart out."

"Goddamn you, why Rochelle? She didn't do anything to you."

"She was only another piece on my board I played. She spoke very highly of you though, going on about how hardworking you are, and how good you are." I grabbed my nail file off the nightstand as Myrick paced the floor, going on about the brutal way he killed Rochelle. "But let's not go on about all that. Being locked up gave me a lot of time to think about what happened and I just want you to know that I forgive you, that I hold no grudges. I love you. You're my girl." I cringed to Myrick's touch. "I want to forget everything that's happened, and move on with a fresh start."

"Fuck you!" I yelled, as I plunged the file in Myrick's chest and ran out of the bedroom.

"Fucking bitch!" Myrick let off a shot as I ran. The bullet missed me by a hair. I gasped to find Emjay lying motionless on the floor in a pool of blood. I frantically pulled the front door open and ran out into the cold night, dirt and gravel wet under my feet as I ran through a thicket of brush and trees. "Shariece!" Myrick yelled. He wasn't too far behind. "I'm going to kill you, you fucking bitch." The full moon was the only light I had to illuminate my way. I was familiar with the area. Sedrick and I used to play tag and hide-and-seek in these woods when we were children. "So that's how you want to play this? I confess my love for you and you stab me?" I made my way toward an old tool shed that wasn't far from the cabin. It was cold, wet and reeked of rot. My heart was beating like a stampede of bulls in my chest as I searched the shed for something to protect myself with. I noticed a rusty screwdriver on one of the tables. I grabbed it and hid into a cold, dark corner, gripping the tool.

"You can come out, baby. I'm not mad. Let's talk about this," Myrick said as he kicked open the door of the shack. "There you are, beautiful. Why are you running away from me?"

"I ain't running from you anymore. If you want me, then come and get me, you sick, psycho fuck." Myrick tucked his gun in the waist of his jeans. As he lunged for me, I plunged the screwdriver into his stomach. I screamed as he grabbed me by the throat. His hold on me weakened as I shoved the screwdriver in deeper. "Die, motherfucker, die!" Myrick collapsed to the floor. He struggled to pull the screwdriver out, coughing up blood, but was too weak in his efforts. I ran out of the shed back toward the house.

I turned Emjay over on his back and felt for a pulse. "He's alive." I grabbed my cell phone and dialed 9-1-1. "Stay with me, baby. Stay with me," I repeated.

SIXTY
LEANDRA

Two Months Later

The aroma of turkey and dressing, both turnip and collard greens, chitterlings, and honey-baked ham filled the house. Every cap on my stove had a pot on it. I had the platter of macaroni and cheese sitting on the counter to cool along with a pot of black-eyed peas and four sweet potato pies. I was going to make a chocolate cake, but Shariece said she would handle dessert, so that was one less thing I had to fool around with. "Damn, baby, it smells amazing in here," Taj said, sliding his arms around my waist as I stirred the turnip greens.

"Thank you. These turnip greens are almost done and I'm warming the turkey and dressing up in the oven. Did you set the table?"

"All set and ready for company." Things were going better than I expected between me and Taj. It took a while, but I finally was able to accept him making porn films. I figured as long as he was safe and not sticking dicks in his mouth, I was cool with it. A lot of women would say that I'm crazy as hell, but they're not in a relationship with Taj; I am, and I love him. He had told me about the mess going on with Jimi, and that the best thing was to cut ties with him. With all the drugs that were running in and out of his place, getting as far away from Jimi as he could was a good idea. "What time did Emjay and Shariece say they were coming?"

"I told them that everything would probably be ready by four o' clock, so I suspect that they should be here around three-thirty."

"I could not be happier right now," Taj said.

"Why is that?"

"Spending Thanksgiving with the woman I love. I'm going to be a father. What's not to be happy about?" I finished stirring both pot of greens, turned around and gave Taj a long, sweet kiss.

"This is one of the craziest years I've had, and I'm glad that it's over, that we can move on with our lives," Leandra said.

With everything that had gone on, I was more than ready to say good-bye to 2012 and usher in 2013, which could not come quick enough for me. "Amen to that, you and me both."

"Did you get a chance to speak with Deandre's mother?"

"Yeah, and I could tell from the crack in her voice that she was still very upset about his death."

"You didn't tell her about all the other stuff, did you?"

"His tapes? Of course not. She's better off not knowing that about her son. Best that she remembers him like she always saw him. She came down last week to pick up his body and take him back to St. Pete for burial."

"Well, even though Deandre had his issues, I could only hope that he can find peace in death that he couldn't find in life. My prayers are with his family."

"I can't imagine what they must be going through this Thanksgiving," Taj said.

"They'll get through it." Taj pulled me close and hugged me. "Time heals all as they say. You want to get the ham sliced up for me?" I said.

"Oh, that reminds me. Where's the electric carver I bought?"

"I think I put it in that last drawer at the end of the counter."

Taj took the carving knife and rinsed the blade off under water. I was about to grab a few bowls to put the black-eyed peas and creamed corn in when my cell phone rang. It was Nishelle. I pressed the green icon on my phone. "Hello?"

"Happy Thanksgiving, Ms. Fox."

"Hey, girl, Happy Thanksgiving."

"What are you doing?" Nishelle asked.

"I'm just over here cooking. I'm almost done." When Taj began cutting the ham in slices, I walked into the dining room to drown out the buzzing sound the electric carver gave off. I checked the glasses and plates to make sure there weren't any spots on them.

"What did you cook? 'Cause, ma, I know you can throw down in the kitchen."

"Girl, what didn't I cook? I got turkey and dressing, greens, both turnips and collards, honey baked ham, creamed corn, black-eyed peas, and you know I have to have me some chitterlings."

"Uh-uh, you can have that swine. That stuff stinks."

"It only smells like that when you're cleaning them, but once you get these babies going in the pot with some salt, put some onions and bell pepper in them, that takes the smell right off of them."

"I will have to take your word for it, but I'm still not putting my mouth anywhere near pig intestines."

"Listen to you. Are you cooking?"

"Me? Cook? L, you know me better than that. I can boil water, maybe toast some bread, but I'm no Martha Stewart. Wish I could cook like that sister, though. I'm over at my auntie's house."

"Is that all that noise I hear in the background?"

"Yes. The house is filled with uncles, aunties, cousins, second cousins and third cousins all in one house. I'm hiding out in Latoya's bedroom upstairs. It's too much. I need a break from all the craziness."

"Nishelle, you past crazy," I said, laughing. "I know it ain't that bad."

"It's not, really, but you know how family can be."

I heard someone in the background laughing hard and loud. "Who is that laughing like a witch?"

"That's one of my first cousins, Kora. She likes to laugh at her own jokes, thinking she's Sommore, and honey, don't let her start drinking. She's a hot-ass mess when she's had too much Hennessy. I stay as far away from her as any beautiful black woman can possibly get when she's had too much to drink."

I burst out laughing. "Listen to you."

"Once everybody fills their bellies, they'll leave Kora with auntie to clean up. They always do. No one wants to put up with her. She'll be spending the night, I'm sure."

I noticed one of the wineglasses had a few spots, so I rubbed them out with my thumb. Taj came with the turkey and dressing and placed it at the head of the table. I chuckled when I saw him wearing my other cherry-printed apron. He gave me a kiss. "Girl, she sounds like a mess."

"And don't even get me started on all these bad-ass kids running around here, Lee. I don't know if I can take a whole weekend of this."

"I think you'll manage. What time did you get to Gainesville last night?"

"A little before ten o' clock."

"Is it cold there?"

"It's cool enough for a sweater, but not cold-cold. Only a day, and I already want to jump in my Saab and drive back to Tallahassee. I should have taken you up on your offer to spend the holidays with you." Nishelle could be the biggest drama queen. She had no idea how lucky she was to have a family that loved and cared about her. Some people don't have anyone to spend Thanksgiving with.

"Well, I'm sure you will tell me all about it when you get back, but until then, enjoy Turkey Day. Your drunk, bad joke-telling auntie, your crazy cousins, enjoy it all, because that's the kind of stuff you will laugh about when you get to my ripe old age."

"Yeah, I guess."

"Baby, cut the heat down on the greens for me, and I think the turkey and dressing is ready to take out of the oven," I told Taj. I heard someone call Nishelle's name in the background.

"Well, let me go before Latoya has the entire house looking for me."

"I know how crazy things can be with family this time of year, but that's what makes it all worthwhile. Family is family."

"I'll give you a call tomorrow; let you know that I survived unscathed."

"Sounds good, and don't be so hard on your people, crazy aunties, cousins, uncles or otherwise. They are all you have. Trust me, I know."

"I'll talk to you later, Lee. Happy Thanksgiving."

"You too, baby girl."

I went back to the kitchen to help Taj with the food. Who knew he could be so handy? "Who was that?" he asked.

"That was Nishelle. She's spending Thanksgiving with her family in Gainesville. It sounds like she—" I paused when I felt the baby kicking.

"What is it?" Taj asked. "Lee, is everything all right?"

"The baby just kicked again. Here, feel." I placed Taj's hand on my baby bump.

"Oh shit, I felt that." Taj rested his head against my belly. "Cut that out in there. It's not time for you to come out yet."

I laughed. "Boy, you so silly."

"I can't believe I'm going to be a daddy."

"You? I can't believe somebody's going to be calling me Mama again after twenty-two years."

"Stop talking like you're old. You look damn good."

"Aww, you're so sweet." As I gave Taj a kiss for his kindness, the doorbell rang. I looked at the cookie jar clock above the sink. It read, *4:20*. "That must be Emjay and Shariece."

"You want me to get it?"

"No. I like you in that apron. It brings out your eyes. Finish putting the food out. I'll get the door." I wiped my hands on my own apron printed with cherries. I answered the door to find Emjay and Shariece standing there in their Sunday best. "Hey, Happy Thanksgiving," I said, as I threw my arms around Shariece. She wore a navy wrap dress with six-inch heels to match.

"Hey, girl, Happy Thanksgiving."

"Happy Thanksgiving, Mama."

"Happy Thanksgiving to you, too, baby." It was hard to get my arms around Emjay with the five-layer chocolate cake he was holding in his hands. "You look so handsome in your suit." I got all teary-eyed looking over my son and best friend. And it wasn't because of seeing them together, but because I was glad to see them both alive. Emjay had white gauze wrapped around his head from the concussion he had suffered from being bludgeoned by Myrick, and I could still see a few cuts and bruises on Shariece. I led them into the living room.

"Mama, you ain't crying again, are you?"

"I'm happy to see you two, that's all. I'm truly blessed." Shariece gave me another hug. "You don't know how thrilled I am to have my best friend back."

Taj made his way into the living room where we were standing. "Hey, ya'll made it. Happy Thanksgiving." He shook Emjay's hand and hugged Shariece.

"You too, man," Emjay said.

"Thank you, Taj. Happy Thanksgiving," said Shariece.

"Cute apron," Emjay said.

"You like this? I think we might have another one with flowers on it. I can hook you up," Taj joked.

"No, brother, I'm good." All of us laughed.

"Here, I'll take this cake to the kitchen. Girl, this cake looks so good we might as well skip dinner and start on dessert."

"Six layers."

"Oh, six layers this time?"

"It's Thanksgiving. You know how extra I like to get. Besides, you're eating for two now."

"Ain't that the truth. I'm avoiding the scale until I push this human being out of me."

"Ya'll want something to drink, some champagne?" Taj asked.

"Sounds good," Shariece said.

"Apple cider for me, baby."

"Ma, so how's the baby? What did the doctor say?"

"Everything is fine. The baby is healthy and other than my blood pressure being a little high, I'm fine too."

"Do you think you should be on your feet? Shouldn't you be lying down or something?"

"Emjay, I'm fine. Dr. Winn gave me some medication for the high blood pressure, so everything is good."

"Okay, if you say so."

I got four wineglasses out of the cabinet while Taj twisted the corks off a bottle of Chardonnay and apple cider. "Speaking of doctors, how are you doing?"

"She gave the both of us a clean bill of health. Other than the bruises and scratches Shariece endured, and the bump on my head, we should be fine."

"Thank the Heavenly Father for that." Taj poured wine and cider into the glasses and passed them around. "Let's make a toast," I said. The four of us raised our glasses. "Here's to good friends and family." We raised our glasses, clanging them together and took sips of the white wine.

"Lee, did you talk to Rochelle's brother?" Shariece asked.

"Yeah, I did."

"How is he?"

"He seemed okay. He came down to make arrangements to have Rochelle's body shipped to Blacksburg for the funeral. He didn't think it was a need to tell their mama about Rochelle's death. With the dementia, he said she doesn't even know her own son."

"That's so sad," Shariece said.

"It is sad," Emjay said.

"Was she the only daughter?" Taj asked.

"It was just her and Edmond. She had told me about how sick her mama was, and that she was thinking about leaving here to move back to Blacksburg to take care of her because Edmond had his hands full with his own family."

"So what is he going to do now?"

"He didn't say, but I would imagine he's going to put her in a home. He's got his wife and kids to take care of, so who's going to see about his mama?"

"I'm sorry, ya'll," Shariece said.

"Sorry for what, baby?" Emjay asked.

"Just for…bringing Myrick into our lives."

"Shariece, don't even go there. You had absolutely nothing to do with what that sick bastard did. If anyone is to blame, it's the cops for not informing you that he was released. The blood of all his victims is on their hands, not yours, so don't blame yourself."

"Mama's right, Shariece. Nobody here blames you for what that freak did."

"Have the police made any progress to his whereabouts?" Taj asked.

"They're still searching," Emjay said. "They searched his house and found more bodies in the basement and in a storage building in the backyard. One of the victims was a good friend of Chadae."

Shariece rubbed her arms like a cold chill ran up her limbs as Emjay explained. "Deputy Newburn says the FBI has stepped in," she said.

"Good. If anyone is going to dig him out, the feds will. It's about time some real cops took over with these sad-ass excuses for police officers around here."

"He could be all the way to Alaska by now," Shariece said.

"Baby, you can't keep living in fear of the guy."

"Emjay's right," I said. "No matter what happens, you have to move on with your life. Living in fear is exactly what that crazy bastard wants. The best thing you can do is live your life. The FBI will deal with Myrick."

"I don't want them to catch him," Shariece said. "I want them to kill him. No courts, no jury of his peers, just shoot him dead."

"I second that," said Emjay.

The conversation was getting way too eerie. "You know what? Enough talk about Myrick. It's Thanksgiving and the worst is over. It's safe to say that it's been a difficult year for us all. Why don't we all go around and say what we're thankful for. Taj, you start."

"Well, I'm thankful for the health and happiness of myself, my lady and our baby's health." I gave Taj a kiss for his lists of warm, heartfelt thanks. I was next. "I'm thankful for the Almighty Heavenly Father for letting me see another Thanksgiving and my beautiful son who is growing up to be a man any mother would be proud of." I began to get choked up again. "Damn, these hormones." Everyone laughed. I took Shariece's hand. "I'm thankful to have my best friend and my sister back in my life as well as a wonderful man. Praise Jesus for you all." I looked at Emjay to let him know that he was next.

"Dang, I don't know how I can top that one, but I will try. I'm thankful for God for getting us all through these past few months and allowing me to continue to live a happy, healthy life. I'm thankful for my beautiful mother who has worked so hard over the years in making sure I have the best of everything, and never giving up on me, and last but certainly not least, I'm thankful for Shariece who has been my rock. I love you." I smiled warmly when she kissed Emjay. Seeing them together made me realize just how in love they were. She was next.

"I'm thankful for my God allowing me to see another light of day. Thankful for my best friend, my heart and my sister, Leandra Fox, and for leading me to my hero, my rock and other half, Emjay Fox. Rest in peace, Rochelle, Deandre, and all of those who have fallen victim to Myrick Nickels. May all of the families be blessed."

"Amen," we all said.

"My stomach has been growling all day," Emjay said. We all chuckled.

"When are you not hungry?" Shariece asked. "Do you know he actually liked that hospital food they were feeding him?"

"He will eat anything that isn't tied down," I said. "I remember how picky you were as a child. Wouldn't eat nothing green unless it was candy or Jell-O."

"Sounds like me when I was growing up," Taj said. "I couldn't stand broccoli and I couldn't stand cabbage."

"Exactly. Ma wouldn't let me get up from the table unless I ate all of my cabbage. I mean, why cook it if you know we're not going to eat it?"

"Because it's good for you. I'm going to make sure the baby eats plenty of vegetables." We went to the dining room where every corner of the table was occupied with a bowl or dish of something from turkey and ham to oxtails and hot-water cornbread.

"This is a big ol' spread," Shariece said.

"Girl, you know I don't play when I get in the kitchen. I'm going to float away like a Goodyear Blimp after all this food," I said.

"Don't worry. We're getting back on Jenny Craig after the holidays."

Taj sat at one end of the table and me at the other while Emjay and Shariece sat across from one another. "Do ya'll know the sex of the baby yet?" Emjay asked. "Am I going to have a little brother or a little sister?"

I glanced across the table at Taj. "You want to tell them?"

"Only if you want to," he said.

"It's a girl."

"A baby girl," Shariece said, smiling. She rushed over to me and gave me a big hug. "A daughter. Congratulations, baby."

"I don't care if it's a girl or a boy as long as it's healthy," Taj said.

"I've always wanted a baby sister," Emjay said.

"Uh-huh, let's see if you say that when you're changing her diapers and we call you over to babysit."

"What was that about diapers? I'm a little deaf in this ear."

"Yeah, exactly." We all laughed.

"Have ya'll decided on a name yet?" Shariece asked.

"I was thinking of either Jayda or Violet. Like after my favorite flower."

"I like Violet, that's pretty," said Shariece.

"I like it, too. Maybe Violet Jayda. Who would like to say the blessings?"

"I'll have a go at it," Taj said. We all held hands and bowed our heads as Taj began. "God, thank you for this good food we are about to receive, for life, love and health. Bless all the families that are gathered around the table this day, and may those who are without find their way into your grace and the arms of their loved ones. Thank you for your blessings, God, Amen."

"Amen, Hallelujah. All right, everybody, dig in." As we all spooned food on our plates, I looked around and could not have been happier to see all of us at the dinner table together. I was truly blessed.

ABOUT THE AUTHOR

Shane Allison is a Florida native, noted poet and writer. His poems and stories have graced the pages of over a dozen anthologies, and online and literary magazines. When he's not hard at work writing short stories, he's busy working on new novels and collections of poetry.

If you enjoyed "Harm Done," be sure to check out

YOU'RE THE ONE I WANT

BY SHANE ALLISON
AVAILABLE FROM STREBOR BOOKS

BREE

What the fuck is he doing here?

I thought I was going to lose my shit when I saw Deanthony walk through the door of Mama Liz's house. Deanthony's skin glowed under the living room lights. He was wearing a red durag, a black tank top, and black, baggy jean shorts. A trace of red from his boxers was showing from the waistband. I'm not going to lie, he looked good, but still, what the hell was he doing here? It took everything in me to keep from dropping the cup of punch that Tangela had spiked with vodka when nobody was looking. Suddenly, my heart was pounding like a drum in my chest. I gawked at Deanthony like the devil himself had walked in Mama Liz's house, and as far as I was concerned, the devil was exactly who Deanthony was, a demon spawn. Tangela startled me when she crept up behind me, grazing my arm.

"Girl, did you see who just walked up in here?"

Deanthony looked dead at me as he shook hands, gave dap and half-hugs to friends and family. You would think he was some famous athlete or some shit, the way everybody gathered around him.

"I didn't think he was going to come."

"He looks good," Tangela said. "Damn good."

"You're not helping," I said, annoyed by Tangela stating the obvious.

I watched Kashawn from the kitchen window where he and Tyrique stood on the deck, nursing on beers.

"Hey, baby, you came," Mama Liz shouted, damn near knocking me down to get to her son. She wiped her hands dry from dish water on the apron that was draped around her, and gave Deanthony a big, mama bear hug.

"Hey, Mama. Of course I came. It's only my brother's birthday."

"You look so skinny. What, you don't eat up there in Hollywood Land?"

"I can't believe he's got the balls to show his face here, yet I don't know why I'm surprised."

"You want me to get rid of him?" Tangela asked.

"No, forget it. It's all good. I don't know why I was stupid enough to think that he wouldn't have the guts to show up for Kashawn's birthday party."

Everyone but me was happier than flies on shit to see Deanthony, especially since he didn't come around that much. You would think he had just returned from some space mission from Mars the way everyone was hovered around him like he was some golden child they needed to protect. I noticed Yvonne, Kashawn, and Deanthony's cousin staring at me from across the room. I knew right then and there that she must have had something to do with getting Deanthony to show up at the party, just so she could see my reaction. That nosey bitch needed to get herself some business.

"You're going to be all right, girl?" Tangela asked.

"Shit, girl, you know me. Calm, cool, and collected." I could tell by the look Tangela gave me, she didn't believe a word that tumbled past my lips.

I made my way out to the deck where Kashawn, Tyrique, and friends were talking, drinking, and playing spades. I ran to Kashawn's side like there was some evil thing hungry on my red-bottom, fuchsia Christian Louboutins.

I leaned in and whispered, "Deanthony's here."

Kashawn gawked at me as if I'd just told him I had six weeks to live.

"He just arrived. He's in the living room with your mama."

"Where my brother at?" Deanthony hollered.

Always gotta be the ham, I thought.

He stood in the doorway that divided the deck from the house. The rest of the birthday party guests gathered around him like he was Tallahassee royalty.

Kashawn started toward him. I was scared shitless, not sure what Deanthony was going to say or do. My nerves settled when Kashawn greeted Deanthony with a grizzly bear hug of warmth and affection after three years of being away from the family. I couldn't help but wonder what brought Deanthony back to Tallahassee other than to ring in his thirtieth birthday.

"Man, where the hell have you been?"

"Bro, you know how I do. Still out here on this grind."

I nervously sipped spiked fruit punch from my red Dixie cup.

"What's up, Bree?" Deanthony asked, looking at me as if nothing happened.

He wrapped an arm around my waist, hugging me. I could feel

his hand on my ass and prayed to God that Kashawn hadn't noticed the advance he made.

"You look good, girl, damn!" he said, shouting loud enough for the whole neighborhood to hear.

My plan was simple: avoid his ass like an STD. I could feel pearls of sweat dripping from the roof of my armpits. I knew damn well that Deanthony didn't have the balls to put what we did on blast at the fish fry birthday party here in front of all his friends and family. I learned the hard way not to put anything past Deanthony's sneaky ass. He might have had Mama Liz, Kashawn, and everybody else fooled, but I knew firsthand what a sinister bastard he could be, especially when he wanted something he couldn't have.

"All right, y'all come on and get it. The food's ready!" Uncle Ray-Ray, Kashawn and Deanthony's uncle, yelled while forking mullet, bream, hushpuppies, and fried oysters in an aluminum pan. The smell of fresh fried fish infiltrated the hot June air. Uncle Ray-Ray was known around Tallahassee for serving up the best of everything when it came down to food. The best fish, the best barbecue, the best banana pudding, the best pork chops, the best chittlins, not to mention being the go-to guy for installing stereo systems.

Everyone started to line up along the table, grabbing paper plates. Tyrique's big ass was the first in line, of course, forking what had to be five pieces of bream and mullet on his plate, followed by a mess of cole slaw and cheese grits. No matter where he was—restaurant, party, fish fry—Tyrique always ate like every meal was his last. I grinned, watching his wife, Ebonya, nudge him, scolding him to save some fish for everyone else. Tyrique had always been kind of this big, dumb jock, teddy bear of a man. Kashawn got him on as an orderly at Tallahassee Memorial Hospital.

"Baby, you hungry? You want me to fix you a plate?" I asked.

"Um, yeah, baby, would you please? You know what I like."

"You still eat them fried oysters like that?" Deanthony asked.

"Hell yeah, with some hot sauce. That ain't nothin' but good eatin'.'"

Kashawn grabbed another beer from the wash basin filled with ice and an assortment of beer and Chek sodas. Deanthony would nonchalantly look off in my direction, smiling, knowing something only he and I knew. If the truth ever came to light, it would kill Kashawn.

After seeing Deanthony, I had lost my appetite. The smell of fish and fried oysters was making me nauseous as I plated the seafood on a paper plate for Kashawn. Shit, I wish I could blame it on fish. Seeing Deanthony was the real reason behind my queasy stomach. Kashawn and Deanthony sat at one of the patio tables, drinking beer.

"There you go."

"You're not going to eat anything, baby?" Kashawn asked, roping his arm around my waist, resting his hand on my booty.

I looked over at Deanthony and said, "I'm not really hungry." With laughter in those big penny-brown eyes of his, he took another swig from a Corona. "I left my cigarettes in the car. I'll be back."

"You all right?" Kashawn asked.

"Yeah, baby, I'm fine. Stomach bothering me, that's all."

"It's that cheap Winn-Dixie liquor Tangela put in the punch that's got you sick. I told you about drinking that stuff."

"Yeah, I guess." I gave Kashawn a kiss on the forehead. "I'm going to the car to relax."

"Okay. Feel better."

"Thank you, baby."

I ignored Deanthony as I walked off, easing my way through the crowd of guests armed with plates of food.

Tangela made her way over to me, sensing that I was in need of her best friend forever benefits. "Girl, what happened?"

"Come outside. I need a cigarette, bad."

Tangela's black Mustang was parked behind a row of cars in Mama Liz's pine-needle-strewn driveway.

"I got something better than cigs," she said, pulling a plastic sandwich bag of weed out of the glove box.

"Damn, bitch, you ride around with this in your car?"

"No, I just brought it today in case my best friend had to sneak out of her man's birthday party to get away from his brother whom she fucked around with." Tangela laughed, but I didn't find what she said the least bit funny.

"Whatever, bitch. Light that shit up."

Tangela was a slightly plumper version of me with apple butter–brown skin, hazel eyes that made her look like a vampire, and a weave that flowed luxuriously down her back. The low-cut red blouse she wore barely held in her round, cantaloupe breasts she loved showing off every chance she got. Tangela lit the end of the joint and took a couple of puffs and passed it to me.

"Hold on, let me crack the windows," she said. "Mama Liz isn't going to run out here cursing and screaming for smoking weed in her yard, is she?"

"Hell, she would probably join in. Kashawn told me she smokes weed herself. Medicinal marijuana, he said. Something about her bad knees or some shit."

"Yeah, whatever," Tangela said, taking her joint back. "So I saw you over there with Kashawn and Deanthony. I'm surprised you still keeping it together with him being here."

"Shit, barely. If I didn't get away from him, I was going to lose it."

"I thought he was on the grind in L.A., trying to do that acting thing?"

"That's what Kashawn told me. Deanthony said he had too much going on to come home. You saw that I was as surprised as anyone to see him bust up in here like that." When Tangela passed the blunt back to me, I took a long drag, letting the weed infiltrate my lungs.

"Damn, ma, slow down. That's about all I have until I get back to the house."

"Girl, you would think that out of respect for my marriage, he would have stayed away. That's what I get for taking the word of a high-yellow, Denzel Washington wannabe brother like him. Did you see Yvonne looking at me when Deanthony walked in? That busy bitch wanted to see my reaction and I fell right into that shit. I know she's the one who convinced him to come home."

"Bree, come on, now. Yvonne is family."

"Family, hell. She's had it out for me since the day I said, 'I do.'"

"Why would she mess with you like that, though?"

"Because ever since I told the family that I used to strip at Risqué, she hasn't liked me. I can't stand how she prances around here like she shits potpourri."

"She's so damn uppity since she got sanctified," Tangela added.

"And Akaisha at Radiance Salon, who went to Rickard's High School with her, told me she used to spread those hippo thighs for every dick that swung in her face."

Tangela bucked with laughter as she took a toke from the weed. "Damn, girl, you wrong for that."

"I'm just telling you what I heard. I'm sick of her giving me the stink eye every time she sees me. Matter of fact, I'm going to go in here right now and tell her to back the fuck off. I don't care whose first, second, or third cousin she is."

Tangela grabbed my arm as I opened the car door. "The last thing you need to do is go up in there, making a scene at Kashawn's birthday party of all places. Forget her. Leave it alone."

I sat there, feeling the effects from the weed. "Yeah, you right. Forget that heifer. I'm too high anyway."

"What she needs is some dick," Tangela said. "Some big Mandingo to fuck her cross-eyed." Tangela had me laughing my ass off when she said that.

As the two of us continued getting high, Mama Liz peeked her head out of the screen door.

"Oh shit."

"What are y'all doing out here? Come on inside. We're about to cut the cake."

"Okay, Mama Liz, we coming."

She stared at us, puzzled, like she was trying to make out what we were doing. "I mean it. Come on now."

"Are you going back in?" Tangela asked.

"I'm too fucked up and I don't want to go back in there smelling like weed."

"You wanna get out of here?"

"Yeah. Kashawn will understand. I told him that I don't feel good no way. I don't think I can go through the rest of the afternoon having to make idle chatter with Deanthony in there."

Tangela drove me home where we mellowed out to Beyoncé's "Sasha Fierce" CD.

"Damn, ma, you did your thing on the remodeling."

"You like it? You know I love that Afrocentric shit. Kashawn gave me his credit card and told me to have fun. You know, with his long hours at the hospital, he doesn't always have time. I damn near furnished the whole house in a day."

"I like these tables and the sectional. All this must have set y'all back a couple of stacks."

"Girl, you know I don't look at the price tag. If I like it, I get it."

"That painting of you is cute."

"It's all right. The artist is from Atlanta. I think he made me look too old. I want this artist Fullalove to do it."

"Who?"

"Fullalove. He paints these portraits of athletes and rappers. I'm going to New York in November so he can paint me. It'll be a nice Christmas gift for Kashawn." I walked over to the bar in front of the kitchen. "Hey, you want a drink?"

"Yeah, I'll have whatever you're having."

Tangela continued looking around in awe at all the new furniture like she was in a museum while I poured two glasses of Chardonnay.

"So girl, what are you going to do about Deanthony?" she asked as I handed her a glass of wine.

"No clue. I guess this is what they mean by making your bed and lying in it."

"You don't think he will say anything to Kashawn, do you? Came back to clear his conscience?"

"Deanthony doesn't have a conscience. Family or no family, he doesn't care who he hurts. Just like he showed up at the party without any thought for me. The best thing he can do is stay the hell away from me and Kashawn."

"Well, baby girl, you know I got you if you need anything. He'll have to go through me first if he's thinking about messing shit up with you and Kashawn."

"Thanks, Tange, but I don't think he'll be a problem. I plan on staying away from him." I was about to take another swig from my drink when my cell phone rang. I pulled it out of my clutch. I studied the number on the screen. "Oh, this brother's got brass fucking balls, girl."

"Who is it?"

I showed Tangela Deanthony's number on my phone.

"Don't answer it."

Against Tangela's advice, I pressed the green icon on my phone. "Why are you calling me?"

"I told you, didn't I? I told you I was coming back for you."

"Stay the hell away from me, Deanthony."

"Or what?"

"Or I'll make you wish you had." I pressed END CALL before he could utter another syllable.

"What did he say?"

"He ain't here for the cake. I gotta do something, 'cause if I don't, I'm going to lose Kashawn."